OTHER TIMES THAN PEACE

DAVID DRAKE

OTHER TIMES THAN PEACE

A Baen Book

Baen Publishing Enterprises
P.O. Box 1403
Riverdale, NY 10471
www.baen.com

ISBN 10: 1-4165-5566-8
ISBN 13: 978-1-4165-5566-7

Cover art by Kurt Miller

First paperback printing, August 2008

Library of Congress Control Number: 2006012261

Distributed by Simon & Schuster
1230 Avenue of the Americas
New York, NY 10020

Pages by Joy Freeman (www.pagesbyjoy.com)
Printed in the United States of America

For David G. Hartwell
Who first bought a story from me in 1977
and has bought many things since,
Though not any of the pieces in this collection.

CONTENTS

Introduction:

A RANGE OF TREATMENTS

I started out writing horror stories. To be precise, I started out by writing a pastiche of August Derleth pastiches of H.P. Lovecraft horror stories. (It was very bad. The only collection I can imagine reprinting it in is a retrospective where I can point to it and say, "See how much better I've gotten?" Which, believe me, will be damning my later work with faint praise.)

From horror I moved to heroic fantasy (sword and sorcery, if you prefer), to mainstream SF, to space opera, to military SF (I distinguish between those two subgenres), and even to humor. I've also written quite a lot of fantasy—the Isles series of Tolkienesque fantasies for Tor of course, but quite a lot before I started that series as well.

There aren't any fantasies in this collection, but I've included samples from the other named subgenres. I read widely across the spectrum of SF/fantasy, and I don't see much difference between writing one type and another. The stories I like are about characters—about people—and that's a constant in all genres.

These stories include one of my earliest as well as the two most recent (as of this writing). Some are self-standing, some were written for series of my own, and several were written for shared universes. There are light stories and some of the grimmest things I've ever written. (Yes, I know what I'm saying.) Some are carefully researched historicals, some take place in the far future, and one was set in the place and time where I wrote it.

What the stories have in common is that they're all about war. Some of the protagonists are fighting for the survival of the human species; some are fighting for national political ends; and many are simply fighting because it's their job. The reasons don't really matter to the people at the sharp end.

And above all, these are stories about people.

Dave Drake

david-drake.com

LAMBS TO THE SLAUGHTER___

A trumpet called, giving the go-ahead to a detachment leaving by one of the other gates of the Harbor. Half of Froggie's bored troopers looked up; a few even hopped to their feet.

The century's band of local females roused, clucking like a hen-coop at dinner time and grasping the poles of the handcarts holding the troopers' noncombat gear. Slats, the six-limbed administrator who Froggie was escorting out to some barb village the gods knew where, clambered into his palanquin and ordered his bearers to lift him.

"Everybody sit down and wait for orders!" Froggie said in a voice that boomed through the chatter. "Which will come from me, Sedulus, so you can get your ass back into line. When I want you to lead the advance, I'll tell you."

That'd be some time after Hermes came down and announced Sedulus was the son of Jupiter, Froggie guessed.

Three days after Froggie was born, his father had

3

lifted him before the door of their hut in the Alban Hills and announced that the infant, Marcus Vibius Taena, was his legitimate son and heir. He'd been nicknamed Ranunculus, Froggie, the day the training centurion heard him bellow cadence the first time. Froggie's what he'd been since then; that or Top, after he'd been promoted to command the Third Century of the Fourth Cohort in one of the legions Crassus had taken east to conquer Parthia.

Froggie'd continued in that rank when the Parthians sold their Roman prisoners to a man in a blue suit, who wasn't a man as it turned out. A very long time ago, *that* was.

The girls subsided, cackling merrily. Queenie, the chief girl, called something to the others that Froggie didn't catch. They laughed even harder.

The barbarians in this place were pinkish and had knees that bent the wrong way. They grew little ruffs of down at their waists and throat, and the males had topknots of real feathers that they spent hours primping.

Froggie's men didn't have much to do with the male barbs, except to slaughter enough of them the day after the legion landed that the bottom lands flooded from the dam of bodies in the river. As for the girls—they weren't built like real women, but the troopers had gotten used to field expedients; and anyway, the girls were close enough.

"Don't worry, boys," Froggie added mildly. "We'll get there as soon as we need to."

And maybe a little sooner than that. Froggie didn't understand this operation, and experience had left him with a bad feeling about things he didn't understand.

Commanding the Third of the Fourth didn't give Froggie much in the way of bragging rights in the legion, but he'd never cared about that. Superior officers knew that Froggie's century could be depended on to get the job done; the human officers did, at least. If any of the blue-suits, the Commanders, bothered to think about it, they knew as well.

Froggie's men could be sure that their centurion wasn't going to volunteer them for anything, not even guard duty on a whore house, because there was always going to be a catch in it. And if the century wound up in the shit anyway, Froggie'd get them out of it if there was any way in Hell to do that. He'd always managed before.

The howl of the Commander's air chariot rose, then drummed toward the gate. Froggie stood, using his vinewood swagger stick as a cane.

"*Now* you can get your thumbs out, troopers!" he said in a roar they could hear inside the huge metal ship that the legion had arrived on. Froggie was short and squat—shorter than any but a handful of the fifty-seven troopers in his century—but his voice would have been loud in a man twice his size.

The troopers fell in with the skill of long practice; their grunts and curses were part of the operation. Men butted their javelins and lifted themselves like codgers leaning on a staff, or else they held their heavy shields out at arm's length to balance the weight of their armored bodies as their knees straightened.

They wore their cuirasses. They'd march carrying their shields on their left shoulders, though they'd sling their helmets rather than wear them. Marching all day in a helmet gave the most experienced veteran a throbbing headache and cut off about half the sounds around him besides.

Froggie remembered the day the legion had marched in battle order, under a desert sun and a constant rain of Parthian arrows. They all remembered that. All the survivors.

Besides his sword and dagger, each trooper carried a pair of javelins meant for throwing. Their points were steel, but the slim neck of each shaft was soft iron that bent when it hit and kept the other fellow from pulling it out and maybe throwing it back at you. After you hurled your javelins it was work for the sword, and Froggie's troopers were better at that than anybody who'd faced them so far.

Slats stood on his two legs with his four arms crossed behind his back. He'd travelled in the same ship as the legion for the past good while. Slats wasn't a Commander any more than Froggie was, but he seemed to have a bit of rank with his own people. Like all the civilians who had to deal with the barbs, Slats wore a lavaliere that turned the gabble from his own triangular mouth into words the person he was talking to could understand.

"The bug's been around a while, right?" murmured Glabrio, a file-closer who could've had more rank if he'd been willing to take it. Though Slats looked a lot like a big grasshopper, he had bones inside his limbs the same as a man did.

"Yeah, Slats was in charge of billeting three campaigns ago," Froggie said. "He's all right. He'd jump if a fly buzzed him, but seems to know his business."

Glabrio laughed without bitterness. "That's more'n you could say about some Commanders we've had, right?" he said.

"Starting with Crassus," Froggie agreed.

Froggie'd stopped trying to get his mind around the whole of the past; time went on too far now. Little bits of memory still stuck up like rocks in a cold green sea. One of those memories was Crassus, red-faced with the effort of squeezing into his gilded cuirass, telling the Parthian envoys that he'd explain the cause of the war at the same time as he dictated terms in the Parthian capital.

The Commander's flying chariot came over a range of buildings. The guards in the gate tower here, a squad from the Ninth Cohort, leaned over the battlements to watch. One of them made a joke and the others laughed. Glad they weren't going, Froggie guessed.

The Harbor, the Commanders' city across the river from what had been the barb capital, had started as a Roman palisade thrown up half a mile out from the huge metal ship from which the legion had landed. The open area had immediately begun to fill with housing for civilians: those from the metal ship and also for barbs quick to take allegiance with the new masters whom Roman swords had imposed.

Glabrio must've been thinking the same thing Froggie was, because he eyed the barbs thronging the streets and said, "If anybody'd asked me, I'd have waited till I was damned sure the fighting was over before I let any of the birds this side of my walls. The men, I mean. They strut around like so many banty roosters."

"Next time I'm having dinner with the Commander," Froggie said sourly, "I'll mention it to him."

The flying chariot settled majestically onto the space left open for it beside the gate. Froggie felt the hair on the back of his arms rise as it always did when the machines landed or took off nearby. This was a big example of the breed. It carried the Commander and his driver; two of the Commander's huge, mace-wielding toad bodyguards; Pollio, the legion's trumpeter; and five of the male barbs who'd joined the Commander's entourage almost from the moment he'd strode into the palace still splashed with the orange blood of the barb king.

The top barb aide was named Three-Spire. Froggie had seen him before and would've been just as happy never to see him again.

The troopers clashed to attention. Froggie crossed his right arm over his cuirass in salute, sharply enough to make the hoops clatter.

"Sir!" he boomed. "Third Century of the Fourth Cohort, all present or accounted for!"

The Commander stood up, though he didn't bother to get out of his chariot. The barbs sharing the vehicle with him—all this Commander's aides were barbs, the first time Froggie remembered that happening—continued to talk among themselves.

"Very good, warrior," the Commander said. He wore a thin, tight suit that might have almost have been blue skin, but his face was pale behind the enclosing bubble of a helmet. His garb was protection of some sort, but he wouldn't need the huge bodyguards if he didn't fear weapons. "Don't let sloth degrade your unit while you're on this assignment. No doubt my Guild will have fighting for you in the future."

Even without using the chariot for a reviewing stand, the Commander would be taller than any trooper in the legion. Back in the days before Crassus, though,

Froggie had seen Gauls who were even taller, as well as heavier-bodied than the blue-suited race.

The Commander turned to Slats and spoke again; this time the words that came from the lavaliere around the Commander's neck sounded like the squeak of twisted sinews: they were in Slats' language, not Latin or any other human tongue. The administrator spread his six limbs wide and waggled submissively, miming a bug flipped on its back.

Fixing Froggie with a pop-eyed glare that was probably meant to be stern—language could be translated; expressions couldn't—the Commander resumed, "Obey the orders of the administrator I've provided you with as though his orders were mine. You have your duty."

Three-Spire said something to the Commander. The barb wore one of the little translator plates and must have spoken in the Commander's own language, instead of speaking barb and letting the Commander's device translate it.

The Commander flicked his left arm to the side in his equivalent of a nod. "I'll be checking up on you," he added to Froggie. "Remember that!"

"Yes, sir!" Froggie boomed, his face impassive. "The Third of the Fourth never shirks its duty!"

Three-Spire looked at the girls with dawning comprehension; his topknot bristled with anger, bringing its three peaks into greater prominence. "You! Warrior!" he said. "Where's the leader of these females?"

"Hey, Queenie!" Froggie said—in Latin. He could've called the chief girl in a passable equivalent of her own language, but he didn't think it was the time or place to show off. The troopers didn't have lavalieres to translate for them, but they'd had a lot of experience getting ideas across to barbs. Especially female barbs.

Queenie obediently stepped forward, but Froggie could see that she was worried. Well, so was he.

"No, not a female!" Three-Spire said. The lavaliere wouldn't translate a snarl, but it wasn't hard to figure there should've been one. "I mean the male who's leading this contingent!"

The Commander looked from Queenie to his aide, apparently puzzled. He didn't slap Three-Spire down the way Froggie expected. Hercules! Froggie remembered one Commander who'd had his guards smash a centurion to a pulp for saying the ground of the chosen campsite was too soft to support tent poles. The legion had slept on its tents that night, because spread like tarpaulins the thick leather walls supported the troopers enough that they didn't sink into the muck in the constant rain.

"We take care of that ourself, citizen," Froggie said, more polite than he wanted to be. Something funny was going on here, and Froggie'd learned his first day in the army that you usually win if you bet "unusual" meant "bad."

"That's not permitted!" Three-Spire said. "Sawtooth here will accompany you."

He spoke to the barb beside him, then opened a bin that was part of the chariot and handed the fellow a lavaliere from it. Sawtooth walked toward the girls clustered around the carts. He didn't look any too pleased about the assignment.

"What's this barb mean 'not permitted'?" Glabrio said in a ragged whisper. "If he don't watch his tongue, he's going to lose it!"

"Take your own advice," Froggie said out of the side of his mouth. Loudly, facing the Commander, he said, "Yes, sir!" and saluted again. "Century, form marching order and await the command!"

The Commander blinked inner eyelids that worked sideways the way a snake's do. He spoke to Pollio, who obediently stood and raised his trumpet.

"You're going to take this from a barb?" Glabrio demanded.

Pollio blew the long attention call, then the three quick toots for Advance. He looked past the tube of his instrument at his fellow troopers, his eyes troubled.

"March!" Froggie called. The century was too small a unit to have a proper standard to tilt forward, so Froggie swept his swagger stick toward the open gateway instead. To Glabrio, in a voice that could scarcely be heard over the crash of boots and equipment, he added, "For a while, sure. Look what Crassus bought by getting hasty, trooper."

Before his Third Squad was out of the gate, Froggie heard the chariot lift with a frying-bacon sizzle. A moment later he saw it fly over the palisade, heading for the next gate south where the Fifth of the Fourth waited to escort another administrator out into the sticks. Pollio looked down at the troops; none of the others aboard the vehicle bothered to.

Froggie stepped out of line, letting Lucky Castus of the first squad lead. Sunlight winked on the battle monument which the legion had set up outside the main gate of the Harbor: a pillar of rough-cut stonework, with captured armor set in niches around it and a barb war chariot filled with royal standards on top.

The barbs used brass rather than bronze for their helmets and the facings of their wicker shields. Polished brass shone like an array of gold, but verdigris had turned this equipment to poisonous green in the three months since the battle.

A lot of things had gone bad in the past three months. Froggie'd be glad to get out of this place. If it could be done alive.

The girls came through the gate, pushing the carts. Froggie'd heard Sawtooth shouting, "March! March! March!" for as long as the Commander's chariot was visible, but the barb was silent now.

Queenie saw Froggie watching. She twitched the point of her shoulder in Sawtooth's direction. Froggie smiled and moved his open hand in a short arc as though he were smoothing dirt.

That was a barb gesture. For men with damage to the spine or brain that even the Commanders' machines couldn't repair, the legion continued the Roman practice of cremating corpses. The barbs here buried their dead in the ground.

Slats came through the gate after the last cart, swinging in his palanquin. His four girls handled the weight all right, but they didn't seem to have much sparkle. Well, that'd change when they started eating army rations along with the century's girls.

As soon as Slats saw Froggie, he desperately beckoned the Roman to him. Froggie didn't care for anybody calling him like a dog, but there wasn't much option this time. As clumsy as Slats was, he'd probably break his neck if he tried to climb out of the palanquin hastily. Froggie sauntered over and walked beside the vehicle. That wasn't hard; the carts were setting the pace.

"Centurion Vibius," the administrator said, "I'm pleased to see you. I have studied your record. There is no unit whose escort on this expedition I would prefer to yours."

Froggie thought about that for a moment. You'd rarely go wrong to assume whatever your officers told you was a lie . . . but Slats wasn't exactly an officer. Also, Froggie'd gotten the impression back when Slats was billeting officer that his race of bugs couldn't tell lies any better than they could fly.

"If we're going to be stuck in the middle of nowhere for however long," the centurion said, "then you may as well learn to call me Froggie. And I'm not sorry we're with you, Slats, if we've got to be out here at all."

Pollio's trumpet called again, ordering Postumius and his boys into the back of beyond. Three centuries from each cohort, half the strength of the legion, had been sent off these past two days on individual escort missions.

"Exactly!" said Slats. He spoke through his mouth— not every race serving the Commanders did—but he had three jaw plates, not two, and he looked more like a lamprey talking than he did anything Froggie wanted to watch. "*If* we have to be here. What do you think of the expedition, Centurion Froggie?"

Froggie thought it was the worst idea he'd heard since Crassus marched into Parthia with no guides and no clue, but he wasn't going to say that to *any*damnbody. Aloud he said, "I would've thought that maybe waiting till this place was officially pacified so you guys could move in your burning weapons and so forth . . . that that might be a good idea."

The First Squad with Glabrio in front was entering

the forest. It niggled Froggie that he wasn't up with them, though he knew how sharp Glabrio's eyes were. The file-closer had served as the unofficial unit scout ever since Froggie got to know him.

"Exactly!" Slats repeated. "It is extremely dangerous to treat the planet as pacified when it is *not* pacified. What if the Anroklaatschi—"

The barbs; Froggie never bothered to learn what barbs called themself. Most times you couldn't pronounce it anyway.

"—attack the Harbor in force as they attacked when we landed? They could sweep right over the few troops remaining, could they not?"

Froggie thought about the question. The barbs came riding to battle on chariots. One fellow with only a kinked sword drove while two warriors with long spears and full armor stood in the back. The driver held the "horses" behind the lines while his betters stomped forward in no better order than a flock of sheep wearing brass.

The barbs had gotten a real surprise when—instead of spending half the afternoon shouting challenges—the legion had advanced on the double, launched javelins, and then waded in for the real butcher's work with swords. That surprise couldn't be repeated, but so long as whoever was in command of the understrength legion kept his head . . .

"Some folks' swordarms are going to be real tired by the time it's over," Froggie said judiciously, "but I guess they'd come through all right."

The smooth-barked trees in this place were tall, some of them up to two hundred feet. The branches came off in rows slanting up the trunks to end in sprays of tassels like willow whips instead of proper leaves.

Froggie hadn't seen real trees since he'd marched into Mesopotamia. He'd seen a date palm there and wondered what he was doing in a place so strange. He'd been right to worry.

Slats and the Commander called this place a planet, just like the Commanders did every place they took the legion to. The only thing "planet" meant to Froggie was the stars that he used to watch move slowly across the sky while he tended sheep before he enlisted. *Hercules!* but he wished he was back in the Sabine Hills now.

"Well, all right, the Harbor may hold," Slats said peevishly, "but what about you and I, Centurion Froggie? What chance do we have if the Anroklaatschi attack?"

"Well, Slats . . ." Froggie said. "That depends on a lot of things. I'd just as soon it didn't happen, but me and the boys'll see what can be done if it does."

Froggie and the palanquin reached the shade of the forest. This wasn't a proper road but it was a lot more than an animal track. Two and generally three men could march abreast, though their outside knees and elbows brushed low growth which looked like starbursts from a peglike stem.

Tassels closed all but slivers of the sky overhead, and the trunks cut off sight of the Harbor. Froggie knew the Commander had ways to see through trees or even solid rock, but he still relaxed a little to have the feeling of privacy.

"I'm wondering . . ." Slats said. He spoke softly and seemed to be afraid to meet Froggie's eyes. "I'm wondering if perhaps the Commander is sending us and the others out to give him warning if the Anroklaatschi are planning an attack? They would hit us first, and of course I would call a warning to the Harbor."

He waggled a little rod that Froggie had taken for a writing stylus.

Froggie sighed. "Well, I tell you, Slats," he said. "A long time ago I gave up expecting what officers did to make a lot of sense. But I gotta say, as a plan that'd *really* be a bad one. He's weakening his base too much."

"Nothing about this planet makes sense!" Slats burst out. "None of the products are of real value to the Guild. Oh, in the long term, certainly—but nothing worth the loss of warrior slaves as valuable as you are, Roman. And to lose my life as well over this wretched planet! Oh, what a tragedy!"

"I can see you'd feel that way about it," Froggie said. "Well, you worry about your business, Slats, and me and the boys'll worry about ours."

He stepped aside and let the column tramp on by him. He'd see how Verruca, his number two, was making out at the end of the line; then he'd go up with Glabrio again where he belonged.

It didn't make Froggie feel good that the administrator was just as worried about this business as he was, but sometimes it's nice to know that you can trust your instincts *even* when they're telling you you're stepping into a pool of hog manure.

After all, you had to trust something.

Froggie looked at the sun, a hand's breadth past zenith. He thought the days here were about the

same length as those in Italy—that wasn't true a lot
of places the legion had been—but home was too
long ago for him to be sure.

A few big trees sprang from the protection of a
limestone outcrop, but only saplings grew in the rest
of the broad floodplain. At the moment the river was
well within its channel.

"Queenie!" Froggie said. The chief girl, older than
the others by a ways, didn't actually push one of the
carts. She trotted over to him. "River there—much
water come down? Quick quick happen?"

Half his words were Latin, most of the rest were
in Queenie's chirps or as close as Froggie could come
to the sounds. Trooper pidgin had bits and pieces
of other tongues, too, some of them going back to
the Pahlevi the legions had picked up marching into
Parthia.

Queenie glanced at the river, using Froggie's gestures
as much as his words to figure out what he was asking. Some troopers had a knack for jawing with barbs.
Froggie didn't, but he could make out. It wasn't like
they were going to be talking philosophy, after all.

"No way, boss-man!" Queenie said. "Sky get cold
first, then get warm, then *hoosh!* sweep all shit down-
stream. Long time, boss-man."

Then, hopefully, "We camp here?"

"We camp here," Froggie agreed. The century had
already halted and the men were watching him; it
wasn't like they were recruits who couldn't figure out
what was going to happen next.

"Fall out!" Froggie said. "First and Third Squads
provide security, Second digs posts every twelve feet—"
for a marching camp there was no need to set every

timber of the palisade in the ground, the way you'd do for a more permanent structure "—and the rest of you start cutting timber. I want this complete before sunset, and I *don't* mean last light."

Verruca and Blasus already had the T-staff and measuring cord out. Any of the troopers could survey a simple camp by now, and with the right tools Blasus could've set an aqueduct.

He'd never have occasion to do that, of course. The Guild didn't use the legion for that kind of work. Well, Blasus was a good man to have at your side with a sword, too.

Troopers unlimbered axes, saws and shovels from the leading cart. The first job was to remove trees from the campsite, but they'd need to clear a wider area to complete the palisade. There wasn't a high likelihood that the barbs would try anything, but—

"Hey, Froggie!" Galerius called. "You know it's a waste of time to fort up in the middle of a nowhere like this. Ain't the blisters on our feet enough for today that we got to blister our hands, too?"

"Yeah, Froggie," Laena said. "Give it a rest for tonight, why don't you? We all know you're boss—you don't got to prove it."

There was a chorus of agreement, though Froggie was glad to notice the grumblers continued to pick up their tools. "You're damned right I don't have to prove it!" Froggie said. "And if you don't start working your shovel instead of your tongue, Laena, you're going to have four shifts of night watch on top of the post-holing!"

"By Hercules!" Laena said as he strode toward the line the surveyors were laying out. "One of these days

I'll get some rank myself so I can stand and watch other guys sweat!"

It was the same thing every halt, whether they were operating as the whole legion or in detachments like now: the centurions ordered the troopers to fortify the camp and the troopers complained. *Every* damned time!

And the troopers went ahead and fortified the camp anyway, with palisades, turf walls, drystone, or even fascines of spiky brush. Whatever there was that'd make a wall, that's what the legion used.

The troopers didn't obey because they were afraid of Froggie. Oh, he was tough enough—but Froggie'd seen Laena strangle a barb half again his own size in a place where the grass grew to the height of a small tree.

They obeyed, Laena and the rest, because they knew Froggie was right: that one of these nights they'd bed down in a spot just as empty as this one, and the walls Froggie had forced them to build would be the difference between seeing the dawn and having barbs cut all their throats. But they'd still complain and fight the orders, just like Froggie had before he got promoted.

The girls were starting cookfires and getting ration packs out of the third cart. The barbs here used wooden pistons to light wads of dry moss, quicker and at least as easy as striking sparks off steel with a flint. Queenie'd called something to Slats' porters, who obediently put him down.

The barb aide, Sawtooth, trotted over to Froggie. "You, warrior!" he said, his words coming out of the translator on his chest. "Why are we stopping?"

Glabrio put a hand on his swordhilt. Froggie waved him to calm down and walked over where Slats was cautiously stepping out of his vehicle. Sawtooth continued to jabber, but Froggie ignored him.

"Slats, this is a good place to set up," Froggie said. "When we get out of this bottom the trees'll be too big for us to build a stockade with the manpower we got. Besides, I don't want to work the girls too hard. This is a damned poor road for carts."

"Do not be concerned for the females," Sawtooth said. His barb chattering was an overtone to the accentless Latin coming out of the lavaliere. "We must push on till dark. Then we will reach Kascanschi by tomorrow!"

"Another thing, Slats," Froggie said without turning to look at the aide. "I wish you'd tell that barb who got wished on us that all he has to do to live a long, happy life is to keep his mouth shut and let me forget he's around. If he can't do that, then there's going to be a problem and he ain't going to like the way it gets solved."

"What?" said Sawtooth. "What do you mean? Three-Spire gave me complete authority over the females!"

"But Centurion Froggie . . . ?" Slats said. The translated words were without inflection, but the way the bug flicked his middle arms to the side indicated puzzlement. "Sawtooth has a translator. He has heard your words directly."

"No fooling?" said Froggie. He turned and tapped the barb's nose with his left index finger. Sawtooth yipped and jumped backward. "Well, I hope he was listening. I hate trouble."

❖   ❖   ❖

"All right," Froggie ordered. "One man from each squad stands wall guard, and the rest of you are dismissed for dinner. Squad leaders, set up a roster for the night watches."

The stockade wasn't fancy—you could stick your arm between posts in a lot of places—but it'd slow down a barb attack in the unlikely event that there was one. Froggie eyed it with approval. His boys hadn't forgotten how to work during the past three months in the Harbor.

The tents were up. Normally there'd have been six big ones holding a squad apiece, plus a pair of little bell tents with Slats in one and the other for Froggie and Verruca together. Slats still was separate, but Froggie'd traded the other little one for three more squad tents. He and Verruca would bunk down with the men—that was a better idea anyway, when you were out in the back of beyond with only a century—and the girls didn't have to make their own shelters.

One tent was for the unattached girls; the rest bunked with the soldiers they'd paired off with. If you wanted privacy you shouldn't have joined the army, but the extra tents provided a little elbow room when otherwise things would've been pretty crowded.

Froggie wondered where Sawtooth thought he was going to sleep. The question didn't concern him; he just wondered.

Because he wasn't especially hungry, Froggie paused for a moment on the low fighting step that let the troopers look over the top of the six-foot palisade. Glabrio walked over to him.

"The tree tassels are going yellow," Glabrio said. "They were dirty blue when we landed, do you remember?"

Froggie shrugged. "You think it's turning Fall?" he said. "I sure haven't noticed it getting colder."

The sky still looked bright, but the cookfires illuminated circles of ground. The green wood gave off clouds of smoke that looked oily but didn't smell too bad. Girls dipped stew into troopers' messkits, then sat beside them on split-log benches to share the food.

There was a lot of laughter. Froggie didn't like this operation one bit, but even he had to admit that it felt good to get away from the Harbor and the eyes of hundreds of bureaucrats.

Slats watched them from across the encampment, his upper and middle arms twitching to separate rhythms. Froggie nodded toward the administrator. To Glabrio he murmured, "The poor bastard's probably lonely. This can't be a picnic for him either."

There was a high, clucking scream. Sawtooth burst into the circle around the First Squad's cookfire and began to shriek at Queenie. Froggie sighed and strode over to the commotion. He'd been as clear as he could be, but some people—and some barbs—just wouldn't listen.

"What's the problem?" Froggie demanded, not shouting but making sure that Sawtooth and Queenie both would hear him over their gabble. He couldn't make out a word of it, they were talking so quick and angry.

"These sluts were proposing to eat meat!" the barb aide shouted, through the lavaliere now because he was speaking to Froggie. "They have no right to meat!"

"Is everything all right, Centurion Froggie?" Slats demanded nervously. He barely poked his head around the edge of one of the tents where he was hiding from the threat of violence.

"All's fine, Slats," Froggie called. Because Froggie was on top of things, the troopers kept a bit back. They were all steaming, though, and more than one man had his hand on his swordhilt.

"Look, buddy," Froggie said to the barb aide. "I decide who eats what here. The girls do better work with a little sausage in their mush, and—"

"They are not breeders!" Sawtooth shouted. He struck the mess tin out of Queenie's hand, spraying the savory brown stew across the ground in an arc. "I will not permit them to eat meat!"

"Top?" said Glabrio. He was standing right behind the barb.

"Yeah," said Froggie, "but you have to clean it up."

"What do you—" Sawtooth said. Glabrio grabbed his topknot with his left hand and pulled the barb's head back.

Most troopers used their daggers for the odds and ends of life in the field: trimming leather for bootsoles, picking a stone out of a draft animal's hoof, that sort of thing. Glabrio often carried only the dagger when he went scouting and didn't want the weight and clatter of full equipment. He kept a working edge on one side of the blade, but the other was honed to where he could slice sunbeams with it.

It was the sharp edge that he dragged across Sawtooth's throat, cutting through to the spine. The barb's blood was coppery in the firelight.

Glabrio twisted and flung Sawtooth on the ground behind him to finish thrashing. Bending, he wiped the daggerblade on the barb's kilt. Over his shoulder he asked, "Is the river all right, Froggie?"

"Dis, no! The river's not all right!" Froggie said.

"I want him buried deep enough nobody's going to find him till we've shipped out of this place. I want the ground smooth so you don't see there's a grave there, too!"

Glabrio stood and sheathed his dagger with a clack of the guard against the lip of the tin scabbard. "Sounds good to me, Froggie," he said.

Froggie grimaced. "Caepio and Messus," he said to the pair of men nearest, both of them members of the First Squad. "Get your shovels out and give him a hand."

Queenie stepped over to Froggie and held his hands as she touched cheeks, the right one and then the left. That was what the barbs did instead of kiss; they didn't really have lips, just a layer of skin over their mouth bones.

"You great boss-man!" she said. "We proud we be in your flock!"

Froggie patted her. "Hey, Marcellus!" he said to the guard from the Fourth Squad who was watching the excitement. "All of you who've got the duty—you think the barbs are going to pop up out of the campfires? Turn your heads around or you'll find 'em decorating somebody's lodgepole!"

Glabrio chose a patch of ground without many roots and started breaking it with his mattock; the rest of the squad was getting its tools out, not just the two troopers who'd been told off for the job. That was more people than you needed to dig a hole, but they were making a point that Froggie could appreciate.

Slats had vanished. Very slowly, he raised his triangular face around the edge of the tent again. Froggie smiled, raised his hands to show that they were empty, and walked over so he could talk to the administrator without shouting. Slats trembled, but he didn't run screaming toward the back gate the way Froggie half expected him to do.

"I was . . ." Slats said. "I . . ."

The bug turned his head around so that he was looking over his left shoulder, then repeated the gesture in the other direction. As if that had been his way of clearing his throat, he resumed, "Centurion Froggie, was that action necessary?"

"Yeah," Froggie said, "it was. Or anyway, it was going to be necessary before long. I figured it was better to take care of it out here where there wasn't anybody to watch. Right?"

"Hey, Top?" Glabrio called. "What about this?"

He held up Sawtooth's lavaliere, dangling on the tip of his finger. It winked in the firelight, except where tacky blood covered the metal.

"Hercules, bury it with him!" Froggie said. "If the barb deserted, he wasn't going to give us his gadget first, was he?"

He turned to the administrator again. "How about it, Slats?" he said. He didn't touch his swordhilt or do anything that might be taken as threatening; the poor bug was set to shake himself apart already. "Do you agree?"

"Centurion Froggie," Slats said finally, "I trust you to keep us all safe if it is possible to be safe. But the next time, the next time . . ."

He did his spin-your-head-around-twice trick again.

"The next time, Centurion Froggie, please warn me so that I know not to be watching!"

❖   ❖   ❖

Tatius and Laena were talking in low voices at the corner where their guard posts met. They heard the crunch of Froggie's boots and moved apart, each down his own stretch of palisade. Froggie didn't mind the guards chatting on duty if it didn't get out of hand.

Which it wouldn't, so long as Froggie made a pass around the posts once or twice each night. He didn't even have to speak.

A couple—or maybe it was a pair of the girls—sat in the shelter of the carts and shared a mug of something. Guild rations were pretty good, but the troopers had learned to supplement them from whatever was available locally. The wine here was first-rate, though the barbs made it from a root that looked like a beet.

The fires had burned down. Slats' tent was leather like all the rest, but the cold light that the Guild bureaucrats used leaked out the seams and underneath the tent walls. It didn't look like the administrator was going to make trouble over the business this evening. Froggie knew there'd been a risk in killing Sawtooth, but *Hercules!* he just couldn't feel in his heart that one barb more or less made a difference.

"Hey, boss-man!" Queenie called in a fluting whisper from the tower protecting the front gate. "Come up, we talk-talk."

Froggie looked at the night sky. He missed having a moon. In all the places the legion had been, there'd only been half a dozen where the moon was as big and bright as it ought to be. There was no moon at all here.

"Yeah, sure," Froggie said. He wriggled the pole that served as a ladder, making sure it was solid, then climbed. They'd trimmed a young tree, leaving stubs of branches on alternating sides for steps. The sap of the trees here dried hard and as smooth as glass.

Calling a platform with a waist-high parapet "the gate tower" was bragging a bit, but this was a damned impressive marching camp for a single century to lay out. The Third of the Fourth would survive this business if anybody could.

Of course, they might be in for nothing but a short march and a few days of boredom. Froggie'd been a soldier too long to complain about being bored. There was lots worse that happened.

"This bad shit, boss-man," Queenie said as she offered Froggie a skin of wine. "We watch out or we get chopped, right?"

"You can break your neck stepping off the curb, Queenie," Froggie said. Hercules, did *everybody* think they were all marching off a cliff? He squirted a stream of wine into his mouth like he was milking a ewe.

The girls and the troopers had gotten together pretty quick after the legion stood down from the battle; within a few hours, mostly. A lot of them were widows and orphans, but not by any means all. Females turned to strength as sure as the sun rises in the east; and when the legion was in town, strength spoke Latin.

Queenie spat over the parapet. She said, "Three-Spire a—" Froggie didn't catch the word, but she mimed squishing something against the platform. "A little bug, you know? He nasty bug serving king, he same-same nasty bug now. You chop him like you chop Sawtooth, boss-man?"

Froggie shrugged and passed the wine back. "No chance, Queenie," he said. "King boss-man, the blue guy, him love Three-Spire. Me just little boss-man."

Queenie patted him. "You find way, boss-man. You find way."

Far off in the night an animal gave a long, rising shriek. It wasn't a cry of pain because nothing that hurt so much could live to finish the call.

"New girls virgin," Queenie said unexpectedly. "Feed 'em up meat, they be ready in one day, two day. Want me save them for you, boss-man?"

"What?" said Froggie. Frowning, he took the offered wine and drank deeply. "Oh, Slats' porters, you mean. So it's the meat that warms 'em up, huh?"

He hadn't known that, but he'd seen that the girls on army rations had a lot more life in them than those eating mush in labor teams bossed by male barbs. Sometimes he wondered—he always wondered, every place they went where there were girls—what happened when the legion pulled out for the next campaign. Froggie'd met a cute little Armenian girl in Samosata while Crassus was getting ready to march east. . . .

Froggie sighed. "Naw, me no care, Queenie," he said.

Queenie finished the wine and clucked contentedly. She turned and fixed Froggie with eyes larger than a human's and perfectly round. "You no want me, boss-man?" she said. "Queenie too old?"

Froggie thought about it, then reached for the girl. "Naw, Queenie first rate," he said.

After all, with what they were getting into, he didn't know how many more chances he'd be getting.

"What do you think of Kascanschi, Centurion Froggie?" Slats asked. He'd climbed out of his palanquin as soon as they came into sight of the walls.

"I've seen worse towns," Froggie replied. "It'll do, I guess."

The village was a whole lot bigger than Froggie'd figured. If the barbs lived as tight together as they did in the old capital, there must be nigh onto three thousand of them here. They weren't all warriors, and a lot of what warriors there'd been had probably joined their king for the battle. Most of *those* had been feeding the eels for the past three months.

It was still a damned big place for one century to garrison.

The troops remained in marching order, but everybody wore his helmet with the crest mounted. Froggie's crest was transverse and twice as wide as those of the common troopers. Originally they'd been made of bleached horsehair. These most recent replacements weren't from a horse's tail—Froggie hadn't seen a real horse since Parthia—but they did the job.

The village gates were hung from towers made of irregularly shaped stones mortared together. A mound with a timber stockade on top surrounded the rest of the village. The posts were thicker than those of the troopers' marching camps, but the wall wasn't in good repair.

"It looks very strong, Centurion Froggie," Slats said. "Does it not?"

Froggie snorted. "Give us two hours to build a siege shed and we'll bore through that sorry excuse for a wall in another ten minutes," he said.

That was bragging; it'd take a bit longer. Though if wet rot had eaten the posts as bad as it just might have done . . .

After the battle in the bow of the river, the barb

king had escaped inside the thick stone walls of his capital. It had taken the legion just two days to undermine them, replace the pilings with props of dry timber, and then set the timbers ablaze. The barbs ran around like a stirred-up anthill when smoke started coming out of the ground, but even then they didn't seem to realize that the walls were going to collapse into a fiery pit along with everybody who was on the battlements at the time.

The Fourth Cohort was the lead unit through the breach. The barbs were too stunned by the disaster to put up much of a fight, but the troopers still had to kill like a plague to show what'd happen anytime the barbs didn't do just what the Guild said. The muscles of Froggie's right shoulder still twinged at the thought of how he'd lifted his sword again and again and again.

The gates of Kascanschi were open. From inside, barbs clacked the flat blocks of wood they used instead of trumpets. A procession of males came out: the six village elders, like enough, and a section of forty soldiers. Froggie felt his muscles tighten, but he hoped nothing showed on his face.

Slats stepped forward and started jawing the village chief, using his lavaliere. Glabrio edged toward Froggie and slid his shield out of the way so he could whisper. He saw it too. Dis, they all did, they were all veterans.

And so were the soldiers who'd just come through the gates.

They weren't big. One by one they were shorter than the warriors the legion had slaughtered three months before. These troops didn't *move* one by one, though:

they moved like a team, like disciplined soldiers, and that was all the difference between being sheep and being the butcher.

"They're a funny color pink," Glabrio said. "And look, they got axes instead of spears."

The knives Froggie had seen previously in this place were of brittle iron that he wouldn't have used for a plow coulter back in Latium. These short-hafted axes had blades of real steel, and the iron-strapped wooden bucklers were a lot solider than the brass-faced wicker that the royal army had died with.

Slats returned to Froggie. "The chief bids us welcome," he said. Because of the translator, it was hard to tell if Slats was as worried about the situation as he ought to be. "They've prepared housing for us in the village temple, the big building just inside the gate."

Froggie looked around instead of immediately answering Slats or giving the troops an order. For most of the past mile they'd been marching between fields of broad-leafed root vegetables, each growing in a little mound of compost. The area for nearly a bowshot outside the walls wasn't planted. At one time it must have been cleared for defensive purposes, but for at least a decade it'd grown up in brush.

"Glabrio," Froggie said, "you come with me. The rest of you wait for orders."

Slapping his swagger stick into his left palm, he strode through the gate with Glabrio at his side. Queenie trotted along two paces behind, which was fine. Slats rotated his head in desperation, then scuttled after Froggie like a nervous cockroach.

Four of the barb axemen came too, which was no

more than Froggie expected. Close up, the pink of their skins had a lot more blue and less red than the village elders did. They looked tough and no mistake.

"That's the temple, huh?" Froggie said, eyeing the structure. It was impressive, all right: sixty feet at least to the top of the main spire. Ten or a dozen lesser peaks sprang from other parts of the wooden roof. The walls were built up from staves, not heavy timbers, and every finger's breadth of the pieces had been carved with the images of plants and animals before they were pegged together.

"According to my briefing cube . . ." Slats said, facing Froggie very deliberately so that he could pretend that the four funny-looking barbs weren't standing close holding their axes, ". . . the chiefs are also priests just as the king is the high priest. This would be the chief's residence as well as the temple."

The temple's lines were all up and down, but it covered a fair stretch of ground besides. There'd be room for the century to fit inside even if the height wasn't divided into several floors.

"It looks impressive, doesn't it?" Slats said nervously.

"It looks like a bloody firetrap!" said Glabrio, who'd come from Sicily a long time ago. "I'd sooner bunk in Etna than there!"

"Right," said Froggie. "Slats, we're not going to billet inside the walls, but it won't be any problem—"

"Company coming!" Verruca called from the other side of the gate. "The bluebird's returning to our happy meadows."

"Seems the Commander's paying us a visit, Slats," Froggie said. "What do you suppose he's got in mind?"

"If he were ordering us home," Slats said in obvious

disquiet, "he would call me instead of coming out here. It must be a tour of inspection."

Froggie walked out and caught the wink of sunset on metal as the Commander's chariot came over the eastern horizon. When the sun's angle was just right, the light twisted as though Froggie were seeing the vehicle through the clear water of a pond.

Usually when barbs saw a flying chariot for the first time, they threw themselves face-down and prayed—the ones who didn't run off screaming. The village elders looked scared, no mistake, but the axemen stood rock solid. In fact when the chief turned like he planned to run, the guard with gold wristlets—the others wore black—caught him and faced him around with a firm grip. It made you wonder who was really in charge of things.

The flying chariot hissed to the ground alongside where Slats had spoken to the village chief. The vehicle was the same one that had seen the century out of the Harbor, but the only ones aboard were the driver, the Commander and his two bodyguards, and Three-Spire.

"Is he sick?" Glabrio whispered. The Commander had a glassy expression and didn't move when the chariot landed.

My guess'd be drunk, Froggie thought, but he didn't let those words or any touch his lips.

While the Commander remained in his comatose half-sprawl, Three-Spire stood in the chariot and spoke to the village chief. The elders bent their heads back in a gesture of submission.

Their posture reminded Froggie of Sawtooth's last moments, so he was smiling when Three-Spire turned and spoke to Slats. The administrator replied and, to Froggie, said, "Three-Spire says we are to enter our assigned quarters at once and dismiss the porters. Sawtooth will lead them back to the Harbor, Three-Spire says. He speaks with the authority of the Commander, who is indisposed. Three-Spire says."

"I guess you'll want to assure the Commander that you'll inform your escort and other interested parties," Froggie said. This wasn't the perfect time to explain where Sawtooth was at, but Froggie wouldn't have gotten as old as he was if he counted on perfection. "We'll find a way to deal with the girls ourselves in the absence of Sawtooth."

"What?" said Three-Spire, his translator croaking in Latin. He hopped out of the chariot and stepped so close to Froggie that the centurion had to look up if he wanted to see anything above the barb's neckline. "Where is Sawtooth? He should be—"

Changing tack in the middle of the question, Three-Spire cawed a demand at Queenie. Before she could speak—not that Froggie was worried about Queenie forgetting the story they'd worked out together—Froggie said, "Sawtooth went off last night with one of the girls, citizen. The others tell me he'd been feeding her meat from army rations."

That set the barb back like Froggie'd caught him at throat level with a shield-rim—an image which'd been going through Froggie's mind, sure enough. "Sawtooth did that?" Three-Spire said.

This time Queenie answered, speaking slowly enough that Froggie caught the word for disgrace. She even squatted down and raised her hips, the way the girls here did to honor a man.

Three-Spire's translator shot a question at Slats. The administrator answered just as smooth and polite as he would've the Commander. Speaking of Blue-Suit, he'd stuck a finger in his mouth and was rolling it around like a pestle in a handmill.

The aide bobbed his head, indicating a complete lack of understanding. To Froggie he said, "Well, the females must return on their own, then. They won't need food—it's a short journey since they no longer have burdens."

"Ah . . ." said Froggie. It griped his soul to have to treat this barb like he was real people, but whatever was going on was deeper waters than Froggie was ready to swim in yet. "I guess the girls can stay with us. We'll need cooks and washing done, so—"

Three-Spire's crest twitched, sticking straight up and then spreading out like a drop of water splashing on bone-dry ground. Instead of talking to Froggie, he turned and flung another load of gabble at Slats through the lavaliere. Slats twice tried to reply, but the barb snarled him down before he got out more than a few clicking words. When Three-Spire finally finished, he glared at Froggie.

Slats spread his limbs in acceptance. Very carefully he said to Froggie, "Three-Spire, speaking in the Commander's name, says that the females cannot remain within Kascanschi because they are not of this tribe. He says that would cause offense—"

The administrator flicked his middle limbs out minusculely.

"—although my briefing cube failed to note this cultural peculiarity. Furthermore, Three-Spire rejects my suggestion that we could camp outside the walls as

we did on the way here. That would be a rejection of
the villagers' hospitality that again would give offense,
Three-Spire says. Speaking for the Commander."

In Latin Three-Spire said, "The Commander wishes
to inform you that if you do not carry out his orders
at once, his terrible weapons will burn all you warriors to ash for mutiny. To ash!"

"I see," Froggie said. He looked over his troopers.
Verruca had lined them up five squads abreast with
the carts behind them and the Sixth Squad acting as a
rear guard and reserve. "Century, mount up! We'll be
billeted in that big-ass building right inside the gates
until we hear different. By squads, march!"

In truth Froggie didn't see very much, but at least
he knew for sure where he stood. He'd met plenty of
Three-Spire's type, politicians who always landed on
their feet. By now all of that sort had been weeded
out of the legion. No matter how well you sucked
up to the high command, in a battle there was a lot
of stuff happening. Sometimes javelins flew from a
funny direction.

Glabrio joined his fellows as they clashed off on
their left feet. He gave Froggie a hard glance from
beneath the brim of his helmet.

The Commander had slumped down onto the chariot's floor. The bodyguards remained stolidly motionless
but the driver was peering over his seat-back at the
Commander, her scaly hide turning mauve in concern.

The Guild had long ago made sure the legion
knew about those weapons that could find a man
wherever he hid and burn him alive through solid
rock. It was interesting that a barb aide knew about
them, though. Froggie wasn't about to bet that those

weapons wouldn't be used on him and his boys, even though the Commander didn't look in much shape to give orders.

"Slats," Froggie said aloud, "please inform our Commander that I hear him talking."

Some things translate, others—with luck—don't. Nodding to Three-Spire, Froggie turned and strode into the village behind his last squad.

The temple or whatever was built even stranger on the inside, but it was comfortable enough if you avoided thinking of it as the setup for the world's biggest funeral pyre. You could look up to the open sky from the central court. At the back of the ground floor was a sanctum set off by heavy doors; inside was a black stone on a plinth. At six levels above the ground were rooms for sleeping and storage, reached by stairs that snaked up both sides of the walls.

Froggie was overseeing the squad that stowed the century's gear when one of the pair of guards at the entrance called, "Hey Top? The bug wants to come in."

"Well, let him in, Calamus," Froggie said with a touch of irritation in his tone. He strode toward the door, his feet drumming *thump/squeal* on floor timbers. "He's our commanding officer, remember."

"Right, Froggie," a trooper called from halfway up the open staircase. "And I'm Venus rising from the seafoam!"

Froggie really hadn't meant Slats when he said not to let any but their own people into the billets even if that meant putting twelve inches of steel through a few of them. He'd damned well meant it about the barbs, though. He guessed he ought to be glad Slats wasn't the sort who'd try to push through a door when a guard stopped him.

Slats entered, his middle limbs quivering. "Centurion Froggie," he said, "the village chief says—"

He turned, apparently expecting to see the barb following him. Instead, the guards had locked their shields across the entrance. The chief jumped back like he'd stepped on a hot griddle, but the four axe-men who tagged along might have been inclined to try something.

Calamus and Baldy both had their swords drawn; door-guard was no job for javelins. The barb soldiers backed away, looking angry but not afraid.

"Slats, tell the barbs that this building is now Guild territory," Froggie said. "Tell them that any attempt to enter it while we're billeted here is an attack on the Guild, to which we'll respond with all necessary force."

"Well, really, Centurion Froggie," the administrator said. "I don't think—"

"Tell them!" Froggie said.

Slats spread his limbs, then clicked to the barbs through his translator. The chief twisted his throat back. His bodyguards' faces didn't change a bit, but Froggie figured those boys had understood the deal before they were told.

Slats turned to Froggie. He went into his submissive posture again and said, "The chief informs me that your men are constructing a camp outside the walls. The Commander—we must accept that it was the Commander speaking—was explicit that you warriors and I live within Kascanschi. *Please*, Centurion Froggie!"

"Sirmius?" Froggie called to the squad leader. Poor

Slats was scared enough to turn into a pile of the little green pellets he shit. "Finish up here. I'm going to take our leader on a tour of the make-work I've got the other squads doing."

He put his arm around the administrator and walked him into the evening. There were a lot of women and children in the town; they'd come out a few at a time and headed for the fields when they saw the century was settling into a routine that didn't include rape and slaughter. Now they were returning.

There weren't many males, though, except for the forty axemen who'd escorted the chief and elders. Those were keeping pretty much out of the way since they and the century had sized each other up. The four shepherding the chief in the wake of Froggie and Slats were the only ones in sight now.

"You see, sir," Froggie said to the administrator as they walked through the gate, "I've got to keep the men busy. You'll recall the Commander gave me specific orders about that when he sent us out. I've got the boys building a fort in this waste ground, just for the exercise. They've got a good start, wouldn't you say?"

"You're not going to live there?" Slats said in desperate hope. His triangular head moved back and forth in quick jerks, the way a human might have done with his eyes alone. "I thought . . ."

Froggie had left Verruca to deal with the fort because he was more worried about the way the temple had been constructed. The wall was well begun already. The ground cover here didn't bind the soil the way grass did, so the squads were trading off on the task of weaving brush into rough baskets to hold dirt.

This sort of construction would keep out prying eyes better than a stockade. Besides, when the troopers had time in a day or two to wet and tamp the soil, the result'd be as good as a turf wall.

The men had stripped off their helmets and body armor, but they still wore their sword belts. Four fully-equipped troopers guarded the gear of the others in the center of the rising fort. No point in taking chances.

"But the female barbarians?" Slats said. "They have remained, against the Commander's clear orders."

"Huh!" Froggie said. "I guess you're right. Who'd have thought it?"

Most of the girls were helping with the work, but a pair were coming back from the stream with buckets of water for the evening meal. They waved gaily to Froggie. Queenie came out from behind the barrier that protected the fort's gateway and walked over.

"But they must leave," Slats said in frightened animation. "You must order them to leave!"

"Oh, I did," Froggie said. He'd said the words to Queenie, true enough. He'd sooner not tell a lie if he could avoid it, and a long career in the army had taught him lots of ways to avoid it. "Maybe you should try yourself, Slats."

The administrator rotated his head toward the approaching girl. Froggie patted Slats on the back and said, "Go ahead. Maybe you'll have better luck."

And maybe pigs would fly. The troopers had seen stranger things since they'd been bought by the Guild.

Slats' translator blurted a demand that was so full of apologies you'd have thought he was talking to the Commander. Slats really didn't like saying things the listener might not want to hear.

"Go fuck tree, bug-man," Queenie said in cheerful pidgin. "We stay."

"I guess they can camp out in the fort," Froggie said. "Since it's built, after all."

"But—" said Slats. "They're supposed to go—"

The village chief spoke to Queenie. She'd known to be politic when Three-Spire was here with the Commander, but the local hick got out less than ten words when Queenie lit into him.

Queenie didn't kick the barb in the balls, but she did everything short of that. He bobbed and fluttered his arms up and down. Other girls called raucous support, and half a dozen of the nearest troopers rested their hands on their swordhilts as they smiled and watched.

Slats turned to Froggie. "She says—" he began.

Queenie whirled toward the centurion and administrator. "We no need him shitpot village!" she cried. "We stay out here, take care boss-man and great warriors like always!"

The village chief skittered back when Queenie let him go, but the captain of his guards caught him by the arm and pushed him forward again. Froggie stepped between the chief and Queenie.

"Slats," he said without looking around, "to make sure that none of the girls leave their quarters at night, I'm going to station an outpost here during the four watches."

"An outpost?" Slats said. Froggie could hear the administrator's limbs rubbing against the slick, copper-colored robe he wore.

"Just two men," Froggie said reassuringly. "Tell the chief that if he's got problems with Guild personnel and their slaves using waste ground outside his village, he'd better keep them to himself."

The administrator's lavaliere began chirping away in rapid barb. Froggie looked the head of the axemen in the eye and said, "And by the way, Slats. I don't guess the girls'll have any trouble with the local barbs . . . but you might let the chief know that we were the first troops through the breach when the capital fell. If there *is* any trouble, we won't stop killing while there's one barb alive here. And we'll burn the houses down over their bodies."

Slats looked at the centurion and opened his mouth as if to comment. Then he spread his limbs and resumed his directions to the village chief, speaking with great earnestness.

Froggie woke before the man coming down the ladder had reached the top level of the temple's own staircase. There were two sentries on the temple roof as well as the pair at the entrance. Froggie was with the squad sleeping in the nave of the temple, while for official purposes the other men were distributed in the rooms on higher levels.

When he'd gotten his boots laced, Froggie started up the stairs to meet the messenger. He hadn't put on his cuirass, but he carried it on his left forearm. The information coming down from the roof wasn't an immediate crisis—there was a gong for that—but something might blow up while Froggie was talking to the messenger. He didn't want to be in the dark and a level away from his armor if that happened.

"Top?" Glabrio whispered. Froggie figured it'd be him. "There's a couple guys went out through the wicket in the gate tower. They started west toward the hills, but from up in the tower we couldn't see 'em once they got into the brush."

"A couple of the bodyguards, did it look?" Froggie said.

Glabrio nodded. "Hard to see much by starlight, but they had axes," he said. "Besides, who else would it be?"

Slats came through the curtained doorway of the room beside them. "Centurion Froggie?" he said. "There is trouble?"

"Naw," said Froggie. He'd forgotten that the room was occupied. "Not just yet, anyhow. Glabrio tells me a couple barb soldiers went out of the village tonight. Tomorrow night him and me'll be in the fort with the girls, so if it happens again we'll follow them."

Glabrio grinned. "Hoped you might say that," he murmured.

"Do you think that's . . . ?" Slats began, but his voice trailed off. He twisted his head fiercely.

"Centurion Froggie," he said, facing away from the two Romans. The words still whispered from the translator on his chest. "I do not understand what is happening and I'm very concerned."

"Well, sir," Froggie said judiciously, "that's true of the rest of us too. We ought to know more soon, though; and anyhow, we're working on ways to handle whatever might come up."

Slats faced around. "I am glad to hear that," he said, though he didn't sound glad about much of anything. "I have heard at the Harbor that the aide Three-Spire visits the Commander often in private. And I have heard—I have never seen this!—that sometimes after those private meetings, the Commander dances to music only he can hear."

"The barb's fixing up our blue-suited leader with drugs, you mean," Froggie said bluntly. Glabrio was holding as still as a hare in covert. Froggie trusted Glabrio with anything there was to know, but he doubted the administrator would feel that way except he was so upset.

"I don't know that!" Slats said, flailing his middle limbs like they were wings. "And even if it were true, why would Three-Spire want to split the legion up into tiny groups? How would *he* gain if we were all killed?"

"I wouldn't guess Three-Spire was in charge of whatever's going on," Froggie said. "But we'll know more soon. Why don't you go back to bed, Slats?"

"To sleep?" Slats said. His mouth gave a clack that the lavaliere couldn't translate. "How could I do that? But I will try."

He paused and cocked his head. "Centurion Froggie?" he said. "I hear the sound of tools."

"No," Froggie said. "You don't hear tools. Remember that, Slats. It's important."

"Ah," said the administrator. "I will remember that, Centurion Froggie. And perhaps I will sleep after all."

Froggie could stay awake constantly for half an eight-day market cycle if he had to, but pieces started coming off his concentration early on. He'd napped because there was no reason not to. Now he got up, cinched his swordbelt tighter—he hadn't actually unbuckled it or taken his boots off—and sauntered out of the temple. The guards murmured politely.

Slats was checking the village's warehouses, great thatch-roofed rounds of basketry. Brush filled the space between the double walls, so air could circulate among the vegetables on shelves inside but rain couldn't get in even when the wind was driving it.

Froggie knew Slats was in the warehouse because a squad of troopers waited at the doorway, taking it easy. There wasn't room within for both of the squads Slats insisted on having around him at all times. He was a nervous little bug, he was; not that he didn't have reason to be.

The troopers started to rise when they saw their centurion. Froggie waved them back. They'd been putting in long hours, and there'd be more work for them tonight. It wasn't safe to keep on with the real job during daylight; there were too many barbs up and moving around the streets near the temple.

Laena came out of the fort scratching himself. He'd probably been sleeping, which was fine under the circumstances; the men had orders just not to lay about where the barbs could see them, since somebody might wonder what they were doing at night to be so tired.

Laena saw Froggie and came trotting over. He leaned his face close to the centurion's ear and said, "Hey, Top? You know my girl Glycera?"

"I believe I've seen her," Froggie said carefully. Every place that relative anatomy permitted it, Laena paired off with a local girl and called her Glycera. For most of his existence, Laena seemed to have no desire except to argue about orders. You didn't want to touch—or even look hard at—any of his current Glyceras, though.

"Our girls talk with the ones from the town while they're all down at the creek doing wash, you know?" Laena said. "You know them guards the chiefs got around him? They're not from here!"

"Right," said Froggie mildly. He'd have thought Laena was smart enough that he wouldn't have to be told that the axemen weren't local.

Laena looked miffed at the centurion's lack of surprise. He was one of the real linguists of the legion: give Laena three days anydamnplace and he'd be chattering to "Glycera" like they'd grown up in the same hamlet. Like a lot of other specialists, though, he tended to think that his way of learning things was the only one there was. Froggie never got beyond basic pidgin, but he knew how to keep his eyes open.

"Well, it's more'n that," Laena said. "The local girls say that under those kilts they wear, them guys are more different from the barbs here than we are. What do you think of that?"

Froggie mulled the question. Queenie was coming toward him, her neck ruff in an angry flare.

"I'll tell you the truth, Laena," he said. "I don't know what I think. Did the girls say anything about a metal ship landing like, you know, when we came?"

"Nope," said Laena. "They just come out of the hills. The Commander's pet barb Three-Spire come along with them and told the elders the new guys were in charge now. They looked tough enough that the local guys didn't argue matters. The warriors left here were the ones who'd run fast enough when they met *us*, after all."

"Boss-man!" Queenie said. She didn't even bother

to look at Laena. Froggie was boss-man and she was the leader of Froggie's women, so nothing a mere trooper had to say was important when *she* needed to talk. "Fucking barb warriors here—they mean bastards! You chop them quick-quick, yes?"

Queenie's notion of how to solve a problem usually involved somebody getting chopped. That was probably why she got along so well with troopers.

And if the bodyguards had been bothering the girls . . . Froggie's hand touched the ivory hilt of his sword, smoother than silk by now from all the use it'd gotten. He'd warned them, hadn't he?

"What's the problem, Queenie?" he asked, his tone quiet but a little thicker than usual.

"Them take girls from village," Queenie said. "They no feed meat, boss-man!"

Froggie frowned at Laena. An argument about how much some other soldier paid his whore didn't strike either of them as a killing business.

"No meat, girl not *right* inside!" Queenie said. "Girl hurt, girl scream! Bastards laugh, they like girl to hurt! All them bastards!"

"Ah," said Froggie as he understood. Not that he hadn't known soldiers who liked their girls to scream; pretty good soldiers, some of them, and it wasn't something he figured he'd need to interfere with if they'd been his men.

But these weren't his men. And it wasn't one or two of them, it was the whole troop. And truth to tell, when Froggie'd had a guy like that in his squad, the fellow'd got all the dirty jobs there were till he transferred to another cohort.

"I hear you, Queenie," he said. "We no chop-chop

yet. Right now, you slip other girls meat, yes? Me tell boys this all right."

He slapped his armored breast with the flat of his hand.

Queenie clucked happily. "Me fix!" she said. "Later you chop-chop, all right?"

"I wouldn't be a bit surprised," Froggie said. "Not one little bit."

The trail was as dark as the inside of a grave. A piece of quartz clicked under Froggie's hobnails. The barefoot Glabrio turned and glared, but Froggie met the trooper's gaze with cold unconcern. He knew it was important to follow as quietly as possible, but he also knew the pair of axemen ahead were talking in normal voices and occasionally clearing branches from the trail with a swipe of their weapons. He gestured Glabrio on with a flick of his finger.

Some of the trees here had thorns. Glabrio might be able to avoid stepping on one as he trotted down the shadowy track, but Froggie wasn't that confident. He wouldn't make near the racket with his heavy bootsoles as he might if a thorn drove into the ball of his foot and jolted loose a curse.

Glabrio grimaced and went on. Froggie kept Glabrio in sight. He could've followed the barbs by ear alone if he'd had to, as nonchalant as they were, but Glabrio was the real expert.

Froggie wasn't as good a tracker as Glabrio. He wasn't the best swordsman in the century, he didn't have the best range with a javelin, and there were three or four of the troopers who could take him apart in a barehanded fight.

But Froggie could do every job in the unit *nearly* as well as his best man; and there was nobody the Third of the Fourth trusted more to bring them alive out of the sort of ratfuck they were surely in the middle of now.

They'd come nearly a mile from the village. The barbs had left at midnight, same as the night before; as soon as they reached the woods, they'd started acting like there was nothing to worry about except maybe tearing their clothes on a prickly branch. As a veteran, Froggie was pleased to see how badly the enemy was underestimating him; but he was human enough to feel insulted, too.

Glabrio started around a tree with six trunks braided together like a horsehair rope. He stopped and flashed his hand toward Froggie, palm out and fingers spread. Froggie stopped dead, then hunched forward to a curtain of tasseled vegetation on the other side of the trail. He extended his left arm carefully to make an opening so he could watch the pair of barbs.

The axemen stood at the base of a thirty-foot basalt thumb poking through the weathered shale. Only a few sprays of vegetation blotched the hard rock, but trees growing nearby shaded all but the very peak of the intrusion. The barb leader took something from a pouch on his harness and pointed it at the basalt.

There was a clicking sound like a treefrog winding up for its mating call. A circle of rock dissolved.

Glabrio had the point of his dagger clear of the sheath before his mind got control of his instincts. The barbs could've heard his blurted curse if they been paying attention to anything but what was in front of them.

Froggie didn't move. He hadn't expected this, exactly, but he'd expected something.

The rock opened into a tunnel ten feet in diameter; the walls were of glowing blue ice. A Commander waited behind a waist-high screen of the same translucent blue, guarded by a pair of armored apes wearing metal gloves with knives welded onto the knuckles. Those were good weapons for the tunnel's close quarters.

Three-Spire stood at the Commander's side. The bastard sure did get around.

The barbs from the village walked into the tunnel. There was another click, click, click-clickclick, and the opening fused to solid rock again.

Glabrio turned to his centurion, his face white. The dagger trembled in his hand. He wasn't worried by flying chariots or the way the metal ships climbed through the air, but this was new.

It was new to Froggie too, but he was a centurion. He couldn't let anything show on his face, or his boys might go off in a panic that got some of them killed.

He motioned to Glabrio and backed out of sight of the outcrop before turning to start down the trail again. He heard the muted *tunk* of the dagger going home in its sheath; then Glabrio whispered, "Aren't we gonna follow 'em when they leave, Top?"

"Hercules, we know where they're going back to, don't we?" Froggie said. "And if they didn't, that'd be two fewer to take care of when the time comes. Not that I'd mind the extra work in this case."

The blue glow hadn't been real bright, but it was enough to leave Froggie just better than stone blind on the starlit trail. He'd like to have hurried, though he didn't suppose it mattered. However long the barbs stayed inside the tunnel, they weren't going to see well enough to run up the Romans' back when they got out.

"The thing I don't figure . . ." Glabrio said—and if there was only one thing, he was doing better than Froggie—". . . is what the Commander's doing there? Does he have some kinda plan?"

"Your people were farmers, weren't they, Glabrio?" Froggie said. As his sight came back, he was stepping up the pace. His left foot flicked a spark off into the night.

"Huh?" Glabrio said. "Yeah, wheat and a garden, the usual. So what?"

"We were shepherds," Froggie said. "Now, if you're not used to them, all sheep look alike—but they don't all act the same way. You learn to tell them apart by the way they stand, by the way one's left ear curls back—that sort of thing."

"Yeah?" said Glabrio.

"So the guy in a blue suit we just saw was standing straight, not hip-shot, and when he called the barbs inside he tapped his left fingertips into the other palm," Froggie said. "He was a Commander, son, but he wasn't the guy who's supposed to be in command of us."

The sun had just come over the horizon, and the birds that roosted in treetops at night were lifting into the sky. They flew on sheets of skin rippling along either side of their snake-slim bodies, more like flounders swimming through the air than the birds Froggie'd grown up with.

These would fly to the sea three days march to westward. They'd gorge on the jellyfish swarming in sheltered waters between the mainland and the chain of offshore islands, then fly back. The birds were free to go anywhere they pleased—and it pleased them to go the same place every day.

Glabrio was sleeping but Froggie stood at the fort's west gate, facing Kascanschi. He thought about the birds and all the similar birds he'd seen in scores of places, and he tried to imagine his life if he'd never been sold to the Guild. Maybe for him there wouldn't have been any difference between being a freeborn Roman citizen and a Guild slave . . . but he knew he hated his Commanders as he'd never hated a Roman general, not even that idiot Crassus who put him here.

The city gates creaked open. Local women shoved the sagging panels outward, supervised by one of the squad of axemen who'd spent the night in the gatehouse.

The guard noticed Froggie. He balanced his long-hafted axe on the fingers of one hand, then did a complicated series of sweeps that involved him stepping forward and back through the spinning weapon. His eyes remained locked with the centurion's.

One of the girls chirruped in fear as steel flicked toward and past her. Given the blade's weight and edge, the axe would've taken her arm off if she'd lurched in the wrong direction as she stepped back from the gate. Froggie was willing to bet that the axeman wouldn't have let that prevent him from finishing with the flourish that brought his weapon to rest precisely as it had been at the start.

The village women were lined up to go to the fields now that the gate was open, but today Slats and his guards were ahead of them. The administrator chirped an order through his lavaliere. His four bearers left the group of girls at the fort and lifted him in his palanquin. Slats sat bolt upright with both sets of arms crossed behind his back, wearing what Froggie was coming to recognize as a sour expression on his pointed face.

Froggie nodded. He didn't especially want to talk to Slats, but he wasn't surprised when the palanquin came to a stop beside him.

"No more warehouse inventory to take, Slats?" Froggie asked. "Can we head home now?"

"Of course not, Centurion Froggie," Slats said severely. "I am to remain here in charge of the district even after the planet is classed as pacified and you warriors are dispatched to another location."

"I'm sorry to hear that," Froggie said. He'd miss the bug now that he'd gotten to know him on this detached duty; but what Froggie *really* regretted was that he and the boys wouldn't be leaving here until the place was officially pacified.

Froggie suspected pacification was a long way off. He just hoped the Third of the Fourth wouldn't be massacred to prove he was right.

"I am going into the fields to watch the work," Slats said. "The crops being harvested are less by one half than they should be."

The palanquin lurched as the bearers set it down without orders. They'd apparently decided that if their cargo was going to stay in one place and talk, they didn't need to hold his weight on their shoulders.

Froggie braced Slats with a hand to keep him from tumbling out on his face.

"They're eating meat, remember?" Froggie said. "It makes them perkier."

The women from the town were trudging out to the fields, moving in pairs and small groups the way it always happens, even in a flock of sheep. Queenie, striding with the assured direction of a thrown javelin, entered a clot of a dozen local girls and brought them to a halt. She didn't look around as she talked, but her listeners turned and stared straight at Froggie. It was like walking by a fishmonger's stall, all eyes and gaping mouths. He hoped the barb axemen weren't watching.

"Anyway," he continued to Slats, "two days isn't much time to decide what's a normal amount of work."

"Do I tell you how to use your sword, warrior?" Slats said, his tone the first hint Froggie'd gotten that the bug was capable of an emotion other than fear. "Do not tell me how to assess labor against output; this is what I *do*. I tell you the crops entering Kascanschi these past two days are only half what they should be, based on the surplus earmarked for transport to the royal capital immediately before the battle."

"That's 'cause half the women have been put to slicing the tops of kiro trees out in the forest, buddy," Laena said. Slats chirped and jumped against the back of his palanquin in surprise at being addressed by a man he'd thought of as furniture.

Froggie was surprised too. Laena was part of the administrator's guard section today, but while Slats talked he'd been taking it easy with "Glycera" same as the other troopers and girls were. The last thing you'd expect from Laena was for him to volunteer a comment about farm output.

"Yeah," Laena continued. He didn't notice or didn't care that he'd scared Slats into an early molt. "My girl Glycera says that since this new lot come in, they've put half the workers to cutting the tops, that's where they fruit, of the kiro trees. The sap bleeds out and hardens, and the seeds don't ripen the way they ought to."

"Dis!" Froggie said. "What's good does that do?"

"Not a bit, the girls say," said Laena. "The guys with axes tell them they'll carry the heads away in a couple weeks, but none of the girls can see why. It just makes a black gunk."

Slats patted his middle arms together. "I will examine the kiro trees," he said, his eyes focused on a point in space. "Perhaps they provide a valuable product which the survey informing my briefing cube failed to note. But if they do not—"

The administrator clasped his hands, upper left with middle right and vice versa, in a gesture of emphasis.

"—then I will put a stop to this diversion of effort. I am the Guild administrator for this district!"

"Our friends with the axes might have something to say about that," Froggie said quietly.

"Then you and your warriors will remove them, Centurion Froggie!" Slats said. "It is your duty!"

"Yeah," said Froggie. "Though in this case, it'd probably be a pleasure as well."

The native women had been drifting back from the fields for some while before Froggie saw Slats and his troopers returning. The administrator took his job seriously, which Froggie generally would've been glad of.

The fort was small—as it had to be for a single century to defend it—but it was a clean, professional piece of work. There were gates in all four walls and fighting towers kitty-corner on the northwest and southeast angles. The walls were eight feet high, and the earth-filled hurdles were actually more difficult to bore through than stone because gravity would fill the holes between pick-strokes.

"We don't have a proper ditch around it, Top," said Glabrio, beside Froggie and leaning against the baffle protecting the north gate.

"It'd get in the way," Froggie said. "Besides, with maybe three thousand barbs in the town, how long d'ye think a ditch would slow them down? Dis, they could take the thatching off a few houses and fill any ditch sixty men could dig."

Glabrio frowned, but he didn't argue the point. He was tense because he knew things were about to happen and he couldn't tell for sure how it was going to turn out.

Froggie sighed. He couldn't tell either.

The bearers carried Slats to where Froggie was waiting. Slats grabbed the sides of the palanquin and chirped an order so that he could seem to be telling the girls what to do this time. They set him down.

As the administrator got out, one of the girls stroked his shoulder the way you'd polish a nice piece of pottery. He hopped away sideways; all the bearers giggled.

"Come on inside here, Slats," Froggie said. "I'll show

you the way we've been carrying out the Commander's orders to keep busy."

Slats looked at his palanquin. He could walk fine, so it was just a status thing that he wanted to be carried.

"Come on, Slats," Froggie repeated gently. "There's not room enough to turn that travelling couch between the gate baffle and the main wall anyway."

He reached out his hand, but Slats was already scuttling down the open-topped passage. The gate looked crude, but the leaf pivoted on a bearing of hollowed stone. Everywhere workmanship would affect function, the job had been accomplished to the highest standards.

"I am very angry, Centurion Froggie," Slats said. "What Warrior Laena said was true: half of the labor force is wasting its efforts on mutilating kiro trees. This sabotage of Kascanschi's output is as pointless as it is deliberate."

"Step over here by the wall, Slats," Froggie said. Somebody—meaning somebody with an axe—on the city gates could see down into some of the fort's interior; that was the disadvantage of having had to build so near to the city. Froggie could've taken the administrator into the timber-roofed barracks, but the light was better if they stood close to the wall nearest the town.

Froggie brought an oval tube the length of a man's middle finger out of his wallet. There were indentations at several places on the surface, perhaps intended for finger pressure.

"What?" said Slats in amazement. He snatched the gadget. Froggie had to tug him back or he'd have stepped into plain view with it. "Where did you find this?"

"The head of the guys with axes had it," Froggie explained. "The feathers're dyed, by the way. His girlfriend slipped it to Queenie. Only *girlfriend* isn't exactly the right word, because I guess she'd rather he was dead and a long time dying."

"This is the key to a dimensional portal!" Slats said. "There's nothing on this planet that would justify the cost of constructing a portal! Even ordinary stardrive is a marginal proposition for the products available here."

"If it turns solid rock into a hole with blue ice around it," Froggie said, "then somebody disagrees with you about it being worthwhile to put one here."

He reached for the key. The administrator kept hold of it and said, "This is incredible! I must take this—"

"Nowhere," Froggie said, closing his fist around the little tube despite Slats' attempt to retain it. "The girl has got to get it back before her master finds it's missing. Whatever else happened, she'd be chopped for sure. You coming back late pushed the time more than I'd have chosen to do."

"This is more important than one—" Slats said.

Froggie tapped the bug's mouth, not the lavaliere, with his index finger. "No," he said, "it isn't. I've got nothing against killing barbs, but I'm not going to have somebody else kill 'em because I didn't do what I promised. Understood?"

"Understood, Centurion Froggie," Slats said in a tiny voice. "I must go to my room, now. This is very important."

"Yeah," said Froggie, "I thought it might be."

Queenie waited nearby, tense and silent. When

Froggie nodded to her, she snatched the key and slipped it beneath her kilt before scurrying out of the fort. Froggie smiled faintly.

"Do you have any idea what this is all about, Slats?" he asked as he followed the administrator out of the fort. Slats didn't bother with status and the palanquin in his haste to get back to his room in the temple.

"I do not!" he said. "It is inconceivable, Centurion Froggie!"

Froggie sighed again. "I kinda thought that too," he said.

During previous nights a fire on the central slate hearth illuminated the temple's interior adequately. Tonight the space was full of troopers: sharpening weapons, polishing armor, and talking in hushed voices about the future. Because so many bodies blocked the light, Froggie'd had a fatigue detail string the nut-oil lanterns they'd found in a storage room on the sixth level. The shades were rinds of something like a beet, pierced with fanciful shapes.

The lamplight was creamy, but it waked sword-edges into sparkles like fangs winking in the night.

Slats came down the stairs, eyeing the assembled troopers warily. Froggie broke off his conversation with Verruca about the guard roster and went to meet the administrator.

"Are you expecting trouble, Centurion Froggie?" Slats whispered, twitching one of his middle limbs to indicate the soldiers. The courtyard would've held at least five hundred worshippers, but men in armor filled the space in a way that civilians could not have done.

"Not anything special, Slats," Froggie said. "The men're getting a break tonight except for the guards. A lot of them thought it'd be a good time to put their equipment in order."

Slats moved his head in tiny jerks, looking across the array of bronze and iron. "You had them busy on other duties before?" he asked.

"Yeah," said Froggie. "I did."

"I have been talking to the Commander," Slats said. He held up the little wand that he'd said could summon help. "Trying to talk with him, that is."

"You have?" Froggie said. "Dis, if whoever's behind Three-Spire gets wind of what we've found here, they'll come for us sure. And I sure don't believe the Commander's going to keep anything private. We're going to have to head back to Harbor at first light!"

"We can't do that," the administrator said. "Our orders are to remain here until recalled. In any case, I doubt that the Commander will even remember that we talked. He seemed disconnected. By the end of the conversation he was almost comatose."

Froggie shook his head. "Slats," he said, "I'm a big believer in following orders, at least when people are going to know if you don't, but Three-Spire's bound to have listened to everything you said to the Blue Boy. As soon as he gets a messenger out here, the guys with the axes are going to send the whole village at us. We can't fight that many barbs, even if most of 'em are women."

"If they have a dimensional portal," Slats said, "surely they would have holographic communicators—"

He waggled his wand in the air again.

"—as well. But even so I cannot permit you to—"

The sentries on the roof parapet began to whang their gong violently. An instant after the first bronze note echoed down the temple's interior, a barb outside screamed like she was being disemboweled—which was likely enough to be the truth.

"By squads and wait for orders!" Froggie bellowed. He strode to the door with the certainty of an ox pacing through stubble, sliding men off his shoulder to either side even though many of them were bigger than he was.

The few troopers not already wearing their cuirasses began locking them on with the help of friends. Swords clashed into sheathes; the air filled with the jangling of hinged cheekpieces as men donned their helmets.

Froggie'd ordered the door kept closed but not barred. Two men stood in full armor just inside, ready to support the sentries in the street. Froggie waved them back and jerked the door open.

Laesio and Five Metellus hunched in the door alcove behind their upraised shields. Beyond them, mobs streamed down the three approaching streets, waving torches and shouting. The front ranks were local warriors with spears and wicker shields. Froggie caught glimpses of the foreign axemen, but they were staying back a little—safe from Roman javelins and able to prod the locals forward if they hesitated.

"Inside!" Froggie shouted, clapping the armored shoulders of his two guards. Even if he'd been able to deploy the whole century in the plaza, they wouldn't have a chance against five or six hundred warriors with a couple thousand women to throw stones down from the roofs of the surrounding buildings.

Turning his head he added in the loudest voice he

could manage, "Head for the fort by squads! Move 'em out, Verruca!"

The guards backed into the building, guided by their centurion's touch. Stones banged off the wall of the building. Froggie felt the doorpanel shake as he held it closed while the back-up team slid the bar into place.

When the Romans arrived, the temple door had a catch that was barely strong enough to keep the panel from blowing open in a storm. A timber as thick a man's thigh had replaced it immediately. The barbs could batter a hole in the walls quicker than they'd get through that bar.

They weren't planning to do either thing, of course. The mob's torches weren't just for light.

"Centurion Froggie!" Slats cried as Froggie turned around. His mouth chirped close to the centurion's ear but the Latin words came disconcertingly from the chest-level lavaliere. "What is happening? Are we in danger?"

"Keep your mouth shut and do exactly what I tell you!" Froggie said. "Then at least you've got a better chance than a lot of them barbs outside do."

The administrator jerked his head back and wrapped all four arms around his thin chest. He stood upright, quivering like a poplar tree in a storm.

Verruca had the evacuation in hand. First and Second Squads had already disappeared through the doors to the sanctum in back. Third Squad was providing the guards at this hour, so Fourth had fallen in behind Second.

There wasn't any pushing or open panic, but the troopers were tense. They were veterans, but nobody likes the thought of being burned alive.

"We've got plenty of time, boys," Froggie called cheerfully. "It'll be a good ten minutes before you'll even smell smoke in here—and I'm the last one out, remember!"

"Smoke?" Slats said, forgetting to stay silent. "Is there a fire, Centurion Froggie?"

"Sure, they're going to burn this place down," Froggie said, rubbing the side of his neck with his swagger stick. His nonchalance was a pose, but calming other people in a crisis had the effect of settling the tribe of field mice dancing in Froggie's own stomach. "Don't worry about it, Slats. You and me ain't staying much longer."

"But there's no other way . . ." the administrator began, then quivered to a halt.

Laena had been one of the roof sentries. He joined Froggie as his partner fell in with the rest of his squad, at the end of the line that shuffled toward the sanctum.

"Top?" he said. "We saw one of the girls—not one of ours I don't think—run down the street toward here. There was the whole damned town right after her, it looked like. The guys in front threw spears and scragged her. You think she was trying to warn us?"

"Could be, Laena," Froggie said. "The men probably figure this is getting even for the way we handed them their heads when we landed; but to the women these foreigners took, we probably look better'n the swans from Venus' chariot."

The Romans hadn't needed the warning, and the girl had been a damned fool to try and give it so openly, but it still gave Froggie a cold itch to think about. He twitched his swagger stick toward the line of troopers.

"Fall in, Laena," he said. "We'll pay them back pretty quick."

He could smell smoke already and it hadn't been any ten minutes. The temple was old, and when the little staves dried out they left gaps that sucked the smoke through.

The gaps sucked in the fire as well. The interior was already brighter than daylight with flames thin as snake tongues slipping in and out of the panelling. Froggie heard thumps as barbs flung bales of brushwood against the outer walls, but that was a waste of effort. Torches had already ignited the bare wood without need for additional fuel.

"Please, Froggie," Slats whimpered. "What are we to do?"

"First get out of here," Froggie said. "Then kick some ass."

He put his arm around the bug's thin shoulders and pointed the swagger stick in that hand toward the end of Third Squad, disappearing into the sanctum. The flames were beginning to heat the temple's cavernous interior. Had any of the barbs objected to burning the place down this way? Not that an objection would've lasted longer than the time it took one of the foreigners to swing an axe. . . .

The stone spindle the barbs prayed to—or whatever they did; it wasn't like there'd been any ceremonies since the Third of the Fourth arrived—had been shoved into a corner, wooden base and all. The troopers had taken up the rest of the floor and gone ten feet straight down before heading east with a tunnel so level that water wouldn't flow along it.

Verruca'd wanted to slope the entrance so they

wouldn't have to turn part of the flooring into stairs, but Froggie insisted on a full five feet of dirt between every part of the tunnel roof and the street around the temple. Going up and down the stairs took a little more time, but the troopers *had* plenty of time—unless the barbs discovered the tunnel.

"Down ahead of me, Slats," Froggie said. He stood, taking a last look over the temple's interior; his left arm held his shield slightly out from his body instead of letting the neck strap support all its weight.

The barbs were probably staying well back, expecting the century to cut a hole through a sidewall and make a desperate sally. That'd be suicide, of course, when a dozen warriors would be waiting for each trooper who stumbled through the flames. Better to die on a spearpoint than be cooked alive, though.

Better still to send the other bastard to Dis with his skull split or trying to stuff guts back through the rip in his belly.

Froggie turned. Slats still stood at the top of the stairs. "Move!" Froggie said, barely a heartbeat from slamming the administrator forward with his shield.

Slats hopped twice, to the landing midway and then the floor of the tunnel. The motion reminded Froggie of a crane flying, graceless but seemingly without weight.

Froggie followed, thumping on stair treads already scarred by many hobnails. They'd stored the excavated dirt in the sanctum at first; then, when the inside squad met the tunnel being driven from the fort, they'd used the spoil to fill baskets and add to the strength of the fort's walls. On this side the floors of upper-level rooms had provided the pit props; on the other, green timber like that of the fort's barracks and gates kept the tunnel from collapsing.

It was a neat job with plenty of room for a fully-equipped legionary to pass along it. He'd have to hunch over, but that was just as true for most of the huts and tenements the troopers had lived in before they'd been recruited.

"This tunnel goes to your new fort?" Slats asked. His head turned but his translator was still on his chest, and the echo of boots muffled his words. "You will protect me there until help comes?"

Froggie snorted. "You're a fool if you expect help from any farther away than my sword-edge, Slats," he said. "But yeah, we'll protect you."

The far end did slope till it came out in the barracks. Two grim-faced men from First Squad were waiting at the top of the ramp.

"I'm the last," Froggie said. The troopers grunted and swung the heavy trapdoor down over the opening, then slid a crossbar through the staples to hold it closed. There was next to no chance that the barbs would break into the burning temple, follow the Romans down the tunnel, and come up in the middle of the fort while everybody was looking the other way . . . but there was no chance at all if the tunnel was closed and barred.

Froggie stepped out of the barracks. The sky was orange from the flames that shot from the top of the temple, reflecting on the base of the clouds. The fire roared louder than a storm. It was like standing at the seashore as the surf comes in, a dull sound but one so loud that you have to shout to be heard over it.

Like he'd been ordered to, Verruca had the troopers crouching on the fighting step so that they couldn't be seen from outside the fort. Maybe the barbs were too sure of themselves to notice a line of helmeted heads where there were supposed to be only women, but Froggie wasn't the sort to take chances.

The girls stood in a close group beside the barracks. Froggie'd figured they'd be in a funk, either cackling in terror or frozen like open-mouthed statues while they waited to be chopped.

He should've known better. Queenie trotted over to him, holding a Roman dagger and looking as grim as a Fury. Every one of the girls had a weapon: a spear, a narrow-bladed barb hatchet, or at least a club.

"We chop now, boss-man!" Queenie said. "Yes?"

"Yes," Froggie said. "We chop."

Verruca, his normally ruddy face further brightened by the pillar of fire, came around the back of the barracks and saw Froggie. "I just put Third Squad with First at the west gate, Top," he said, shouting over the flames. "We don't need a reserve in the camp, not with the girls here."

The city gates opened, their creaking audible despite the fire's deep thrum. A trooper reached for the bar that held the camp's north gate closed.

"Wait for it, Sedulus!" Froggie said. The trooper jerked his hands away as though the timber had burned him.

The barb mob spilled out of the city. Froggie couldn't see them from where he crouched, but the varied shouts of "Kill!" and "Burn!" spilled around the fort like surf on a rock. Torches and a few spears flew over the walls. The green timber of the barracks wasn't going to catch fire easily, not that it mattered if it did.

"Ready the gates!" Froggie said. The men chosen for the duty at the north, west and south gates lifted the crossbars out of their staples; other members of their squads braced the panels against the unskilled efforts of barbs pushing from the other side.

A few crested heads appeared over the wall, enterprising barbs who'd been lifted on the shoulders of their fellows. They didn't have either siege equipment *or* discipline. It was like watching sheep trying to invade the butcher's stall. . . .

Froggie tossed his swagger stick over his shoulder and drew his sword. "Get 'em, troopers!" he bellowed.

The troopers bracing the gates stepped back and let the panels fly inward. The barbs pushing against them lurched into a flurry of sword-strokes that lopped them to pieces.

The rest of the mob didn't know what was happening. Two troopers at each gate strode forward with their shields raised, hacking barbs who were packed too tight to protect themselves or use their weapons. Outside the fort the leading pair spread slightly so that a third man could step between them. Another pace and two more troopers joined the wall of shields and slaughter. And two more . . .

The squads advanced only a little slower than if they'd been sauntering down the market square of a village when they were civilians. Every time a heavy, broad-bladed sword slashed, a barb died—though he might not be able to fall for a moment because of the crush of his fellows against him. Troopers stumbled and cursed as bodies writhed beneath their hobnails.

Froggie stepped forward. Mamurra, leader of the Third Squad, was about to take his boys out now that

First was clear of the gateway. Froggie tapped him aside and stepped through in his place, placing himself beside Glabrio on the right end of the line.

The flames were a hammer. The fort's walls had blocked more of the heat than Froggie'd realized as he waited till he was sure his job as centurion was over and he could be a soldier again. The temple was a roiling, red-orange tower trying to pierce the clouds.

An axeman short-gripped his weapon and thrust at Froggie's face. Froggie lifted the edge of his shield and cut low with his sword. He missed the knee joint but the blade sank so deep in the barb's thighbone that it cracked when Froggie twisted his blade free.

The barb howled and fell sideways with his axe sticking for a moment in the cross-laminated wood. Froggie thrust beneath the lower edge. He couldn't see the barb's belly and chest but he could guess close enough for the work.

The barb slumped out of sight with blood spewing from his mouth. Another axeman had figured out what was happening quicker than the local warriors. He turned to cut his way out the back of the mob with his shield slung behind him. Froggie stabbed upward from just beneath the barb's rib cage. That did the job, but Froggie had a bitch of a job tugging his blade free from a stroke so deep.

The axemen would've been nasty opponents on an open battlefield. One blow from their weapons would split a Roman shield, and a second would take off whichever body part it landed on, armor be damned. But the axe helves were too long to use in a mob like this, and the axemen's cuirasses of flexible cloth wouldn't even slow down the point of a Roman sword.

The barbs hadn't been expecting a battle; they'd come out to butcher the Roman girls so there wouldn't be any witnesses. What they'd found was butchery, all right. Froggie swung his sword and his shield edge, killing with every blow and striding forward.

The screams were loud, but for the first several minutes the roaring flames muffled the sound enough that those in the rear ranks thought their leaders were calling in triumph, not terror. When they finally understood and tried to flee, the real slaughter began.

The squads from the fort's north and south gates had circled the mob, compressing it sideways while the troopers from the west gate pushed the barbs toward the city. In panic the barbs tried to run back inside their own walls.

There must've been five hundred of them, easy, maybe even a thousand; all the men and a lot of boys and women, some of them carrying a kid in one hand and a rock to throw in the other. Mobs are like that; they've got no more brains than water pouring out a hole.

The barbs in this mob didn't have brains enough to know they couldn't all fit through the city gate at one time—and if they *had* known, they still didn't have the discipline to feed through in at least as much order as they'd come out for the attack. They piled up in the gateway and died, crushed and suffocated and puling with fear as blind as the brutal anger that had filled them only minutes before.

The temple fell with a rending crash, sweeping a wave of fire over the plaza and the buildings beyond. Sparks curled over the wall and fell on the battle indiscriminately. Helmet brims and shoulder pieces protected the troopers from the worst of it, but the flaming shower still made men step back and lift their shields overhead.

It wasn't as though there was much work remaining for them, after all. The barbs' own panic had seen to that.

"Save me a couple prisoners!" Froggie shouted. "I need a couple of the bastards with axes for prisoners!"

Dis! he could barely croak. He hadn't been this dry or this tired since . . .

Dis. Since three months back when the legion entered the barb capital over the smoking ruins of its wall. Same as the time before that, and the one before that, back to the day Cataline thought to become consul by the sword when he couldn't muster the votes. One of the people proving to Cataline that he didn't have enough swords either was a new recruit whose buddies called him Froggie.

Queenie offered a skin of wine. Froggie tried to sheathe his sword, but the blade was bloody and he didn't have a hand free to wipe it. Queenie put the wooden teat between his lips and squeezed, perfectly judging when to let up.

Froggie swizzled the unmixed wine, cleansing his mouth of dust and the stench of barb blood. He spewed out the first mouthful, then let Queenie take his sword so that he could drink at his own greedy choice.

Queenie ripped the kilt off a warrior's corpse and rubbed at the tacky blood on the blade. "You chop bastards good, boss-man," she said. "You chop them real good!"

❖   ❖   ❖

Half the town of Kascanschi was in flames or in ashes; most of the rest would burn before daylight.

"Thank Hercules and the luck of a soldier that the wind was from the east," Froggie muttered. "If it'd changed, the temple would've toppled right on top of us here."

He glanced at the huge mound of bodies and added, "It wouldn't make much difference to the barbs, would it?"

"Who gives a fuck about barbs?" Glabrio said. He reached out to scratch his left forearm, covered with tarry ointment the girls had daubed on it.

Glycera grabbed his hand and chittered, stopping him from disarranging her bandage. Glabrio clucked apologetically and put his right hand back on his knee. He'd forget in a moment and try to scratch his burn again.

Slats came from where he'd been interrogating the prisoners. His head pecked back and forth, more like the play of raindrops on a pond than an animal looking about him.

Froggie wondered whether the bug's sense of smell was the same as a man's. If it was, then no wonder he looked about ready to collapse. You never really got used to the smell of a battlefield. Especially not one where there'd been fire.

"They talked?" Froggie said. He supposed he should've been overseeing the questioning, but he'd decided to sit on a low pile of bodies instead and get his breath back for a while.

"Yes," the administrator said. "I cannot believe it, Centurion Froggie. The warriors with axes were mercenaries from another planet. A rival Guild was interloping on our claim. We've been granted development rights here, but they'd put in a survey team before the Federation Council made the assignment. They had found a product so valuable that they were violating Guild rules to reverse the assignment!"

"Do tell," Froggie said. He started to laugh at Slats' earnestness, but a fit of coughing broke him up instead.

"They were engineering a massacre of our pacification team!" Slats continued. "It would appear that the natives had been responsible. Their Guild would have bought the development rights from ours at a low price, and no one would be the wiser . . . but I would be dead!"

"It happens to everybody sooner or later," Froggie said; though "later" could be a long time if you were a Guild slave, and maybe longer than . . .

He looked to where the foreigners had been interrogated. They'd captured six of them alive, which was doing pretty well under these circumstances. Two of them had been hoisted with their wrists and ankles tied together so they hung belly down over a slow fire. The first pair had talked. If they hadn't, well, there were four more.

Naw, life was better. Even as a Guild slave.

"The product is a drug," Slats said. He kept his head rigid and avoided Froggie's eyes. "Three-Spire is in the pay of the rival Guild. The Commander is addicted to the drug which Three-Spire supplies to him."

Glabrio's face changed from dreamy somnolence to full, focused awareness of the world around him. A battle like the one just past could put a fellow, even a veteran, into a numb place that he might not come out of for days.

"Are we the only ones left?" he demanded. "Have they chopped the rest of the legion?"

Slats looked shocked. "I do not know," he said. "Centurion Froggie took my communicator—"

"To keep you from putting us deeper in the hole than you'd done when you called in the last time," Froggie snapped. He was coming back up from the gray depths too. "Don't worry, I'll give it back when I'm good and ready to."

Slats mimed submission. "I do not know," he repeated to Glabrio, "but I do not think the others have been attacked. Our rivals planned to wait for another ten days, when they would have been ready to capture the Harbor as well as eliminate the detachments. We were made an exception because of what we had discovered."

He made a kak-kak-kak sound which the lavaliere didn't translate; maybe it was a cough of embarrassment. "That is, what Centurion Froggie had discovered."

Froggie got up slowly and took stock. Barbs were starting to come out of the town, using other gates or just climbing over the walls. Most all of them were women. They picked over bodies, looking up fearfully whenever a trooper moved but continuing to search anyway.

"How many times have we seen that, Glabrio?" Froggie asked, nodding to the women. Glabrio shrugged but didn't answer.

The notch in the upper rim of Froggie's shield meant he'd need a replacement as soon as he got back to the Harbor, but it'd serve for now. He'd sharpen his sword when he got a moment but the edge wasn't notched the way you'd expect from as much work as the blade had done tonight. The barbs didn't wear proper armor, and not a one of them had tried to block Froggie's stroke with a blade of his own.

Six troopers would be out of action till they got back to the Guild's mechanical surgeons, but nobody was dead or in real danger. Froggie looked at the piles and long windrows of barb corpses. That's the way battles ended, in cheap victories till the day one went the other way and the legion didn't have enough survivors to form a burial party.

"The Anroklaatschi were not really responsible," Slats said. He'd turned to see where Froggie was looking. "It is a pity that so many of them died."

"Slats," Froggie said. His tone drew the eyes of everybody within twenty paces, despite the continuing snarl of the flames. "I don't really give a fuck what somebody's reasons are when he tries to burn me alive. I wouldn't give a fuck if we'd chopped every fucking barb there was!"

Queenie rubbed her cheek against his. Froggie hugged her and let her go. The girls weren't barbs, not now. They belonged to the Third of the Fourth.

"I understand, Centurion Froggie," Slats said quietly; and perhaps he did.

Froggie walked over to the prisoners. One of them was their leader, still wearing the gold wristlets. He glared at Froggie but didn't speak.

"Top?" said Laena, offering the lavaliere the barb had been wearing openly during the battle. Froggie took it, weighing it absently in his palm.

"I am very angry at this violation of Council regulations," Slats said. "If rules are ignored, how can the structure stand?"

He'd followed Froggie the way a puppy would. Queenie was close by also, her dagger thrust through a fold of her sash. It'd been bloody after the battle, same as Froggie's sword was. Nobody was going to confuse Queenie with a puppy.

"Don't get mad about that, Slats," Froggie said, dropping the lavaliere around his neck. The barb leader was one of the pair who'd been questioned. The down singed off his belly stank even with so many competing smells. "It's just business, you know."

Troopers had cut off the leader's harness so that the leather cross-belts wouldn't get in the way of questioning. The scraps lay on the ground with the pouch still attached. Froggie pulled the ties back and took out the key which the leader's girlfriend had returned.

Wonder where that barb woman was now? Maybe she'd been the one who tried to warn the Romans when the mob moved on them.

"What do you want us to do with the prisoners, Froggie?" Laena asked.

Froggie gave the field a quick, cold appraisal. "Leave the locals be," he said. "Slats is right—they weren't the problem. The foreigners here—"

He toed the leader in the ribs. The fellow twisted, trying to bite Froggie's ankle. Froggie gave him a bootheel in the face in an absent gesture.

"Take 'em into the town and toss them into a building that's still burning good," Froggie went on, pointing with his thumb.

"Do we untie them first, Top?" Laena asked.

"Dis, why would you want to do that?" said Froggie. He glanced over the battlefield until he saw Lucky Castus, the leader of First Squad.

"Hey Lucky!" he called. Froggie's throat was back in service; like its owner, it recovered quick if it got a bit of rest and some wine. "Get your boys together and we'll go visiting. Verruca, you're in charge here till we get back. Set up some kinda chain of command for what's left of the locals, all right?"

"Where are you going, Centurion Froggie?" Slats asked. All four arms were wrapped around his chest again.

"I'm going to go finish this business, Slats," Froggie said. "Want to come along?"

The administrator's body didn't move. His head swivelled, then swiveled back. "You are going to the dimensional portal," he said. "That is so?"

"That is so," Froggie said. Castus had his boys lined up. Caepio was using a broken javelin as a crutch. He'd have to stay, but they'd still be nine swords counting Froggie. That was plenty for the job.

"Yes, Centurion Froggie," Slats said. "I will come along. And we will finish the business!"

Glabrio led and Froggie was at the end of the line, since they were the two who knew the way. Froggie guessed the squad sounded like a drove of cattle—hobnails, shields clanking against cuirasses, and every couple of strides a man tripping on a root and swearing like a, well, a trooper. Slats said the folks inside the portal couldn't see or hear till it opened; that had better be true.

The administrator walked right in front of Froggie, making just as good time as the troopers. The bug's legs were plenty strong enough for his thin frame, and he seemed to see better than a man in this shadowed forest.

"We're getting close, now," Froggie said, as much to remind himself as to encourage Slats. Froggie'd come back mentally after the battle, but his body was still weaker than it'd been this morning. "It'll be right over the next rise."

Slats swivelled to look over his shoulders. He kept on walking and didn't stumble. Did he have eyes someplace besides the ones on the front of his face?

"I am still surprised that our rivals found it worth the expense of a dimensional portal," Slats said. "Though of course that is the only way they could carry out their regulation-breaking activities. The product must be of remarkable value."

"The Commander seems to think so," Froggie said. "If 'thinks' is the right word for the state he's in."

"Yes," Slats said. His words came eerily to Froggie's ears through the administrator's translator and directly to Froggie's mind, he guessed because of the lavaliere he'd taken from the barb. "The mercenary leader said the dose Three-Spire gives the Commander is a dangerously heavy one. It saps the user of all will, but our rivals were concerned that only slightly more would be fatal. The Commander's death would require a replacement and cause them problems."

Froggie caressed the hilt of his well-used sword. "They'll learn about problems," he said quietly.

Word came down the line over the shoulder of each trooper in turn. Froggie already knew what it was. "We've arrived, Slats," he said.

Lucky lined the squad up to face the spike of rock. Everybody had his sword drawn. Froggie took the key out of his pouch and handed it to the administrator.

"Open it when I tell you, Slats," he said. "Not before."

Now that the troopers' clattering equipment didn't mask it, the night was bright with animal sounds: chirps, peeps, and a *thoom, thoom,* that could almost have been a bullfrog sounding from a bog in the Sabine Hills. Froggie missed being able to wander around in the countryside at night the way he had as a kid . . . but Hercules! that was asking to get chopped in a place the legion had just conquered. Since the Guild bought him, Froggie was only going to see places just before or just after the legion had smashed the local king or chief or priestess.

"All right, boys," Froggie said. His breathing was under control and his body ready now. His sword was the only one still sheathed. "When Glabrio and me was here before it was just a guy in a blue suit—he's not our Commander, don't worry—"

"Who was worried?" Glabrio muttered.

". . . along with two bodyguards and that barb Three-Spire from the Harbor," Froggie continued. "These bodyguards look like monkeys, but they're big and they've got spiked gloves."

A trooper spit on the ground and grinned.

"There was two axemen besides from the town," Froggie added with a gesture back the direction they'd come, "but they won't be there this time."

"There may be messengers from the other locations, however," Slats said. "This same portal can serve many local sites. I would expect our rivals to keep in touch with all thirty locations to which detachments from your legion were sent."

Froggie shrugged. "Regardless," he said. "There's not room inside for more than maybe a dozen people, and they won't be expecting us. Glabrio and I lead in, then the rest of the squad by pairs till the job's done. Lucky, you watch our rear. There's the off chance that a few of the barbs got loose back at the town. They could be waiting for us to get focused on what's inside the cave before they weigh in."

"Pollux, Froggie!" Lucky said. "I ought to be in front with you. It's my squad!"

"Lucky," Froggie said, "if I thought you had anything to prove, you wouldn't be here. Now, carry out my orders or it *won't* be your squad."

Lucky nodded. "Sorry, Top," he said through tight lips.

Froggie drew his sword and walked close enough to the rock that he could touch it with the outstretched blade. He hefted his shield, making sure that the heavy oblong was balanced to swing or smash. A shield was a better weapon than a sword, often enough.

"All right, Slats," he said calmly. "Do it!"

Solid basalt dissolved into a cave. The vanishing rock gave Froggie an instant of vertigo: his mind told him he'd plunged over a cliff. He strode forward.

The Commander looked up angrily and said, "You're off your sched—"

His face blanked. He shrieked and dived behind his bodyguards.

Three-Spire was talking to the barbs behind the Commander. Two were axemen like the batch who'd been running things at Kascanschi, but the third was a real local with strings of quartz and coral beads woven through his topknot. He was taking a cake of tarry-looking stuff from the sack he held.

A guard drove a spiked fist at Froggie. Froggie raised his shield a hand's breadth and twisted his body out of the line of impact.

It was like being punched by a battering ram. Froggie heard two boards of the outer lamination split; the shield's lower edge rocked up, using Froggie's grip as a fulcrum and absorbing the force of the blow. Froggie thrust at the ape's knee, feeling the thin armor over the joint separate an instant before gristle and spongy bone did.

The ape bellowed. He swung with his other fist but he was already toppling toward his crippled leg. The spike that brushed Froggie's helmet gouged through the bronze and even nicked the leather harness within.

Bald Lucius, a pace behind Froggie, stabbed for the ape's head. His blade sparkled into the upright of the helmet's T opening, grinding on teeth and then the creature's spine. Baldy put his right boot on the helmet and tugged his sword free with both hands.

Glabrio was down but twisting as he grappled with the other guard. Two troopers stood over the pair, chopping at joints in the ape's backplate. Three more troopers had sprinted past that part of the melee to get at the mercenaries beyond. Velio blocked an axe with his shield as his two companions hacked at the barb from either side.

At Froggie's feet, the Commander tried to squirm around a console of translucent blue ice. Froggie grabbed him by the throat and pulled him upright.

"You cannot—" the Commander shrilled. Froggie punched his sword home, all the way to the hilt. He felt ribs grate, then a snap! and a shock that numbed his arm. He'd driven his point into the ice beyond.

The Commander's eyes rolled up. The blood that spewed from his mouth was as red as a man's.

Froggie couldn't grip his sword. Ice was boiling

away from where the steel pierced it; the Commander's staring body toppled backward, no longer supported by the blade.

All the barbs were down. A trooper was helping Glabrio get out from under the bodyguard. The hilt of his dagger stuck from beneath the ape's chin like a hazelwood beard.

Everybody was all right, everybody who counted. Slats hopped over the litter of bodies with the bag the local—his head now sitting on the stump of his neck with a startled expression—had brought to show.

"Get out!" Slats screamed. "The wormhole generator has been damaged!"

Something had been damaged, sure enough. The ice into which Froggie'd pinned the Commander had burned completely away, and the hissing scar was spreading across the floor. Froggie grabbed a trooper's shoulder and jerked him toward the mouth of the cave.

"Go!" he said. He reached for another man, but they were all moving in the right direction, stumbling and cursing. Glabrio bent to pick up his shield but thought again and lunged through the opening instead.

There was a smell like the air gets sometimes just *before* a thunderbolt. Froggie stamped out of the cave with only Slats behind him. "Venus Mother of Men!" he said as the forest enfolded him, blissfully cooler than the place he'd just left.

Three-Spire, unhurt and unnoticed, sprang from the sizzling, sparking portal. "I will help you—" he cried.

Slats put his four hands on the ground and kicked with both feet. The barb aide toppled backward, into the cave again. His scream stopped while he was still in the air.

The walls of the cave vanished. It was like looking into the green depths of the sea. Three-Spire fell, his body shrinking but remaining visible even when it was smaller than a gnat glimpsed through an emerald lens.

Froggie blinked. The basalt spike was before him again. His right arm ached, and the night was alive with noises of the forest.

Nobody spoke for a moment. Lucky was bandaging Messus' left forearm; it was a bad cut, definitely a job for the medics from the Harbor.

Froggie rubbed his right wrist against his thigh, trying to work the feeling back into it. His shield was scrap, but he guessed he'd carry it to Kascanschi.

"We're done here," he said. "Let's get back to the damned town and Slats can call for help. It's safe to do that now."

"Top?" said Lucky. He glanced toward where the cave had been, then straightened his head very quickly. "Is there going to be trouble? Because of, you know, what happened?"

"No," said Slats forcefully. When they left the Harbor just a few days ago, Froggie wouldn't have believed the bug had the balls to do what he'd done—any of the things he'd done—tonight. "The event will never be reported. Our rivals have lost their considerable investment when we destroyed the dimensional portal; they will fear severe sanctions in addition if the truth comes out. We will gain credit for discovering a product of unexpected value on this planet."

"Lets go," said Froggie, slinging what was left of his shield behind him. "I'll lead."

"*We'll* gain, you say," Glabrio muttered. "The Commander gains, you mean. Third of the Fourth don't get jack shit."

"You're alive, aren't you, Glabrio?" Froggie said as he stepped off on his left foot. "You'd bitch if they crucified you with golden nails!"

The squad swung into motion behind him. Over the noise of boots and equipment Slats said, "The first thing the Commander will gain is this satchel of prepared drug which I rescued before the portal collapsed. I will present it to him myself. I estimate there are three thousand euphoric doses in it. And one fatal dose, I suspect."

Froggie chuckled. He was looking forward to seeing Queenie. After a night like this, you needed to remind yourself you were alive.

Not that it'd been a bad night. Froggie thought again about the way his sword had slid through a blue suit and the ribs beneath it.

He chuckled again. In some ways this had been the best night of Froggie's life.

_____*End note to* Lambs to the Slaughter

In 1976 I wrote "Ranks of Bronze," a short story which postulated that the Roman soldiers captured when the Parthians defeated Crassus in 54 BC had been sold as mercenaries to alien merchants, who then used them to fight colonial wars for trade rights. Jim Baen, who bought the story for *Galaxy*, liked it so much that he asked me to expand it into a novel when he started his own publishing company, Baen Books. I was pleased to do so. So far, so good.

Even before the novel version of *Ranks of Bronze* appeared, Jim got on me to write a sequel. This I resolutely refused to do, since I had written a Novel of Education: the viewpoint character grows in the course of the novel into a mature adult with a final resolution of his situation. Jim didn't see that as a problem for a sequel, but I stuck to my guns.

Finally—remember the fable about the water wearing down the rock?—I did agree to edit an anthology set in the *Ranks* universe. I would do one novella, and four other writers would do their own takes on the milieu. The volume came out as *Foreign Legions*.

"Lambs to the Slaughter" was my entry for the volume. None of the characters had appeared in the original volume, and the planetary setting was also new. (To my amusement, two of the other writers—Eric Flint and Steve Stirling—used preexisting characters from *Ranks* just as Jim had wanted me to do. I still think I was right.)

The situation of the novella is based on what happened to the Roman Army of Upper Germany in 9 AD, when the Emperor Augustus put a political crony named Quinctilius Varus in command of what Varus thought was a conquered province. A lot of good men died as a result of that miscalculation, which depresses me (I'm a Nam vet). But this is fiction. . . .

MEN LIKE US

There was a toad crucified against them at the head of the pass. Decades of cooking in the blue haze from the east had left it withered but incorruptible. It remained, even now that the haze was only a memory. The three travellers squatted down before the talisman and stared back at it.

"The village can't be far from here," Smith said at last. "I'll go down tomorrow."

Ssu-ma shrugged and argued, "Why waste time? We can all go down together."

"Time we've got," said Kozinski, playing absently with his ribs as he eyed the toad. "A lot of the stories we've been told come from ignorance, from fear. There may be no more truth to this one than to many of the others. We have a duty, but we have a duty as well not to disrupt needlessly. We'll wait for you and watch."

Smith chuckled wryly. "What sort of men would there be in the world," he said, "if it weren't for men like us?"

All three of them laughed, but no one bothered to finish their old joke.

The trail was steep and narrow. The stream was now bubbling twenty feet below, but in springtime it would fill its sharp gorge with a torrent as cold as the snows that spawned it. Coming down the valley, Smith had a good view of Moseby when he had eased around the last facet of rock above the town. It sprawled in the angle of the creek and the river into which the creek plunged. In a niche across the creek from the houses was a broad stone building, lighted by slit windows at second-story level. Its only entrance was an armored door. The building could have been a prison or a fortress were it not for the power lines running from it, mostly to the smelter at the riverside. A plume of vapor overhung its slate roof.

One of the pair of guards at the door of the powerplant was morosely surveying the opposite side of the gorge for want of anything better to do. He was the first to notice Smith. His jaw dropped. The traveller waved to him. The guard blurted something to his companion and threw a switch beside the door.

What happened then frightened Smith as he thought nothing in the world could frighten him again: an air-raid siren on the roof of the powerplant sounded, rising into a wail that shook echoes from the gorge. Men and women darted into the streets, some of them armed; but Smith did not see the people, these people, and he did not fear anything they could do to him.

Then the traveller's mind was back in the present, a smile on his face and nothing in his hands but an oak staff worn by the miles of earth and rock it had butted against. He continued down into the village, past the fences and latrines of the nearest of the houses. Men with crossbows met him there, but they did not touch him, only motioned the traveller onward. The rest of the townsfolk gathered in an open area in the center of the town. It separated the detached houses on the east side from the row of flimsier structures built along the river. The latter obviously served as barracks, taverns, and brothels for bargees and smelter workers. The row buildings had no windows facing east, and even their latrines must have been dug on the river side. A few people joined the crowd from them and from the smelter itself, but only a few.

"That's close enough," said the foremost of those awaiting the traveller. The local was a big man with a pink scalp. It shone through the long wisps of white hair which he brushed carefully back over it. His jacket and trousers were of wool dyed blue so that it nearly matched the shirt of ancient polyester he wore over it. "Where have you come from?"

"Just about everywhere, one time or another," Smith answered with an engaging grin. "Dubuque, originally, but that was a long time ago."

"Don't play games with the Chief," hissed a somewhat younger man with a cruel face and a similar uniform. "You came over the mountains; and *nobody* comes from the Hot Lands."

Chief of Police, Smith marveled as he connected the title and the shirts now worn as regalia. Aloud he said, "When's the last time anybody from here walked over the mountains? Ever?"

Bearded faces went hard. The traveller continued, "A hundred years ago, two hundred, it was too hot for you to go anywhere that side of the hills . . . but not now. Now—maybe I'll never sire children of my own, but I never needed that, I needed to see the world. And I have done that, friends."

"Strip him," the Chief said flatly.

Smith did not wait for the grim-looking men to force him. He shrugged off his pack and handed it to the nearest of the guards armed with crossbows and hand-forged swords. He said, "Gently with it, friend. There's some of it that's fragile, and I need it to trade for room and board the next while." He began to unhook his leather vest.

Six of the men besides the Chief wore the remnants of police uniforms over their jackets. They were all older, not lean warriors like the crossbowmen—but they carried firearms. Five of them had M16 rifles. The anodized finish of the receivers had been polished down to the aluminum by ages of diligent ignorance. The sixth man had a disposable rocket launcher, certain proof that the villagers here had at some time looted an army base—or a guard room.

"Just a boy from the Midwest," Smith continued pleasantly, pulling out the tails of his woolen shirt. "I wanted to see New York City, can you believe that? But we'll none of us live forever, will we?"

He laid the shirt, folded from habit, on his vest and began unlacing his boots of caribou leather. "There's a crater there now, and the waves still glow blue if there's even an overcast to dim the sun. Your skin prickles."

The traveller grinned. "You won't go there, and I won't go there again; but I've seen it, where the observation deck of the World Trade Towers was the closest mortal man got to heaven with his feet on man's earth. . . ."

"We've heard the stories," the Chief grunted. He carried a stainless-steel revolver in a holster of more recent vintage.

"Trousers?" Smith asked, cocking an eyebrow at the women in dull-colored dresses.

The Chief nodded curtly. "When a man comes from the Hot Lands, he has no secrets from us," he said. "Any of us."

"Well, I might do the same in your case," the traveller agreed, tugging loose the laces closing the woolen trousers, "but I can tell you there's little enough truth to the rumors of what walks the wastelands." He pulled the garment down and stepped out of it.

Smith's body was wiry, the muscles tight and thickly covered by hair. If he was unusual at all, it was in that he had been circumcized, no longer a common operation in a world that had better uses for a surgeon's time. Then a woman noticed Smith's left palm, never hidden but somehow never clearly seen until that moment. She screamed and pointed. Others leveled their weapons, buzzing as a hive does when a bear nears it.

Very carefully, his face as blank as the leather of his pack, Smith held his left hand toward the crowd and spread his fingers. Ridges of gnarled flesh stood out as if they had been paraffin refrozen a moment after being liquified. "Yes, I burned it," the traveller said evenly, "getting too close to something the—something the Blast was too close to. And it'll never heal, no . . . but it hasn't gotten worse, either, and that was years ago. It's not the sort of world where I could complain to have lost so little, hey?"

"Put it down," the Chief said abruptly. Then, to the guard who was searching the pack, "Weapons?"

"Only this," the guard said, holding up a sling and a dozen dense pebbles fitted to its leather pocket.

"There's a little folding knife in my pants pocket," Smith volunteered. "I use it to skin the rabbits I take."

"Then put your clothes on," the Chief ordered, and the crowd's breath eased. "You can stay at the inn, since you've truck enough to pay for it"—he nodded toward the careful pile the guard had made of Smith's trading goods—"and perhaps you can find girls on Front Street to service you as well. There's none of that east of the Assembly here, I warn you. Before you do anything else, though, you talk to me and the boys in private at the Station."

The traveller nodded and began dressing without embarrassment.

The Police and their guards escorted Smith silently, acting as if they were still uncertain of his status. Their destination was a two-story building of native stone. It had probably been the Town Hall before the Blast. It was now the Chief's residence as well as the headquarters of the government. Despite that, the building was far less comfortable than many of the newer structures which had been designed to be heated by stoves and lighted by lamps and windows. In an office whose plywood panelling had been carefully preserved—despite its shoddy gloominess—the governing oligarchs of the town questioned Smith.

They were probing and businesslike. Smith answered honestly and as fully as he could. Weapons caches? Looted by survivors or rotted in the intervening centuries. Food depots? A myth, seeded by memories of supermarkets and brought to flower in the decades of famine and cold which slew ten times as many folk as the Blast had slain directly. Scrap metal for the furnaces? By the millions of tons, but there would be no way to transport it across the mountains . . . and besides, metals were often hot even at this remove from the Blast.

"All right," said the Chief at last, shutting the handbook of waxed boards on which he had been making notes. The room had become chilly about the time they had had to light the sooty naphtha lamp. "If we think of more during the night, we can ask in the morning." His eyes narrowed. "How long are you expecting to stay?"

Smith shrugged. "A few days. I just like to . . . wander. I really don't have any desire to do anything else." He raised his pack by the straps and added, "Can one of you direct me to your inn?"

Carter, the youngest of the six Policemen, stood. He was a blocky man with black hair and a pepper and salt beard. He had conducted much of the questioning himself. "I'll take him," he said. Unlike his colleagues, he carried a heavy fighting knife in addition to his automatic rifle. He held the door for Smith.

The night sky was patchy. When the sliver moon was clear, there was more light outside than the bud of naphtha gave within. The pall of steam above the powerplant bulged and waned like the mantle of an octopus. Tiny azure sparks traced the power lines across the bridge and down into the smelter.

Smith thumbed at the plant. "They made light from electricity, you know? Before the Blast. You ever try that?"

His guide looked at his sharply. "Not like they did. Things glow, but they burn up when we can't keep all the air away from 'em. But you'd be smarter not to ask questions, boy. And maybe you'd be smarter to leave here a little sooner than you planned. Not to be unfriendly, but if you talk to us, you'll talk to others. And we don't much care for talk about Moseby. It has a way of spreading where it shouldn't."

The Policeman turned through an open gate and up a gravelled pathway. Rosy light leaked around the shutters of a large building on the edge of the Assembly. Sound and warm air bloomed into the night when he opened the door. In the mild weather, the anteroom door was open within.

"Carter!" shouted a big man at the bar of the tap-room. "Just in time to buy us a round!" Then he saw Smith and blinked, and the dozen or so men of the company grew quieter than the hiss of the fire.

"Friends, I don't bite," said Smith with a smile, "but I do drink and I will sleep. If I can come to an agreement with our host here, that is. . . ." he added, beaming toward the barman.

"Modell's the name," said the tall, knob-jointed local. Neither he nor the traveller offered to shake hands, but he returned the other's smile with a briefer, professional one of his own. "Let's see what you have to trade."

The men at the bar made room as Smith ranged his small stock on the mahogany. First the traveller set out an LP record, still sealed in plastic. Modell's lips moved silently as his finger hovered a millimeter above the title. "What's a 'Cher'," he finally asked.

"The lady's name," said Smith. "She pronounced it 'share'." Knowing grunts from the men around him chorused the explanation. "You've electricity here, I see. Perhaps there's a phonograph?"

"Naw, and the power's not trained enough yet anyhow," said Modell regretfully. His eyes were full of the jacket photograph. "It heats the smelters, is all, and—"

"Modell, you're supposed to be trading, not running your mouth," interrupted the Policeman. "Get on with it."

"Well, if not the record, then—" Smith said.

"I might make you an offer on the picture," one of the locals broke in.

"I won't separate them, I'm afraid," Smith rejoined, "and I won't have the record where it can't be used properly. These may be more useful, though I can't guarantee them after the time they've been sitting . . ." and he laid a red and green box of .30-30 cartridges on the wood.

"The Chief keeps all the guns in Moseby besides these," spoke Carter, patting the plastic stock of his M16. "It'll stay that way. And there's a righteous plenty of ammunition for them already."

"Fine, fine," said Smith, unperturbed, reaching again into his pack. He removed a plastic box which whirred until a tiny green hand reached out of the mechanism to shut itself off. It frightened the onlookers as much as Smith's own radiation scars had. The traveller thoughtfully hid the toy again in his pack before taking out his final item, a GI compass.

"It always shows North, unless you're too close to iron," Smith said as he demonstrated. "You can turn the base to any number of degrees and take a sighting through the slot there . . . but I'll want more than a night's lodging for it."

"Our tokens're good up and down the river," one of the locals suggested, ringing a small brass disk on the bar. It had been struck with a complex pattern of lightning bolts on one side and the number '50' on the other. "You can redeem'em for iron ingots at dockside," he explained, thumbing toward the river. "'Course, they discount'em the farther away you get."

"I don't follow rivers a great deal," the traveller lied with a smile. "Let's say that I get room and board—and all I care to drink—for a week . . ."

The chaffering was good-natured and brief, concluding with three days' room and board, or—and here Smith nodded toward the stern-faced Carter—so much shorter a time as he actually stayed in the village. In addition, Smith would have all the provisions he requested for his journey and a round for the house now. When Modell took the traveller's hand, extended to seal the bargain, the whole room cheered. The demands for mugs of the sharp, potent beer drew the innkeeper when he would far rather have pored over his pre-Blast acquisition—marvelous, though of little enough use to him.

Dealing over, Smith carried his mug to one of the stools before the fire. Sausages, dried vegetables, and a pair of lanterns hung from the roof joists. Deer and elk antlers were pegged to the pine panelling all around the room, and above the mantle-piece glowered the skull of a rat larger than a German Shepherd.

"I wonder that a man has the courage to walk alone out there," suggested a heavy-set local who tamped his pipe with the ball of his thumb, "what with the muties and all."

Smith chuckled, swigged his beer, and gestured with the mug at the rat skull. "Like that, you mean? But that's old. The giant rats were nasty enough, I have no doubt;

but they weren't any stronger than the wolves, and they were a good deal stupider. Maybe you'd find a colony now and again in ruins downwind of a Strike . . . but they'll not venture far into the light, and the ones that're left—not many—are nothing that a slingstone or arrow can't cure if needs be." He paused and smiled. "Besides, their meat's sweet enough. I'm told."

Despite the ruddy fire, the other faces in the circle went pale. Smith's eyes registered the reaction while his mouth continued to smile. "Now, travellers tell stories, you know," he said, "and there's an art to listening to them. There's little enough to joke about on the trail, so I have to do it here."

His face went serious for a moment and he added, "But I'll tell you this and swear to the truth of it: when I was near what may have been Cleveland, I thought I'd caught a mouse rummaging in my pack. And when I fetched it out, it was no bigger than a mouse, and its legs were folded under it so it could hop and scurry the way a mouse can. But its head . . . there was a horn just there"—the traveller touched the tip of his nose—"and another littler one just behind it. I figure some zoo keeper before the Blast would have called me a liar if I'd told him what his rhinos would breed to, don't you think?"

He drank deep. The company buzzed at the wonder and the easy fellowship of the man who had seen it.

"Scottie meant the half-men, didn't you, Scottie?" said a bulky man whose moustache and the beard fringing his mouth were dark with beer. He mimed an extra head with his clenched fist. "Monsters like that in the Hot Lands."

Smith's head bobbed sagely against the chorus of

grim assent from the other men. "Sure, I know what you mean," he said. "Two-headed men? Girls with an extra pair of legs coming out of their bellies?"

Sounds of horror and agreement.

"You see," the traveller went on, "the Blast changed things . . . but you know as I do that it didn't change them to be easier for men. There've always been children born as . . . monsters, if you will. Maybe more born nowadays than there were before the Blast; but they *were* born, and I've seen books that were old at the Blast that talk of them. And they don't live now, my friends. Life everywhere is too hard, and those poor innocents remind folk of the Blast; and who would remember that?"

He looked around the room. The eyes that met his dropped swiftly. "There's been some born here in Moseby, haven't there?" Smith asked, his words thrusting like knifeblades and no doubt to them. "Where are they now?"

The man they had called Scottie bit through the reed stem of his pipe. He spluttered and the front legs of his stool clacked on the puncheon floor.

"Say, now, I'm not here to pry," Smith continued swiftly. "What you do is your own business. For my own part, I'd appreciate another mug of this excellent beer."

Chairs scraped in agreement as all the men stood, stretched, and moved to the bar. Modell drew beer smoothly, chalking drinks on the board on the back wall—everyone but Smith was a local. The innkeeper even broached a new cask without noticeable delay. Several of the company went out the rear door and returned, lacing their trousers. There was a brief pause as everyone settled back around the fire. Then Scottie swallowed, scowled, and said belligerently, "All right, what about the Changlings?"

"Pardon?" The traveller's eyes were friendly above the rim of his mug, but there was no comprehension in them.

"Oh, come on!" the local said, flushing in embarrassment. "You know about the Changlings, everybody does. The Blast made them. They were men before, but now they glow blue and change their shapes and walk around like skeletons, all bones!" Scottie lowered his eyes and slurped his beer in the silence. At last he repeated, "Everybody knows."

Gently, as if the suggestion did not appear as absurd to him as it suddenly did to everyone else in the room, Smith said, "I've seen some of the Strike Zones. . . . I guess I've said that. There's nothing there, friend. The destruction is total, everything. It isn't likely that anything was created by the Blast."

"The Blast changed things, we can all agree there," said Carter unexpectedly. Eyes turned toward the Policeman seated at one corner of the hearth. "Random change," Carter continued to muse aloud. "That generally'll mean destruction, yes. But there was a lot of power in the bombs, and a lot of bombs. So much power that . . . who knows what they could have done?"

Smith looked at the Policeman, raising his eyebrows. He nodded again. "Power, yes. But the *chance* that the changes, cell by cell, atom by atom, would be . . . not destructive. . . . That's a billion to one against, Mr. Carter."

"Well, the books say there were billions of men in the world before the Blast," the Policeman said, spreading the fingers of his left hand, palm upward.

The traveller's scarred left hand mirrored the Policeman's. "It's a wide world," he said, "as you must know and I surely do." He drank, smiled again, and said, "You're familiar with bombs it would seem, friend. I've heard talk in my travels that there was a stockpile of bombs in the mountains around here. Do you know that story?"

Carter looked at Smith with an expression that was terrible in its stillness. "Modell," he said in the silence, "it's time to throw another log on the fire." He paused; the innkeeper scurried to do as directed. "And it's time," the Policeman continued, "to talk of other things than the Blast. What sort of game do you find in the Hot Lands, for instance?"

"Well, I snare more than I knock on the head with my sling," Smith began easily, and the room relaxed a little.

They talked and drank late into the night. Smith told of gnarly woods and following miles of trails worn no higher than a hog's shoulder. The locals replied with tales of their farms in the river bottoms, managed for them by hirelings, and the wealth they drew from shares in the smelter's profits. Few of them actually did any of the heavy, dangerous work of steel production themselves. Moseby was a feudal state, but its basis was the powerplant rather than land.

When Carter finally left, only Scottie and another local remaining in company with Smith and Modell, the talk grew looser. Finally Scottie wheezed, "They drift in here to Moseby, up the river and down—you're the first across the mountains, boy, I'll tell the world. We put'em to work in the fields or the smelter, or they crew the barges for us. But they're not Moseby, they're not of the Assembly. It's *us* who've got the power, under the Chief and the Police, that is. We keep the Light and the—"

Modell touched the line of Scottie's jaw, silencing him. Scottie's surprise bloomed into awakened fright. "You've had enough tonight, old man," the innkeeper said. "Pook, you too. Time for you both to get home, and for me to get to bed."

"And me," Smith agreed—Modell had already brought out blankets and opened a side bench into a cot. "Though first I'll take a leak and, say, a walk to settle my head. If you leave the door on the latch?"

Modell nodded dourly. "You've been listening to that fool Howes and his talk of the girls across the Assembly. Him with a wife and six children, too! Well, don't try to bring one back here with you. They should know better, but if one didn't, it'd be the worse for both of you." The innkeeper blew out one of the lamps and moved toward the other.

Smith urinated in the open ditch behind the building, letting his eyes readjust to the moonglow. Then he began to walk along the sewer with a deceptive purposelessness. In the shadow of the house nearest the creek he paused, eyeing the nodding guards across the gorge. The traveller took off his boots. He ducked into the ditch and used its cover to crawl down onto the creek bank.

The rock was steep, but it was limestone and weathered into irregularity enough for Smith's practiced digits to grip. Smoothly but without haste, the traveller slipped along below the line of sight of the guards at the powerplant. When he reached the bridge trestles he paused again, breathing carefully. His hands examined the nearest of the handsawn oak timbers, tracing it from where it butted into the rock to where it crossed another beam half-way to the stringers. Smith swung onto the trestle and began to negotiate the gorge like an ant in a clump of heavy grass.

Any sounds the traveller might have made were hidden by the creek. Its clatterings beneath echoed in a backdrop one could not easily talk over. That itself was a danger for Smith when he reached the far end of the bridge and would have listened to the guards' conversation before going on. Carefully, because a crook in the gorge threw most of the spray onto the rocks on this side, Smith edged left toward the west corner of the building. The wall there was built almost to the rim of the gorge. Smith's clothing matched the color of the wet stone so that his outline was at least blurred for a potential watcher from the village; but lack of alertness on the guards' part was his real defense.

Smith raised his head. Both guards were nodding in their chairs, crossbows leaning against the doorposts beside them. The traveller swung lithely up. A step later he was hugging the greater concealment of the powerplant's west wall. The stone hummed.

The building was as massive a construction as anything Smith had seen created after the Blast. The walls were drystone, using the natural layering of limestone and their two-foot thickness to attain an adequate seal without mortar. Their weathered seams made it easy for one of Smith's strength and condition to mount the fifteen feet of blank wall to the lighted slits just below the roof. The interior was much as the traveller had expected it to be, much as he had seen it before here and there across the face of the world.

Six huge electric motors were ranked below him. They were being used as generators, driven by a complex pattern of shafts and broad leather belts. Only one of them was turning at the moment. When the smelters were working at full capacity and called in turn for the maximum output of the plant, the room would be a bedlam of machines and their attendants. Now a man and a woman, scarcely less somnolent than the guards outside, were sufficient. The light of the naphtha lanterns illuminating the chamber may have exaggerated the attendants' pallor, but they certainly saw less of the sun than the villagers across the stream did. It was hard to believe that control of this apparatus was left to slaves; yet it was even more unlikely that free men who knew what they were doing would be willing to enter the chamber below.

In the center of the north wall, built against the living rock of the mountainside, was the reactor.

Its genesis was evident, for the black hulls of ten fusion bombs were ranged along the partition wall to the east. Smith, his head framed in the narrow window, licked his lips when he saw the bombs. They would no longer be weapons; the plutonium of their fission cores would have decayed beyond the capacity to form critical mass when compacted. But those cores, taken from their cocoons of lithium hydride and the inner baths of deuterium, could still fuel a reactor.

The latter was an ugly mass of stone blocks, overshadowed by a mantis-like derrick. Steam from the reactor drove the pistons of a crude engine. Unlike the pre-Blast electric motors, the steam engine had been manufactured for its present purpose. Inefficient, it leaked vapor through seams and rope gaskets—but the power to create steam from water was practically inexhaustible on the scale required here.

Manufacturing skill and not theoretical knowledge had frequently been the brake on human progress: da Vinci could design a workable aircraft, but no one for four hundred years could build an engine to drive it. Nuclear power technology was so simple, given the refined fuel and expendable humans to work it, that an age which could not manufacture smokeless powder could nonetheless build a fission plant. All it would have taken was a weapons stockpile and a technician or two from Oak Ridge, vacationing in the mountains at the time of the Blast.

It was what Smith had come to learn.

There was a new sound in the night. A score or more of men were thudding across the bridge to the powerplant. Smith ducked his head beneath the sill of the window. As he did so, the siren on the roof hooted ferally. Knowing that there was no escape downward if he had been seen, the traveller slipped sideways and began to clamber up between a pair of the windows. As his fingers touched the edge of the slates, a voice from below shouted, "There he is!"

Smith gathered himself to swing onto the gently-sloped roof; something tapped his knuckles. He looked up. The muzzle of Carter's M16 stared back at him. The Policeman smiled over the sights. "I saw something block one of the plant windows," the local man said. "Thought it might be worth waking the guards for. Now, 'friend,' you just climb down easy to where the people are waiting, or me and the boys here won't wait for the ceremony."

The pair of guards flanking Carter had faces as

tense as their cocked crossbows. Smith shook his head ruefully and descended into the waiting manacles.

The siren gave three long cries as the guards marched Smith back across the bridge. Citizens, warned by the initial signal, began walking out of their houses; the men armed, the women bleak as gray steel. They drifted toward the shrouded platform across the long axis of the Assembly from the bridge. None of the citizens seemed to want to be the first to reach the common destination. They dawdled in pairs and trios, turning aside as Smith and his captors passed through them.

The Chief and the remaining Policemen had hurried up the steps to what was clearly a covered altar by the time Smith reached it. Cords fluttered as the canvas roof was gathered within the screen of hoardings built on a base of stone blocks. Something mechanical purred and paused. Sparks hissed about the powerline strung to the platform along a line of low posts on the western edge of the Assembly.

"On up," Carter said, smiling. He tweaked Smith's manacles toward the steps. The guards were taking position at the base of the altar, facing out toward the Assembly. Despite the siren calls, there was no sign of life or movement from the smelter and its associated buildings. Their blank walls were no more than a physical reminder of the grip the freeholders of Moseby held on the minds and lives of those who would work in their village. The business tonight was no business of a bargee or a factory hand.

Smith mounted the steps. Two Policemen received him, holding their rifles by the pistolgrips as if they were still functional weapons. Well, perhaps they were.

There were other improbable things in this place. . . .

The moonlight was shadowed by the flimsy walls. It gave only hints of the enclosed area: the Policemen in their ragged uniforms; two large, vertical cylinders, the one mounted somewhat higher than the other; and, at the front of the platform, a wooden block the height of a man's knee.

"There," muttered one of the Policemen, guiding the traveller's neck onto the block. No force was necessary; Smith was as docile as a babe at its mother's breast. Carter took a quick lashing from Smith's right wrist to a staple set for the purpose in the flooring. "If it wasn't that you know too much," the Policeman said conversationally, "we'd let you spend the rest of your life inside the plant. But somebody's who's travelled as you have, seen what you have . . . we don't want to be like Samson, chaining you in the temple so you can bring it down on us, hey?"

"Tie him and we'll get this over with," the Chief growled.

Carter unlocked the manacles and bound Smith's left wrist to another staple. "It was a good idea when they chopped muties here every week," he said. "It's a good idea now. The ceremony reminds us all that it's us against the world and all of us together. I'll take the axe if you like."

Smith, facing the wooden panels, could not see the exchange. The air licked his neck and cheek as something passed from hand to hand between the two men. "Drop the walls," the Chief ordered. "And turn on the Light."

The pins locking together the corners of the hoardings slipped out. The panels arced down simultaneously in a rush of air and a collective sigh from the Assembly. The purring of an electric motor awoke under the platform, rising and becoming sibilant in the absence of competing sound. A taut drive-belt moaned; then the moan was buried in a sudden crackle and white light played like terror across the upturned faces.

Smith twisted his head. The Policemen stood in a line across the width of the platform. Carter, in the middle, gripped the haft of a fire axe. Its head was still darkened by flecks of red paint. He grinned at the traveller. Behind the rulers of the village glared another burst of lightning between the static generator's heads: the polished casings of a pair of fusion bombs. No objects could have been more fittingly symbolic of Moseby's power. The van de Graff generator provided a crude but effective way of converting electricity to light. Its DC motor pulled a belt from which electrons were combed into one bomb casing. The static discharges to the grounded casing were all the more spectacular for being intermittent.

"You still have a chance to save yourselves if you let me go," said Smith, shouting over the ripping arcs. "There is no punishment too terrible for men who would use atomic power again, but you still have time to flee!"

Carter's smile broadened, his teeth flickering in light reflected onto his face. He roared, "We dedicate this victim to the power that preserves us all!" and he raised his axe.

"You fool," the traveller said quietly. He did not try to slide back from the block, even as he watched a multiple discharge strobe the edge of the descending axe. The hungry steel caught him squarely, shearing like a shard of ice through his flesh. His vertebrae popped louder in his ears than the hollow report of the blade against the wood. The axe head quivered, separating all but a finger's breadth of the traveller's neck. He blinked at Carter.

The Policeman rocked his blade free. Static discharges sizzled behind him at three-second intervals. Smith felt a line of warmth as his Blast-changed flesh knit together again as the steel withdrew.

Still kneeling, the Changling turned toward the crowd. "People!" he shouted. "Whatever it costs men today, men tomorrow must know that nuclear power is death! Nuclear power made this world what it is. Nuclear power is the one evil that cannot be tolerated, never again! For Man's sake, for the world's—"

Screaming, Carter slammed the axe down on the traveller's temple. The blade bit to the helve. Smith reached up with his right hand, tearing the staple from the flooring. He gripped the wood and it splintered as he drew the axe from where it was lodged in his bone. The Changling stood, his head flowing together like wax in a mold. His left wrist reformed as the rawhide lashing cut through it.

Sparks like shards of sunlight clawed through the high windows of the powerplant. That gush of light died. The siren began to wind, higher and higher. The motor of the van de Graff generator was speeding also, the current that drove it no longer controlled. The arcs were a constant white sheet between the bomb casings. Someone—two figures—crossed the bridge from the powerplant. The blue glow from the building backlighted them.

"Flee!" Smith cried, lifting to the crowd the scarred

hand he had thrown up two centuries before to the flare of a hundred megaton bomb. "Flee this abomination before it devours you—as it surely will, as it did the world before this world!"

Carter screamed again and struck with his riflebutt, hurling the Changling off the platform. Smith picked himself up. The guards backed away from him, their eyes wide, their cocked bows advanced as talismans and not threats.

The two figures on the bridge threw back their cloaks. The lapping arcs played across the half of Kozinski's face and torso that was naked bone. The bare organs pulsed within, and his one eye darted like a black jewel. The Blast had sometimes preserved and had sometimes destroyed; this once it had done both in near equality.

Ssu-ma would have stood out without the artificial lightning. She had the same trim, beautiful figure as the girl she had been the night she stared into the sky above Lop Nor and saw dawn blaze three hours early. Now that figure shone blue, brighter even than the spreading fire that ate through the wall of the power-plant behind her.

The crowd was scattering toward homes and toward the river. No one approached the platform except the two Changlings walking toward their fellow.

The Chief threw up his revolver and snapped it three times, four, and at the fifth attempt an orange flash and the thump of a shot in the open air. Five of the Policemen were triggering their automatic weapons and tugging at the cocking pieces to spill misfired rounds on the platform. But the old guns could still fire. Shots slapped and tore at the night in short bursts that pattered over the flesh of the Changlings like raindrops on thick dust. And still they came, walking toward Smith and the platform.

Incredibly, the anti-tank rocket ignited when the sixth Policeman tugged its lanyard. In ignorance he was holding the tube against his shoulder like a conventional weapon. The back-blast burned away the man's arm and chest in a ghastly simulacrum of Kozinski's mutilation. The rocket corkscrewed but chance slammed it into Ssu-ma's chest. The red blast momentarily covered the Changling's own fell glow. Her body splattered like the pulp of a grapefruit struck by a maul. Simultaneously, the front wall of the powerplant tore apart, snuffing the arcs dancing madly between the bomb casings.

Then, evident in the sudden darkness, the bits of Ssu-ma's glowing protoplasm began to draw together like droplets of mercury sliding in the bowl of a spoon. Her head had not been damaged. The waiting eyes smiled up at the platform.

Only Carter still stood before the casings. He had thrust the muzzle of his M16 into his mouth and was trying to fire the weapon with his outstretched finger. The round under the hammer misfired.

The powerplant exploded again, a gout of lava that loosened the hillside beneath it and sprayed the village. Wood and cloth began to burn in a pale imitation of what was happening across the creek. In slagging down, the reactor was fusing the rock and the hulls of the remaining bombs. Plutonium flowed white-hot with its own internal reactions, but it was spread too thin to self-trigger another Blast. The creek roared and boiled away as the rain of rock and metal spewed into it. The vapor that had been a plume over the power-plant was now a shroud to wrap the burning village.

"I hadn't called you yet," Smith said, shouting over the tumult as he clasped Kozinski's hand with his own left hand. He extended his right to the smiling Ssu-ma.

"We heard the siren," the Ruthenian said, his voice strange for coming from a mouth that was half bone . . . the half that had been turned away from the Strike which vaporized his infantry company, he had once explained.

"We could all tell they weren't burning coal, couldn't we?" Ssu-ma added.

The three travellers began groping through the night, through the smoke and the screaming. "I don't think we've ever checked whether the Oconee plant was still operable," Smith said. "It'd be a good time to see."

Kozinski shrugged. "We ought to get back to England some time. It's been too long since we were there."

"No, there's time for that," Smith argued. "Nobody there is going to build a fission plant as long as there's one man left to tell what we did when we found the one at Harewell."

A pair of burning buildings lighted their path, sweeping the air clear with an angry updraft. Kozinski squinted, then reached out his hand to halt Ssu-ma. "Your birthmark," he said, pointing to the star-shaped blotch beneath the girl's left breast. "It used to be on the right side."

She shrugged. "The rocket just now, I suppose."

Kozinski frowned. "Don't you see? If we can change at all, we can die some day."

"Sure," Smith agreed with a nod. "I've got some white hairs on my temples. My hair was solid brown the . . . when I went to New York."

"We'll live as long as the world needs us," Ssu-ma said quietly, touching each of the men and guiding them onward toward the trail back through the mountains. The steam and the night wrapped them, muffled them. Through it her words came: "After all, what sort of men would there be in the world if it weren't for men like us?"

And all three of them spoke the final line of the joke, their voices bright with remembered humor: "Men like us!"

_____*End note to* Men Like Us

I said in the introduction that this collection didn't include fantasy, but I will add here that I don't imagine that scientifically proper thermonuclear weapons could have the effects I imply in the background to this story. More to the point, whether you want to view it as SF or fantasy, it's quite clearly horror.

"Men Like Us" was written as a conscious variation on Poul Anderson's 1953 novella "UN-Man." When Poul wrote "UN-Man" he was an Internationalist in political outlook. By the time he wrote "No Truce with Kings" a decade later, he'd become a Libertarian. Both these (excellent; I strongly recommend that you read them) novellas reflected Poul's political beliefs at the time he wrote them.

"Men Like Us," on the other hand, says nothing about my own political, economic or social beliefs. Nothing. All it says is that I know a good story when I see one—

And that I steal from the best.

THE DAY OF GLORY

The locals had turned down the music from the sound truck while the bigwigs from the capital were talking to the crowd, but it was still playing. "I heard that song before," Trooper Lahti said, frowning. "But that was back on Icky Nose, two years ago. Three!"

"Right," said Platoon Sergeant Buntz, wishing he'd checked the fit of his dress uniform before he put it on for this bloody rally. He'd gained weight during the month he'd been on medical profile for tearing up his leg. "You hear it a lot at this kinda deal. *La Marseillaise*. It goes all the way back to Earth."

This time it was just brass instruments, but Buntz' memory could fill in, "*Arise, children of the fatherland! The day of glory has arrived. . . .*" Though some places they changed the words a bit.

"Look at the heroes you'll be joining!" boomed the amplified voice of the blonde woman gesturing from the waist-high platform. She stood with other folk in uniform or dress clothes on what Buntz guessed in peacetime was the judges' stand at the county f

"When you come back in a few months after crushing the rebels, the cowards who stayed behind will look at you the way you look at our allies, Hammer's Slammers!"

Buntz sucked in his gut by reflex, but he knew it didn't matter. For this recruitment rally he and his driver wore tailored uniforms with the seams edged in dark blue, but the yokels saw only the tank behind them. *Herod*, H42, was a veteran of three deployments and more firefights than Buntz could remember without checking the Fourth Platoon log.

The combat showed on *Herod's* surface. The steel skirts enclosing her plenum chamber were not only scarred from brush-busting but patched in several places where projectiles or energy weapons had penetrated. A two-meter section had been replaced on Icononzo, the result of a fifty-kilo directional mine. Otherwise the steel was dull red except where the rust had worn off.

Herod's hull and turret had taken even a worse beating; the iridium armor there turned all the colors of the spectrum when heated. A line of rainbow dimples along the rear compartment showed where a flechette gun—also on Icononzo—had wasted ammo, but it was on Humboldt that a glancing 15-cm powergun bolt had flared a banner across the bow slope.

If the gunner from Greenwood's Archers had hit *Herod* squarely, the tank would've been for the salvage yard and Lahti's family back on Leminkainen would've been told that she'd been cremated and buried where she fell.

Normally Lahti'd have been in the salvage yard too, and there wouldn't be any way to separate what was left of the driver from the hull. You didn't tell families all the details. They wouldn't understand anyway.

"Look at our allies, my fellow citizens!" the woman called. She was a newsreader from the capital station, Buntz'd been told. The satellites were down now, broadcast as well as surveillance, but her face'd be familiar from before the war even here in the boonies. "Hammer's Slammers, the finest troops in the galaxy! And look at the mighty vehicle they've brought to drive the northern rebels to surrender or their graves. Join them! Join them or forever hang your head when a child asks you, 'Grampa, what did you do in the war?'"

"They're not *really* joining the Regiment, are they, Top?" Lahti said, frowning again. The stocky woman'd progressed from being a fair driver to being a bloody good soldier. Buntz planned to give her a tank of her own the next time he had an opening. She worried too much, though, and about the wrong things.

"Right now they're just tripwires," Buntz said. "Afterwards, sure, we'll probably take some of 'em, after we've run 'em through newbie school."

He paused, then added, "The Feds've hired the Holy Brotherhood. They're light dragoons mostly, but they've got tank destroyers with 9-cm main guns. I don't guess we'll mop them up without somebody buying the farm."

He wouldn't say it aloud, even with none of the locals close enough to hear him, but he had to agree with Lahti that Placidus farmers didn't look like the most hopeful material. Part of the trouble was that they were wearing their fanciest clothes today. The feathers, ribbons, and reflecting bangles that passed for high fashion here in Quinta County would've made the toughest troopers in the Slammers look like a bunch of dimwits. It didn't help that half of 'em were barefoot, either.

The county governor, the only local on the platform, took the wireless microphone. "Good friends and neighbors!" he said and stopped to wheeze. He was a fat man with a weather-beaten face, and his suit was even tighter than Buntz' dress uniform.

"I know we in Quinta County don't need to be bribed to do our duty," he resumed, "but our generous government is offering a lavish prepayment of wages to those of you who join the ranks of the militia today. And there's free drinks in the refreshment tents for all those who kiss the book!"

He made a broad gesture. Nearly too broad: he almost went off the edge of the crowded platform onto his nose. His friends and neighbors laughed. One young fellow in a three-cornered hat called, "Why don't *you* join, Jeppe? You can stop a bullet and save the life of somebody who's not bloody useless!"

"What do they mean, 'kiss the book?'" Lahti asked. Then, wistfully, she added, "I don't suppose we could get a drink ourself?"

"We're on duty, Lahti," Buntz said. "And I guess they kiss the book because they can't write their names, a lot of them. You see that in this sorta place."

"*March, march!*" the sound truck played. "*Let impure blood water our furrows!*"

It was hotter'n Hell's hinges, what with the white sun overhead and its reflection from the tank behind them. The iridium'd burn'em if they touched it when they boarded to drive back to H Company's laager seventy klicks away. At least they didn't have to spend the night in this Godforsaken place. . . .

Buntz could use a drink too. There were booths all around the field. Besides them, boys circulated through the crowd with kegs on their backs and metal tumblers chained to their waists. It'd be rotgut, but he'd been in the Slammers thirteen years. He guessed he'd drunk worse and likely *much* worse than what was on offer in Quinta County.

But not a drop till him and Lahti stopped being a poster to recruit cannon fodder for the government paying for the Regiment's time. Being dry was just part of the job.

The Placidan regular officer with the microphone was talking about honor and what pushovers the rebels were going to be. Buntz didn't doubt that last part: if the Fed troops were anything like what he'd seen of the Government side, they were a joke for sure.

But the Holy Brotherhood was another thing entirely. Vehicle for vehicle they couldn't slug it out with the Slammers, but they were division-sized and bloody well trained.

Besides, they were all mounted on air cushion vehicles. The Slammers won more of their battles by mobility than by firepower, but this time their enemy would move even faster than they did.

"Suppose he's ever been shot at?" Lahti said, her lip curling at the guy who spoke. She snorted. "Maybe by his girlfriend, hey? Though dolled up like he is, he prob'ly has boyfriends."

Buntz grinned. "Don't let it get to you, Lahti," he said. "Listening to blowhards's a lot better business than having the Brotherhood shoot at us. Which is what we'll be doing in a couple weeks or I miss my bet."

While the Placidan officer was spouting off, a couple men had edged to the side of the platform to talk to the blonde newsreader. The blonde snatched the microphone back and cried, "Look here, my fellow citizens! Follow your patriotic neighbors Andreas and Adolpho deCastro as they kiss the book and drink deep to their glorious future!"

The officer yelped and tried to grab the microphone; the newsreader blocked him neatly with her hip, slamming him back. Buntz grinned: this was the blonde's court, but he guessed she'd also do better in a firefight than the officer would. Though he might beat her in a beauty contest. . . .

The blonde jumped from the platform, then put an arm around the waist of each local to waltz through the crowd to the table set up under *Herod*'s bow slope. The deCastros looked like brothers or anyway first cousins, big rangy lunks with red hair and moustaches that flared into their sideburns.

The newsreader must've switched off the microphone because none of her chatter to one man, then the other, was being broadcast. The folks on the platform weren't going to use the mike to upstage her, that was all.

"Rise and shine, Trooper Lahti," Buntz muttered out of the side of his mouth as he straightened. The Placidan clerk behind the table rose to his feet and twiddled the book before him. It was thick and bound in red leather, but what was inside was more than Buntz knew. Maybe it was blank.

"Who'll be the first?" the blonde said to the fellow

on her right. She'd cut the mike on again. "Adolpho, you'll do it, won't you? You'll be the first to kiss the book, I know it!"

The presumed Adolpho stared at her like a bunny paralyzed in the headlights. His mouth opened slackly. *Bloody Hell!* Buntz thought. *All it'll take is for him to start drooling!*

Instead the other fellow, Andreas, lunged forward and grabbed the book in both hands. He lifted it and planted a kiss right in the middle of the pebble-grain leather. Lowering it he boomed, "There, Dolph, you pussy! There's one man in the deCastro family, and the whole county knows it ain't you!"

"Why you—" Adolpho said, cocking back a fist with his face a thundercloud, but the blonde had already lifted the book from Andreas. She held it out to Adolpho.

"Here you go, Dolph, you fine boy!" she said. "Andreas, turn and take the salute of Captain Buntz of Hammer's Slammers, a hero from beyond the stars greeting a Placidan patriot!"

"What's that?" Andreas said. He turned to look over his shoulder.

Buntz'd seen more intelligence in the eyes of a poodle, but it wasn't his business to worry about that. He and Lahti together threw the fellow sharp salutes. The Slammers didn't go in for saluting much—and to salute in the field was a court-martial offense since it fingered officers for any waiting sniper—but a lot of times you needed some ceremony when you're dealing with the locals. This was just one of those times.

"An honor to serve with you, Trooper deCastro!" said Lahti. That was laying it on pretty thick, but you really couldn't overdo in a dog-and-pony show for the locals.

"You're a woman!" Andreas said. "They said they was taking women too, but I didn't believe it."

"That's right, Trooper," Buntz said briskly before his driver replied. He trusted Lahti—she wouldn't be driving *Herod* if he didn't—but there was no point in risking what might come out when she was hot and dry and pretty well pissed off generally.

"Now," he continued, "I see the paymaster—" another bored clerk, a little back from the recorder "—waiting with a stack of piasters for you. Hey, and *then* there's free drinks in the refreshment car just like they said."

The 'refreshment car' was a cattle truck with slatted steel sides that weren't going to budge if a new recruit decided he wanted to be somewhere else. A lot of steers had come to that realization over the years and it hadn't done 'em a bit of good. Two husky attendants waited in the doorway with false smiles, and there were two more inside dispensing drinks: grain alcohol with a dash of sweet syrup and likely an opiate besides. The truck would hold them, but a bunch of repentant yokels crying and shaking the slats wouldn't help lure their neighbors into the same trap.

Buntz saluted the other deCastro. The poor lug tried to salute back, but his arm seemed to have an extra joint in it somewhere. Buntz managed not to laugh and even nodded in false approval. It was all part of the job, like he'd told Lahti; but the Lord's truth was that he'd be less uncomfortable in a firefight. These poor stupid bastards!

The newsreader had given the mike back to the

county governor. It was funny to hear the crew from the capital go on about honor and patriotism while the local kept hitting the pay advance and free liquor. Buntz figured *he* knew his neighbors.

Though the blonde knew them too, or anyway she knew men. Instead of climbing back onto the platform, she was circulating through the crowd. As Buntz watched she corralled a tall, stooped fellow who looked pale—the locals were generally red-faced from exposure, though many women carried parasols for this event—and a stocky teenager who was already glassy-eyed. It wouldn't take much to drink in the truck to put him the rest of the way under.

The blonde led the sickly fellow by the hand and the young drunk by the shirt collar, but the drunk was really stumbling along quick as he could to grope her. She didn't seem to notice, though when she'd delivered him to the recorder, she raised the book to his lips with one hand and used the other to straighten her blouse under a jumper that shone like polished silver.

They were starting to move, now, just like sheep in the chute to the slaughter yard. Buntz kept saluting, smiling, and saying things like, "Have a drink on me, soldier," and, "Say, that's a lot of money they pay you fellows, isn't it?"

Which it was in a way, especially since the inflation war'd bring—war *always* brought—to the Placidan piaster hadn't hit yet except in the capital. There was three months pay in the stack.

By tomorrow, though, most of the recruits would've lost the whole wad to the trained dice of somebody else in the barracks. They'd have to send home for money then; that or starve, unless the Placidan government fed its soldiers better than most of these boondock worlds did. Out in the field they could loot, of course, but right now they'd be kept behind razor ribbon so they didn't run off when they sobered up.

The clerks were trying to move them through as quick as they could, but the recruits themselves wanted to talk: to the recorder, to the paymaster, and especially to Buntz and Lahti. "Bless you, buddy!" Buntz said brightly to the nine-fingered man who wanted to tell him about the best way to start tomatoes. "Look, you have a drink for me in the refreshment car and I'll come back and catch you up with a couple more as soon as I've done with these other fellows."

Holding the man's hand firmly in his left, Buntz patted him on the shoulders firmly enough to thrust him toward the clerk with the waiting stack of piasters. The advance was all in small bills to make it look like more. At the current exchange rate three months pay would come to about seventeen Frisian thalers, but it wouldn't be half that in another couple weeks.

A pudgy little fellow with sad eyes joined the line. A woman followed him, shrieking, "Alberto, are you out of your mind? Alberto! Look at me!" She was no taller than the man but easily twice as broad.

The woman grabbed him by the arm with both hands. He kept his face turned away, his mouth in a vague smile and his eyes full of anguish. "Alberto!"

The county governor was still talking about liquor and money, but all the capital delegation except an elderly, badly overweight union leader had gotten down from the platform and were moving through the crowd. The girlishly pretty army officer touched the screaming woman's shoulder and murmured something Buntz couldn't catch in the racket around him.

The woman glanced up with a black expression, her right hand rising with the fingers clawed. When she saw the handsome face so close to hers, though, she looked stunned and let the officer back her away.

Alberto kissed the book and scooted past the recorder without a look behind him. He almost went by the pay table, but the clerk caught him by the elbow and thrust the wad of piasters into his hand. He kept on going to the cattle truck: to Alberto, those steel slats were a fortress, not a prison.

A fight broke out in the crowd, two big men roaring as they flailed at each other. They were both blind drunk, and they didn't know how to fight anyway. In the morning they'd wake up with nothing worse than hangovers from the booze that was the reason they were fighting to begin with.

"I could take 'em both together," Lahti muttered disdainfully. She fancied herself as an expert in some martial art or another.

"Right," said Buntz. "And you could drive *Herod* through a nursery, too, but they'd both be a stupid waste of time unless you had to. Leave the posing for the amateurs, right?"

Buntz doubted he *could* handle the drunks barehanded, but of course he wouldn't try. There was a knife in his boot and a pistol in his right cargo pocket; the Slammers had been told not to wear their sidearms openly to this rally. Inside the turret hatch was a sub-machine gun, and by throwing a single switch he had control of *Herod*'s tribarrel and 20-cm main gun.

He grinned. If he said that to the recruits passing through the line, they'd think he was joking.

The grin faded. Pretty soon they were going to be facing the Brotherhood, who wouldn't be joking any more than Buntz was. The poor dumb bastards.

The county governor had talked himself out. He was drinking from a demijohn, resting the heavy earthenware on the cocked arm that held it to his lips.

His eyes looked haunted when they momentarily met those of Buntz. Buntz guessed the governor knew pretty well what he was sending his neighbors into. He was doing it anyway, probably because bucking the capital would've cost him his job and maybe more than that.

Buntz looked away. He had things on his conscience too; things that didn't go away when he took another drink, just blurred a little. He wouldn't want to be in the county governor's head after the war, though, especially at about three in the morning.

"*Against tyrants we are all soldiers,*" caroled the tune in the background. "*If our young heroes fall, the fatherland will raise new ones!*"

The union leader was describing the way the army of the legitimate government would follow the Slammers to scour the continent north of the Spine clean of the patches of corruption and revolt now breeding there. Buntz didn't know what Colonel Hammer's strategy would be, but he didn't guess they'd be pushing into the forested highlands to fight a more numerous enemy. The Brotherhood'd hand 'em their heads if they tried.

On the broad plains here in the south, though. . . . Well, *Herod*'s main gun was lethal for as far as her

optics reached, and that could be hundreds of kilometers if you picked your location.

The delegation from the capital kept trying, but
not even the blonde newsreader was making headway
now. They'd trolled up thirty or so recruits, maybe
thirty-five. Not a bad haul.

"Haven't saluted so much since I joined," Lahti
grumbled, a backhanded way of describing their success. "Well, like you say, Top, that's the job today."

The boy kissing the book was maybe seventeen
standard years old—or not quite that. Buntz hadn't
been a lot older when he joined, but he'd had three
cousins in the Regiment and he'd known he wasn't
getting into more than he could handle. Maybe this
kid was the same—the Army of Placidus wasn't going
to work him like Hammer's Slammers—but Buntz
doubted the boy was going to like however long it
was he wore a uniform.

The last person in line was a woman: mid-30s, no
taller than Lahti, and with a burn scar on the back
of her left wrist. The recording clerk started to hand
her the book, then recoiled when he took a look at
her. "Madame!" he said.

"Hey Hurtado!" a man said gleefully. "Look what
your missus is doing!"

"Guess she don't get enough dick at home, is that
it?" another man called from a liquor booth, his voice
slurred.

"The proclamation said you were enlisting women
too, didn't it?" the woman demanded. "Because of
the emergency?"

"Sophia!" cried a man stumbling to his feet from
a circle of dice players. He was almost bald, and his

long, drooping moustaches were too black for the color to be natural. Then, with his voice rising, "Sophia, what are you doing?"

"Well, maybe in the capital," the recorder said nervously. "I don't think—"

Hurtado grabbed the woman's arm. She shook him off without looking at him.

"What don't you think, my man?" said the newsreader, slipping through what'd become a circle of spectators. "You don't think you should obey the directives of the Emergency Committee in a time of war, is that what you think?"

The handsome officer was just behind her. He'd opened his mouth to speak, but he shut it again as he heard the blonde's tone.

"Well, no," the clerk said. The paymaster watched with a grin, obviously glad that somebody else was making the call on this one. "I just—"

He swallowed whatever else he might've said and thrust the book into the woman's hands. She raised it; Hurtado grabbed her arm again and said, "Sophia, don't make a spectacle of yourself!"

The newsreader said, "Sir, you have no—"

Sophia bent to kiss the red cover, then turned and backhanded Hurtado across the mouth. He yelped and jumped back. Still holding the book down at her side, she advanced and slapped him again with a full swing of her free hand.

Buntz glanced at Lahti, just making sure she didn't take it into her head to get involved. She was relaxed, clearly enjoying the spectacle and unworried about where it was going to go next.

The Placidan officer stepped between the man and

woman, looking uncomfortable. He probably felt pretty much the same as the recorder about women in the army, and maybe if the blonde hadn't been here he'd have said so. As it was, though—

"That will be enough, Senor Hurtado," he said. "Every family must do its part to eradicate the cancer of rebellion, you know."

Buntz grinned. The fellow ought to be glad that the blonde'd interfered, because otherwise there was a pretty fair chance that Lahti would've made the same points. Lahti wasn't one for words when she could *show* just how effective a woman could be in a fight.

"We about done here, Top?" she said, following Sophia with her eyes as she picked up her advance pay.

"We'll give it another fifteen minutes," Buntz said. "But yeah, I figure we're done."

"Arise, children of the fatherland. . . ." played the sound truck.

"It's gonna be a hot one," Lahti said, looking at the sky above *Herod*. The tank waited as silent as a great gray boulder where Lahti'd nestled it into a gully on the reverse slope of a hill. They weren't overlooked from any point on the surface of Placidus—particularly from the higher ground to the north which was in rebel hands. Everything but the fusion bottle was shut down, and thick iridium armor shielded that.

"It'll be hot for somebody," Buntz agreed. He sat on the turret hatch; Lahti was below him at the top of the bow slope. They could talk in normal voices this way instead of using their commo helmets. Only the most sophisticated devices could've picked up the low-power intercom channel, but he and Lahti didn't need it.

He and Lahti didn't need to talk at all. They just had to wait, them and the crew of *Hole Card*, Tank H47, fifty meters to the north in a parallel gully.

The plan wouldn't have worked against satellites, but the Holy Brotherhood had swept those out of the sky the day they landed at New Carthage on the north coast, the Federation capital. The Brotherhood commanders must've figured that a mutual lack of strategic reconnaissance gave the advantage to their speed and numbers. . . . and maybe they were right, but there were ways and ways.

Buntz grinned. And trust Colonel Hammer to find them.

"Hey Top?" Lahti said. "How long do we wait? If the Brotherhood doesn't bite, I mean."

"We switch on the radios at local noon," Buntz said. "Likely they'll recall us then, but I'm just here to take orders."

That was a gentle reminder to Lahti, not that she was out of line asking. With *Herod* shut down, she had nothing to see but the sky—white rather than really blue—and the sides of the gully.

Buntz had a 270 degree sweep of landscape centered the Government firebase thirty klicks to the west. His external pickup was pinned to a tree on the ridge between *Herod* and *Hole Card*, feeding the helmet displays of both tank commanders through fiber optic cables.

There were sensors that could *maybe* spot the pickup, but it wouldn't be easy and even then they'd have to be searching in this direction. The Brotherhood wasn't likely to be doing that when they had the Government battalion and five Slammers combat cars to hold their attention on the rolling grasslands below.

The Placidan troops were in a rough circle of a dozen bunkers connected by trenches. In the center of the encampment were four 15-cm conventional howitzers aiming toward the Spine from sandbagged revetments. The trenches were shallow and didn't have overhead cover; ammunition trucks were parked beside the guns without even the slight protection of a layer of sandbags.

According to the briefing materials, the firebase also had two calliopes whose task was to destroy incoming shells and missiles. Those the Placidan government bought had eight barrels each, arranged in superimposed rows of four.

Buntz couldn't see the weapons on his display. That meant they'd been dug in to be safe from direct fire, the only decision the Placidan commander'd made that he approved of. Two calliopes weren't nearly enough to protect a battalion against the kind of firepower a Brotherhood commando had available, though.

The combat cars of 3d Platoon, G Company, were laagered half a klick south of the Government firebase. The plains had enough contour that the units were out of direct sight of one another. That wouldn't necessarily prevent Placidans from pointing their slugthrowers up in the air and raining projectiles down on the Slammers, but at least it kept them from deliberately shooting at their mercenary allies.

Buntz' pickup careted movement on the foothills of the Spine to the north. "Helmet," he said, enabling the voice-activated controls. "Center three-five-oh degrees, up sixteen."

The magnified image showed the snouts of three air-cushion vehicles easing to the edge of the evergreen shrubs on the ridge nearly twenty kilometers north of the Government firebase. One was a large armored personnel carrier; it could carry fifteen fully-armed troops plus its driver and a gunner in the cupola forward. The APC's tribarrel was identical to the weapons on the Slammers' combat cars, a Gatling gun which fired jets of copper plasma at a rate of 500 rounds per minute.

The other two vehicles were tank destroyers. They used the same chassis as the APC, but each carried a single 9-cm high intensity powergun in a fixed axial mount—the only way so light a vehicle could handle the big gun's recoil. At moderate range—up to five klicks or so—a 9-cm bolt could penetrate *Herod*'s turret, and it'd be effective against a combat car at *any* distance.

"Saddle up, trooper," Buntz said softly to Lahti as he dropped down into the fighting compartment. "Don't crank her till I tell you, but we're not going to have to wait till noon after all. They're taking the bait."

The combat cars didn't have a direct view of the foothills, but like Buntz they'd raised a sensor pickup; theirs was on a pole mast extended from Lieutenant Rennie's command car. A siren wound from the laager; then a trooper shot off a pair of red flare clusters. Rennie was warning the Government battalion—which couldn't be expected to keep a proper radio watch—but Buntz knew that Platoon G3's main task was to hold the Brotherhood's attention. Flares were a good way to do that.

The Government artillerymen ran to their howitzers

from open-sided tents where they'd been dozing or throwing dice. Several automatic weapons began to fire from the bunkers. One was on the western side of the compound and had no better target than the waving grass. The guns shooting northward were pointed in the right direction, but the slugs would fall about fifteen kilometers short.

The Brotherhood tank destroyers fired, one and then the other. An ammunition truck in the compound blew up in an orange flash. The explosion dismounted the nearest howitzer and scattered the sandbag revetments of the other three, not that they'd been much use anyway. A column of yellow-brown dirt lifted, mushroomed a hundred meters in the air, and rained grit and pebbles down onto the whole firebase.

The second 9-cm bolt lashed the crest of the rise which sheltered the combat cars. Grass caught fire and glass fused from silica in the soil sprayed in all directions. Buntz nodded approval. The Brotherhood gunner couldn't have expected to hit the cars, but he was warning them to keep under cover.

Brotherhood APCs slid out of the shelter of the trees and onto the grasslands below. They moved in companies of four vehicles each, two east of the firebase and two more to the west. They weren't advancing toward the Government position but instead were flanking it by more than five kilometers to either side.

The sound of the explosion reached *Herod*, dulled by distance. A little dirt shivered from the side of the swale. Twenty klicks is a hell of a long way away, even for an ammo truck blowing up.

The tank destroyers fired again, saturated cyan flashes that Buntz' display dimmed to save his eyes.

Their target was out of his present magnified field of view, a mistake.

"Full field, Quadrant Four," Buntz said, and the lower left corner of his visor showed the original 270 degree display. A bunker had collapsed in a cloud of dust though without a noticeable secondary explosion, and there was a new fire just north of the combat cars. The cars' tribarrels wouldn't be effective against even the tank destroyers' light armor at this range, but the enemy commander wasn't taking any chances. The Brotherhood was a good outfit, no mistake.

Eight more vehicles left the hills now that the advanced companies had spread to screen them. Pairs of mortar carriers with pairs of APCs for security followed each flanking element. The range of Brotherhood automatic mortars was about ten klicks, depending on what shell they were firing. It wouldn't be any time before they were in position around the firebase.

Rennie's combat cars were moving southward, keeping under cover. Running, if you wanted to call it that.

The Brotherhood APCs were amazingly fast, seventy kph cross-country. They couldn't fight the combat cars head-on, but they wouldn't try to. They obviously intended to surround the Slammers platoon and disgorge their infantry in three-man buzzbomb teams. Once the infantry got into position, and with the tank destroyers on overwatch to limit the cars' movement, the Brotherhood could force Lieutenant Rennie to surrender without a shot.

One of the Government howitzers fired. The guns could reach the Brotherhood vehicles in the hills, but this round landed well short. A red flash and a spurt of sooty black smoke indicated that the bursting charge was TNT.

The gunners didn't get a chance to refine their aim. A 9-cm bolt struck the gun tube squarely at the trunnions, throwing the front half a dozen meters. The white blaze of burning steel ignited hydraulic fluid in the compensator, the rubber tires, and the hair and uniforms of the crew. A moment later propellant charges stacked behind the gun went off in something between an explosion and a very fierce fire.

Two howitzers were more or less undamaged, but their crews had abandoned them. Another bunker collapsed—a third. Buntz hadn't noticed the second being hit, but a pall of dust was still settling over it. Government soldiers started to leave the remaining bunkers and huddle in the connecting trenches.

Flashes and spurts of white smoke at four points around the firebase indicated that the mortars had opened fire simultaneously. They were so far away that the bombardment seemed to be happening in silence. That wasn't what Buntz was used to, which made him feel funny. Different generally meant bad to a soldier or anybody else in a risky business.

The tank destroyers fired again. One bolt blew in the back of a bunker; the other ignited a stand of brushwood ahead of the combat cars. That Brotherhood gunner was trying to keep Rennie off-balance, taking his attention off the real threat: the APCs and their infantry, which in a matter of minutes would have the cars surrounded.

Buntz figured it was time. "Lahti, fire 'em up," he said. He switched on his radios, then unplugged the lead from his helmet and let the coil of glass fiber spring back to the take-up reel on the sensor. The hollow *stoonk-k-k* of the mortars launching finally reached him, an unmistakable sound even when the breeze sighing through the tree branches almost smothered it.

The hatch cover swivelled closed over Buntz as *Herod*'s eight drive fans spun. Lahti kept the blades in fine pitch to build speed rapidly, slicing the air but not driving it yet.

"Lamplight elements, move to start position," Buntz ordered. That was being a bit formal since the Lamplight call-sign covered only *Herod* and *Hole Card*, but you learned to do things by rote in combat. A firefight's no place for thinking. You operated by habit and reflex; if those failed, the other fellow killed you.

The fan note deepened. *Herod* vibrated fiercely, spewing a sheet of grit from beneath her skirts. She didn't move forward; it takes time for thrust to balance a tank's 170 tonnes.

A calliope—only one—ripped the sky with a jet of 2-cm bolts. The burst lasted only for an eyeblink, but a mortar shell detonated at its touch. The gun was concealed, but Buntz knew the crew was slewing it to bear on a second of the incoming rounds before it landed.

They didn't succeed: proximity fuses exploded the three remaining shells a meter in the air. Fragments sleeted across the compound. Because mortars are low pressure, their shell casings can be much thinner than those of conventional artillery; that leaves room for larger bursting charges. The blasts flattened all the structures that'd survived the ammo truck blowing up. One of the shredded tents ignited a few moments later.

Herod's fans finally bit deeply enough to start the

tank climbing up the end of the gully. Buntz had a panoramic view on his main screen. He'd already careted all the Brotherhood vehicles either white—*Herod's* targets—or orange, for *Hole Card*. That way both tanks wouldn't fire at the same vehicle and possibly allow another to escape.

Buntz' smaller targeting display was locked on where the right-hand Brotherhood tank destroyer would appear when *Herod* reached firing position. *Hole Card* would take the other tank destroyer, the only one visible to it because of a freakishly tall tree growing from the grassland north of its position.

"*Top, I'm on!*" shouted Cabell in *Hole Card* on the unit frequency. As Cabell spoke, Buntz' orange pipper slid onto the rounded bow of a tank destroyer. The magnified image rocked as the Brotherhood vehicle sent another plasma bolt into the Government encampment.

"Fire!" Buntz said, mashing the firing pedal with his boot. *Herod* jolted backward from the recoil of the tiny thermonuclear explosion; downrange, the tank destroyer vanished in a fireball.

Hole Card's target was gone also. Shrubbery was burning in semicircles around the gutted wreckage, and a square meter of deck plating twitched as it fell like a wounded goose. It could've come from either Brotherhood vehicle, so complete was the destruction.

There was a squeal as Cabell swung *Hole Card's* turret to bear on the plains below. Buntz twitched *Herod's* main gun only a few mils to the left and triggered it again.

The APC in the foothills was probably the command

vehicle overseeing the whole battle. The Brotherhood driver slammed into reverse when the tank destroyers exploded to either side of him, but he didn't have enough time to reach cover before *Herod*'s 20-cm bolt caught the APC squarely. Even from twenty kilometers away, the slug of ionized copper was devastating. The fires lit by the burning vehicles merged into a blaze of gathering intensity.

Now for the real work. "Lahti, haul us forward a couple meters, get us onto the forward slope!" Buntz ordered. The main gun could depress only 5 degrees, so any Brotherhood vehicles that reached the base of the rise the tanks were on would otherwise be in a dead zone.

They shouldn't get that close, of course, but the APCs were very fast. Buntz hadn't made platoon sergeant by gambling when he didn't need to.

The Brotherhood troops on the plains didn't realize—most of them, at least—that their support elements had been destroyed. The mortar crews had launched single rounds initially to test the Placidan defenses. When those proved hopelessly meager, the mortarmen followed up with a Battery Six, six rounds from each tube as quickly as the automatic loaders could cycle.

The calliope didn't make even a token effort to meet the incoming catastrophe; the early blasts must've knocked it out. The twenty-four shells were launched on slightly different trajectories so that all reached the target within a fraction of a same instant. Their explosions covered the interior of the compound as suddenly and completely as flame flashes across a pool of gasoline.

The lead APC in the western flanking element glared

cyan; then the bow plate and engine compartment tilted inward into the gap vaporized by *Hole Card*'s main gun. As Lahti shifted *Herod*, Buntz settled his pipper on the nearest target of the eastern element, locked the stabilizer, and rolled his foot forward on the firing pedal.

Recoil made *Herod* stagger as though she'd hit a boulder. The turret was filling with a gray haze as the breech opened for fresh rounds. The bore purging system didn't get *quite* all of the breakdown products of the matrix which held copper atoms in alignment. Filters kept the gases out of Buntz' lungs, but his eyes watered and the skin on the back of his hands prickled.

He was used to it. He wouldn't have felt comfortable if it *hadn't* happened.

The lead company of the commando's eastern element was in line abreast, aligning the four APCs—three and a dissipating fireball now—almost perfectly with *Herod*'s main gun. Buntz raised his pipper slightly, fired; raised it again as he slewed left to compensate for the APCs' forward movement, fired; raised it again—

The driver of the final vehicle was going too fast to halt by reversing the drive fans to suck the APC to the ground; he'd have pinwheeled if he'd tried it. Instead he cocked his nacelles forward, hoping that he'd fall out of his predicted course. The APC's tribarrel was firing in *Herod*'s general direction, though even if the cyan stream had been carefully aimed the range was too great for 2-cm bolts to damage a tank.

As Buntz' pipper steadied, the sidepanels of the APC's passenger compartment flopped down and the infantry tried to abandon the doomed vehicle. Buntz barely noticed the jolt of his main gun as it lashed out. Buzzbombs and grenades exploded in red speckles on his plasma bolt's overwhelming glare. The back of the APC tumbled through the fiery remains of the vehicle's front half.

Half a dozen tribarrels were shooting at the tanks as the surviving APCs dodged for cover. The same rolling terrain that'd protected Platoon G3 from the tank destroyers sheltered the Brotherhood vehicles also. Buntz threw a quick shot at an APC. *Too* quick: his bolt lifted a divot the size of a fuel drum from the face of a hillock as his target slid behind it. Grass and topsoil burned a smoky orange.

The only Brotherhood vehicles still in sight were a mortar van and the APC that'd provided its security. They'd both been assigned to *Hole Card* originally, but seeings as all of *Herod's* targets were either hidden or blazing wreckage—

Cabell got on the mortar first, so as its unfired shells erupted in a fiery yellow mushroom Buntz put a bolt into the bow of the APC. The sidepanels were open and the tribarrel wasn't firing. Like as not the gunner and driver had joined the infantry in the relative safety of the high grass.

The mortars hadn't fired on Rennie's platoon, knowing that the combat cars would simply put their tribarrels in air-defense mode and sweep the bombs from the sky. The only time mortar shells might be useful would be if they distracted the cars from line-of-sight targets.

The Brotherhood commando had been well and truly hammered, but what remained was as dangerous as a wounded leopard. One option was for Rennie to claim a victory and withdraw in company with the tanks. In the short term that made better economic sense than sending armored vehicles against trained, well equipped infantry in heavy cover. In the longer term, though, that gave the Slammers the reputation of a unit that was afraid to go for the throat . . . which meant it wasn't an option at all.

"*Myrtle Six to Lamplight Six,*" said Lieutenant Rennie over the command push. "*My cars are about to sweep the zone, west side first. Don't you panzers get hasty for targets, all right? Over.*"

"Lamplight to Myrtle," Buntz replied. "Sir, hold your screen and let me flush 'em toward you while my Four-seven element keeps overwatch. You've got deployed infantry in your way, but if we can deal with their air defense—right?"

Finishing the commando wouldn't be safe either way, but it was better for a lone tank. Facing infantry in the high grass the combat cars risked shooting one another up, whereas *Herod* had a reasonable chance of bulling in and out without taking more than her armor could absorb.

Smoke rose from a dozen grassfires on the plain, and the blaze on the hills to the north was growing into what'd be considered a disaster on a world at peace. A tiny part of Buntz' mind noted that he hadn't been on a world at peace in the thirteen standard years since he joined the Slammers, and he might never be on one again until he retired. Or died.

He'd been raised to believe in the Way. Enough of the training remained that he wasn't sure there was peace even in death for what Sergeant Darren Lawrence Buntz had become. But that was for another time, or probably no time at all.

While Buntz waited for Myrtle Six to reply, he
echoed a real-time feed from *Hole Card's* on a section
of his own main screen, then called up a topographic
map and overlaid it with the courses of all the Brotherhood vehicles. On that he drew a course plot with
a sweep of his index finger.

"Lamplight, this is Myrtle," Lieutenant Rennie
said at last. The five cars had formed into a loose
wedge, poised to sweep north through the Brotherhood anti-armor teams and the remaining APCs. *"All
right, Buntz, we'll be your anvil. Next time, though,
we get the fun part. Myrtle Six out."*

"Four-seven, this is Four-two," Buntz said, using the
channel dedicated to Lamplight; that was the best way
to inform without repetition not only Sergeant Cabell
but also the drivers of the two tanks. "Four-two will
proceed on the attached course."

He transmitted the plot he'd drawn while waiting for
Rennie to make up his mind. It was rough, but that
was all Lahti needed—she'd pick the detailed route
by eyeball. As for Cabell, knowing the course allowed
him to anticipate where targets might appear.

"I'll nail them if they hold where they are, and you
get'em if they try to run, Cabell," he said. "But you
know, not too eager. Got it, over?"

"Roger, Four-two," Cabell replied. *"Good hunting.
Four-seven out."*

Lahti had already started *Herod* down the slope,
using gravity to accelerate; the fans did little more
than lift the skirts off the ground. Their speed quickly
built up to 40 kph.

Buntz frowned, doubtful about going so fast cross-
country in a tank. Lahti was managing it, though.

Herod jounced over narrow, rain-cut gullies and on hillocks which the roots of shrubs had cemented into masses a hand's breadth higher than the surrounding surface, but though Buntz jolted against his seat restraints the shocks weren't any worse than those of the main gun firing.

The fighting compartment displays gave Buntz a panoramic view at any magnification he wanted. Despite that, he had an urge to roll the hatch back and ride with his head out. Like most of the other Slammers recruits, whatever planet they came from, he'd been a country boy. It didn't feel right to shut himself up in a box when he was heading for a fight.

It was what common sense as well as standing orders required, though. Buntz did what he knew he should instead of what his heart wanted to do. When he'd been ten years younger, though, he'd regularly ridden into battle with his torso out of the hatch and his hands on the spade grips of the tribarrel instead of slewing and firing it with the joystick behind armor.

"Boomer Three-niner-one, this is Myrtle Six," Lieutenant Rennie said, using the operation's command channel to call the supporting battery. *"Request targeting round at point Alpha Tango one-three, five-eight. Over."*

Herod tore through a belt of heavy brush in the dip between two gradual rises. Ground water collected here, and there might be a running stream during the wet season. The tank's skirts sheared gnarled stems, and bits that got into the fan nacelles were sprayed out again as chips.

Hole Card fired. Buntz had been concentrating on the panoramic screen, poised to react if the tank's AI careted movement. Now he glanced at his echo of Cabell's targeting display. The bolt missed, but a Brotherhood APC fluffed its fans to escape the fire spreading from the scar which plasma'd licked through thirty meters of grass.

Cabell fired again. Maybe he'd even planned it this way, spending the first round to startle his target into the path of the second. The APC flew apart. There was no secondary explosion because the infantry had already dismounted, taking their munitions with them.

A shell from the supporting rocket artillery screamed out of the southern sky. While the round was still a thousand meters in the air, a tribarrel fired from near the predicted point of impact. Plasma ruptured the shell, sending a spray of blue smoke through the air. It'd been a marking round, harmless unless you happened to be exactly where it hit.

Herod had just reached the top of another rise. The APC that'd destroyed the shell was behind a knoll seven kilometers away, but Buntz fired, Cabell fired, and two combat cars on the east end of Rennie's wedge thought they had a target also.

None of them hit the target, but Buntz got a momentary view of a Brotherhood soldier hopping into sight and vanishing again. He'd leaped from his cupola, well aware that it was only a matter of time—a matter of a short time—before the Slammers' concentrated fire hit the vehicle that'd been spared by such a narrow margin.

Lahti boosted her fans into the overload region to lift *Herod* another centimeter off the ground without letting their speed drop. The side-slopes were harsh going: the topsoil had weathered away, leaving rock exposed. Rain and wind deposited the silt at the bottom of the swales, so the Brotherhood troops waiting on the other side of the hill would expect *Herod* to come at them low.

Buntz'd angled his main gun to their left front, fully depressed. The cupola tribarrel was aimed up the hill *Herod* was circling. He saw the infantry on the crest rise with their buzzbombs shouldered. Before his thumb could squeeze the tribarrel's firing tit, his displays flickered and the hair on the back of his neck rose. The top of the hill erupted, struck squarely by a bolt from *Hole Card*'s main gun. Cabell's angle had given him an instant's advantage.

Twenty-odd kilometers of atmosphere had spread the plasma charge, but it was still effective against the infantry. There'd been at least six Brotherhood soldiers, but when the rainbow dazzle cleared a single figure remained to stumble downhill. Its arms were raised and its hair and uniform were burning. The fireball of organic matter in the huge divot which the bolt blasted from the hilltop did most of the damage, but the troops' own grenades and buzzbombs had gone off also.

Cabell'd taken a chance when he aimed so close to *Herod* at long range, but a battle's a risky place to be. Buntz wasn't complaining.

Herod rounded the knob, going too fast to hold its line when the outside of the curve was on a downslope. The tank, more massive than big but big as well, skidded and jounced outward on the turn. The four Brotherhood APCs sheltered on the reverse slope fired before *Herod* came into sight, willing to burn out their tribarrels for the chance of getting off the first shot. The gunners knew that if they didn't cripple the blower tank instantly they were dead.

They were probably dead even if they did cripple the tank. They were well-trained professionals sacrificing themselves to give their fellows a chance to escape.

2-cm bolts rang on *Herod*'s bow slope in a brilliant display that blurred several of the tank's external pickups with a film of redeposited iridium. The Brotherhood commander hadn't had time to form a defensive position; his vehicles were bunched to escape the tank snipers far to the west, not to meet one of those tanks at knife range. Three vehicles were at the bottom of the swale in a rough line-ahead; the last was higher on the slope.

Buntz fired his main gun when the pipper swung on—on *anything*, on any part of the APCs. His bolt hit the middle vehicle of the line; it swelled into a fiery bubble. The shockwave shoved the other vehicles away.

The high APC continued to hose *Herod* with plasma bolts, hammering the hull and blasting three fat holes in the skirts. That tribarrel was the only one to hit the tank, probably because its gunner was aiming to avoid friendly vehicles.

Herod's main gun cycled, purging and cooling the bore with a jet of liquid nitrogen. Buntz held his foot down on the trip, screaming with frustration because his gun didn't fire, couldn't fire. He understood the delay, but it was maddening nonetheless.

The upper half of the APC vanished in a roaring coruscation: the explosion of *Herod*'s target had pushed it high enough that *Hole Card* could nail it. Cabell wouldn't have to pay for his drinks the next night he and Buntz were in a bar together.

Two blocks of *Herod*'s Automatic Defense Array

went off simultaneously, making the hull chime like a gong. Each block blasted out hundreds of tungsten barrels the size of a finger joint. They ripped through long grass and Brotherhood infantry, several of them already firing powerguns.

A soldier stepped around the bow of an APC, his buzzbomb raised to launch. A third block detonated, shredding him from neck to knees. Pellets punched ragged holes through the light armor of the vehicle behind him.

Herod's main gun fired—*finally*, Buntz' imagination told him, but he knew the loading cycle was complete in less than two seconds. The rearmost APC collapsed in on itself like a thin wax model in a bonfire. The bow fragment tilted toward the rainbow inferno where the middle of the vehicle had been, its tribarrel momentarily spurting a cyan track skyward.

Lahti'd been fighting to hold *Herod* on a curving course. Now she deliberately straightened the rearmost pair of fan nacelles, knowing that without their counteracting side-thrust momentum would swing the stern out. The gunner in the surviving APC slammed three bolts into *Herod*'s turret at point-blank range; then the mass of the tank's starboard quarter swatted the light vehicle, crushing it and flinging the remains sideways like a can kicked by an armored boot.

Herod grounded hard, air screaming through the holes in her plenum chamber. "Get us outa here, Lahti!" Buntz ordered. "Go! Go! Go!"

Lahti was already tilting her fan nacelles to compensate for the damage. She poured on the coal again. Because they were still several meters above the floor of the swale, she was able to use gravity briefly to accelerate by sliding *Herod* toward the smoother terrain.

Buntz spun his cupola at maximum rate, knowing that scores of Brotherhood infantry remained somewhere in the grass behind them. A shower of buzzbombs could easily disable a tank. If *Herod's* luck was really bad, well . . . the only thing good about a fusion bottle rupturing was that the crew wouldn't know what hit them.

The driver of an APC was climbing out of his cab, about all that remained of the vehicle. Buntz didn't fire; he didn't even think of firing.

It could of been me. It could be me tomorrow.

Lahti maneuvered left, then right, following contours that'd go unremarked on a map but which were the difference between concealed and visible—between life and death—on this rolling terrain. When *Herod* was clear of the immediate knot of enemy soldiers, she slowed to give herself time to diagnose the damage to the plenum chamber.

Buntz checked his own readouts. Half the upper bank of sensors on the starboard side were out, not critical now but definitely a matter for replacement before the next operation.

The point-blank burst into the side of the turret was more serious. The bolts hadn't penetrated, but another hit in any of the cavities just might. Base maintenance would probably patch the damage for now, but Buntz wouldn't be a bit surprised if the turret was swapped out while the Regiment was in transit to the next contract deployment.

But not critical, not right at the moment. . . .

As Buntz took stock, a shell screamed up from the

south. He hadn't heard Lieutenant Rennie call for another round, but it wasn't likely that a tank commander in the middle of a firefight would've.

Six or eight Brotherhood APCs remained undamaged, but this time their tribarrels didn't engage the incoming shell. It burst a hundred meters up, throwing out a flag of blue smoke. It was simply a reminder of the sleet of antipersonnel bomblets that *could* follow.

A mortar fired, its *choonk!* a startling sound to a veteran at this point in a battle. *Have they gone off their nuts?* Buntz thought. He set his tribarrel to air defense mode just in case.

Lahti twitched *Herod*'s course so that *Herod* didn't smash a stand of bushes with brilliant pink blooms. She liked flowers, Buntz recalled. Sparing the bushes didn't mean much in the long run, of course.

Buntz grinned. His mouth was dry and his lips were so dry they were cracking. *In the long run, everybody's dead. Screw the long run.*

The mortar bomb burst high above the tube that'd launched it. It was a white flare cluster.

"All personnel of the Flaming Sword Commando, cease fire!" an unfamiliar voice ordered on what was formally the Interunit Channel. Familiarly it was the Surrender Push. When a signal came in over that frequency, a red light pulsed on the receiving set of every mercenary in range. *"This is Captain el-Khalid, ranking officer. Slammers personnel, the Flaming Sword Commando of the Holy Brotherhood surrenders on the usual terms. We request exchange and repatriation at the end of the conflict. Over."*

"All Myrtle and Lamplight units!" Lieutenant Rennie called, also using the Interunit Channel. *"This is Myrtle*

Six. Cease fire, I repeat, cease fire. Captain el-Khalid, please direct your troops to proceed to high ground to await registration. Myrtle Six out."

"Top, can we pull into that firebase while they get things sorted out?" Lahti asked over the intercom. "I'll bet we got enough time to patch those holes. I don't want to crawl all the way back leaking air and scraping our skirts."

"Right, good thinking," Buntz said. "And if there's not time, we'll make time. Nothing's going to happen that can't wait another half hour."

Herod carried a roll of structural plastic sheeting. Cut and glued to the inside of the plenum chamber, it'd seal the holes till base maintenance welded permanent patches in place. Unless the Brotherhood had shot away all the duffle on the back deck, of course, in which case they'd borrow sheeting from another of the vehicles. It wouldn't be the first time Buntz'd had to replace his personal kit, either.

They were within two klicks of the Government firebase. Even if they'd been farther, a bulldozed surface was a lot better to work on. Out here you were likely to find you'd set down on brambles or a nest of stinging insects when you crawled into the plenum chamber.

As Lahti drove sedately toward the firebase, Buntz opened his hatch and stuck his head out. He felt dizzy for a moment. That was reaction, he supposed, not the change from chemical residues to open air.

Sometimes the breeze drifted a hot reminder of the battle past Buntz' face. The main gun had cooled to rainbow-patterned gray, but heat waves still shimmered above the barrel.

Lahti was idling up the resupply route into the firebase, an unsurfaced track that meandered along the low ground. It'd have become a morass when it rained, but that didn't matter any longer.

There was no wire or berm, just the circle of bunkers. Half of them were now collapsed. The Government troops had been playing at war; to the Brotherhood as to the Slammers, killing was a business.

Lahti halted them between two undamaged bunkers at the south entrance. Truck wheels had rutted the soil here. There was flatter ground within the encampment, but she didn't want to crush the bodies in the way.

Buntz'd probably have ordered his driver to stop even if she'd had different ideas. Sure, they were just bodies; he'd seen his share and more of them since he'd enlisted. But they could patch *Herod* where they were, so that's what they'd do.

Lahti was clambering out her hatch. Buntz made sure that the Automatic Defense Array was shut off, then climbed onto the back deck. He was carrying the first aid kit, not that he expected to accomplish much with it.

It bothered him that he and Lahti both were out of *Herod* in case something happened, but nothing was going to happen. Anyway, the tribarrel was still in air defense mode. He bent to cut the ties holding the roll of sheeting.

"Hey Top?" Lahti called. Buntz looked at her over his shoulder. She was pointing to the nearest bodies. The Government troops must've been running from the bunkers when the first mortar shells scythed them down.

"Yeah, what you got?" Buntz said.

"These guys," Lahti said. "Remember the recruiting rally? This is them, right?"

Buntz looked more carefully. "Yeah, you're right," he said.

That pair must be the DeCastro brothers, one face-up and the other face-down. They'd both lost their legs at mid-thigh. Buntz couldn't recall the name of the guy just behind them, but he was the henpecked little fellow who'd been dodging his wife. Well, he'd dodged her for good. And the woman with all her clothes blown off; not a mark on her except she was dead. The whole Quinta County draft must've been assigned here.

He grimaced. They'd been responsible for a major victory over the rebels, according to one way of thinking.

Buntz shoved the roll of sheeting to the ground. "Can you handle this yourself, Lahti?" he said. He gestured with the first aid kit. "I can't do a lot, but I'd like to try."

The driver shrugged. "Sure, Top," she said. "If you want to."

Recorded music was playing from one of the bunkers. Buntz' memory supplied the words: "*Arise, children of the fatherland! The day of glory has arrived. . . .*"

_____*End note to* The Day of Glory

The Hammer's Slammers series isn't in any sense a future history. It's made up of individual stories exploring one aspect or another of what war means to the men and women at the sharp end. In these stories I've been translating into an SF setting what I learned in 1970 with the 11th Armored Cavalry Regiment in Viet Nam and Cambodia.

We—the Blackhorse—were an elite unit. I was very fortunate to have been assigned to a regiment in which you never had to worry if the guy next to you was going to do his job: he was, and so were you—whatever you thought of war or The War or our Vietnamese allies. (Generally the answer to all those questions was, "Not much.")

The flip side was that the distinction between the categories Not Blackhorse and Enemy got blurred. We didn't view our job as winning hearts and minds: we were there to kill people and then go home. And we didn't much care about the cost of victory so long as somebody else was paying it.

That's something civilians ought to consider long and hard before they send tanks off to make policy. Because I can tell you from personal experience, it isn't something the tankers themselves are likely to worry about.

THE INTERROGATION TEAM

The man the patrol brought in was about forty, bearded, and dressed in loose garments—sandals, trousers, and a vest that left his chest and thick arms bare. Even before he was handed from the back of the combat car, trussed to immobility in sheets of water-clear hydroclasp, Griffiths could hear him screaming about his rights under the York Constitution of '03.

Didn't the fellow realize he'd been picked up by Hammer's Slammers?

"Yours or mine, Chief?" asked Major Smokey Soames, Griffiths' superior and partner on the interrogation team—a slim man of Afro-Asian ancestry, about as suited for wringing out a mountaineer here on York as he was for swimming through magma. Well, Smokey'd earned his pay on Kanarese. . . .

"Is a bear Catholic?" Griffiths asked wearily. "Go set the hardware up, Major."

"And haven't I already?" said Smokey, but it had been nice of him to make the offer. It wasn't that mechanical interrogation *required* close genetic correspondences

153

between subject and operator, but the job went faster and smoother in direct relation to those correspondences. Worst of all was to work on a woman, but you did what you had to do. . . .

Four dusty troopers from A Company manhandled the subject, still shouting, to the command car housing the interrogation gear. The work of the firebase went on. Crews were pulling maintenance on the fans of some of the cars facing outward against attack, and one of the rocket howitzers rotated squealingly as new gunners were trained. For the most part, though, there was little to do at midday, so troopers turned from the jungle beyond the berm to the freshly-snatched prisoner and the possibility of action that he offered.

"Don't damage the goods!" Griffiths said sharply when the men carrying the subject seemed ready to toss him onto the left-hand couch like a log into a blazing fireplace. One of the troopers, a non-com, grunted assent; they settled the subject in adequate comfort. Major Soames was at the console between the paired couches, checking the capture location and relevant intelligence information from Central's data base.

"Want us to unwrap 'im for you?" asked the non-com, ducking instinctively though the roof of the command car cleared his helmet. The interior lighting was low, however, especially to eyes adapted to the sun hammering the bulldozed area of the firebase.

"Listen, me 'n my family *never,* I swear it, dealt with interloping traders!" the York native pleaded.

"No, we'll take care of it," said Griffiths to the A Company trooper, reaching into the drawer for a disposable-blade scalpel to slit the hydorclasp sheeting over the man's wrist. Some interrogators liked to keep a big fighting knife around, combining practical requirements with a chance to soften up the subject through fear. Griffiths thought the technique was misplaced: for effective mechanical interrogation, he wanted his subjects as relaxed as possible. Panic-jumbled images were better than no images at all; but only *just* better.

"We're not the Customs Police, old son," Smokey murmured as he adjusted the couch headrest to an angle which looked more comfortable for the subject. "We're a lot more interested in the government convoy ambushed last week."

Griffiths' scalpel drew a line above the subject's left hand and wrist. The sheeting drew back in a narrow gape, briefly iridescent as stresses within the hydorclasp readjusted themselves. As if the sheeting were skin, however, the rip stopped of its own accord at the end of the scored line. "What're you doing to me?"

"Nothing I'm not doing to myself, friend," said Griffiths, grasping the subject's bared forearm with his own left hand so that their inner wrists were together. Between the thumb and forefinger of his right hand he held a standard-looking stim cone up where the subject could see it clearly, despite the cocoon of sheeting still holding his legs and torso rigid. "I'm George, by the way. What do your friends call you?"

"You're drugging me!" the subject screamed, his fingers digging into Griffiths' forearm fiercely. The mountaineers living under triple-canopy jungle looked pasty and unhealthy, but there was nothing wrong with this one's muscle tone.

"It's a random pickup," said Smokey in Dutch to

his partner. "Found him on a trail in the target area, nothing suspicious—probably just out sap-cutting—but they could snatch him without going into a village and starting something."

"Right in one," Griffiths agreed in soothing English as he squeezed the cone at the juncture of his and the subject's wrist veins. The dose in its skin-absorbed carrier—developed from the solvent used with formic acid by Terran solifugids for defense—spurted out under pressure and disappeared into the bloodstreams of both men: thrillingly cool to Griffiths, and a shock that threw the subject into mewling, abject terror.

"Man," the interrogator murmured as he detached the subject's grip from his forearm, using the pressure point in the man's wrist to do so, "if there was anything wrong with it, I wouldn't have split it with you, now would I?"

He sat down on the other couch, swinging his legs up and lying back before the drug-induced lassitude crumpled him on the floor. He was barely aware of movement as Smokey fitted a helmet on the subject and ran a finger up and down columns of touch-sensitive controls on his console to reach a balance. All Griffiths would need was the matching helmet, since the parameters of his brain were already loaded into the database. By the time Smokey got around to him, he wouldn't even feel the touch of the helmet.

Though the dose *was* harmless, as he'd assured the subject, unless the fellow had an adverse reaction because of the recreational drugs he'd been taking on his own. You could never really tell with the sap-cutters, but it was generally okay. The high jungles of York produced at least a dozen drugs of varying effect, and the producers were of course among the heaviest users of their haul.

By itself, that would have been a personal problem; but the mountaineers also took the position that trade off-planet was their own business, and that there was no need to sell their drugs through the Central Marketing Board in the capital for half the price that traders slipping into the jungle in small starships would cheerfully pay. Increasingly-violent attempts to enforce customs laws on men with guns and the willingness to use them had led to what was effectively civil war—which the York government had hired the Slammers to help suppress.

It's a bitch to fight when you don't know who the enemy is; and that was where Griffiths and his partner came in.

"Now I want you to imagine that you're walking home from where you were picked up," came Smokey's voice, but Griffiths was hearing the words only through the subject's mind. His own helmet had no direct connection to the hushed microphone into which the major was speaking. The words formed themselves into letters of dull orange which expanded to fill Griffiths' senses with a blank background.

The monochrome sheet coalesced abruptly, and he was trotting along a trail which was a narrow mark beaten by feet into the open expanse of the jungle floor. By cutting off the light, the triple canopies of foliage ensured that the real undergrowth would be stunted—as passable to the air-cushion armor of Hammer's Slammers as it was to the locals on foot.

Judging distance during an interrogation sequence was a matter of art and craft, not science, because the "trip"—though usually linear—was affected by ellipses and the subject's attitude during the real journey. For the most part, memory was a blur in which the trail itself was the major feature and the remaining landscape only occasionally obtruded in the form of an unusually large or colorful hillock of fungus devouring a fallen tree. Twice the subject's mind—not necessarily the man himself—paused to throw up a dazzlingly-sharp image of a particular plant, once a tree and the other time a knotted, woody vine which stood out in memory against the misty visualization of the trunk which the real vine must wrap.

Presumably the clearly-defined objects had something to do with the subject's business—which was none of Griffiths' at this time. As he "walked" the Slammer through the jungle, the mountaineer would be mumbling broken and only partly intelligible words, but Griffiths no longer heard them or Smokey's prompting questions.

The trail forked repeatedly, sharply visualized each time although the bypassed forks disappeared into mental fog within a meter of the route taken. It was surprisingly easy to determine the general direction of travel: though the sky was rarely visible through the foliage, the subject habitually made sunsightings wherever possible in order to orient himself.

The settlement of timber-built houses was of the same tones—browns, sometimes overlaid by a gray-green—as the trees which interspersed the habitations. The village glowed brightly by contrast with the forest, however, both because the canopy above was significantly thinner and because the place was home and a goal to the subject's mind.

Sunlight, blocked only by the foliage of very large

trees which the settlers had not cleared, dappled streets which had been trampled to the consistency of coarse concrete. Children played there, and animals—dogs and pigs, probably, but they were undistinguished shadows to the subject, factors of no particular interest to either him or his interrogator.

Griffiths did not need to have heard the next question to understand it, when a shadow at the edge of the trail sprang into mental relief as a forty-tube swarmjet launcher with a hard-eyed woman slouched behind it watching the trail. The weapon needn't have been loot from the government supply convoy massacred the week before, but its swivelling base was jury-rigged from a truck mounting.

At present, the subject's tongue could not have formed words more complex than a slurred syllable or two, but the Slammers had no need for cooperation from his motor nerves or intellect. All they needed were memory and the hard-wired processes of brain function which were common to all life forms with spinal cords. The subject's brain retrieved and correlated the information which the higher centers of his mind would have needed to answer Major Soames' question about defenses—and Griffiths collected the data there at the source.

Clarity of focus marked as the subject's one of the houses reaching back against a bole of colossal proportions. Its roof was of shakes framed so steeply that they were scarcely distinguishable from the vertical timbers of the siding. Streaks of the moss common both to tree and to dwelling faired together cut timber and the russet bark. On the covered stoop in front, an adult woman and seven children waited in memory.

At this stage of the interrogation Griffiths had almost as little conscious volition as the subject did, but a deep level of his own mind recorded the woman as unattractive. Her cheeks were hollow, her expression sullen, and the appearance of her skin was no cleaner than that of the subject himself. The woman's back was straight, however, and her clear eyes held, at least in the imagination of the subject, a look of affection.

The children ranged in height from a boy already as tall as his mother to the infant girl looking up from the woman's arms with a face so similar to the subject's that it could, with hair and a bushy beard added, pass for his in a photograph. Affection cloaked the vision of the whole family, limning the faces clearly despite a tendency for the bodies of the children to mist away rather like the generality of trees along the trail; but the infant was almost deified in the subject's mind.

Smokey's unheard question dragged the subject off abruptly, his household dissolving unneeded to the answer as a section of the stoop hinged upward on the end of his own hand and arm. The tunnel beneath the board flooring dropped straight down through the layer of yellowish soil and the friable rock beneath. There was a wooden ladder along which the wavering oval of a flashlight beam traced as the viewpoint descended.

The shaft was seventeen rungs deep, with a further gooseneck dip in the gallery at the ladder's end to trap gas and fragmentation grenades. Where the tunnel straightened to horizontal, the flashlight gleamed on the powergun in a niche ready to hand but beneath the level to which a metal detector could be tuned to work reliably.

Just beyond the gun was a black-cased directional mine with either a light-beam or ultrasonic detonator—the subject didn't know the difference and his mind hadn't logged any of the subtle discrimination points between the two types of fusing. Either way, someone ducking down the tunnel could, by touching the pressure-sensitive cap of the detonator, assure that the next person across the invisible tripwire would take a charge of shrapnel at velocities which would crumble the sturdiest body armor.

"Follow all the tunnels," Smokey must have directed, because Griffiths had the unusual experience of merger with a psyche which split at every fork in the underground system. Patches of light wavered and fluctuated across as many as a score of simultaneous images, linking them together in the unity in which the subject's mind held them.

It would have made the task of mapping the tunnels impossible, but the Slammers did not need anything so precise in a field as rich as this one. The tunnels themselves had been cut at the height of a stooping runner, but there was more headroom in the pillared bays excavated for storage and shelter. Flashes—temporal alternatives, hard to sort from the multiplicity of similar physical locations—showed shelters both empty and filled with villagers crouching against the threat of bombs which did not come. On one image the lighting was uncertain and could almost have proceeded as a mental artifact from the expression of the subject's infant daughter, looking calmly from beneath her mothers worried face.

Griffiths could not identify the contents of most of the stored crates across which the subject's mind skipped, but Central's data bank could spit out a list of probables when the interrogator called in the dimensions and colors after the session. Griffiths would do that, for the record. As a matter of practical use, all that was important was that the villagers had thought it necessary to stash the material here—below the reach of ordinary reconnaissance and even high explosives.

There were faces in the superimposed panorama, villagers climbing down their own access ladders or passed in the close quarters of the tunnels. Griffiths could not possibly differentiate the similar, bearded physiognomies during the overlaid glimpses he got of them. It was likely enough that everyone, every male at least, in the village was represented somewhere in the subject's memory of the underground complex.

There was one more sight offered before Griffiths became aware of his own body again in a chill wave spreading from the wrist where Smokey had sprayed the antidote. The subject had seen a nine-barrelled powergun, a calliope whose ripples of high-intensity fire could eat the armor of a combat car like paper spattered by molten steel. It was deep in an underground bay from which four broad "windows"—firing slits—were angled upward to the surface. Preparing the weapon in this fashion to cover the major approaches to the village must have taken enormous effort, but there was a worthy payoff: at these slants, the bolts would rip into the flooring, not the armored sides, of a vehicle driving over the camouflaged opening of a firing slit. Not even Hammer's heavy tanks could survive having their bellies carved that way. . . .

The first awareness Griffiths had of his physical surroundings was the thrashing of his limbs against the sides of the couch while Major Soames lay across his body to keep him from real injury. Motor control returned with a hot rush, permitting Griffiths to lie still for a moment and pant.

"Need to go under again?" asked Smokey as he rose, fishing in his pocket for another cone of antidote for the subject if the answer was 'no.'"

"Got all we need," Griffiths muttered, closing his eyes before he took charge of his arms to lift him upright. "It's a bloody fortress, it is, all underground and cursed well laid out."

"Location?" said his partner, whose fingernails clicked on the console as he touched keys.

"South by southeast," said Griffiths. He opened his eyes, then shut them again as he swung his legs over the side of the couch. His muscles felt as if they had been under stress for hours, with no opportunity to flush fatigue poisons. The subject was coming around with comparative ease in his cocoon, because his system had not been charged already with the drug residues of the hundreds of interrogations which Griffiths had conducted from the right-hand couch. "Maybe three kays—you know, plus or minus."

The village might be anywhere from two kilometers to five from the site at which the subject had been picked up, though Griffiths usually guessed closer than that. This session had been a good one, too, the linkage close enough that he and the subject were a single psyche throughout most of it. That wasn't always the case: many interrogations were viewed as if through a bad mirror, the images foggy and distorted.

"Right," said Smokey to himself or the hologram map tank in which a named point was glowing in response to the information he had just keyed. "Right, Thomasville they call it." He swung to pat the awakening subject on the shoulder. "You live in Thomasville, don't you, old son?"

"Wha . . . ?" murmured the subject.

"You're sure he couldn't come from another village?" Griffiths queried, watching his partner's quick motions with a touch of envy stemming from the drug-induced slackness in his own muscles.

"Not a chance," the major said with assurance. "There were two other possibles, but they were both north in the valley."

"Am I—" the subject said in a voice that gained strength as he used it. "Am I all right?"

Why ask us? thought Griffiths, but his partner was saying, "Of course you're all right, m'boy, we said you would be, didn't we?"

While the subject digested that jovial affirmation, Smokey turned to Griffiths and said, "You don't think we need an armed recce then, Chief?"

"They'd chew up anything short of a company of panzers," Griffiths said flatly, "and even *that* wouldn't be a lotta fun. It's a bloody underground fort, it is."

"What did I say?" the subject demanded as he regained intellectual control and remembered where he was—and why. "Please, please, what'd I say?"

"Curst little, old son," Smokey remarked. "Just mumbles—nothing to reproach yourself about, not at all."

"You're a gentle bastard," Griffiths said.

"Ain't it true, Chief, ain't it true?" his partner agreed. "Gas, d'ye think, then?"

"Not the way they're set up," said Griffiths, trying

to stand and relaxing again to gain strength for a moment more. He thought back over the goose-necked tunnels; the filter curtains ready to be drawn across the mouths of shelters; the atmosphere suits hanging beside the calliope. "Maybe saturation with a lethal skin absorptive like K3, but what's the use of that?"

"Right you are," said Major Soames, tapping the console's preset for Fire Control Central.

"You're going to let me go, then?" asked the subject, wriggling within his wrappings in an unsuccessful attempt to rise.

Griffiths made a moue as he watched the subject, wishing that his own limbs felt capable of such sustained motion. "Those other two villages may be just as bad as this one," he said to his partner.

"The mountaineers don't agree with each other much better'n they do with the government," demurred Smokey with his head cocked toward the console, waiting for its reply. "They'll bring us in samples, and we'll see then."

"Go ahead," said Fire Central in a voice bitten flat by the two-kilohertz aperture through which it was transmitted.

"Got a red-pill target for you," Smokey said, putting one ivory-colored fingertip on the holotank over Thomasville to transmit the coordinates to the artillery computers. "Soonest."

"Listen," the subject said, speaking to Griffiths because the major was out of the line of sight permitted by the hydorclasp wrappings, "let me go and there's a full three kilos of Misty Hills Special for you. Pure, I swear it, so pure it'll float on water!"

"No damper fields?" Central asked in doubt.

"They aren't going to put up a nuclear damper and warn everybody they're expecting attack, old son," said Major Soames tartly. "Of course, the least warning and they'll turn it on."

"Hold one," said the trooper in Fire Control.

"Just lie back and relax, fella," Griffiths said, rising to his feet at last. "We'll turn you in to an internment camp near the capital. They keep everything nice there so they can hold media tours. You'll do fine."

There was a loud squealing from outside the interrogators' vehicle. One of the twenty-centimeter rocket howitzers was rotating and elevating its stubby barrel. Ordinarily the six tubes of the battery would work in unison, but there was no need for that on the present fire mission.

"We have clearance for a nuke," said the console with an undertone of vague surprise which survived sideband compression. Usually the only targets worth a red pill were protected by damper fields which inhibited fission bombs and the fission triggers of thermonuclear weapons.

"Lord blast you for sinners!" shouted the trussed local, "what is it you're doing, you blackhearted devils?"

Griffiths looked down at him, and just at that moment the hog fired. The base charge blew the round clear of the barrel and the sustainer motor roared the shell up in a ballistic path for computer-determined seconds of burn. The command vehicle rocked. Despite their filters, the vents drew in air burned by exhaust gases.

It shouldn't have happened after the helmets were removed and both interrogator and subject had been dosed with antidote. Flashback contacts did sometimes occur, though. This time it was the result of the very solid interrogation earlier; that, and meeting the subject's eyes as the howitzer fired.

The subject looked so much like his infant daughter that Griffiths had no control at all over the image that sprang to his mind: the baby's face lifted to the sky which blazed with the thermonuclear fireball detonating just above the canopy—

—and her melted eyeballs dripping down her cheeks.

The hydorclasp held the subject, but he did not stop screaming until they had dosed him with enough suppressants to turn a horse toes-up.

_____*End note to* The Interrogation Team

My Military Occupational Specialty was 96C2L94: interrogator with Vietnamese language training. I know of only two SF stories about interrogators: *Tomb Tapper* by James Blish, and this one.

One of my editors pointed out to me that not only did I start out writing horror stories, I continued to write horror in the form of Military SF. I believe it was "The Interrogation Team" in particular that he was thinking of when he made the observation.

A DEATH IN PEACETIME

The brothel was too upscale to have an armored street entrance, but the doorman was a wall of solid muscle beneath a frock coat in the latest style. He frowned when the nondescript aircar hummed to a halt in front of the door.

Four hard-looking men got out. Hesitating only long enough to press the button warning those upstairs to keep an eye on the closed-circuit screen, the doorman stepped into the street. "I'm sorry, gentlemen," he said, "but we're closed tonight for a private party. Perhaps—"

"We're the party, buddy," one of the men said, placing himself alongside the doorman while his partner took the other side. The other two men faced the street in opposite directions. All four wore short capes which concealed their hands and whatever they might be holding.

A fifth man, small and dapper, followed the others out of the car. His suit was exquisitely tailored. The fabric had tawny dappling on the shoulders which faded imperceptibly into the gray undertone as one's eye travelled downward.

The man nodded pleasantly toward the doorman and started toward the stairs. Movement lifted the tail of his jacket enough to disclose the pistol holstered high on his right hip.

"I'm sorry, sir!" the doorman said. "We don't allow guns—"

He tried to step in front of the little man. The guards to either side of him—they were obviously guards—shoved him back against the wall.

"You're making an exception tonight," the little man said. His shoes touched the stair treads with the tsk-tsk-tsk of a whisk broom sweeping up ashes; the men who'd initially stayed with the car followed him. "I promise I won't tell anybody."

Madame opened the upper stairway door to let the little man into the parlor. Straight-backed and dressed in severe black, she was the only woman in the establishment. In the muted lighting which the mirrors diffused rather than multiplied, she might've been anything from forty years old to twice that age.

Her face was stony and her tone coldly furious. "You have no business here!" she said. "We have all our licenses. Everything is perfectly legal!"

Six youths had been reclining on couches of plush and dark wood. They'd sprung to their feet when the doorman gave the alarm. Though Madame had gestured them back to their places, they still had the look of startled fawns.

The barman and waiter had retreated into their small lounge off the parlor. The usher had slipped into the back hallway so recently that the door was still swinging shut.

All three had the size and hard features of the doorman. The waiter in particular looked upset at being ordered away, but Madame had reacted instantly when she recognized the visitor in the closed-circuit image from the street door. No matter how badly things went, she knew she'd make things worse if she used force.

It was possible that things were going to go *very* badly.

"Everything legal?" the little man said. He giggled. "Oh, I very much doubt that, my dear. I suspect that we wouldn't have to search very hard to find drugs that're illegal even in these unsettled times, and. . . ."

He stepped past Madame and traced his left index finger along the jawline of a youth as slim as a willow sapling. The boy didn't flinch away, but when the finger withdrew he shuddered. His head was a mass of gleaming black ringlets; all other hair had been carefully removed from his nude body.

" . . . I'm *quite* sure that that some of your staff is under age."

He turned and faced Madame. "That's why I'm here, you see. I've come on your business, not mine, and I assure you my money's good."

The boy he'd caressed looked like an ivory carving against the red velvet upholstery. His expression was unreadable. "You're Joachim Steuben," he said.

"Rafe!" said Madame in a harsh, desperate whisper.

"You kill people," Rafe said. He didn't seem to have heard Madame. His eyes were locked with the little man's. "You killed thousands of people other places, and now you're on Nieuw Friesland."

"Rafe, if you don't—" Madame said.

"I'll quiet him!" the waiter said. He stepped out of the lounge, his fists bunched.

The little man made a barely-perceptible gesture.

One of the guards who'd come up with him clipped the waiter behind the ear with the edge of his hand, dropping him in a boneless heap.

"I don't know about 'thousands', Rafe," the little man said without glancing back at the waiter. "I'm Joachim Steuben, though."

He giggled. "And perhaps thousands, yes. One loses track, you know."

Rafe rose in an eel-like wriggle. Joachim held out his hand, but the boy slipped past and through the door into the back hall.

Madame stood transfixed, her mouth open, then closing again. Touching her lips with her tongue she said at last, "Sir, I'll bring him back if you'll permit me. Rafe's new here, you see, and a little. . . ."

She didn't know how to end the phrase, so her voice trailed off.

Another boy rose as if to follow. He was black-haired also, but his skin was darker and he was probably several years older.

"Felipe," Madame said, gesturing urgently but continuing to watch Joachim.

Felipe sat down again reluctantly. "Rafe's brother was killed last month so he had to come here," he said to Joachim. "He's a sweet boy, please?"

"My name's Sharls, Baron Steuben," said the muscular youth on the next couch. His naturally blond hair was so fine that it clung to his scalp like a halo. "I won't run away from you."

Joachim glanced at Sharls' erection. "Indeed," he said. "Well, we'll see how things develop."

The waiter began to groan. The guard who'd slugged him gestured. The barman came out warily, gripped the waiter by collar and belt, and dragged him into the lounge. His eyes never left the grinning guard.

"Can I get you some refreshment, Baron Steuben?" Madame said, raising an eyebrow. "Or something for the gentlemen with you?"

She'd recognized her guest instantly, though she'd have preferred that he remain formally incognito. If Steuben's name hadn't been spoken, they could all pretend afterwards that this evening had never occurred.

"Those gentlemen are working," Joachim said. He seated himself on the couch Rafe had vacated. His movements were so supple that they appeared relaxed to a casual observer. "I'll have some light wine while I consider the rest of the evening, though."

Steuben had been the bodyguard and enforcer of Colonel Alois Hammer while the latter was a mercenary leader. Hammer, originally from Nieuw Friesland himself, had returned in the pay of one of the contenders in a presidential race turned violent. When his employer had been killed, supposedly by a stray pistol shot, Hammer himself had become president of Nieuw Friesland.

At Hammer's inauguration the former Major Joachim Steuben had become Baron Steuben, Director of Security for Nieuw Friesland. Joachim remained, as anyone who looked into his eyes could tell, the same sociopathic killer he'd been since birth.

"Of course, sir," said Madame, turning toward the barman with birdlike quickness. "Some Graceling, Kedrick! Red Seal, mind you."

He was already reaching beneath the bar. The nearer

guard watched the barman's movements intently, but he rose cradling a fat, fluted bottle.

"Come here, Felipe dearest," Joachim said, smiling as he crooked a finger toward the black-haired boy. "You can help me drink my wine."

A panel concealed as a pilaster between two mirrors opened. Rafe stood in the doorway, still nude but pointing a heavy service pistol in both hands at Joachim.

"You bastard!" he screamed. "You killed my brother!"

Rafe's head exploded in a cyan flash. The *whack!* of the shot that killed him was echoed an instant later as the boy's finger spasmed on the trigger of his own weapon. It blasted a similar bolt of copper plasma into the molding above where Joachim had been sitting. His body thrashed into the center of the parlor.

The air was hazy. Plaster dust, ozone from the pistol bolts, and the stench of Rafe's voided bowels combined to grip the guts of those who breathed it. A red-haired youth with the face of a cherub looked stricken. He tried to cover his mouth with his hands but only succeeded in deflecting the surge of vomit back over himself.

Joachim stood with his back to the wall, his pistol raised at a slight angle. Its iridium muzzle glowed white; he wouldn't be able to holster it again until it cooled. Not even the guards, crouching horrorstruck with their sub-machine guns openly displayed, had seen him draw and shoot.

He looked at Rafe and giggled. "And now I've killed you too," he said.

The 1-cm plasma bolt had hit the boy between the eyes. At this short range, its energy had turned the boy's brain to steam and ruptured the skull.

Joachim gently toed the pistol from Rafe's hand. "Where do you suppose he got this?" he said. "It's standard military issue, but he scarcely seems a soldier."

One of the guards snatched Rafe's pistol up in his left hand and wheeled to put his sub-machine gun in Madame's face. "Where did he get it, bitch?" he shouted. "I'll kill you anyway, but you get to decide if it's fast or slow!"

"Calm down, Detrich," Joachim said. "There's no harm done, after all. But—"

He looked pointedly around the room. Even before the shooting his eyes had continually flicked from one side to the other, never resting.

"—I *do* need to know where the weapon came from."

Joachim's pistol had cooled below red heat, but he still didn't holster it. It was similar to Rafe's weapon, but the receiver was carved and filled with golden, silvery, and richly-purple inlays.

"Rafe's brother was Captain of Baron Herscholdt's bodyguards," the boy Felipe said unexpectedly. "Rafe lived with him. Rafe *loved* his brother."

"I'll check the serial number," said the guard holding the pistol, calm and professional again. He dropped the weapon into a side-pocket attached to the armored vest he wore under his cape.

"Sir . . ." Madame said. Her legs slowly buckled; she looked like she was kneeling to pray, but her posture may simply have been the result of weakness. "Sir, I beg you, I didn't know. I didn't have any idea. . . ."

"You're a monster," Felipe said. He'd gotten to his feet when Joachim summoned him. He remained where he'd been at the moment of the shot, one foot advanced. "You'll burn in Hell."

Madame turned to look over her shoulder. "Felipe," she said. "For *God's* sake, shut up!"

"You've never done a decent thing in your life!" Felipe said, his face distorted in a rictus of fear and loathing. Tears ran down his cheeks, but his eyes were open and staring. "Not one thing!"

"*Felipe!*" Madame shouted.

The guard who'd been watching Madame when Rafe opened the door behind him now muttered, "Punk *bastard*." He stepped forward, raising his sub-machine gun to smash the butt of it down on the boy's face.

"Painter, I'll handle this," Joachim said. He didn't raise his voice, but the guard jerked back as though he'd been struck.

Felipe's lips moved, but the words had stopped coming out. Joachim walked closer.

"You're too sure of me on short acquaintance," he said, tracing the curve of the boy's jaw with the tip of his left index finger. He giggled again. "But you may be right at that."

"Baron . . ." Sharls said. He hadn't moved during the shooting. "Take me, Baron. Take me *now*."

Joachim looked at the blond youth without expression, then let his eyes travel over Madame and each of her boys in turn. "I could kill you all," he said. "Nobody would even care. I could kill almost anyone and nobody'd say a word. But tonight I don't think I will."

He put his left hand, as delicate as a woman's, on Felipe's shoulder. "Come along, boy," he said. "I prefer to transact our business in privacy."

As Joachim walked into the back hallway, his fingers on the boy's pale flesh, he holstered his pistol.

The motion was as smooth and graceful as that of a lizard snatching a fly.

Whitey Bernsdorf jiggled the earthenware brandy bottle; it made a hollow rattle. He set it back on the workbench they were using for a table and said morosely, "We just about killed it, Spence, and Sally's going to be closed by now. Via, she'll be asleep."

"Then we'll wake her up, won't we?" Spencer growled. "Bloody Hell, Whitey. It's not like we don't have real problems that you have to borrow more!"

Someone knocked on the sliding back door of the garage; not loud, but sharply. The men looked up, momentarily very still. "Go the Hell away!" Spencer called.

The door opened. The man who stepped in wore a distortion cape which blurred his face and torso into a smoky haze.

Whitey got up and walked across the shop to his toolbox, moving with quick economy. Spencer remained seated, but he picked up the brandy bottle by the neck. He was balding and heavy, but much less of his weight was fat than a stranger might've guessed.

"You come the wrong place, buddy," Spencer said. "Go rob somebody else."

"I'm here to offer you money, not rob you," the figure said. The voice was male; the cape concealed even the sex. "I want you to kill a man for me."

The toolchest's lower right-hand drawer slid open when Whitey thumbed the lock, but he didn't pick up the pistol nested in foam within. Instead he glanced at Spencer, the first time his eyes had left the stranger.

Spencer laughed harshly and set the bottle down.

"We're outa that business," he said. "I bought this garage with my retirement bonus. Come back in the morning and see our grand opening. We'll get your aircar running the way it ought to."

"I'm his wrench," Whitey said proudly. He hesitated, then closed the drawer over the gun. "I never could keep two trissies rubbing together in my pocket, but I'll balance your fans so you think it's a new car."

"You'll be sold up before the year's out, Sergeant Spencer," the stranger said calmly. "It'll take six months to build your clientele, and your suppliers will keep you on cash terms for at least that long. You've spent your entire savings buying the operation, so you don't have a cushion to see you through."

Spencer stood, gripping the bottle again. "Look, buddy," he said. "I told you to stay out, and now I'm telling you to *get* out. I won't tell you again."

"You know it's the truth," the stranger said. "That's why you're getting drunk tonight. The money I'll pay you will see you through."

Whitey stared at the blurred shape, then frowned and said to his partner, "Seems like we could talk to him, Spence. Right?"

Spencer's knuckles mottled as he squeezed the earthenware; then he relaxed and set the bottle down. "This is political?" he said in a challenging voice.

"Not for me," said the stranger. "It's purely personal. For somebody else it might be political, though."

His shrug beneath the cape looked like watching fog swirl. "I'll pay you a hundred thousand thalers for the job," he added in the same cool tone as everything else he'd said since he entered the garage.

"Are you crazy?" Whitey said. "Or is this some

bloody game? There's so many guns around now that you can get a man killed for three hundred, not a hundred *thousand*!"

"Not this man," the stranger said. His left hand came out from under his cape with a holochip which he set on the table. He wore a pale gray glove, so thin that it could've been a second skin.

He squeezed the chip to activate it, then withdrew his hand. The two ex-soldiers stared at the image in disbelief.

"It's a trap, Spence!" Whitey said. He reached for the toolchest again, but he couldn't find the print-activated lock with his thumb. "He's setting us up for the chop!"

The stranger turned. "You little fool," he said. The cape concealed his features, but his tone of poisonous scorn was unmistakable. "How do you think you're worth setting up? If you were worth killing, you'd have been shot out of hand. *He* would've shot you himself!"

Whitey banged the heel of his hand on the tool-chest and scowled. "It's still crazy!" he said, but his voice had dropped from a shout to an embarrassed mutter.

Spencer prodded the holochip with a thick, hairy index finger, then looked up at the stranger's smoky face. "Why do you want him dead?" he said. His voice was suddenly husky and soft, as though he'd just awakened.

"I told you," said the stranger. He shrugged. "Personal reasons."

"It happens I've got personal reasons too," Spencer said. "He shot a buddy of mine on Dunderberg for thinking there was better use for a warehouse of good liquor than burning it. That was twelve years ago; Hell, fourteen. But it's a good reason."

"Robbie shouldn't've gone for his gun, Spence," Whitey said sadly. "He'd been into that whiskey already or he'd have known better."

"Did I ask your opinion?" Spencer said. "Just belt up, Whitey! D' you hear me? Belt up!"

"Sorry, Spence," the mechanic said in a low voice. He pretended to study the travelling hoist latched against the wall of the garage.

"Anyway," Spencer said, his voice harsh again, "it don't matter what your reasons are or mine either one. It can't be done. Not without taking out a couple square blocks, and even then I wouldn't trust the bastard not to wriggle clear. I don't care how much money you promise."

"I'll guarantee you a clean shot at the target," the stranger said. He made a sound that might have been meant for laughter. "You won't be close, but you'll have a clear line of sight. Then it's just a matter of whether you're good enough."

"I don't believe it," Whitey said. "I don't *believe* it."

The stranger shrugged. "I'll give you a day to think about it," he said. "I'll be back tomorrow."

He paused in the doorway and looked back at them. "He has to die, you know," he said in his soft, precise voice. "*Has* to."

Then he was gone, sliding the door closed behind him.

Spencer lifted the bottle to his lips and finished it in a gulp. "I'm good enough, Whitey," he said. "But bloody *Hell. . . .*"

They stared at the fist-sized image of Joachim Steuben projected by the holochip.

Danny Pritchard stood at the balcony railing, looking out over Landfall City. A few fires smudged the clear night, and once his eye caught the familiar cyan flash of a powergun bolt somewhere in the capital's street. Those were merely incidents of city life: the real fighting had been over for nearly a month.

Danny'd been born on Dunstan, a farming world where everybody was pretty much equal: equally in debt to the Combine of off-planet merchants who bought Dunstan's wheat and shipped it to hungry neighboring worlds at a fat profit. Nobody on Dunstan would've known what a baron was except as a name out of a book, so for that whimsical reason Danny'd refused the title of Baron when President Hammer offered it to him. He was simply Mister Daniel Pritchard, Director of Administration for Nieuw Friesland.

Danny hadn't been back to Dunstan since he left thirty-odd standard years before. His homeworld was a peaceful place. It didn't need soldiers, and until he took off his uniform on the day Colonel Hammer became President Hammer, Danny Pritchard had been a soldier.

Nobody on Dunstan could've afforded to pay Hammer's Slammers anyway. The Slammers weren't cheap, but in cases where victory was the difference between having a future or not . . . well, what was life worth?

"Danny?" Margritte said, coming out onto the balcony with him. She'd put a robe over her nightgown. He hadn't bothered with clothing; the autumn chill helped bring his thoughts into perfect clarity.

That didn't help, of course. When there's no way out, there's little pleasure in having a clear view of your own doom.

"Just going over things," Danny said, smiling at his wife. He wished that she hadn't awakened. "I didn't mean to get you up too."

Margritte had been as good a communications officer as there was in the Slammers, and as good a wife to him as ever a soldier had. There was nothing she could do now except give him one more problem to worry about.

Danny chuckled. No, when you really came down to it, he had only one real problem. Unfortunately, that one was insoluble.

"You're worried about Steuben, aren't you," Margritte said. The words weren't a question.

"Joachim, yes," Danny said, following the path of a low-flying aircar. It was probably a police patrol. The repeal of the ban on private aircars in Landfall City wouldn't come into effect till the end of the month, though a few citizens were anticipating it.

They were taking more of a risk than they probably realized. There were still military patrols out, and the Slammers' motto wasn't so much 'Preserve and Protect' as 'Shoot first and ask questions later.'

Danny grinned faintly. Troops blasting wealthy citizens out of the sky would make more problems for the Directorate of Administration, but relatively minor ones. A number of Nieuw Friesland's wealthy citizens had been gunned down in the recent past—the former owners of this palace among them.

He had a breathtaking view from this balcony. The palace was a rambling two-story structure, but it was built on the ridge overlooking Landfall City from the south. It'd belonged to Baron Herscholdt, the man who'd regarded himself as the power behind President Van Vorn's throne though he stayed out of formal politics.

Herscholdt was out of life, now; he and his wife as well, because she'd gotten in the way when a squad of White Mice, the security troops under the direct command of Major Steuben, came for the Baron.

Danny was used to being billeted in palaces. He was even used to the faint smell of burned flesh remaining even after the foyer'd been washed down with lye. What he wasn't used to was owning the palace; which he did, for as long as he lived. It was one of the perquisites of his government position.

For as long as he lived.

"Steuben has to go," Margritte said, hugging herself against more than the evening chill. "Can't the Colonel see that? There's no place for him any more."

"Joachim's completely loyal," Danny said. He tried put an arm around his wife. Now she flinched away, too tense for even that contact. "He won't permit the existence of anything that threatens the Colonel."

Danny sighed. "That works in a war zone," he said, letting out the words that'd spun in his mind for weeks. "We go in and then we leave. The people who hired us can blame everything that happened on us evil mercenaries. Then they can get on with governing without the bother of the folks who'd have been in opposition if we hadn't shot them."

Margritte shook her head angrily. "Maybe it'll work here too," she said. Her voice was thick, and Danny thought he caught the gleam of starlight on a tear. He looked away quickly.

"President Hammer isn't leaving this time," he explained quietly. "Shooting everybody who might be a threat will only work if you're willing to kill about ninety percent of the population."

He barked a laugh of sorts. "Which Joachim probably is," he added. "But it isn't *possible*, which is something else entirely."

"Steuben isn't stupid," Margritte said. She suddenly reached for Danny's hand and gripped it between hers; she still wouldn't turn to look at him. "He's . . . I don't think he's human, Danny, but I believe he really does love the Colonel. Can't he see that unless he steps aside, the Colonel's government can't survive?"

"There're fish that have to keep swimming to breathe," Danny said—to Margritte; to himself; to the night. "For Joachim, retirement would mean suffocating. He won't retire, and the Colonel—"

He grimaced. He was trying to remember that Alois Hammer was no longer a mercenary leader and that Danny Pritchard was no longer his Adjutant.

"And President Hammer," he went on, "won't force him out. The Colonel—"

Again!

"—is loyal too. And besides, he *needs* a Director of Security. He knows as well as I do that there's nobody better at it than Joachim. Nobody. The problem is that Joachim's only willing to go at the job in one way, and that way's going to be fatal to the civil government."

Danny shook his head. "Maybe he *can* only go at it one way," he said. "I've known Joachim for half my life, but I won't pretend I understand what goes on in his head."

"He's a monster!" Margritte said to the night in

sudden, fierce anger. She turned and glared at her husband. "Danny?" she said. "If he won't leave but he has to go . . . ?"

Danny laughed. He gave Margritte a quick hug, but that was to permit him to ease back and look toward the city before speaking.

"Sure," he said. "I've thought about killing Joachim. Having him killed. It'd be possible, though it might take a platoon of tanks to make sure of him."

He looked at his wife, his face hard in the starlight. Danny Pritchard was only a little over average height, but there were times—this one of them—that he seemed a much bigger man.

"And I could get a platoon of tanks for the job, sure," he said harshly. "If this was a war, I'd do just that. I've done it, done worse, and we both know it. But that's the whole point, it's not a war: it's the civil government of the planet where I'm going to spend the rest of my life. Unlike Joachim, I won't try to preserve that government by means that I know would destroy it."

Margritte hugged herself again. "What is there to do then, Danny?" she said. "What are we going to do?"

Danny reached out and hugged her with real affection. "We're going to deal with the situation as it develops, I suppose," he said softly, stroking his wife's hair. She cut it short to fit under a commo helmet, but it retained a springy liveliness that always thrilled him. "War gives you a lot of experience in doing that, and war's been my whole life."

He kissed Margritte's forehead. "Now," he said with mock sternness. "Go back to bed and let me stand here for a little while more, all right?"

She kissed him passionately, then stepped away. "All right, Danny," she said as she went back into the bedroom. "I know you'll find a way."

I wish I knew that, thought Danny Pritchard, looking down on the nighted city. *I sure don't.*

All he knew was that if he stood here alone, an assassin wouldn't kill anybody besides his intended target. Joachim Steuben certainly realized that the Director of Administration was a potential danger to him, which he'd read as meaning a danger to President Hammer.

And Joachim didn't have Danny Pritchard's compunctions about how to deal with a threat.

They were expecting the knock on the back door, but even so Whitey's hand jerked the bottle; brandy splashed onto the workbench, beading on the oil-soaked wood.

Spencer said, "Bloody *Hell*, Whitey." Then, louder and with the anger directed at the real cause, he said, "Come in then, curse it!"

The shop's harsh overhead lights were on. The stranger's distortion cape was a deeper pool of shadow than it'd been in the light of the small table lamp the night before. He closed the door and said, "How was your first day's business, then?"

Spencer didn't speak. "It was fine," Whitey said, a trifle too loudly. "Anyway, things'll pick up."

"What have you decided about my proposition?" the stranger said. His voice was like the paw of a cat playing with a small animal; it was very delicate, but points pressed through its softness.

Whitey looked at his partner. Spencer took the

holochip from his pocket, activated the image of Joachim Steuben, and tossed it onto the bench.

"All right," he said in a challenging tone. "We'll do it on one condition: you pay us *all* the money up front."

"Every thaler!" Whitey said. His index finger had been drawing circles in the spilled brandy. When he realized what he was doing, he jerked his hand into his lap.

"Yes, that's reasonable," the stranger said. His gloved left hand slipped from beneath his cape, this time holding a small bag of wash leather. He placed it on the bench, then withdrew his hand. "I think you'll find the full amount there."

"What the hell is this?" Spencer muttered. After a moment's general silence he tugged open the drawstring closure and spilled the bag's contents, several dozen credit chips, onto the wood.

"A hundred thousand thalers in one chip," the stranger said mildly, "might present you with difficulties. But the total is correct."

Spencer began rotating the semiconductor wafers so that the amounts printed on the edges faced him. Whitey picked one up. His lips moved; then he read aloud, "Four . . . four-thousand-one-hunnert-forty-nine."

"Most of the chips range from three to five thousand thalers," the stranger said. "One's for eleven thousand, but you shouldn't have any trouble banking it if you build up a pattern of deposits over the course of a month."

"What the hell," Spencer repeated, scowling at the chips and then looking up at the stranger. "You agreed just like that?"

The shadow rippled in a shrug. "It was a reasonable condition," the stranger said. "You have no reason to trust me, after all. And as for me trusting you. . . ."

He gave a chittering laugh. "You may fail, Sergeant Spencer," he said, "but you won't try to cheat me."

"No, I don't guess we will," Spencer said grimly. "But just how are *you* so sure of that, buddy?"

The gloved hand pointed to the holochip image. "Because if you did, he'd learn that you took money to kill him," the stranger said. "What do you think would happen next?"

"We'll do the bloody job," Spencer said, pushing the credit chips back into the bag. He hadn't counted them; at this point the money wasn't the most important thing. "We'll do it *if* we get a clear shot."

He glowered at the stranger's blurred face. "How d'ye plan to arrange it?" he demanded. "Because I'll tell you, nothing *I* know about that bastard makes me think you can do it."

The stranger put a small data cube beside the image of Joachim Steuben. "This will run in your inventory reader," he said. "It contains the full plan. I suggest you take the machine off-line before you view it, though. It's unlikely that the Directorate of Security would be doing key-word sweeps detailed enough to pick up the contents, but—"

His laugh was like bats quarrelling.

"—it would only take once, wouldn't it? So better safe than sorry."

"How are you going to manage it?" Whitey demanded, angry because he was so nervous. He's been shot at many times; he knew how to handle himself in a firefight. The thing that was happening now made him feel as though the ground was streaming away beneath his feet. "You say 'here's the plan', but what d' you know about this kinda job? You think it's easy?"

Spencer looked at the stranger's smoky features, pursed his lips, and said to his partner, "Whitey, we'll take a look at it—"

He prodded an index finger in the direction of the cube.

"—and make our go, no-go on what we think."

He shifted his gaze back to the stranger. "That's how Whitey and me've always worked, buddy," he said, raising his voice slightly. "If we don't like the mission, we don't take it. We figure we're not paid to commit suicide, we're paid to kill other people. And we're *bloody* good at it!"

"I know, Sergeant," the stranger said; there was more real humor in his voice now than there had been in his previous cracklings of laughter. "That's why I'm here."

His blurred visage turned to Whitey. Occasionally his eyes glinted through the polarizing fabric.

"Next week there'll be privy council meeting in the Maritime Commission building on Quetzal Point, Trooper Bernsdorf," the stranger said. "There's a knoll three kilometers west of the building. When the meeting breaks up, the Sergeant will have a shot."

The distortion cape rippled as he gestured through it toward the data cube.

"The details are in there. If you decide there's anything else you need—a tribarrel, for example, or perhaps a vehicle—hang a white rag on your rear doorlatch. I'll come back to get the details."

Spencer rose and walked to the degreasing tank in

which air bubbled through a culture of petroleum-eating bacteria. "I don't need a tribarrel," he said, reaching into the tank and coming out with a long sealed tube. "You want to knock down a wall, a tribarrel does the job a treat. But if you're just trying to drop one man—"

He twisted the top off the container and slid a shoulder-stocked powergun onto the workbench. It should've been turned in when Spencer retired from the Slammers. An unassigned weapon, picked up in the bloody shambles that'd been an Iron Guard barracks, had gone into the armory in its place.

"—this old girl has always done the job for me."

Spencer shook his head as he lifted the weapon. The stubby iridium barrel's 2-cm bore channeled plasma released from precisely-aligned copper atoms in the breech. The bolts were as straight as light-beams and remained lethal to a human at any range within the curvature of a planet's surface.

"I don't remember how many times I've rebarreled her," Spencer said affectionately. "She never let me down."

"Five-hunnert-an-three kills," Whitey said proudly. "Planned shots, I mean, not firefights where you never know who nailed what."

"I'll use a sandbag rest," Spencer said, facing the hidden figure. "Whitey'll spot for me and pull security, like always. I don't see any bloody thing but what's in my sight picture when I'm waiting, and at three klicks that's not very much. If there's a shot, I'll take it."

He was a different man with the big weapon cradled in his arms. The change wasn't so much that Spencer projected confidence as that he'd become an utterly stable *thing*: a boulder or a tree with centuries of growth behind it.

"All right, Sergeant," the stranger said. "That appears satisfactory. I don't suppose I'll be seeing you again."

He touched the vertical door handle, then reached back beneath the cape and did something hidden. When his gloved hand came out again, it held a coin of gold-colored crystal that'd been pierced for a chain. He dropped it on the bench between the sack of credit chips and the image of Joachim Steuben.

"This is my lucky piece," he said. He chuckled. "If you ever get to Newland I suppose it's still worth a hundred wreaths, but I think you're going to need the luck more than you will the money."

He closed the door behind him, a shadow returning to the night's other shadows.

Whitey carried the data cube to the inventory computer in the service port between the work bay and the front office. "If he gets you a clear line of sight, you don't need luck, Spence," he said.

Spencer didn't reply. He was sliding a 20-round tube of ammunition into the butt-well of his weapon.

President Hammer rested his elbows on the top of the table and massaged his forehead with the fingers of both hands. He muttered something, but the words were lost in his palms. The meeting had been going on since dawn, and it was now late in the afternoon.

"We really need to settle this quickly, sir," said Danny Pritchard, seated to the right of Hammer at the head of the table. "Every day there's another hundred people being added to the camps. Releasing them won't gain us back nearly the amount of good will we lose by arresting them in the first place. And there's too many being shot during arrest, too."

"There's always going to be a few fools who think they can outrun a powergun bolt," said Joachim Steuben with a grin. "I think we're benefiting the race by removing them from the gene pool. And as for the ones who choose to shoot it out with *my* men, well, that's simply a form of suicide."

Joachim was in a khaki uniform, identical except for the lack of rank tabs to those he'd worn during his years in the Slammers. Instead of a normal uniform's tough, rip-stopped synthetic and utilitarian fit, Joachim's was woven from natural fabrics and tailored with as much skill as a debutante's ball gown. He'd always dressed that way. Strangers who'd met Joachim for the first time had often mistaken him for Hammer's lover instead of his bodyguard and killer.

He didn't wear body armor; he rarely had except on battlefields where shell fragments were a threat. He said that armor slowed him down and that his quickness was better protection than a ceramic plate. Thus far he'd been right.

Hammer lowered his hands and looked at the twelve officials—nine men and three women—seated at the table with him. No aides were present within the temporary privacy capsule erected within the volume of the large conference room.

"We're not going to decide this today," Hammer said. His voice was raspy and his face had aged more in a month as president than it had in the previous five years of combat operations. "I've had it for now."

"Then we'll settle it tomorrow?" Danny said in a carefully emotionless tone.

"Blood and martyrs!" said Hammer. "Not tomorrow. Maybe next week. I don't want to hear about it tomorrow."

"Sir," said Danny, "no decision is a decision, and it's the wrong one. We've—"

Hammer lurched up from the table and slammed the heel of his right fist down on the resin-stabilized wood. "This meeting is over!" he said. "Mister Pritchard, Baron Steuben—remain with me for a moment. Everyone else leaves *now*."

Council members got to their feet and moved quickly to the capsule's exit. Guards stationed there opened the doors of the room itself onto the corridor. Aides waited there with additional guards and a number of the people who ordinarily worked in the building.

The locations of privy council meetings were kept secret from all but the attendees and were never held in the same place twice in succession. The first the staff of the site knew what was happening was when workmen arrived an hour ahead of time to erect the privacy capsule that sealed the meeting from the eyes and ears of non-participants.

Half the councillors dressed in civilian clothes; the other half were in uniform, either Slammers khaki or the blue-piped gray of the Frisian Defense Forces. Hammer himself wore a civilian tunic and breeches, but he'd deliberately had them tailored in the style that'd been popular when he left Nieuw Friesland half a lifetime ago.

Hammer's wife Anneke, nee Tromp, was present as the Director of Social Welfare. "Shut the door!" he called to her as she went out.

Anneke turned, met her husband's eyes, and walked

on through to the corridor without responding. A guard swung the panel closed, sealing the capsule again.

Hammer sighed. "Now listen, both of you," he said in a voice that didn't hold the same key from word to word. "I'll make a decision on the detention policy when I'm ready to. Nobody—neither of you—will say another word to me on the subject till then. Do you *hear* me?"

"As you wish, Alois," said Joachim Steuben.

Danny Pritchard grimaced. "Yes sir, I hear you," he said.

"Pritchard, I mean it!" Hammer said in sudden fury.

"I've never doubted your word, Colonel," Danny said, letting his anger show also. "Don't you start doubting mine now!"

"Via, I'm not getting enough sleep," Hammer muttered. He put his left hand over Danny's right, squeezed it, and stepped out of the capsule.

Danny made a wry face and gestured to the exit. "After you, Baron," he said.

Joachim grinned and walked out ahead of the other man. Without turning he said, "I wouldn't shoot you in the back, Mister Pritchard."

Danny laughed. Workmen moved into the meeting room behind him to tear down the privacy capsule for use in another few days or a week. It was simply a framework with an active sound-cancellation system between two layers of light-diffusing membrane.

"Joachim, we've known each other too long for nonsense," Danny said. It was battlefield humor, but this was surely a battlefield. "You'd shoot me any way you felt like at the moment."

Joachim giggled. They'd reached the hallway, but guards had formed a bubble of space around them without being directed to.

Margritte had been standing with the rest of the aides and clerks. They'd gone off with the remaining council members, leaving her alone. She was as still-faced as a statue in a wall niche.

"If I thought it was necessary, I suppose I would at that," Joachim said. "As you would do in similar circumstances. Wouldn't you, Daniel?"

Danny looked at the shorter man. They'd known each other for such a long time. . . .

Aloud he said, "If you mean, 'Would I shoot you if I thought that was necessary to bring an end to policies that I'm sure will destroy the government?' then the answer is apparently, 'No.' Even though I believe that if I don't kill you, nobody in that council meeting is going to die in bed. *None* of us."

"You have your beliefs," Joachim said, shrugging. "I have mine. I don't believe that I should wait to see if a man who threatens the President is really serious; or if maybe he'll change his mind before acting; or if he's simply too incompetent to carry through with that threat."

"Joachim . . ." Danny said. He and the other man were so focused on one another that the bustle of the hallway could have taken place on another planet. "You know I'm right. You can follow a chain of consequences as far as anybody I've ever met."

"Yes, Daniel," Joachim said. "And so can you, which is why you know that *I'm* right also."

He giggled. "A pity that we can't run the experiment both ways before we make our decision, isn't

it?" he said. "Well, perhaps in another universe Nieuw
Friesland is being governed according to other principles. For now . . . well, go to your wife, Daniel. The
only thing *I* know about is killing."

Danny opened his mouth, then closed it and smiled.
He said, "That's been our job for a long time, Joachim.
Maybe you're right and it still is. If so, the Lord
help us."

Joachim frowned. "I left my hat," he said, stepping
back into the meeting room.

"Watch it!" a workman shouted as he and his partner
swung one of the last panels of the privacy capsule out .
of its frame. When the fellow looked over his shoulder
and saw who he'd spoken to, the panel slipped from
his hands.

Joachim ignored him and bent to retrieve the
saucer hat on the frame bracing the chair legs. He
turned with a smile and called to Danny, "You have
to remember, Daniel, that dying in bed has never
been a goal of mine."

One of the west-facing windows shattered in a cyan
flash. The bolt caught Joachim between the shoulder-
blades. His body fluids flashed into steam, flinging his
trim figure in a somersault that landed him face-up at
Danny's feet. The shot had torn the right arm from
his torso, but his cherubic face was still smiling.

Mister Daniel Pritchard wasn't carrying a gun, but
his reflexes were still in place. He threw himself to
the floor, snatched the pistol from the cutaway holster
on Joachim's right hip, and rose. He fired three times
out the window through which the shot had come.

Danny didn't expect to hit anything but empty sky,
but he'd gotten to be a veteran by learning that you

always shot back instantly. At the worst it wasn't going to do their aim any good, and every once in a while you might nail the bastard.

People were shouting and running. The meeting room's other high vitril windows cascaded in splinters as guards smashed them out with gun-butts. They began raking shots along the distant hills.

Danny lifted himself into a crouch to get a better view. A trooper wearing body armor, one of Joachim's White Mice, landed on his back and flattened him again.

"Keep the fuck down, sir!" she shouted. "We already lost the Major!"

"Roger!" Danny said, trying to breathe against the weight of the trooper protecting him with her own body. "I'll stay down!"

The guard got up and scuttled to join her fellows as they fired into the distance. Danny didn't have commo, so he could only hope that the captain commanding the security detail was doing something more useful than the nearest personnel were.

"What happened?" said a voice nearby. He looked back, expecting to see Margritte. She was in the corridor under a guard twice her size.

President Hammer hunched at Danny's side. In one hand he held the pistol he'd worn in a shoulder holster, but the fingers of the other traced Joachim's cheek with a feather-light touch.

"A two-see-em bolt through the window," Danny said, gesturing with his pistol. The inlays winked festively, reminding him whose weapon it'd been. "One round only, so the shooter was either really good or really lucky."

He set the gun down. A floor-tile *crack*ed, broken by the glowing iridium barrel.

"Joachim wouldn't've given him more than one round," Hammer whispered. His face was set, but tears ran down his cheek. "I never thought I'd see this. Never."

Hammer holstered his own pistol and rose to his knees. The guards had stopped shooting. Under a sergeant's bellowed orders they backed away from the windows and stood shoulder to shoulder, a living wall between the direction of the shot and the men they were here to protect.

The bolt had blown the remainder of Joachim's tunic away. His chest was as white and hairless as an ivory statue.

"Where's his lucky piece?" Hammer said.

"What?"

Hammer looked at Danny, his expression suddenly blank and watchful. "Joachim always wore a coin from Newland around his neck," Hammer said. "That was the only thing he'd brought from home. He said it was his luck."

"Colonel?" Danny said harshly. He got to his feet. "I'm not behind this. I don't care if you believe me, but it's the truth anyway. This is the best piece of luck you and the whole planet could've gotten."

Joachim's corpse smiled at him from the floor.

_____*End note to* A Death in Peacetime

Very much to my surprise, Joachim Steuben became many readers' favorite character in the Hammer series. He's a murderous sociopath, cruel as well as ruthless—but also intelligent, cultured, and loyal to Colonel Hammer. I mentioned his death early in the series, but I never described or explained it. Over the years I received many requests to provide those details.

I wasn't willing to write that story, because a man of Joachim's sort is almost impossible to kill unless he's been betrayed. I don't like betrayal, and I don't like to look closely at it.

But then I thought about the death of Periander, the Tyrant of Corinth: a real figure whom later Greek historians both reviled as an emblem of cruelty and praised as one of the Seven Sages, the wisest men of their time. That became the key to telling the last portion of Joachim's story.

DREAMS IN AMBER

The man in the tavern doorway was the one whom
Saturnus saw in the dreams which ended in nightmare.
The bead on Saturnus's chest tingled, and the frag-
mented dream-voice whispered in the agent's mind,
Yes. . . . Allectus.

Allectus paused to view the interior, smoky with the
cheap oil of the tavern lamps. He was a soft-looking man
whose curly beard and sideburns were much darker
than his flowing ginger moustache. Allectus wore boots,
breeches, and a hooded cape buttoned up the front. All
his clothing was farm garb, and all of it was unsuited
to the position Saturnus knew Allectus held—Finance
Minister of Carausius. The Emperor Marcus Aurelius
Mausaeus Carausius, as he was styled on this side of the
British Ocean which his fleet controlled. The onetime
Admiral of the Saxon Shore now struck coins to show
himself as co-emperor with his "brothers," Diocletian
and Maximian. In the five years since disaster engulfed
Maximian's fleet off Anderida, there had been no attempt
from the mainland to gainsay the usurper's claim.

No attempt until now, until Gaius Saturnus was sent to Britain with instructions from an emperor and a mission from his dreams.

Allectus stepped aside as the agent approached him. He took Saturnus for another sailor leaving the tavern on the Thames dockside, the sort of man he had come to hire perhaps . . . but the finance officer was not ready to commit himself quite yet.

Saturnus touched his arm. "I'm the man you want," the agent said in a low voice.

"Pollux! Get away from me!" the finance officer demanded angrily. Allectus twitched loose as he glared at Saturnus, expecting to see either a pimp or a catamite. Saturnus was neither of those things. In Allectus's eyes, the agent was a tall, powerful man whose skin looked weathered enough to fit the shoddy clothes he also wore.

The finance officer stepped back in surprise. He had been tense before he entered the dive. Now, in his confusion, he was repenting the plan that had brought him here.

"I know what you want done," Saturnus said. He did not move closer to Allectus again, but he spoke louder to compensate for the other's retreat. "I'm the man you need." And Saturnus's arm tucked the cloak momentarily closer to his torso so that it molded the hilt of his dagger. The voice in Saturnus's mind whispered . . . *need* . . . to him again.

A customer had just left one of the blanket-screened cribs along the wall. It was a slow night, no lines, and the Moorish prostitute peered out at the men by the door as she settled her smock. Allectus grimaced in frustration. He looked at Saturnus again. With a curse

and a prayer in Greek—Allectus was a Massiliot, no
more a native Briton than the Batavian Carausius—he
said, "Outside, then."

Three sailors blocked the door as they tried to
enter in drunken clumsiness. Normally the finance
officer would have given way, even if he had his
office to support him. Now he bulled through them.
Anger had driven Allectus beyond good judgment;
though the sailors, thank Fortune, were too loose to
take umbrage.

Taut himself as a drawn bow, the Imperial agent
followed the official. Maximian had sent him to pro-
cure the usurper's death. The dreams . . .

The air outside was clammy with a breeze off the
river. All the way from the docks to the fort there
were taverns similar to the one in which Saturnus had
been told to wait: one-story buildings with thatched
roofs and plaster in varying states of repair covering
the post and wattle walls. The shills were somnolent
tonight. Only a single guard ship remained while the
Thames Squadron joined the rest of the fleet at some
alert station on the Channel. Saturnus knew that the
mainland emperors planned no immediate assault. He
could not tell, however, whether the concentration
were merely an exercise, or if it were a response to
some garbled news of a threat. The threat, perhaps,
that he himself posed.

There was some fog, but the moon in a clear sky
gave better light than the tavern lamps in the haze of
their own making. Allectus had composed himself by
the time he turned to face Saturnus again. In a voice
as flat and implacable as the sound of waves slapping
the quay, the finance officer demanded, "Now, who are

you and what do you think you're playing at?" The metal of an armored vest showed beneath Allectus's cloak as he tossed his head. His right hand was on the hilt of a hidden sword.

Saturnus laughed. The sound made Allectus jump. He was aware suddenly of his helplessness against the bigger, harder man who had accosted him. "My name doesn't matter," the agent said. "We both want a man killed. I need your help to get close to him, and you need . . ." the men looked at one another. "You were looking for a man tonight, weren't you?" Saturnus added. "A tough from the docks for a bit of rough work? Well, you found him."

The finance officer took his hand from his weapon and reached out slowly. His fingers traced the broad dimple on Saturnus's forehead. It had been left by the rubbing weight of a bronze helmet over years of service. "You're a deserter, aren't you?" Allectus said.

"Think what you like," Saturnus replied.

Allectus's hand touched the other man's cape. He raised the garment up over the agent's shoulder. Saturnus wore breeches and a tunic as coarse as the cape itself. The dagger sheathed on his broad leather belt was of uncommon quality, however. It had a silver-chased hilt and a blade which examination would have shown to be of steel watermarked by the process of its forging. The knife had been a calculated risk for the agent; but the meanest of men could have chanced on a fine weapon in these harsh times.

On the chain around Saturnus's neck was a lump of amber in a basket of gold wire. The nature of the flaw in the amber could not be determined in the light available.

Allectus let the garment flop closed. "Why?" he asked very softly. "*Why* do you want to kill Carausius?"

Saturnus touched the amber bead with his left hand. "I was at Anderida," he said.

The truth of the statement was misleading. It did not answer the question as it appeared to do. It was true, though, that in the agent's mind shimmered both his own memories and those of another mind. *Transports burned in scarlet fury on the horizon, driven back toward the mainland by the southwest wind against which they had been beating. With the sight came the crackle of the flames and, faintly—scattered by the same breeze that bore it—the smell of burning flesh. Maximian had clutched the stern rail of his flagship in his strong, calloused hands. His red cloak and those of his staff officers, Saturnus then among them, had snapped like so many pools of quivering blood. The emperor cursed monotonously. Still closer to their position in the rear guard a sail was engulfed in a bubble of white, then scarlet. Maximian had ordered withdrawal. A trumpet had keened from the flagship's bow, and horns answered it like dying seabirds.*

No one in the flagship had seen a sign of the hostile squadron. In shattered but clear images in Saturnus's mind, however, a trireme painted dark gray-green like the sea struggled with waves that were a threat to its low freeboard. The decks of the warship were empty, save for the steersmen and a great chest lashed to the bow . . . and beside the chest, the stocky figure of Carausius himself. The usurper pointed and spoke, and a distant mast shuddered upward in a gout of flame. . . .

The finance officer sagged as if he had been stabbed. "I was at Mona," he whispered. "Eight years ago. He took a chest aboard, bullion I thought, like he was going to run. But he caught the Scoti pirates and they burned. . . . He's a hero, you know? Ever since that." Allectus gave a sweep of his arm that could have indicated anything from the fort to the whole island. "To all of them. But he scares me, scares me more every day."

Saturnus felt a thrill of ironic amusement not his own. He shrugged his cape back over him. Aloud he said, "All right, we can take care of it now. They'll let me into the fort with you, won't they?"

"Now? But . . ." Allectus objected. He looked around sharply, at the empty street and the river blurred in cottony advection fog. "He's gone, isn't he? With the squadron?"

Sure with a faceted certainty where even the high official had been misled, Saturnus said, "No, Carausius is here. He sends the ships out sometimes when he doesn't want too many people around. I've been told where he is, but you'll have to get me into the fort."

The finance officer stared at Saturnus for seconds that were timeless to the agent. "If Carausius knows enough to send you to trap me," mused Allectus, "then it doesn't really matter, does it? Let's go, then." He turned with a sharp, military movement and led Saturnus up the metalled road to the fort.

The Fleet Station at London had been rebuilt by Carausius from the time he usurped the rule of Britain. There had always been military docking facilities. Carausius had expanded them and had raised the timber fort which enclosed also the administrative center from which he ruled the island. Now only a skeleton detachment manned the gates and the artillery in the corner towers. The East Gate, opening onto the central street of the fort, was itself defended by a pair of flanking towers with light catapults. The catapults were not cocked. Their arms were upright, and the slings drooped in silhouette against the sky above the tower battlements. The bridge over the ditch had not been raised either, but the massive, iron-clad gate-leaves were closed and barred against the night.

Someone should have challenged the men as soon as they set foot on the drawbridge. Instead, Allectus had first to shout, then to bang on a gate panel with his knife hilt to arouse the watch. A pair of Frankish mercenaries finally swung open a sally port within the gateway. The Franks were surly and reeked of wine. Saturnus wondered briefly whether the finance officer's help had been necessary to get him within the fort. But the agent was inside safely, now, and a feeling of satisfaction fluttered over his skin.

Allectus looked angrily away from the guards. "All right," he said in a low voice to the agent. "What next?"

Saturnus nodded up the street, past the flanking barracks blocks to the Headquarters complex in the center of the fort. "In there," he said. He began walking up the street, leading Allectus but led himself by whispers and remembered dreams. "In the Headquarters building, not the palace."

The two central buildings were on a scale larger than the size of the fort would normally have implied. Though the fort's troop complement was no more than a thousand men, it enclosed what amounted to an

Imperial administrative center. The Headquarters building closing the street ahead of them was two-storied and almost three hundred feet to a side. Saturnus knew that beyond it the palace, which he had never seen with his own eyes, was of similar size.

The fort's interior had the waiting emptiness of a street of tombs: long, silent buildings with no sign of inhabitants. Occasionally the sound of laughter or an argument would drift into the roadway from partying members of the watch detachment. Others of the troops left behind when the squadron sailed were certainly among the few customers on the strip below the fort. Men who chanced near to Saturnus and the finance officer ducked away again without speaking. Both the men had the gait and presence of officers, and the foggy moonlight hid their rough clothes.

"How do you know this?" Allectus asked suddenly. "How do you know about—about me?"

"It doesn't matter," the agent said. He tramped stolidly along the flagstone street with his left hand clutching the bead against his chest. "Say I dreamed it. Say I have nightmares and I dreamed it all."

"It could be a nightmare," the finance officer muttered. "He must consult sorcerers to bring storms down on his enemies. He must *be* a sorcerer—I've never seen any others of that sort around him."

"He's not a sorcerer," Saturnus remarked grimly. "And he's not alone." *Alone* . . . echoed his mind.

"I can rule without sorcery," Allectus said, aloud but to himself. The agent heard. He did not respond.

The guard at the front door of the Headquarters Building was a legionary, not a barbarian from the Rhine Estuary as those in the gate-tower had been.

The soldier braced to attention when he heard the pairs of boots approaching. "Who goes there?" he challenged in Latin.

"The Respectable Allectus, Chief of Imperial Accounts," the finance officer replied. "We have business inside."

The guard waited two further steps until he could visually identify the speaker. Allectus threw back his cowl to expose his face. The guard's spear clashed as he swung it to port against his body armor. "Sir!" he acknowledged with a stiff-armed salute. Then he unlatched the tall double doors before returning to attention. Saturnus watched with a sardonic smile. There were few enough units back on the mainland which could be expected to mount so sharp an interior guard. Whatever else the source of Carausius's strength, he had some first-class troops loyal to him.

"Who's the officer of the watch?" Saturnus asked.

The guard looked at him, surprised that Allectus's companion had spoken. The agent did not look to be the sort of man who entered headquarters at night. That raised the question of the way Allectus himself was dressed, but . . . "Standard-bearer Minucius, sir," the guard replied. Discipline held. It was not his business to question the authority of one of Carausius's highest officials. "You'll find him in his office."

When the big door closed behind them, it was obvious how much ambient light there had been outside. The clerestory windows were pale bars without enough authority to illuminate the huge hall beneath them. The nave could hold an assemblage larger than the normal complement of the fort. On the south end, the tribunal was a hulking darkness with no hint of the majesty it would assume when lighted and draped with bunting. "We'll need the officer of the watch," Saturnus remarked. He gestured.

Lamplight was showing through the columns from one of the offices across the width of the hall. "We need to get into the strongroom beneath the Shrine of the Standards."

The finance officer looked sharply at his companion. It was absurd to think that all this was a charade dreamed up by a common thief . . . absurd. "There's nothing in the strongroom but the men's private accounts," he said aloud.

Saturnus appeared to ignore the comment.

The gleam from the office was a goal, not an illumination. That did not matter to the agent. He could have walked across the building blindfolded, so often had he dreamed of it bathed in amber light. Now Saturnus strode in a revery of sorts, through the arches of the aisle and finally into the office section beyond the assembly hall. Allectus and present reality had almost disappeared from Saturnus's mind until the Standard-bearer, alerted by the sound of boots, stepped from his office behind an upraised lamp. "Who the hell are you?" the soldier demanded, groping behind him for the swordbelt he had hung over the top of the door.

Allectus stepped into the light as Saturnus paused. "Oh, *you,* sir," said the startled duty officer. "I didn't recognize your, ah, bodyguard."

"We need to check the strongroom," Allectus said unceremoniously. He gestured with his head. "Get your keys and accompany us."

The Standard-bearer reacted first to the tone of

command. He patted the ring of keys he wore on a leather shoulder-belt. Then he frowned, still touching the keys. He said, "Sir, none of that's public money, you know."

"Of course we know!" snapped Allectus. "We need to check it anyway." He did not understand the stranger's purpose, but he was not willing to be balked in any request by an underling.

"Sir, I think . . ." the Standard-bearer said in a troubled voice. "Look, the squadron should be back tomorrow or the next day at the latest. Why don't you—"

He delays us, Saturnus dreamed. His right hand swung from beneath his cape to bury the dagger to its crossguards in the pit of the soldier's stomach.

The Standard-bearer whooped and staggered backward with a look of surprise. Saturnus released the dagger-hilt in time to take the lamp before the soldier collapsed. Minucius was dead before he hit the stone floor.

Saturnus rolled the body over before he withdrew the knife. Blood followed the steel like water from a spring. None of the blood escaped the dead man's tunic and breeches to mark the stones.

"Gods," whispered the finance officer. His hand hovered short of his sword. "You just killed him!"

"We came here to kill, didn't we?" the agent reminded him bleakly. "Help me drag him back behind a pillar where he won't be noticed till morning." As Saturnus spoke, he wiped the dagger on his victim's tunic, then cut the keys loose from the belt that supported them. "Come on, for pity's sake. We haven't much time." *Time . . .* the mind in his mind repeated.

Allectus obeyed with a quickness close to panic. Vague fears and a longing for personal power had brought the finance officer to the point of murder and usurpation. Now the ordinary concerns of failure and execution to which he had steeled himself were giving way to a morass more doubtful than the original causes.

They tugged the murdered man into the empty office next to his own. Allectus then carried the lamp as he nervously followed the agent's striding figure.

The Shrine of the Standards was a small room in the center of the line of offices. It faced the main entrance across the nave, so that anyone entering the building during daylight would first see the sacred standards of the unit in their stone-screened enclosure. They were gone, now, with the squadron. The lamp threw curlicue shadows across the shrine to the equally-twisted stonework on the other side. Saturnus fitted one key, then the next on the ring, until he found the one that turned the lock. His dreams were trying to speak to him, but trial and error was a better technique now than viewing the ring of keys through eyes which were knowledgeable but not his own.

Allectus sighed when the iron door swung open. Saturnus released the keys. They jangled against the lockplate. For safety's sake, the agent should have closed the door behind them. That would have disguised the fact that they were inside. He was too nervous to do so, however. The nightmare was closing on him, riding him like a raft through white water. "Come on," Saturnus said to the finance officer. He had to remember that the other man could not hear the clamor in his own mind. Saturnus bent to lift the ring-handled trap door in the center of the shrine's empty floor. "We'll need the light when we're inside."

The hinges of the door down to the strongroom were well-oiled and soundless. Saturnus did not let the panel bang open. Rather, he eased it back against the flooring. The room beneath was poorly lighted by the lamp which trembled in Allectus's hand. In any case, the strongroom was no more than a six-foot cube. It was just big enough to hold the large iron-bound chest and to give the standard-bearers room to work in their capacity as bankers for the troops of the unit. The walls of the dug-out were anchored by posts and paneled with walers of white oak to keep the soil from collapsing inward.

Saturnus used the ladder on one wall instead of jumping down as Allectus half expected. "Quietly," the agent said with exaggerated lip movements to compensate for the near silence of his command. He took the lamp from Allectus's hands.

As the finance officer climbed down into the cramped space, Saturnus put the lamp on the strongbox and drew his dagger. "Get ready," he said with a grin as sharp and cold as the point of his knife. "You're about to get your chance to be emperor, remember?"

Allectus drew his sword. The hem of his cape snagged on a reinforcing band of the strongbox. The finance officer tore the garment off with a curse. He had seen battle as a line infantryman, but that had been fifteen years before. "Ready," he said.

An ant stared at Saturnus from the wall opposite the strongbox. The creature was poised on what seemed to be a dowel rod set flush with the oak paneling. The agent's right hand held his dagger advanced. Saturnus

set his left thumb over the ant and crushed the creature
against the dowel that sank beneath the pressure. The
whole wall pivoted inward onto a short tunnel.

With his left thumb and forefinger, Saturnus snuffed
the lamp.

Allectus opened his mouth to protest. Before the
whispered words came out, however, the finance officer realized that he was not in total darkness after
all. The door at the tunnel's further end, twenty feet
away, was edged and crossed with magenta light that
slipped through the interstices of the paneling. Allectus
chewed at one point of his bushy moustache. He could
not see his companion until the other man stepped
forward in silhouette against the hot pink lines.

For his own part, Saturnus walked in the monochrome tunnel of his mind. Light suffused the myriad
facets through which he saw. He was walking toward
the climax of his nightmare, the nightmare which had
owned his soul ever since his parents had hung the
lucky amulet of gold and amber around his neck as an
infant. Unlike other well-born children, Gaius Saturnus
had not dedicated the amulet with his shorn hair at
age twelve when he formally became a man. The blade
that would exorcize his childhood was not in the hand
of a barber but rather now in Saturnus's own.

There, whispered the mind beyond Saturnus's mind
as the agent's hand touched the ordinary bronze
latch-lever on the further door. Saturnus had enough
intellectual control over what he was about to do to
check his companion's position. Allectus stood to the
side and a step back. The finance officer's face would
have been white had it not been lighted by the rich
glow. Allectus was clear of the door's arc, however. In

a single swift motion, Saturnus turned the latch and pulled the door open.

The door gave onto a room covered in swaths of ceramic-smooth substance that was itself the source of the magenta light. Carausius stood in the center of the room. Three maggots as large as men hung in the air around him with no evident support. They were vertical, save for tapered lower portions which curled under them like the tails of seahorses. To one side of the room was a large wooden box with its lid raised. The box had been built around a cocoon of the same glowing material that covered the walls. A part of the agent's mind recognized the box as the "treasure chest" which Carausius had strapped to the foredeck of the ship in which he sailed at Mona and at Anderida, where his opponents burned. The cocoon was open also, hollow and large enough to hold the maggot which began to drift soundlessly toward it.

Saturnus's amulet tingled and its commands were white fire in his brain. There were a score, a hundred ants hidden against the whorls of the magenta room. The cocoon pulsed in the myriad facets of their eyes. *The weapon* demanded the gestalt mind behind them all. *It must not turn toward you.*

The burly emperor in the center of the room gurgled like a half-drowned man recovering consciousness. He fumbled for his sword as Saturnus ignored him and leaped past.

The agent brushed the drifting maggot as it and he both made for the cocoon. The creature's skin was dry and yielding. Had Saturnus thought, he could not even have sworn that he touched a natural integument and not some sort of artificial one. He did not think. He reacted with a panicked loathing uncontrollable even by the group intelligence riding him. Saturnus cut at the maggot with the motion of a man chopping away the spider that leaped on his shoulder. There was a momentary resistance to the point. Then the steel was through in a gush and spatter of ochre fluids.

The maggot fell in on itself like a pricked bladder collapsing. It shrank to half its original size before the remainder slopped liquidly to the floor. By that time, the agent had grabbed the side of the cocoon. The object, crate and all, began to twist as if to point one of its ends toward Saturnus.

Neither of the other floating creatures was moving. Besides the way the cocoon shifted, a great lens blacker than matter started to form in place of the wall behind Carausius.

The emperor had cleared his sword as much by reflex as by conscious volition. Allectus, almost mad with fears and the impossible present, struck Carausius before the latter could parry. The blade rang on Carausius's forehead. The finance officer was no swordsman, but panic made his blow a shocking one even when the edge turned on bone and glanced away. The Emperor staggered. His sword clanged as the hilt slipped from his fingers.

Saturnus gripped the cocoon with his left hand. He could not prevent the object from turning. Like a man wrestling a crocodile, however, he kept the end from pointing toward him the way it or what controlled it desired. Then, as the dream-voices demanded, Saturnus stabbed into the spongy wall of the cocoon. His steel hissed in a dazzling iridescence. The cocoon's material boiled away from the metal, disappearing at a rate that increased geometrically as the gap expanded toward itself around its circumference.

There was a crashing sound like lightning. The box that camouflaged the cocoon from human eyes burst into flames.

Saturnus rolled back from the destruction he had caused. The blade of his dagger had warped, though its hilt was not even warm in his hand. One of the floating maggots made a sound like that of water on hot iron.

Allectus ignored the maggots as if he could thus deny their existence. The finance officer stepped between them to thrust with the full weight of his body at the reeling Carausius. His point skidded on the breastplate hidden by the Emperor's tunic. Carausius flung himself back, away from the blade. He fell into the lens and merged with the dim shape already forming there.

Carausius's whole body burned. His iron armor blazed like the heart of the sun. In its illumination, the wall began to powder and the maggots shriveled like slugs on a stove. The mind in Saturnus's mind sparkled in triumph.

Saturnus dragged Allectus back down the tunnel toward the strongroom. The agent acted by instinct rather than from any conscious desire to save the other man. The finance officer had been stunned by events and reaction to his own part in them. His skin prickled where it had been bare to coruscance a moment before, and his eyes were watering.

"What was it?" Allectus whispered. He felt his lips crack as he moved them. "What were they?"

Saturnus had been familiar since infancy with the scene he had just lived and with a thousand variations upon that scene. "Things from far away," he said. It was the first time he had spoken to a human being about the nightmare that had ruled him for so long. "They've been helping Carausius for now, getting his support in turn for their own mission, things they need. When they were ready, more of them would come. Many more. They would smooth this world like a ball of ivory and squirm across its surface with no fellow but themselves."

"What?" mumbled Allectus. They had reached the strongroom. With Carausius gone and no one else aware of that feat, the finance minister could seize the throne himself—if he could organize his mind enough to act. The agent's words rolled off Allectus's consciousness, part of the inexplicable madness of moments before. He did not wait for Saturnus to amplify his remarks, did not *want* to hear more about things whose possible reality could be worse than human imaginings.

Saturnus paused as his human companion began to scramble up the ladder. The agent's left hand closed for the last time over the amulet on his chest. The further door of the tunnel had swung shut on the blazing carnage within. The hinges and latch glowed. As Saturnus watched, the center of the wood charred through and illuminated the tunnel harshly.

Saturnus jerked his hand down and broke the thin gold chain. The amulet was as clear in his mind as if he could see it through his clenched fist. At the heart of the amber bead was the creature trapped in pine resin sixty million years before Man walked the Earth. Trapped and preserved in sap that hardened to transparent stone. . . . Trapped and preserved, an ant like so many billions of others in that age and in future ages. . . .

Saturnus hurled his amulet back toward the flame-shot door. A last memory remained as the amber bead left his hand. It was not the world of his nightmare, the maggot-drifting globe Saturnus had described to Allectus.

Saturnus's Roman world-view had as little concept of duration as did that of the timeless group mind to which he had so long been an appendage. *Thirty million years in the future* would have been no more than nonsense syllables to Saturnus if someone had spoken them. But he could understand the new vision that he saw. The dream-Earth crawled with the one life form remaining to it. To salute Saturnus as they left him, all the billions of six-legged units raised their antennae, under the direction of the single gestalt intelligence which had just saved the world for itself.

Then the amber bead and the vision blazed up together.

_____*End note to* Dreams in Amber

The short-lived Empire of Carausius caught my fancy as soon as I heard about it in the '60s. I remember getting and reading in 1970 the *Panegyric to Constantius Chlorus* which is one of the few literary sources on the subject, but it'd been an interest of mine from well before then.

I'm often asked how much research I do for a story. I could honestly answer either, "Almost none," or "An absurdly great amount." To write "Dreams in Amber," I had to learn the history of a little-known and very ill-documented period, the location and design of the Fleet Station of London, the internal layout of a Roman headquarters building, and any number of lesser bits of data which were necessary to the texture of the final story.

But I'd done that for my own whim many years before I put the "research" into a story. Take your pick of the above answers.

SAFE TO SEA

Even in the first instants they knew that something had gone wrong. The transit that should have jumped them a quarter light year had hung the thirty-four of them as a ragged constellation among totally unfamiliar stars.

"Hey, my drive's going out!"

"Where the cop are we and how—".

"Johnnie, hang on. Perk and I'll get you out but you gotta hold your spin—"

Individually they were forty-foot daggers, maneuvered by solid-fuel rockets but flung between stars by the transit element amidships. Half each vessel's length was a weapons bay, its only reason for existence. They were neither armored nor fitted with damper fields to choke off incoming nuclear weapons, and while their hulls were studded and meshed with a score of sensor inputs that gave them the airflow of a cookie cutter, the sheeting was utterly opaque and left the pilots blind if the power failed. But nobody had ever pretended that an attack ship could last long in an engagement; only that it could last long enough.

A little sun flared as Corcoran's radiation-poisoned star drive failed catastrophically. The chatter ended, frozen by cold-voiced orders and replies as Attack Squadron 18 sorted itself out. Three of the tiny warships snatched at the tumbling one with their docking tractors, killing all motion relative to the sun below. The ship's medicomp went to work on Calvados, the pilot, his senses junked by the wild centrifuging.

Bernstein, Captain in Command—and the thought of how far his command now reached ate at the edges of his mind—lay rigidly suited in the center of his instruments and display screens. He could move his body six inches at most in any direction. His arms had a nearly full sweep, but each centimeter of their circuit took them to control switches of invisible but memorized significance.

"Heavy in IR," Lacie's voice was rumbling, "but visible spectrum too. The planet itself has fairly regular contours, but we'd want the high ground, the low spot's muck, pure muck. Haven't got the trace readout yet, but we oughta be fine with just breathers."

"Not after you redpill the field," Bernstein stated flatly.

"Aw. . . ." Lacie was six-four, a hugely fat man who began to itch the moment he suited up.

"Sorry, Corporal, but we've got major maintenance to pull and I don't want things creeping up on us while we pull it. Slag it."

"Roger." The commo transmitted the clunk of a fusion weapon leaving the scout ship's bay. "No sign of chicks, sir. No sign of people either, of course, just a lot of jungle."

Individually in section order, most of AS 18 dropped

toward the mesa on the pale blue rods of their belly jets. Calvados was an exception, still unconscious and laid down by the straining motors of the ships that had caught his. Herb Wester's craft had been spiked by shrapnel in the instant of transit.

"Look, I can bring her in alone."

"Not until your metering controls get patched up, and we can't do that till you're down."

"Look, sir, it's one hellova lot safer for me to go in alone than with you and the el-tee locked—"

"Shut it off, Wester, I'm through talking about it. You're going in between Lt. Hsi-men and myself and that's all."

Damaged craft locked between the two officers, the trio began dropping toward the surface. Fog or yellow clouds boiled about them. Visibility in the optical ranges was generally nil, but occasional serpents of turbulence gaped unexpectedly. At 8300 meters, Wester's jets surged. All three ships tumbled. Bernstein failed to hit his own motors swiftly enough and the tractor snapped. The jowly captain fought his controls to stasis before tracking the green dots of Hsi-men and Wester on his volume display.

"Cut me, Chen!"

"No no, we'll get you—"

"Goddam slanteye I can't fight this bitch and you! Cut me!"

The dots separated.

Wester dropped his ship alone with the two officers paralleling him at a thousand meters. When an asymmetric surge rippled the damaged vessel, Wester expertly brought it back with a short burst from all motors, then freefell nearly two kays. As the craft dropped below 3400, its green dot blipped out on the other screens. The shock wave of the exploding craft reached Bernstein and Hsi-men a few seconds later. They followed the remainder of the squadron down to the landing site.

"I don't say we're out of the woods yet," the CinC's voice rasped through the suit commo. "At the moment, none of us know where we are."

Jobbins stood on the perimeter, cradling a fat-nosed missile from his ship's defensive cluster; and a damn poor weapon it was for a man on foot. Even if the cannibalized power supply kicked off the motor, the backblast would probably fry him alive; and the high explosive charge in the nose was contact fused, making it suicide just to drop the coppy thing. Then for back-up, all he had was a meter's length of chrome-van tubing cut from Calvados' ship. Calvados' two 15cm power guns had been dismounted onto jury-rigged tripods as well, but only his. With available tools you had to butcher a ship to disarm it, so only the hopeless wreck was being stripped. Besides, the guns were designed for use in vacuum; fired in the thick, scattering atmosphere of this planet they weren't going to last a dozen shots.

"But we have a good chance—a damned good chance—to find out. It'll take another jump. That means more time in suits, I know."

Jobbins' suit made him ache all over, trying to walk in it. Coppy things weren't made for gravity use. But who the hell thought the chicks could slip an intruder into the center of the 1st Fleet undetected? The squadron was lucky at that. If their tender had been going to boost them an instant later instead of precisely when it vaporized, AS 18 wouldn't be around to wonder where the incredible surge of energy had flung them.

"We're picking up heavy diffusion in transit space from a location within ninety minutes' hop of here. Lt. Reikart and I are working together to calibrate for it, and by the time AS 18 is set to move, we'll have a location to move to."

Jobbins fingered the tube. Both ends had been severed at 45 degrees, and he wasn't sure whether he was meant to use it as a spear or a club. Clumsy either way. But even through his IR converters, there was nothing to be seen here but glass and pressure cracks spreading out from ground zero.

"We'll all move together. The signal source may be hostile, may be the chicks themselves. No one stays behind here, and every ship has to be as close to battle-ready as we can make it without shipyards."

Or even the tender's half-assed support, Jobbins thought without humor. Sudden realization of their position hit him, black gut-level knowledge that they would never get back. Nobody even knew they were spending their lives wandering out here instead of already being a gas cloud in space off Rigel XII.

There was movement in the shadowy fringes of Jobbins' vision. Dust devils or the like? But the ground was shaking. "Movement," he called in excitedly. "Ah, Jobbins, position, ah, two-seventy degrees."

"What sort of movement, flyer?"

"Second section, stand by."

"Jeez, it's big. Oh Jesus God my rocket won't fire! This coppy rocket won't fire! Get me some support!"

"Three-sixty, move toward him. Face out, everybody, we'll need—"

"Captain, my volume display's got it, it's like a mountain. . . . Get aloft, for God's sake, it's coming in!"

With the panicked flyer's voice echoing in his mind, Jobbins backed two steps. His left arm clamped the missile, dangerous to himself if not the intruder. His converters weren't running right, he couldn't see anything but a huge blur in front of him. Something snaked out of the fog and rippled past. He jabbed with the tube, feeling tough muscle rip under the point. The power guns opened up simultaneously, on infrared a blinking crisscross aimed high in the air.

The member he had stabbed lashed toward Jobbins cat swift, coiled around his waist and flung him upwards. Even through the suit's rigidity, he felt his ribs groan. The tubing skittered through a separate trajectory as Jobbins fell toward the circular blur. It was too large to possibly be alive. The impact shook him. It didn't shake him so badly that he couldn't see the ring above him like a crater's mouth, feel the fleshy wavelets that washed him farther downward.

"Cop!" he shouted angrily as he aimed his missile down the maw and jabbed in vain at the jerry-built igniter. Still screaming meaninglessly, Jobbins grabbed the base of the missile with both hands and leaped.

Fluids and bits of flesh rained down on the squadron for several minutes. Nothing was ever recovered of Jobbins' body.

They were in communication, at least. Of a sort. Rodenhizer spoke a pretty fair grade of Interspeech, and the beings running the trading station dirtside knew a little of it. Or, filtered through a thousand tongues, a score of races, two languages linked by a few hundred words in common were being spoken.

So far as Rodenhizer could tell, the traders knew nothing about either other humans or the chicks.

"Well," Bernstein said to his officers on the command channel, "I don't see there's any choice. They must have some sort of charts down there. Star atlases look pretty much the same whoever draws them."

The lock channels didn't carry visuals, but there was no mistaking Lt. Reikart's quick tenor blurting, "Kyle, we've got three other sources now—"

"We can't—"

"No no no—"

"We can't hop around to every goddam transit user in the goddam universe!" Hsi-men snarled. "We need charts, and this is the nearest place to get a look at some."

"Well, it's dangerous to split up the force."

"Only for me, Mr. Reikart," the CinC said heavily.

"Look, take Murray down too. He's got some Interspeech, and with him and Juan sardined into one ship. . . ."

Murray dropped his ship in first. Nobody said it, but there was a good chance that with Calvados lying on top of him he'd miss a call. No point in having another ship beneath his then. AS 18 hadn't left anything behind on the nameless fog-world except two irreparably damaged vessels and Jobbins' thinly scattered remains. Murray hadn't complained about the passenger.

The CinC's craft shrieked in beside Murray's seconds later. The field was rammed earth, partly vitrified by something with less tendency to gouge and spatter

than the Terran belly jets. About the field rose the
massive walls of the compound, built more like a
circular fortress than a warehouse. Maybe it was a
fortress—the world had to be inhabited to have a
trading station. At any rate, the structure had been
easy to locate from space.

Murray and Calvados were already unsuiting when
Bernstein locked back his hatch. He said nothing. The
worst environmental threat was the high air temperature
and a sky full of actinics from the blue-white sun. As
for the fact resuiting in a crunch would mean several
minutes' delay—well, the men knew that. The CinC
kept his own armor on, even the faceplate.

"A vehicle's picked them up," Lacie reported from
orbit, his high-resolution sensors trained on the landing field.

"Captain?" Reikart requested. "Captain?" switching
frequencies up and down the scale. "Coppy thing's
shielded, we've got no contact."

"So they shield trucks in the landing—"

"Lieutenant! The towers're opening. They've got missile batteries there, three and. . . . eighteen unmasked!"

Liquid Interspeech rustled on the commo.

"Ransom," Rodenhizer translated. "Somebody's supposed to land . . . they're hostile—they'll kill, attack—"

"Lacie, Where'd the vehicle go?" Hsi-men demanded.

"North tower, just before—"

"Kranski, put an R-60 into the south tower. Combat pass."

"Hey, hold up!"

"Lieutenant, shut your face. I'm senior and I'm giving orders until we get the CinC back. And that's just
what—"

Hsi-men paused as the atmosphere lit up with the attack ship's passage in its star drive envelope. The effect of the penetrator missile that Kranski's computer spat out during a microsecond phase break was shrouded by the flaring pyrotechnics of its delivery. The southern quarter of the huge compound bulged, then crumbled at the explosion within it. All six missiles streaked from the eastern tower. They exploded barely their own length over the launching troughs.

"Bozeman, take out the west tower."

"Air car leaving the north tower, big, it's—" "They're gabbling, they've dropped Inter—" The second explosion was easily visible. "You coppy son of a bitch, I didn't tell you to nuke it!" "Crater radius one-three-ought-ought, depth at—" "Oh, Jesus, the captain, oh Jesus I didn't—" "Car is down, bearing two-two-ought from crater center, range—"

Kranski, perhaps unaware that he was speaking aloud, said it for all of them. "Well, they wasn't chicks. Not with no better dee-fense'n that."

There were forty-one bodies in the shock-flattened wreckage of the air car. None of them were human. The aliens' ropy limbs belied their endoskeletons, though only Doc Bordway, the ex-zoologist, cared much about that. Or the fact that most of the bodies were female and young. One of the few adult males found was clutching a blue case packed with documents. With no one left to translate the multi-colored squiggles, they were valueless to the squadron.

Eighty percent of the horizon was a hell of glass in a thousand dazzling forms: needles and vast, smooth clearings, iridescence and inkiness, sheets smeared vertically when a nearby pair of weapons had detonated simultaneously and conspired to create while destroying.

The three iron-gray towers dwarfed the attack ships huddled in their shadow.

"What're they doing here?" Ceriani asked, bending down to touch helmets with Hsi-men. "Broadcasting like this on all bands, transit space and normal; shut in behind a screen that's only open in the visible and that at damned low intensity—something's going on in there."

The stocky officer, suited against the vacuum and expected radiation—ground sensors showed the surface count was well below that of Colorado soil, but visual evidence to the contrary was all around—stared up the full length of a tower without answering. He had seen more impressive objects in his life, the coruscating ball of this world hanging in space among them; but the towers had a grim majesty he found unsettling.

"Somebody built to last," he said, helmet to helmet. All radio was drowned by the city's enormous output. "That isn't proof they lasted."

"But the signals—"

"Listen to the damn things, listen to them. A nine-word group, over and over, the same on every channel. You don't have to translate a bit of it to know exactly what it's asking. And if these poor damned machines were getting an answer, well, they'd say something else, wouldn't they?"

He snapped off a shard projecting from the ground, hurled it toward the nearest tower. The glass shattered a foot from his hand. "Something got through to them. Maybe age did. It's sure as death that AS 18 isn't going to, though. There's nothing here for us, nothing for men."

"I wish I knew one thing," the gangling, brown-eyed sergeant said morosely.

"Umm?"

"I wish I knew that whoever was fighting them back then was gone too."

Ignoring the hairless "squirrels," Roland turned over to set the sores on his back to the muted sunlight. There could be no true bedsores in freefall, but the constant abrasion by suit irregularities had welted every man in AS 18 during the seventy-nine days since they had suited up on their tender.

Seventy-nine days.

"Could've stayed where the CinC bought it," Lacie muttered from his nearby leaf pallet. "Wasn't so bad there. This jumping from one coppy place to another, before we can take our suits off. . . ."

A breeze riffled the overhanging leaves, a little too yellow for a Terran summer but close enough for men who had shipped on three years in the past. Little beads like scarlet oak galls spattered a number of the prominent veins, brightening the dappled shade.

"What's the matter with here?" Then, "Wish I had a place this nice back home. It's worth waiting for."

"Hellova long drag."

"There were gooks the other place. Here there ain't. Everything here but women. . . ."

That night, Lacie began screaming. Roland used a damp wad of cushion to try to bring his friend around and lower his fever. It wasn't until Bordway wandered over, curious as usual, that anybody realized Lacie was dying.

"Suit up—everybody suit up and get under your

medicomps," Bordway ordered. As he spoke, he was dragging Lacie's armor over the big man's swollen limbs. Part of the diagnostic and injection apparatus was built into the suits, since normally at least the tender's medical facilities would be available any time a flyer was out of his armor.

"What's the matter, Doc?" Hsi-men, squat and unperturbed, held the scout's leg without being asked.

"We're in trouble. Lacie's caught something here."

"Hey, even I know that's cop. You can't catch sick from a non-Earth disease. Everybody—"

"Not everybody's stupid enough to believe that," Bordway snapped. "A protein's a protein, and this place has raised one that's pretty damned compatible with ours. . . ."

Lacie screamed in delirium. Hsi-men pinioned his arms. "He caught a virus from the squirrels? God."

"Not the squirrels." Bordway gestured, his crooked index finger circling one of the abrasion sores on Lacie's chest. Ringing it now were a score of tiny scarlet beads. "The leaves."

He paused a moment, ran a hand through black hair months unshorn and glistening with natural oil. In the glare of the landing light rigged on a convex reflector for illumination, Hsi-men could see the wen on Bordway's elbow was beaded too.

Bordway was the second of the seven victims to die in space as Terran anti-virals proved worthless and supportive treatment insufficient.

Lacie. Bordway. Roland, who screamed to everyone around him as they scrambled into their suits, saying that Lacie was fine, he just had nightmares, that was all. Hamid. Jones, a thin, short man from somewhere in

Britain, one of the few in AS 18 who liked the thought of killing. He had never been happier than the day at the Meadows of Altair when he had ripped open three Ch'koto transports with bursts from his power guns. Reikart took three days to die. There was no cut-off on the command channels, and Hsi-men's fingers crept to the weapons delivery console a dozen times during the hours of uninterrupted raving. Volomir.

The foliage below was bluer than the seas and starred with crystalline cities. There was no sign of highways—or aircraft, for that matter. But words crackled from the commo, loud and static-free: "'Peace, welcome.'"

"You can get it clear, Rodie?"

"Yeah, this is pretty good. Hey, maybe we're back into the trade sphere?"

"Cop, I can't get any of the stars. Wish that little prick Reikart hadn't died just before he was good for something."

Slowly, tentatively, negotiations went on. The flat-faced Chinese officer was no diplomat, but he knew enough Interspeech to keep Rodenhizer from over-modifying his replies.

"We are distressed beings searching for our home."

"All beings are one in peace. Land, remain until your home is in peace."

"Rodie! They must know us if they know about the war. Baby, we're on the way!"

"Can you direct us to our home? We ask nothing but your instruction."

It was very hard to tell from the alien tones and syntax, but Rodenhizer suspected that after a brief pause a new voice came on. It blurred the labials of

Interspeech slightly, but carried, even in its strangeness, a surprising dignity. "We here are beings of peace. We would have you wait with us in peace. While your home is at war, we cannot guide you to war."

Rodenhizer didn't have a command set. When he translated the statement on an open channel, the whole squadron exploded.

"What sorta cop is that? Look—"

"Wait a minute, wait, he can't have—"

Hsi-men let them run for a minute or more. Then he hit the override and ordered, "That's enough. Shut it off." They could hear his breathing alone for the next several seconds. Then, "Tell them we're going home now. We don't mean to hurt them, but they're not going to keep us away from home."

The ex-trader fitted his tongue to the syllables carefully. The answer was liquid, vibrant; uncompromising.

"Sir, he says they won't help us fight the chicks. We can stay or go our own way, but they won't guide us back to the war."

"Tell'em they can start giving us the data we need right now, or I'll give'em a war right here in their backyard."

"Sir, we can't! They've got all sorts of knowledge here, just incredible to have even heard of us and the chicks. We can't just smash them up because they got morals."

"Wanna bet? This is AS 18 and it's going home. You just tell them what I said."

"El-tee—"

"Tell'em or by God I'll blast a couple cities without it! Tell them!"

The answer was even shorter than the demand.

Hsi-men didn't wait for the translation that was stuck in Rodenhizer's throat. "Kranski, pick yourself one of those cities and slag it." He knew the men pretty well. Kranski had already programmed his computer, hoping against hope, and his index finger was poised over the execute switch. A few milliseconds later the fireball bloomed through the false aurora of passage. A crystal glitter rode the edge of the shock wave like palings before a tsunami.

"Say it again, Rodie," Hsi-men thundered. "I've got bombs for a hundred more like that if they've got the cities."

"Dear God how could you do it? They'll guide . . . they'll guide us away, just give some time to match computer language. The whole city—we could have talked, have convinced them, maybe. . . ."

As the data was piped into the navigation units, Mizelle spoke his first words since they had lifted from the fog-world. That was the day Juan Calvados chose to share Murray's ship instead of Mizelle's. "They may be sending us into the center of a star," he said. If there was an emotion in his voice, it was not fear.

"Then they got better guidance systems than us by a long ways. My readout says we'll be jumping for about the next three days, and I'll sure be surprised if we hit anything as small as a star. . . ."

"And if we don't," Kranski purred in a husky whisper, "we know the way back."

On the battleship *Rahab*, the crews felt cramped by the enormous commo and guidance requirements of the flagship of the 3d Fleet; but the *Rahab* held only eight hundred men in a volume seven thousand times that of an attack ship. Vice-Admiral Ceriani stepped with a martinet's precision down the double row of monitors, each an expert overseeing the fraction of the ship's commo load routed to him. Only in the rarest of circumstances would a human override the computer's automatic response. Even more rarely, the datum or question would be forwarded directly to an officer.

As the admiral watched, his third monitor in the right-hand section threw the knife switch on top of his panel, setting the ship on battle alert and clearing a circuit to every officer of staff rank in the fleet. Rather than take the replay, the admiral cut in on the monitor line.

"—main fleet. There's forty-eight blips of thirty kilotonne or over, assorted light craft. And their dampers are down, all down. If those mealy-mouthed peace-lovers hadn't dropped us damn near on top of the chicks, it can't be three minutes, we'd never have known there were any in twelve hours time. God they run clean! But they've got the damper screens down too, so they're wide open to nukes."

"Lieutenant," the Grand Marshal's labored voice queried, "what is your strength?"

"Umm, eighteen Omega-class attack ships, one Epsilon-class command," replied the other voice. They must be nearly at the limits of intelligible transmission, one hell of a long way still. More than far enough for the Ch'koto to catch the broad wake of the oncoming 3d Fleet and activate their dampers for a knock-down, drag-out fight. By now they could afford to lose surprise once. "Mizelle hit his destruct as we came out of transit, I swear to God, and that pansy bastard Rodenhizer took himself off the pattern the second day out, so he's gone too. . . ."

"Lieutenant?"

"God! Sir, I'm sorry; I'm—what do you want us to do?"

"Lieutenant, we are advancing on your plot." The admiral could feel the truth of that, he realized, from the deck's squirreliness; the *Rahab* must be transiting at minimum interval, less than ten seconds. "We need—we *must* have a strike within the next fourteen minutes, before we enter the chicks' detection range."

"Sir, we . . . sir, we have no support."

"Neither do we, Lieutenant. Since last Saturday, we are the only fleet the Terran Federation has in space or is able to put there. Do you understand?"

"Roger. Will do."

Nineteen slivers of electronics and thin alloy, the admiral thought, razoring along some three minutes from destruction. Don't think about the men, there were twenty-one thousand of those in the 3d Fleet and nine billion more on Earth if you had that kind of mind. "Get me into the intership channels for AS 18," he ordered brusquely into his right lapel.

"Sir, we'll have to squelch pretty tight above and below the orals, and there'll still be a lot of background."

"Don't talk—do it."

Hissing sharpened abruptly into words: "—appear on your screens in red."

"Roger."

"Roger."

"Team Nine; Kael, Ceriani, lead and backup. Your four targets appear on your screens in red."

"Roger."

"Roger."

"And they thought one nuke was enough for a command ship. Well, that big mother in the center may not be their flag, but it's sure worth a redpill. Last questions?"

"Sir, we don't have a reserve."

"Hell, we don't have forty-eight battlewagons, either. Bobby, we don't knock 'em down on the first time through, you can write off any reserve along with the rest of us.

"OK, boys, let's take them out."

Hissing silence stalked the battle-lit commo room of the *Rahab*. "Kranski, not so short. Slide in at a flat angle or you'll blow us all."

"Two ready."

"Seven ready."

"El-tee, this is five. We're blocked from our targets unless we do a one-twenty around the whole coppy fleet. Got some alternates?"

"Roger, watch your screens. Clear?"

"Roger, that's fine."

"El-tee, I can zap the others with penetrators. Just run my pass on through—"

"Shut it off, Kranski. You'll reform with the rest of us after your pass. If you're lucky."

Seen in plane, the Ch'koto fleet was a roughly flat-tened zig-zag. The chicks were as disorderly in maneuver as they seemed to be as technicians, draping the gang-ways of their warships with festoons of wire and bare ranks of printed circuitry. But their sloppy formations reacted like bear traps in an engagement, and chick ships had cleaner drivers and better detection gear than the Terran Federation's. Their only technical problem, near enough, was their noisy, clumsy nuclear damper that took upwards of four minutes to build from zero to a level that would squelch a 50-KT bomb.

The volume display danced with beads of four colors: white for the enemy, red for the four targets spotted to Team Three, Womack and Bozeman; green for the rest of AS 18, brilliant sapphire for Womack's own ship as it slid toward a tight knot of red beads and white. At present closing velocity, the chicks were a minute and a quarter away. At maximum thrust—

"Go!"

Womack's stubby right forefinger smashed down. His vision blurred with a rush of sweat from his forehead before the suit dried him with a blast of hot air. Thirty-five seconds at full thrust. And the chicks weren't going to miss nineteen rooster-tails in transit space.

"Six, Chen; we're getting an IFF signal from a destroyer-leader—orange tracer."

"Give'em a random return, Cooper pop them if—"

Womack's volume display overloaded in a blue flare as bolts from the quad 80.3 turret of a chick battleship ripped past his vessel. The chicks were too tightly formed to spray seeker missiles, but big power guns wouldn't leave much if they hit. Womack was screamingly blind for second on second, knowing somewhere nearby an enemy computer was feeding corrections to the guns—

With a treble thump, the redpills unloaded from his weapons bay.

Still blind but able now to react, Womack hurled his ship into a tight helix away from his delivery approach. The display flickered wanly. The sapphire and its trailing green companion winked suddenly into view, diving toward a single red-coded hostile. Another near miss and the cube sagged and crackled in the blue flame.

"Coppy bastards!" the flyer shouted. Without hesitation, he tapped pre-eject, stripping off two square meters of hull above him. He was so close that the battleship hung above him bright as the sun seen from Jupiter. "Boze!" Womack called, "for God's sake *get* the bastard!"

The Ch'koto flashed again. Womack's body strained in the salvo's viscous drag. "Bozeman!"

"Oh Jesus Captain oh Jesus I didn't—"

The next salvo hit both ships of Team Three squarely.

"Team Seven?"

"Farloe, but I've been pushing max too long." "Team Eight?" Silence. "Nobody? Team Nine?" "Kael bought it, I'm OK. Lost some sheeting's all." "El-tee, those bastards're coming up on us and my drive, she just *won't* hang together much longer."

"OK, on the count we all come around. This isn't over yet." "Sir, there's seven of us! We can't—" "We can't take out a dozen chick wagons with HE? Well, we sure as death can't run away from'em in the shape these boats are. On the count, boys. Three, two, one, *hit'em!*"

A wash of static laced the channel. Then, very faintly, "Follow me home, you silly mothers, this squadron's going home."

In the red-lighted commo room of the *Rahab*, a monitor glanced sidelong from under his helmet. You didn't often get to see an admiral cry.

_____*End note to* Safe to Sea

> From too much love of living,
> From hope and fear set free,
> We thank with brief thanksgiving
> Whatever gods there be:
> That no life lives forever;
> That dead men rise up never;
> That even the weariest river
> Winds somewhere safe to sea.

> *The Garden of Proserpine,*
> A. C. Swinburne

I wrote this story in 1973, starting it shortly after I'd sold "Contact!" (my sixth sale) through my new agent, Kirby McCauley. Kirby liked the story a lot—Kirby's enthusiasm for whatever was in front of him is a major reason for his success as an agent—but he couldn't sell it.

"Safe to Sea" had been an experiment; well, everything I wrote at the time was an experiment. I'd been trying to address larger themes than I had in the past. I did that, but to do properly it required a broader canvas than I was capable of using at the time. I basically forgot about the story and went on to other things (which also didn't sell for some while, but that's another matter).

In 1987 Marty Greenberg asked me if I had a story for *Space-Fighters*, an anthology Joe Haldeman would be headlining. I regretted that I didn't, as much because I like Marty as because I needed another hundred bucks. (I'm always happy to find money in the street, but it wasn't going to pay the mortgage.) Kirby then told me that he'd sold "Safe to Sea" to Marty.

My initial reaction wasn't entirely positive. I *didn't* need the money, and I wasn't sure after fifteen years that the story was really of publishable quality. I allowed the sale after I'd reread the piece, though. If I were writing the story today, I'd use at least twice the wordage—but the ellipses work surprisingly well, and there's a lot of good stuff in the parts which I didn't leave out. Enough good stuff that I'm reprinting the piece here.

I once did a short-short about the abduction of the boy who becomes St. Patrick. I wrote it in the desperate hope that perhaps I could sell something to a Roman Catholic magazine when I couldn't sell to anybody else. I failed, and I forgot about the story.

Maybe I should've sent it to Kirby.

THE MURDER
OF HALLEY'S COMET

by Larry Niven and David Drake

Even with half a square kilometer of light-sail deployed, the Khalian projectile was an insignificant blip compared to the four-kilometer diameter of the comet's core. The entire unit weighed just under ten kilograms. There was a terminal-guidance system which incorporated a proximity fuse, a small bursting charge, a reflective shell, and tiny servomotors coupled to the spars of the light-sail.

The sail blazed with a terrible intensity, a tiny, peculiar star, brilliant green. It was traveling at almost 25,000 kilometers per second—8 percent of light speed—when the payload detonated. The cloud of shrapnel grew but continued with the same course and velocity as the missile had before exploding.

Its target was black with age, invisible against the sky.

The projectile had become a cloud over four kilometers across when it splashed across the ancient ice ball. Traveling at a significant fraction of light speed, the shrapnel's effect was that of a blast of gamma rays.

Half of the comet's surface absorbed the impact and vaporized instantly. Stresses transmitted by flash heating shattered the remnant of the loosely compacted ball of snow and slag.

The comet exploded. Thirty-meter chunks of rock and finger-sized shards of ice drifted apart in millions of separate orbits.

The *Admiral Wilhelm Canaris* hadn't moved in nearly a decade. The huge spiky cylinder rested in unstable equilibrium in the L3 point of the Earth-Moon system, at the fringes of Earth's gravity field. Escape craft were positioned to serve as attitude jets. Their main motors fired now and then to adjust the big vessel's orbit.

The heart of the *Willy C* wasn't the vessel's bridge, but rather the office deep in its interior where sat Sector Commander Lars Eriksen, the Fleet's highest ranking officer for thirty light years in any direction. The bridge only controlled the vessel's rare course adjustments: trivial matters to a sector commander.

A sector commander's business was politics.

The spymaster-class command and control ship circled Earth itself, where the Alliance Senate met and deliberated on the Fleet's budget. In an hour Eriksen would be meeting the Senate's Trade and Industry Committee. Deep inside several concentric metal shells within what could still be described as a tremendous warship, Eriksen sat within a ring of heads. He was choosing among the alternative hairstyles that his coiffeur had downloaded into his hologram projector.

Two of the three doors into his office burst open

simultaneously. Eriksen looked up. So did six bodi-
less heads, each slightly different yet each his own,
all rotating, all annoyed.

"Our telemetry links—" blurted Captain Crocker,
head of the sector's Bureau of Military Affairs.

"On the omni—" said Captain Krasnowski, head of
the sector's Bureau of Civil Affairs as he pointed to
the omni unit beside the desk.

The captains were too agitated to notice one another's presence. The admiral gestured with his little finger; his desk's artificial intelligence shut off the omni
hologram projector. The other heads faded.

"—on Halley's comet—" continued Crocker.

"—Noel Li says—" continued Krasnowski.

"—report that the comet has exploded!"

"—that the Khalians have blown up Halley's comet!
Oh, sorry, Grig."

Eriksen pointed to the omni and said, "On."

The AI responded instantly to Eriksen's command.
The omni's surface clothed itself in a three-dimensional
image that appeared to squarely face every human in
the room. Noel Li, Earth's top newsreader, was saying,
"—however, Fleet sources have refused to comment—"

Somebody from Technical Affairs chimed for admit-
tance at the third door to Eriksen's office.

"Come!" the admiral snarled, his eyes on Noel Li.

"—on whether the comet's destruction was the first
action of a Khalian armada headed for Earth."

Halley's had been visible when Eriksen's eldest son
Mark was born; so his wife had told him. Thirty-four
years ago. The comet must be almost at aphelion,
near Neptune's orbit, Eriksen thought; better check
when he had the chance.

Li's face was replaced by an image of what Eriksen took to be Halley's comet. The holocast showed it as a cold gray ball, dimly lit, lumpy. Steam feathered out from some surface crack. Above the image glowed the word SIMULATION—in English, because the men in the office had been speaking English.

Simulation. The real Halley's was black with comet tar, carbon and polymers and other solids left on the surface by evaporating ice. The astronauts had to wear Teflon boots. Water volcanoes peaked all around them, and tiny Jupiter rose every seven hours twenty-four minutes. Thirty-five years ago, when Mark was conceived, they'd left the omni on for the whole four days, with the Halley's expedition as background.

One side of the dark sphere suddenly glared flame-green. A moment later a bright cap of vapor exploded away from almost a third of the original surface. The dark side shattered, a snowball striking a wall. Ice fragments spewed one way, steam the other.

I'm watching computer-programmed guesswork. The map is not the territory. Simulation . . . but Halley's comet is dead.

"Ah, that's what it was," said Commander Mown, who'd entered the third door when the AI opened it. Unlike Crocker and Krasnowski, the head of Technical Affairs didn't have even the option of barging in on the sector commander unannounced. "Just a drive laser—so of course the modulation was random."

"What?" said Admiral Eriksen, twisting to look squarely at the ferally slender Mown.

"Whatwhat?" gabbled Crocker and Krasnowski.

"Do you mean you—" Eriksen began.

"Is this something—" said Crocker.

"How do you mean—" said Krasnowski.

Eriksen turned again and stared at his Civil and Military Affairs chiefs. They were not too flustered by the situation to read danger in the admiral's look.

In the silence, Commander Mown said, "Three days ago, a courier on the Earth-Titan run, the *Sabot*, I believe, with three crew named—"

"Mown."

"Yes, of course, sir. The *Sabot* encountered what appeared to be a powerful laser signal directed inward, across the solar ecliptic. They recorded the data—as a matter of course—and passed them on to us for analysis."

As Mown talked, he tapped the side of the multi-function helmet he wore even here in his superior's office. His eyes focused on the holographic display it projected—visible to the others in the room only as occasional flickers—and his fingers tapped a rapid pattern of keystrokes in the air. The nerve impulses rather than the "touch" of Mown's fingertips controlled the data flow.

"We assumed it was a message. It was modulated. We found coded patches in Old French and English and Japanese. We wondered if the code was changing second by second. Truth was, there was nothing to analyze," Mown's voice continued while his eyes tracked information the others couldn't see. "We think the modulations are partly randomized and partly bits of old messages in obsolete codes, stuff the Khalians must have been picking up for a century. The beam's only a drive laser of considerable—

"*Here* we are. Yes, quite correct. The vector indicates that it was driving a projectile toward Halley's comet."

Mown's fingers danced as though he were executing half of a secret handshake for entry to a lodge. The data terminal opposite the omni obliged: it switched itself on to project visions.

Admiral Eriksen watched a schematic of the solar system from behind the omni. Here was black space where reality held only his office wall. Planetary orbits showed in primary colors, each a ring with a cluster of lumps on it, wound tight around the white dot of the sun. Thousands of spacecraft showed as little vector arrows. Clusters of comets showed as clouds. A bright green path indicated the computed track of the laser beam.

Fury closed Eriksen's throat. *Halley's comet!* Without the capacity for berserk rage, he never would have survived his two decades as a warrior. He'd learned how to swallow rage. But: A thousand years ago, Halley's comet showed us that we can predict. There is more than caprice in the world; there is law. The Weasels have murdered law.

"—listeners fully informed about the crisis," Noel Li's image closed primly.

"Off!" snapped Eriksen, pointing a finger toward the omni and wishing he had a pistol. He pointed at Mown and said, "Commander, stand in front of me where I can see you without pretending to be a contortionist!"

The admiral's tone cut through the hazy reality that surrounded the Technical Affairs chief. He hopped quickly around Eriksen's desk to stand between Crocker and Krasnowski.

Eriksen pointed to the green track of the enemy laser beam. It wasn't a line, it was a narrow fan of probable paths. "Why the blurring? Where's the uncertainty?"

Mown answered, "We don't know very much about the projectile, after all. We can guess how hard it hit, that is, how much kinetic energy it was carrying. We've seen the beam, so we know how much energy was in that. But we don't know the mass of the bullet, or the size of the light-sail, or how long the beam was on—"

A pair of panicked lieutenant commanders, the seconds in command of both Military and Civil Affairs, burst into Eriksen's office behind their chiefs.

"Sir!" blurted the officer from Military Affairs. It was unclear—perhaps even to her—whether she was speaking to her direct superior or to Eriksen himself. "The secretary of the Senate Liaison office just called. He's demanding we sound Red Alert and recall at least three battle squadrons soonest!"

"Sir!" said the junior from Civil Affairs, to Krasnowski. "The president of the Senate's on the line for"—his eyes flicked toward the admiral—"Admiral Eriksen. The president herself is on the line!"

Eriksen's handsome features were a requisite for his position, but there was nothing wrong with his mind, or his ability to act with decision. He pointed toward Krasnowski. "All right," he said. "I'll take President Ssrounish's call."

His finger twitched toward Crocker. He said, "Red Alert. Do it."

"And the recall?" piped Crocker's aide.

"I said alert! If I meant something else—" Keep it simple, especially when giving important orders. Keep it explicit, keep it simple. "Do not send a recall. I have not authorized a recall."

Nodding—both lieutenant commanders white-faced—all the intruders started to leave Eriksen's office. "Wait," the admiral ordered crisply.

He pointed toward Mown. "You," he said. "Can you locate the source of that drive laser?"

Commander Mown's lips pursed. "Very probably, yes," he said. "Yes, I suppose so."

"Make the attempt," Eriksen said. "And you"—Crocker snapped to attention, at the business end of the admiral's finger—"*take* his plot, and if it is Weasels, I want their ears! Dismissed!"

The office cleared. Crocker followed Mown. As they disappeared into the corridor leading to Technical Affairs, Mown was saying, "Actually, Khalians have very small external ears. It's my understanding that the field units take the tails as . . ."

"Why was I not informed of thisss . . . ?" demanded President Ssrounish. Her accent was normally flawless; she drew out the terminal *ess* of her question now to have an excuse to curl her lip above her fangs. "Why was no member of the Ssenate informed?"

The Alliance of Planets was denounced often enough—and with enough truth—as the Alliance of Human Planets. It may be worth noting that such denunciations came generally from humans and Hrrubans. Other species did not find it worthy of comment that a powerful race should favor its own.

But when a thoroughly acceptable nonhuman candidate presented herself for the post of president of the Alliance Senate, her colleagues had voted her in by an overwhelming margin. The duties of president were largely those of a figurehead—

And the head of Madame Ssrounish, the Hrruban senator, was fearfully impressive.

Ssrounish was intelligent by any standards, much less those of politicians. Her grace and beauty were remarkable; and in her social dealings she had invariably proved herself to be as gentle as a butterfly. Nevertheless, as Admiral Eriksen faced the holographic image of the catlike Hrruban, his insides twisted the way those of his remote ancestors had done when a saber-tooth stalked through the entrance of their cave.

"Madame President," Eriksen said with the dignity of absolute truth, "I believe you learned as fast as I did. I've just watched it on the omni. That is all I or my chief aides know about the event."

"What?" Ssrounish's jaws twitched as though she were trying to swallow a bolus too large for her throat. It was simply a gesture, but Eriksen's instincts told him to hurl himself through the doorway behind him.

"Halley's comet has exploded," he said calmly. "We know that much. We'll know more shortly."

Eriksen had commanded the *Tegetthoff* when plasma bolts killed fifty-eight of the seventy men with him on the cruiser's bridge. This wasn't the first time he'd had to function when he was scared green.

Ssrounish blinked but remained silent for a moment. "I don't—" she began. Then her eyes clicked into focus again, and she continued decisively, "What additional measures are you taking to safeguard Earth, Admiral?"

Superimposed over Ssrounish's image in the holovision tank were red letters reading SENATOR PENRYTH— another priority call that Eriksen's aides knew their chief would have to deal with personally. Hugh David

Penryth's votes were so closely identified with policies emanating from Fleet headquarters on Tau Ceti
that he was known—not to his face—as the Senator
From Tau Ceti.

Penryth would be asking the same questions as
Ssrounish, but his priorities would differ. Eriksen
thought vaguely of merging the calls, but this was
going to be unpleasant enough one-on-one.

"Earth's defenses—the Home System defenses—"
Eriksen said, "are already sufficient to meet any
potential threat, Madame President. Until—"

"You say that, wrapped in a Fleet dreadnought!"
Ssrounish roared. She reared up on her hind legs; the
sending unit in her holotank panned back automatically
to show the august president of the Alliance Senate
clawing strips from the three-meter ceiling of her
office. "The Meeting Hall has nothing above it but
clouds—and they are sparse enough in this damned
bright atmosphere!"

Must I step outside to speak further? These
days Eriksen rarely exercised his talent for sarcasm.
"Madame President, the Home System is more heavily
defended—"

"I am old and perhaps ready to die!" Ssrounish
continued, belying her words with the supple fury
of her limbs. "But my colleagues—the senators who
vote the Fleet's appropriations—they are perhaps not
all so philosophical!"

But enough was enough. "One may hope they are
less timid, also," Eriksen said. "Sol system is more
heavily defended than Port Tau Ceti. Any monkey
with a spacecraft can blow a snowball apart, but a
real Khalian attack would require greater force than

they've ever demonstrated . . . if the Khalians are even involved. We have only the news broadcasts to suggest even that."

"You said 'timid,'" President Ssrounish said.

"Have you remembered your dignity, Madame President?"

President Ssrounish settled back into her normal posture, bonelessly, like a house cat. "Admiral, you must be very sure of yourself."

"Why not? This is my skill."

"You say that we have only the omni newscasts to thank for any information about the attack. How is it that Noel Li knew about it before you did? . . . or the Senate either!"

"Madame President," said Eriksen grimly, "I hope to find you an answer very soon."

When Lieutenant Scarlatti's console began making busy chuckling sounds, Scarlatti stood, stretched, then leaned over the divider to see how Lieutenant Stich was doing.

Stich was rising also, sweeping her fingers across her scalp as if to straighten the hair that she'd had stylishly removed. Almost no one really looked good as a baldie, but Jenna Stich was the "almost."

"What do they have you on, Alec?" she asked Scarlatti with a smile that sometimes made him wonder what a female praying mantis looked like to a male. Beautiful. Worth whatever it took . . .

"Ah!" he said, snapping back to the reality of the two of them on duty, ten levels deep inside the *Willy C.*

Of course, their consoles were doing the real work. Still.

"One of the courier ships tracked through a laser.

Somebody's drive laser," Scarlatti explained, glancing back at his console to be sure that it didn't require a human decision. Nope. "I'm to calculate the probable track of the laser and come up with a source . . . assuming it was ship-mounted. Max priority."

Stich frowned and said, "But you can't calculate direction from one point, can you?"

"Well, no, but it's *not* a point." Scarlatti gestured to his console and muttered a command. Stich moved closer to see over the divider; their arms were almost touching. "The courier was in the beam for almost thirty seconds, so there's a good long line to work with."

The ignorance implied by Stich's question bothered him for a moment; it was as though she'd asked him how to turn on her console. But though the units were identical, the operators and their jobs were not. Jenna didn't do the particular sort of number crunching that was second nature to Scarlatti.

The console obediently gave him visuals, a green line hanging in the air. "The intersection line," he explained. The green shrank to a mere dash, then extended in orange from one end, in a narrow flattened cone that stretched to the limit of the hologram display. "And a location cone, depending on the sender's course and speed. I'm checking the extension against known objects before I run à plot from what I have already."

Scarlatti knew that what he had so far wasn't enough to locate the sender, unless a couple of battle squadrons were recalled to the Home System to sift through all the possibilities; but Stich probably didn't realize that. The bit of harmless boasting made the young lieutenant feel good.

Beaming with his promise of success, Scarlatti said,

"What do they have you on, ah, Jenna? Not"—a cloud passed over the sun of Scarlatti's hopes—"a cross-check on my, ah—"

"Oh, no, nothing like that!" Lieutenant Stich warbled in amusement. "One of the omni newsreaders announced—"

Stich cued her console with a gesture Scarlatti failed to catch. The unit said in Noel Li's dulcet, cultured tones, ". . . *the Khalians have blown up . . .*"

"—Halley's comet blew up before anybody here knew about it," Stich continued over the newsreader's voice. "I'm looking for the source of their data—"

". . . *Fleet sources have refused comment on . . .*"

"What?" Scarlatti interjected, pointing as though the recorded words weren't utterly disembodied. "You mean they *did* report it to us before the broadcast and somebody—"

Stich's smile wasn't so much mechanical as electronic in its precision. She gestured again. Li's voice switched in midsyllable to a man saying, ". . . *Landhope, producer of the Morning News. We have a report—*"

"Assistant producer," murmured Stich coldly. "He's calling Commander Brujilla in the Public Information office thirteen minutes before air time."

"—*just been blown up by a Khalian armada incoming to attack Earth. Can you comment on that for the record, Commander?*"

"*What?*" demanded a female voice from the heart of Stich's console. "*Landhope, what are you on?*"

"*Commander Brujilla, I'm not going to be put off by pretended ignorance,*" the producer snapped. "*If the Fleet refuses comment on the biggest security lapse since Pearl Harbor, we'll run what we've got!*"

"Well, run it and be damned, then, Landhope! And if you think your calls here'll ever be answered again, y—"

"Ooh . . ." said Scarlatti.

"Yeah," said Stich. "Brujilla's got about as much chance of promotion as Ito van Pool." Van Pool had docked Admiral Ozul's gig three meters deep into his flagship's hull, sixty years ago. Such things are remembered. "And I'd have said the same thing if anybody'd called me with such an idiot story . . ."

"Sure, anybody would," Scarlatti agreed. The cold feeling in the pit of his stomach had crushed all the pride, all the sexual display, out of his voice. He'd just seen somebody's career get hit by an astrobleme.

Stich gestured again. "This is the call to Broadcast Towers," she said.

"How do you . . . ?" Scarlatti asked. "I mean, are you just pulling these calls out of a file, or . . . ?"

"Of course," Stich agreed. Her quizzical expression reminded Scarlatti of how he'd felt when she asked a ridiculous question about course computation. "They don't name these ships after spymasters and hang them over sector capitals for nothing, Alec. I told my console to sort message traffic to and from Broadcast Towers over the past three days, using the key phrase 'Halley's comet.'"

". . . *Towers,*" said a voice from the console. "*Can I help you, please?*"

"*Record this,*" responded another voice, probably unnecessarily. "*I won't say it again. A—*"

"We don't have a match on the voice, at least yet," Stich explained in an undertone, "but the call originated from Dallas."

"*—Khalian armada is inbound toward Earth. They have already destroyed Halley's comet. Professor Sitatunga at Fermi-Geneva will confirm this.*"

"Thirty-seven minutes before air time," Stich added with professional appreciation. "They were cutting it close."

When Jenna Stich flicked her control hand again, the console generated a hologram of a man with implanted hair—a cheap job that looked as though the surgeon normally specialized in putting greens—oriental features, and a rich black complexion.

"*Yes, yes?*" a voice was saying; the image's lips moved, slightly out of synch with the words. "*I am Sitatunga, yes.*"

Noticing Scarlatti's frown, Stich said, "They didn't have enough warning to arrange pictures for the initial flash, but they got cameras on him later. I'm just manipulating those sends to fit the initial call."

"*. . . told me you'd be calling about my research . . .*"

"Told by the same guy as made the call to the station?" Stich nodded absently.

"*Yes, Professor, but what about the comet exploding?*" The caller from Broadcast Towers was probably Landhope; Scarlatti couldn't tell.

Stich murmured, "Yes, he called Sitatunga from Dallas the day before, pretending to be Noel Li's producer himself."

The holographic face registered amazement and horror. "*Why are you saying this to me? This is no joke! The comet is not exploded, it—*"

"Told him they wanted a feature on Halley's comet, so he'd have the latest telemetry ready when the station called—"

"*See, right here!*" insisted Sitatunga, obviously pointing to a display terminal that would probably have been illegible even if he were on-camera during the conversation. "*It says . . . oh my God! Oh my God! Oh my God!*"

"*Professor?*"

"*All my equipment! Gone! Gone! Exploded as you say! All my life!*"

Stich gestured away the scientist's voice and the sight of his pop-eyed horror.

"He was the greatest authority on the comet in . . . I suppose the universe," she explained. Her mouth moved in what could have been a cold smile. "I suppose he still is, but there isn't as much now to know."

"Except who did it. And even that—" A pulse of red light and the beep in Scarlatti's mastoid implant warned him that his console needed a human decision.

"Go ahead," he ordered as he turned to face his equipment.

CONFIRMATION POINTS appeared in the air in bright amber letters. The heading lifted a hand's breadth. Beneath it—in red, indicating a high degree of probability—appeared MARS, followed by thirty-digit time-location parameters.

"Right," Scarlatti said. "Check it out."

Stich waited a decent five seconds to be sure she wouldn't interrupt further business, then asked, "Check what out?"

"Ah," said Scarlatti. "The calculated course suggests the drive beam may have intersected Mars before it hit the *Sabot*."

"Wouldn't that have been reported?"

"Sure," Scarlatti agreed, "but so what? A laser beam intersecting a Fleet unit is an incident that sets off alarms. But intersect a planet and that's just data . . . until somebody asks about it."

Lieutenant Stich responded with a smile that warmed Scarlatti all the way down to his toes. "My dad thinks my being in Fleet intelligence is exciting. I tell him I'm just a librarian: my job's information retrieval."

Scarlatti nodded toward his unit. "Yeah. Like I could call somebody on Mars myself . . . after the console told me who. But it's a lot simpler to let the console talk to the data storage site directly."

"Computers don't go out to lunch," Stich agreed.

Scarlatti's implant chimed pleasantly, alerting him that new data hung in the air, to replace the calculated parameters. "Three hours?" he said in amazement as he translated the digits into human reality. "The beam was painting Mars for three hours? That's absurd! Unless they were . . ."

Stich said, "And what were the chances that the beam would intersect a Fleet courier by chance?"

Scarlatti pointed to key his console. He had his mouth open to request the calculation when he realized that the other lieutenant hadn't meant the question literally. "Oh," he said, covering his embarrassment with a fixed grin. "Tiny. Had to be an accident, Jenna."

"Maybe not. What about Mars?"

"Yeah. The Weasels meant to be noticed. Jenna, they kept a violently accelerating bomb between Mars and their ship for *three hours.* So people on Mars would look up. And see Halley's comet explode. And that tells me a *lot* about their course." His hands were moving.

At Scarlatti's mutter-gestured command, his console threw up a course calculated with the addition of the new hard data. The intruder's green line danced in the smoothly-perfect curve of masses in vacuum dancing through the sun's gravity well. The cone of extrapolated paths (orange) had narrowed considerably.

"—but we only know this because *Sabot* was in the beam. And that's four points on a line, Jenna. Couldn't have been planned."

A chime from Jenna's console drew the attention of both technicians. Scarlatti couldn't hear the question Stich's mastoid implant was asking her, but when she said, "Run," the console spewed out loud the recorded conversation it had retrieved from *Willy C*'s files.

It made no sense at all. "What language is. . . ." he murmured, too lost in his own ignorance to notice the frown wrinkling his companion's forehead.

Stich crooked a finger at her console. It obediently threw a holographic caption in the air above itself:

NO KNOWN LANGUAGE.
POSSIBLE COGNATES:
WESTERN EUROPEAN/PRE-EMPIRE.

No known cognates within the thousand years since the collapse of the first starborne human civilization.

The speech, unintelligible even to the SCCS *Willy C*, stopped. Without prompting, Stich's console threw up an additional caption:

TIME TO NEXT PORTION OF TRANSMISSION:
FIVE HOURS, THIRTY-TWO MINUTES.

"Well, compress it, then!" Jenna snapped as though the console and not its programming had forced her to give that "obvious" instruction.

"Five and a half hours," muttered Scarlatti, doing the computation for which he didn't need his console's help. "If the delay's due to transmission lag"—and he couldn't imagine it being from anything else—"it's originating from well beyond Neptune. From the inner comets. Of course."

Stich's console began speaking in a different recorded voice, though the language was at least putatively the same. "The console picked the call out on the basis of the voice print—one speaker's a good match with the man who called Sitatunga and Broadcast Towers."

"In Dallas?"

Jenna nodded. "Forty-three days ago. The other half of the circuit is supposed to be Gravitogorsk, Mars."

"Then why the lag?" her companion asked in puzzlement. "Mars should require only a few minutes' delay."

"Supposed to be," Stich repeated with a slight astringency for what she considered to be someone missing an obvious point. "With thirty seconds and a plot of comsat orbits, I can crash a Gravitogorsk circuit too, or any open circuit."

"But could you do it from five and a half light-hours out?" Scarlatti prompted.

Jenna paused, pursed her lips in consideration. She looked beautiful. "With the *Canaris*'s navigational software to steady the transmission beam," she said at last, "yes. Give me a starship's navigational equipment, and I could tickle an orbital satellite any way you like. I could make anyone think a call was coming from Earth instead of. . . . The Oort Cloud is what we're talking about, isn't it? But you normally wouldn't bother . . ."

"Unless you had an agent on Earth," Scarlatti said,

taking the verbal handoff from his companion. "And you wanted to give him the details of your plans so that he could prepare the propaganda campaign."

Stich stared at the holographic solar system glowing above Scarlatti's console. "Alec," she said cautiously, "if you—"

"—factor in the distance and course calculated from the decreasing lag time between call segments. That's their velocity component toward the *Sabot*. Hee hee hee! We'll have their velocity vector. That's more than they wanted to tell us." Scarlatti's fingers danced. The unit began to chuckle as it processed data.

The orange cone was now on the outer end of the green line—the course the intruder might have taken after his laser beam intersected the *Sabot*.

"—then what's on the inner side of the plotted course?" Jenna finished.

The red pulse and mastoid chime from Scarlatti's console drew the eyes of both operators.

It was only a possibility, of course; a computer's estimate based on the assumption that the Weasel ship had a specific intended goal, and that the vessel's computer would choose the most elegant solution when it laid its course.

There was an event point from which a microwave beam from the Khalian ship would almost align with Mars on its way to Earth itself. A later event point from which the beam of a drive laser would intersect the *Sabot* and Mars sequentially. There was an event-point beyond—

"Of course, they could've popped into sponge space and headed home," Scarlatti muttered. "They'd be crazy to do anything else."

"They haven't done it yet," said Stich. "An unscheduled sponge space entry within the solar system would've alerted the whole defensive array. If they stayed in normal space-time, they could assume no one would notice until . . ."

Scarlatti pointed, keying the console; then he paused while he decided whether to inform Commander Mown under the usual procedure, or to alert the Battle Center directly.

They'd have to be crazy.

Weasels are crazy!

"Battle Center," he said. Moments ago he had watched one Commander Brujilla blow her career in six hot seconds. Likely enough he had just done the same. But beside him, Jenna Stich's bald, finely formed skull was nodding approval of his decision.

Even if there were a ship prepared to take off at once, star-drive required incredibly complex equations that took time to complete.

And if the computed guess glowing above Scarlatti's console was correct, the handful of scientists at Tombaugh Station on Pluto didn't have very much time at all.

"Look, this is really some kinda training exercise, isn't it?" said Pilot Trainee Rostislav. The fear was creeping up his spine. "Come on, Chalfond, a courier ship's too small a box for us to be gaming each other."

"It's no exercise, Rostislav," said Warrant Officer Chalfond, captain of the *Sabot*. "Shut up and worry about course coordinates."

Chalfond had been in charge of a destroyer's gun turret before a Khalian torpedo shredded her legs.

Transfer to the command of a courier vessel on intra-system runs could have been considered a promotion. At least it wasn't forcible retirement.

She hadn't considered it a promotion until now, when it seemed there might be a chance of action after all.

"Captain, the coordinates are set," Rostislav said in a frustrated tone. "They've been set for half an hour. It's the calculations to get there through sponge space that're the problem, and I can't speed them up by poking at keys myself." He grimaced at the blank, pulsing depths within his omni.

The *Sabot*'s command console was a meter-thick pillar in the center of the vessel's cabin. The console had three niches offset 120 degrees from one another, with seats facing inward. When the crew was at flight stations, they were almost touching—but they couldn't see each others' faces.

"Moggs, are your guns ready?" Chalfond demanded.

"Is a bear Catholic?" Rostislav muttered with another grimace. Couldn't she just keep quiet and let the software—

"Huh?" said Crewman Third Class Moggs. Moggs spent all his free time running training programs at the gunnery screen, zapping pirates, meteor storms, Khalians, and whatever else the computer chose to throw at him. "I don't get it, Rostislav."

Rostislav wasn't sure Moggs was bright enough to understand the difference between a training program and what was maybe about to happen.

"You know, Moggs," the pilot said. "Does the pope—"

"Shut *up*, Rostislav!" Chalfond snapped. "Moggs, are your—"

"Captain," said Rostislav. "The console is ready to start sequence."

"Action Stations," said Chalfond. "Pilot, start sequence."

"Sequence started." Rostislav tapped a key and waited for the shift. It always felt like being turned inside out. Captain Chalfond never reacted. She claimed that she had become used to it. Rostislav believed that the captain was lying.

"Moggs, are your guns ready?" Chalfond repeated in a calm voice. Rostislav could hear the tap of keys from by her side console, but his screen was loaded with flight data and didn't echo whatever Chalfond was setting up.

"Yes, Captain."

"C-captain Chalfond," said Rostislav. "What if it really is a Weasel armada we're jumping into the middle of? I mean, I know there won't really be anything there, but if there was . . . ?"

"Don't worry, kid," said the legless warrant officer in what she must have thought was reassurance. "They're scrambling everything in the system! All we gotta do is take the Weasels' minds off Tombaugh Station for a couple minutes."

It was a very short transit. The *Sabot* made a blurring lurch back into normal space-time. This time, Rostislav had too much on his plate to notice the momentary nausea.

"I have a target," said Moggs.

"Magnetics up," said Rostislav. The magnetic shielding that dispersed the effect of plasma bolts was one of his responsibilities at Action Stations, though he was only vocalizing what the green sidebar on the captain's screen told her.

"Unidentified vessel," Chalfond ordered over the tight-beam laser communicator. "Drop your screens and prepare to be boarded."

The *Sabot* gave a triple shudder. Its load of ship-to-ship missiles had toggled off in accordance with the engagement sequence that Chalfond programmed while they were still in sponge space.

"Chalfond!" Rostislav shouted. "We can't shoot before we know—"

Six screens, the outside views, flashed green and were blank. The data displays were unchanged, except that the ship's skin temperature was rising fast. High flux on that laser. A merchant ship would be boiling away. Rostislav recognized that shade of green from days ago and said, "Never mind."

"Stay alert," Chalfond said. "That green light can't hurt us much, but—" The *Sabot* shuddered again. A transient of orange light sparkled within the depths of Rostislav's screen, fogging the data there momentarily. Magnetic fields, *Sabot*'s shielding, twisted in the flow of plasma bolts.

"Taking evasive action," said Rostislav in a steady voice pitched an octave above his normal speech. Khalians. *Weasels*.

"Gunnery officer, open fire," Chalfond said.

Six-round bursts from the ball turret in the nose hammered the hull sharply. Training programs didn't duplicate the effect on the *Sabot* of miniature thermonuclear explosions, contained and directed by laser arrays in the breaches of the twin turret.

The outside cameras came back on.

Rostislav had brought the courier vessel out of sponge space at the rim of Pluto's gravity well, on a reciprocal course to that computed for the intruder by the *Canaris*'s Battle Center. *Sabot*'s real-space velocity was low, but somebody on the command and control ship had really been on his toes: the *Sabot* was headed right down the intruder's throat, and the Weasels' own significant fraction of light speed gave Chalfond's missiles a mere thirteen-second trajectory.

Another plasma bolt snapped close enough to set a relay in the *Sabot*'s guts singing, but that was chance. Rostislav had cranked in lateral accelerations that took the courier out of its ballistic path. The side-thrusters pulsed with computer-generated randomness. That was unpleasant to the crew—but not nearly as unpleasant as taking a direct hit that would flatten the magnetics and vaporize the *Sabot*'s forequarters . . .

The green light flashed and was gone, and was back, and held. Not much of a weapon, that, not to today's mirror-surfaced warships.

The red pip of the Weasel in the center of Rostislav's screen calved a trio of additional pips: missiles. They winked out instantly. Moggs couldn't have reacted to the actual target so quickly, so he must be firing at where and when he expected the Weasels to launch.

The gunnery training programs were worth something after all.

So was Moggs, despite his room-temperature IQ.

One of Chalfond's missiles vanished from the screen. The Weasels had switched their guns onto the missiles homing on them, but there wasn't time to—

The red pip blurred.

"She's trying to enter sponge—" Rostislav warned.

The pip sharpened, then expanded into a fuzzy

cloud quite different from the blurring of a moment before.

"—space."

Ships had to lower their magnetic shields before entering sponge space.

"Game's over," said Moggs simply.

The two remaining missiles plunged toward the heart of the cloud. Chalfond detonated them with an abort command. There might be debris worth examining. "Gunnery officer," she ordered, "secure your weapons. Pilot, bring us around."

Pilot Trainee Rostislav found that his hands were shaking so badly that it was several seconds before he dared touch his controls.

Twenty years before, Commander Antonio Soler, a brilliant young officer, made a brilliant marriage and resigned his commission to follow a brilliant academic career. The marriage hadn't lasted, though friends argued about whether Antonio's drinking was the cause or an effect of the failure. The academic career went by the boards at about the same time as the marriage; and, though he dried out, the brilliance remained in eclipse.

Antonio Soler came back to the Fleet, to serve out the seven years remaining before he was eligible for a full pension. Few military positions require brilliance. The Fleet was glad to give the ex-commander warrant rank and command of Mine Warfare Vessel *774T*.

"Region Twelve cleared, sir," reported Yeoman Second Class Teddley as she began to furl the gossamer static lines with which MWV *774T* had cleared another assigned sweep area of debris from the Khalian vessel.

There were a dozen ships involved in the hasty search, but only the *774T* and her sister ship MWV *301A* were really designed for the work. "Shall I proceed to Region Thirteen?"

Warrant Officer Soler was standing with his hands on hips, jaw out-thrust. Slightly tilted on Velcro slippers, he was facing but not really viewing the main navigational screen. He didn't respond to his subordinate's question.

"Ah," Teddley said. "Sir? Shall we proceed to Region Thirteen while we process the drag-load from Region Twelve?"

"What?" said Soler, turning with the confused embarrassment of a man caught viewing himself in the mirror of his mind. "What? Yes, yes, of course."

Teddley chimed a warning of the coming course correction. It was a moment—as Teddley expected—before Soler himself realized he needed to get into his own acceleration couch.

"Have you been considering the enigma of why the Weasels would attack Halley's comet, Teddley?" Soler demanded.

"Yessir," said Teddley. She programmed the burn. It was a rhetorical question; it wouldn't make the slightest difference whether she responded yes, no, or maybe.

"Let me postulate a plan," said Soler, "a plan for Weasels. I'm a brilliant Weasel, yes? I know I can't invade Sol system. It crosses my mind that I barely have the power to destroy an ice ball ten miles across. That shows no immediate personal profit, so as a Weasel I may well stop thinking at this point."

"But let me attempt to think like a human politician. We Weasels know that they're a cowardly lot."

Soler smiled at Teddley; Teddley smiled back. *Burn in twenty seconds.*

Soler said, "If something as prominent as history's most famous comet is suddenly blasted into a vivid cloud of ice crystals, won't the human government panic? The results must be to our favor. Ships from the Fleet will be withdrawn to Earth for defense there, instead of patrolling regions we Weasels can raid."

"Yessir." The vessel's thrusters fired under orders of the navigational computer. The acceleration was mild, less than a tenth-G, as MWV *774T* eased through black sky, sifting vacuum.

"Well, but you see, the threat has to be credible," Soler continued. "The death of Halley's should look like the first move in an invasion. So my next move is to get my tiny ship out of the solar system, quick, before Earth's defenses can get to me. Otherwise—"

Teddley was intrigued despite herself. "Otherwise Earth's navy will find themselves looking at the blasted remains of one little ship—"

"Too small to invade a decent hotel!"

"Right. But they raided Pluto."

"Why?" Soler demanded. "They could have launched and disappeared. They could have been gone while the laser light was still in transit, and the message to their spy, too. Gone before the comet was even touched."

"Um. Well," Teddley said, "they thought they could get away with it. Immediate profit. The captain couldn't make himself go home without something for his trouble. Weasels are like that."

"And now we know there's no invasion fleet."

Teddley shrugged. "They got caught. *Willy C's*

crew was on the ball. But they didn't expect to get caught."

"But Tombaugh Station is a trivial target," Soler protested, treating Teddley as one of his erstwhile graduate students rather than a military subordinate. "Pointless compared to the propaganda effect that was the object of the exercise!"

"Sir," Teddley said, "somebody who's embezzled millions doesn't pass up a wallet he finds on the sidewalk. A crook is a crook. A Weasel's a Weasel."

Soler's console pinged three times, indicating that Karelly, in the vessel's net bay, thought he had an emergency. Recalled to his duties, Soler grimaced and said, "Karelly? Go."

"Sir! We got something this load that I think you gotta see. I think the sector commander's gotta see it!"

"Calm down, man. You're carrying a camera? Show me."

Soler peered at the blurred, off-color image. "It's frozen," Karelly babbled, "and the blast has chewed it, but *look*—"

"Right. Thank you, Karelly. Teddley, do you see what I meant? No Khalian would have thought of any such plan. The rewards can't be eaten or worn or spent. Phone the *Canaris* for me, will you? Sector commander."

From the surface of Mars, from most of the moons of Jupiter and Saturn, from any worldlet with a black sky, a good eye might see the murder of Halley's comet. One would have to know where one was looking; and then the expanding cloud of ice crystals was a tiny pale smudge, quite different from the sharp point that would be a star or planet.

But beneath the murky atmospheres of Venus and Earth, or within the rock of Ceres and Vesta and hundreds of other asteroids, the pale cloud filled a billion omni screens. A million individual shards flowed twinkling toward the eyes of two billion voting citizens.

Noel Li spoke offstage in an edgy voice with precisely chiseled consonants. "The Fleet reports no sign of the invaders. But fourteen years ago, the Khalian invasion of Rand looked like this—"

Ten thousand individual ships flowed twinkling toward the viewer's eye. The fourteen-year-old omnitape of the invasion of Rand looked dauntingly similar to Halley's comet exploding.

Krasnowski of Civil Affairs was professionally calm, almost sleepy-looking, as he met Noel Li's huge dark eyes in the omni. He waited at the edge of the sector commander's office, out of sight of the cameras which would send Eriksen—as a hologram—into the Meeting Hall of the Alliance Senate, as soon as the sector commander had something to say.

Krasnowski's aide had less experience than his chief in the terrors of political brinksmanship. The lieutenant commander wrung his hands as he scurried in and whispered in Krasnowski's ear.

Krasnowski listened, then waved his subordinate back to the commo center where he would be ready to relay the next frantic message from groundside.

Eriksen cocked an eyebrow. Civil Affairs made another negligent gesture and said, "The natives are restless, Admiral. Perhaps you might throw them a few well-turned phrases while we wait for the—"

"Not until—" Eriksen said, turning toward Captain Crocker, who sat beside Krasnowski and Commander Mown.

Military Affairs met his superior's glance with a look of icy indifference. The expression was as false as a papier mâché cannon, but it was perfect in its artistry.

"Not until Captain Crocker reports," Eriksen continued. "We have one chance to retrieve this situation, and we aren't going to lose it by being—" Crocker's aide ducked in through the door, handed him a brief sheet of hard copy, and disappeared at once. "—overanxious."

"Thank God," Crocker muttered. "We're all right," he added, rising from his seat to hand the flimsy to Eriksen. "There was only one small ship, as we conjectured, and it's been destroyed."

Eriksen waved the document away. Nothing would mar the serene polish of his desk when the cameras went on in a few moments. "There's no possibility of a garbled transmission?" he demanded.

Crocker shook his head with a satisfied smile. "None whatever," he said. "The ship that made the kill was a courier, the *Sabot*. They brought the news back themselves while later arrivals continued to check the area."

"All right," Eriksen said, composing his features into stern, fatherly lines. He stood; simultaneously, his desk sank until its top formed a flush surface with the decking. "I'll see them now."

The outlines of the sector commander's office vanished from his vision. He stood instead in an illusory hall large enough to hold the three hundred Senators and more than a thousand accredited Observers who deliberated on the course and finances of the Alliance of Planets. President Ssrounish faced him from her central dais, while rank after rank of seats mounted in curves to either side.

A surprising number of the seats were empty. Or not surprising, given the widely publicized belief that this room would be the first target when the Khalians' ravening armada reached Earth.

"His Excellency Lars Eriksen," boomed the hall's Enunciator. "Admiral of the Red and Commander of Sol Sector!"

Eriksen waited a three-beat pause. "Madame President," he began. "Honorable Senators and Observers of the Alliance of Planets . . ."

Pause.

"Today I come before you to admit error and apologize on behalf of the Fleet."

There were as many gasps as there were filled seats in the Meeting Hall. Several members rose and scuttled toward the exits, certain that they had just received confirmation of their blackest fears.

"For many years," Eriksen continued in rotund tones, as though he were unaware of the commotion he had caused, "the Fleet has maintained a secret testing facility on Halley's comet. I must now admit to you that an inexcusable lapse in safety precautions occurred, causing an experiment to go disastrously wrong."

Pause.

The hall gasped and burbled, like a catfish pond at feeding time.

"Through that error," Eriksen said, "Fleet scientists have destroyed Halley's comet."

Shouts of amazement.

"We must be thankful," Eriksen went on, knowing

that the Enunciator would raise the volume of his voice to compensate for the ambient noise, "that no lives were lost in the occurrence . . . but I realize that this is small comfort to those inhabitants of Earth, and to their unborn descendants, who will lack forever one of the crowning glories of the solar system."

Several of those listening in the Meeting Hall were literally dancing in the aisles. A portly Observer attempted a cartwheel and wound up crashing into a desk three ranks below her own. No one seemed to care.

"There is only one recompense adequate to the scale of the error," Eriksen said. "I have contacted Fleet headquarters"—There hadn't been anything like enough time to inform Port Tau Ceti of the situation, but that lie would be lost in the greater one—"and have received the full approval of my superiors for the following arrangement."

He paused again, letting the room quiet to increase the impact of what he was about to say.

"We of the Fleet," the sector commander boomed, "at our sole effort and expense, will rebuild Halley's comet, using material from the Oort Cloud. The project is expected to take three years"—Eriksen could imagine Mown nodding approval at the fact his superior had remembered the correct figure—"but at the end of that time you will have a comet identical in orbit and composition, not to the Halley's of two days ago, but to a younger Halley's comet as it was seen four thousand years ago by the Chinese. A young Halley's comet with thousands of years of life ahead of it."

It was almost ten minutes before the cheers and clapping died down enough for Eriksen to signal an end to his transmission.

"God!" he said, flopping backward before he checked to be sure that his chair had risen high enough to catch him. It had.

"Brilliant, sir!" Krasnowski was saying. "Absolutely brilliant!"

"Monitor the omni," Eriksen muttered with his eyes closed against the memory of over a thousand politicians with their mouths open. Cheering now; but it could have been his blood for which they shouted.

When the admiral looked up again, he saw to his surprise that Captain Crocker was frowning, and even Commander Mown looked concerned as he read the sheet of hard copy Crocker had passed to him. "Yes?" Eriksen demanded, waiting for the worst, waiting to learn there really was a Khalian invasion force . . .

"There wasn't much left of the ship the *Sabot* nailed, sir," Crocker explained. "Some Khalian protoplasm. And they did find an arm in a uniform that doesn't match anything in our files to date. Here." Crocker gesture-muttered, and the picture in the omni blurred.

"I didn't think Weasels wore uniforms at all," Eriksen said carefully. What was he looking at? A jittery hand held something in front of an omni camera. Eriksen couldn't make it out. Double image?

A human hand held . . . held a human hand, pale with frost, and half of the raggedly torn forearm.

"Yes, that explains it," Mown muttered. "It bothered me that Khalians understood human psychology so perfectly."

Admiral Lars Eriksen's guts felt as though he'd just dropped into sponge space, except that the sinking sensation went on and on.

——*End note to* The Murder of Halley's Comet

In 1989 I was co-editing The Fleet with Bill Fawcett, a space-opera shared universe series. Bill suggested that I ask Larry Niven for a story, which I did. (I'd been working with Larry on another project which, thank goodness, had died quietly.)

Larry didn't have time to write a story, but he said he'd plot one and do a polish pass if I wrote it; that's what we did. The result was "The Murder of Halley's Comet."

THE HUNTING GROUND

The patrol car's tires hissed on the warm asphalt as it pulled to the curb beside Lorne. "What you up to, snake?" asked the square-bodied policeman. The car's rumbling idle and the whirr of its air conditioner through the open window filled the evening.

Lorne smiled and nodded the lighted tip of his cigarette. "Sitting on a stump in my yard, watching cops park on the wrong side of the street. What're you up to, Ben?"

Instead of answering, the policeman looked hard at his friend. They were both in their late twenties; the man in the car stocky and dark with a close-cropped mustache; Lorne slender, his hair sand-colored and falling across his neck brace. "Hurting, snake?" Ben asked softly.

"Shit, four years is enough to get used to anything," the thinner man said. Though Lorne's eyes were on the chime tower of the abandoned Baptist church a block down Rankin Street, his mind was lost in the far past. "You know, some nights I sit out here for a while instead of going to bed."

Three cars in quick succession threw waves of light and sound against the rows of aging houses. One blinked its high beams at the patrol car briefly, blindingly. "Bastard," Ben grumbled without real anger. "Well, back to the war against crime." His smile quirked. "Better than the last war they had us fighting, hey?"

Lorne finished his cigarette with a long drag. "Hell, I don't know, sarge. How many jobs give you a full pension after two years?"

"See you, snake."

"See you, sarge."

The big cruiser snarled as Ben pulled back into the traffic lane and turned at the first corner. The city was on a system of neighborhood police patrols, an attempt to avoid the anonymous patrolling that turned each car into a miniature search and destroy mission. The first night he sat on the stump beside his apartment, Lorne had sworn in surprise to see that the face peering from the curious patrol car was that of Ben Gresham, his squad leader during the ten months and nineteen days he had carried an M60 in War Zone C.

And that was the only past remaining to Lorne.

The back door of Jenkins' house banged shut on its spring. A few moments later heavy boots began scratching up the gravel of the common drive. Lorne's seat was an oak stump, three feet in diameter. Instead of trying to turn his head, he shifted his whole body around on the wood. Jenkins, a plumpish, half-bald man in his late sixties, lifted a pair of canned Budweisers. "Must get thirsty out here, warm as it is."

"It's always thirsty enough to drink good beer," Lorne

smiled. "I'll share my stump with you." They sipped for a time without speaking. Mrs. Purefoy, Jenkins' widowed sister and a matronly Baptist, kept house for him. Lorne gathered that while she did not forbid her brother to drink an occasional beer, neither did she provide an encouragingly social atmosphere.

"I've seen you out here at 3 AM," the older man said. "What'll you do when the weather turns cold?"

"Freeze my butt for a while," Lorne answered. He gestured his beer toward his dark apartment on the second floor of a house much like Jenkins'. "Sit up there with the light on. Hell, there's lots of VA hospitals, I've *been* in lots of them. If North Carolina isn't warm enough, maybe they'd find me one in Florida." He took another swallow and said, "I just sleep better in the daytime, is all. Too many ghosts around at night."

Jenkins turned quickly to make sure of the smile on the younger man's face. It flashed at his motion. "Not quite that sort of ghost," Lorne explained. "The ones I bring with me. . . ." And he kept his smile despite the sizzle of faces in the white fire suddenly in his mind. The noise of popping, boiling flesh faded and he went on, "There was something weird going on last night, though"—he glanced at his big Japanese wristwatch—"well, damn early this morning."

"A Halloween ghost with a white sheet?" Jenkins suggested.

"Umm, no, down at the church," said Lorne, fumbling his cigarettes out. Jenkins shrugged refusal and the dart of butane flame ignited only one. "The tower there was—I don't know, I looked at it and it seemed to be vibrating. No sound, though, and then a big red flash without any sound either. I thought sure it'd caught fire, but it was just a flash and everything was back to normal. Funny. You know how you hold your fingers over a flashlight and it comes through, kind of? Well, the flash was like that, only through a stone wall."

"I never saw anything like that," Jenkins agreed. "Old church doesn't seem the worse for it, though. It'll be ready to fall down itself before the courts get all settled about who owns it, you know."

"Umm?"

"Fellowship Baptist built a new church half a mile north of here, more parking and anyhow, it was going to cost more to repair that old firetrap than it would to build a new one." Jenkins grinned. "Mable hasn't missed a Sunday in forty years, so I heard all about it. The city bought the old lot for a boys' club or some such fool thing—I want to spit every time I think of my property taxes, I do—but it turns out the Rankins, that's who the street's named after too, they'd given the land way back before the Kaiser's War. Damn if some of them weren't still around to sue to get the lot back if it wasn't going to be a church any more. So that was last year, and it's like to be a few more before anybody puts money into tearing the old place down."

"From the way it's boarded up and padlocked, I figured it must have been a reflection I saw," Lorne admitted. "But it looked funny enough," he added sheepishly, "that I took a walk down there last night."

Jenkins shrugged and stood up. He had the fisherman's trick of dropping the pull tab into his beer before drinking any. Now it rattled in the bottom. "Well," he said, picking up Lorne's can as well, "it's bed time for me, I suppose. You better get yourself off soon or the bugs'll carry you away."

"Thanks for the beer and the company," Lorne said. "One of these nights I'll bring down an ice chest and we'll really tie one on."

Lorne's ears followed the old man back, his boots a friendly, even sound in the warm April darkness. A touch of breeze caught the wisteria hedge across the street and spread its sweetness, diluted, over Lorne. He ground out his cigarette and sat quietly, letting the vines breathe on him. Jenkins' garbage can scrunched open and one of the empties echoed into it. The other did not fall. "What the hell?" Lorne wondered aloud. But there was something about the night, despite its urban innocence, that brought up memories from past years more strongly than ever before. In a little while Lorne began walking. He was still walking when dawn washed the fiery pictures from his mind and he returned to his apartment to find three police cars parked in the street.

The two other tenants stored their cars in the side yard of the apartment house. Lorne had stepped between them when he heard a woman scream, "That's him! Don't let him get away!"

Lorne turned. White-haired Mrs. Purefoy and a pair of uniformed policemen faced him from the porch of Jenkins' house. The younger man had his revolver half drawn. A third uniformed man, Ben, stepped quickly around from the back of the house. "I'm not going anywhere but to bed," Lorne said, spreading his empty hands. He began walking toward the others. "Look, what's the matter?"

The oldest, heaviest of the policemen took the porch

steps in a leap and approached Lorne at a barely-restrained trot. He had major's pips on his shoulder straps. "Where have you been, snake?" Ben asked, but the major was between them instantly, growling, "I'll handle this, Gresham. Mr. Charles Lorne?"

"Yes," Lorne whispered. His body flashed hot, as though the fat policeman were a fire, a towering sheet of orange rippling with the speckles of tracers cooking off. . . .

". . . and at any time during the questioning you may withdraw your consent and thereafter remain silent. Do you understand, Mr. Lorne?"

"Yes."

"Did you see Mr. Jenkins tonight?"

"Uh-huh. He came out—when did you leave me, Ben? 10:30?" Lorne paused to light another cigarette. His flame wavered like the blade of a kris. "We each drank a beer, shot the bull. That's all. What happened?"

"Where did you last see Mr. Jenkins?"

Lorne gestured. "I was on the stump. He walked around the back of the house—his house. I guess I could see him. Anyway, I heard him throw the cans in the trash and . . . that's all."

"Both cans?" Ben broke in despite his commander's scowl.

"No, you're right—just one. And I didn't hear the door close. It's got a spring that slams it like a one-oh-five going off, usually. Look, what happened?"

There was a pause. Ben tugged at a corner of his mustache. Low sunlight sprayed Lorne through the trees. Standing, he looked taller than his six feet, a knobbly staff of a man in wheat jeans and a green-dyed T-shirt. The shirt had begun to disintegrate in the years since it was issued to him on the way to the war zone. The brace was baby-flesh pink. It made him look incongruously bull-necked, alien.

"He could have changed clothes," suggested the young patrolman. He had holstered his weapon but continued to toy with the butt.

"He didn't," Ben snapped, the signs of his temper obvious to Lorne if not to the other policemen. "He's wearing now what he had on when I left him."

"We'll take him around back," the major suddenly decided. In convoy, Ben and the other, nervous, patrolman to either side of Lorne and the major bringing up the rear, they crossed into Jenkins' yard following the steep downslope. Mrs. Purefoy stared from the porch. Beneath her a hydrangea bush graded its blooms red on the left, blue on the right, with the carefully-tended acidity of the soil. It was a mirror for her face, ruddy toward the sun and gray with fear in shadow.

"What's the problem?" Lorne wondered aloud as he viewed the back of the house. The trash can was open but upright, its lid lying on the smooth lawn beside it. Nearby was one of the Budweiser empties. The other lay alone on the bottom of the trash can. There was no sign of Jenkins himself.

Ben's square hand indicated an arc of spatters six to eight feet high, black against the white siding. "They promised us a lab team but hell, it's blood, snake. You and me've seen enough to recognize it. Mrs. Purefoy got up at four, didn't find her brother. I saw this when I checked and. . . ." He let his voice trail off.

"No body?" Lorne asked. He had lighted a fresh cigarette. The gushing flames surrounded him.

"No."

"And Jenkins weighs what? 220?" He laughed, a sound as thin as his wrists. "You'd play hell proving a man with a broken neck ran off with him, wouldn't you?"

"Broke? Sure, we'll believe that!" gibed the nervous patrolman.

"You'll believe *me*, meatball!" Ben snarled. "He broke it and he carried me out of a fucking burning Shithook while our ammo cooked off. And by God—"

"Easy, sarge," Lorne said quietly. "If anybody needs shooting, I'll borrow a gun and do it myself."

The major flashed his scowl from one man to the other. His sudden uncertainty was as obvious as the flag pin in his lapel: Lorne was now a veteran, not an aging hippy.

"I'm an outpatient at the VA hospital," Lorne said, seeing his chance to damp the fire. "Something's fucking up some nerves and they're trying to do something about it there. Wish to hell they'd do it soon."

"Gresham," the major said, motioning Ben aside for a low-voiced exchange. The third policeman had gone red when Ben snapped at him. Now he was white, realizing his mortality for the first time in his twenty-two years.

Lorne grinned at him. "Hang loose, turtle. Neither Ben or me ever killed anybody who didn't need it worse than you do."

The boy began to tremble.

"Mr. Lorne," the major said, his tone judicious but not hostile, "we'll be getting in touch with you later. And if you recall anything, anything at all that may have bearing on Mr. Jenkins' disappearance, call us at once."

Lorne's hands nodded agreement. Ben winked as the lab van arrived, then turned away with the others.

Lorne's pain was less than usual, but his dreams awakened him in a sweat each time he dropped off to sleep. When at last he switched on the radio, the headline news was that three people besides Jenkins had disappeared during the night, all of them within five blocks of Lorne's apartment.

The air was very close, muffling the brilliance of the stars. It was Friday night and the roar of southbound traffic sounded from Donovan Avenue a block to the east. The three northbound lanes of Jones Street, the next one west of Rankin, were not yet as clotted with cars as they would be later at night, but headlights there were a nervous darting through the houses and trees whenever Lorne turned on his stump to look. Rankin Street lay quietly between, lighted at alternate blocks by blue globes of mercury vapor. It was narrow, so that cars could not pass those parked along the curb without slowing, easing; a placid island surrounded by modern pressures.

But no one had disappeared to the east of Donovan or the west of Jones.

Lorne stubbed out his cigarette in the punky wood of the stump. It was riddled with termites and sometimes he pictured them, scrabbling through the darkness. He hated insects, hated especially the grubs and hidden things, the corpse-white termites . . . but he sat on the stump above them. A perversely objective part of Lorne's mind knew that if he could have sat in the heart of a furnace like the companions of Daniel, he would have done so.

From the blocky shade of the porch next door came the creak of springs: Mrs. Purefoy, shifting her weight on the cushions of the old wing-back chair. In the early evening Lorne had caught her face staring at a parlor window, her muscles flat as wax. As the deeper darkness blurred and pooled, she had slipped out into its cover. Lorne felt her burning eyes, knowing that she would never forgive him for her brother's disappearance, not if it were proven that Jenkins had left by his own decision. Lorne had always been a sinner to her; innocence would not change that.

Another cigarette. Someone else was watching. A passing car threw Lorne's angled shadow forward and across Jenkins' house. Lorne's guts clenched and his fingers crushed the unlit cigarette. *Light. Twelve men in a rice paddy when the captured flare bursts above them. The pop-pop-pop of a gun far off, and the splashes columning around Lt. Burnes—*

"Christ!" Lorne shouted, standing with an immediacy that laced pain through his body. Something was terribly wrong in the night. The lights brought back memories, but they quenched the real threat that hid in the darkness. Lorne knew what he was feeling, *knew* that any instant a brown face would peer out of a spider hole behind an AK-47 or a mine would rip steel pellets down the trail. . . .

He stopped, forcing himself to sit down again. If it was his time, there was nothing he could do for it. A fresh cigarette fitted between his lips automatically and the needle-bright lighter focused his eyes.

And the watcher was gone.

Something had poised to kill Lorne, and had then passed on without striking. It was as unnatural as if a wall collapsing on him had separated in mid-air to leave him unharmed. Lorne's arms were trembling, his cigarette tip an orange blur. When Ben's cruiser pulled in beside him, Lorne was at first unable to answer the other man's, "Hey, snake."

"Jesus, sarge," Lorne whispered, smoke spurting from his mouth and nostrils. "There's somebody out here and he's a *bad* fucker."

Carrier noise blatted before the car radio rapped a series of numbers and street names. Ben knuckled his mustache until he was sure his own cruiser was not mentioned. "Yeah, he's a bad one. Another one gone tonight, a little girl from three blocks down. Went to the store to trade six empties and a dime on a coke. Christ, I saw her two hours ago, snake. The bottles we found, the kid we didn't. . . . Seen any little girls?"

There was an upright shadow in front of Ben's radio: a riot gun, clipped to the dashboard. "Haven't seen anything but cars, sarge. Lots of police cars."

"They've got an extra ten men on," Ben agreed with a nod. "We went over the old Baptist church a few minutes ago. Great TAC Squad work. Nothing. Damn locks were rusted shut."

"Think the Baptists've taken up with baby sacrifice?" Lorne chuckled.

"Shit, there's five bodies somewhere. If the bastard's loading them in the back of a truck, you'd think he'd spread his pickups over a bit more of an area, wouldn't you?"

"Look, baby, anybody who packed Jenkins around on his back—I sure don't want to meet him."

"Don't guess Jenkins did either," Ben grunted. "Or the others."

"PD to D-5," the radio interrupted.

Ben keyed his microphone. "Go ahead."

"10-25 Lt. Cooper at Rankin and Duke."

"10-4, 10-76," Ben replied, starting to return the mike to its holder.

"D-5, acknowledge," the receiver ordered testily.

"Goddam fucker!" Ben snarled, banging the instrument down. "Sends just about half the fucking time!"

"Keep a low profile, sarge," Lorne murmured, but even had he screamed his words would have been lost in the boom of exhaust as Ben cramped the car around in the street, the left wheels bumping over the far curb. Then the accelerator flattened and the big car shot toward the rendezvous.

In Viet Nam, Lorne had kept his death wish under control during shelling by digging in and keeping his head down. Now he stood and went inside to his room. After a time, he slept. If his dreams were bright and tortured, then they always were. . . .

"Sure, you knew Jackson," Ben explained, the poom-poom-poom of his engine a live thing in the night. "He's the blond shit who . . . didn't believe you'd broken your neck. Yesterday morning."

"Small loss, then," Lorne grinned. "But you watch your own ass, hear? If there's nobody out but cops, there's going to be more cops than just Jackson disappearing."

"Cops and damned fools," Ben grumbled. "When I didn't see you out here on my first pass, I thought maybe you'd gotten sense enough to stay inside."

"I was going to. Decided . . . oh, hell. What's the box score now?"

"Seven gone. Seven for sure," the patrolman corrected himself. "One got grabbed in the time he took to walk from his girl's front porch back to his car. That bastard's lucky, but he's crazy as hell if he thinks he'll stay that lucky."

"He's crazy as hell," Lorne agreed. A spring whispered from Jenkins' porch and Lorne bobbed the tip of his cigarette at the noise. "She's not doing so good either. All last night she was staring at me, and now she's at it again."

"Christ," Ben muttered. "Yeah, Major Hooseman talked to her this morning. You're about the baddest man ever, leading po' George into smoking and drinking and late hours before you killed him."

"Never did get him to smoke," Lorne said, lighting Ben's cigarette and another for himself. "Say, did Jackson smoke?"

"Huh? No." Ben frowned, staring at the closed passenger-side windows and their reflections of his instruments. "Yeah, come to think, he did. But never in uniform, he had some sort of thing about that."

"He sheered off last night when I lit a cigarette," Lorne said. "No, not Jackson—the other one. I just wondered. . . ."

"You saw him?" Ben's voice was suddenly sharp, the hunter scenting prey.

Lorne shook his head. "I just felt him. But he was there, baby."

"Just like before they shot us down," the policeman said quietly. "You squeezing my arm and shouting over the damn engines, 'They're waiting for us, they're waiting for us!' And not a fucking thing I could do—I didn't order the assault and the Captain sure wasn't going to call it off because my machinegunner said to. But you were right, snake."

"The flames . . ." Lorne whispered, his eyes unfocused.

"And you're a dumb bastard to have done it, but you carried me out of them. It never helped us a bit that you knew when the shit was about to hit the fan. But you're a damn good man to have along when it does."

Lorne's muscles trembled with memory. Then he stood and laughed into the night. "You know, sarge, in twenty-seven years I've only found one job I was any good at. I didn't much like that one, and anyhow—the world doesn't seem to need killers."

"They'll always need us, snake," Ben said quietly. "Some times they won't admit it." Then, "Well, I think I'll waste some more gas."

"Sarge—" The word hung in the empty darkness. There was engine noise and the tires hissing in the near distance and—nothing else. "Sarge, Mrs. Purefoy was on her porch a minute ago and she didn't go inside. But she's not there now."

Ben's five-cell flashlight slid its narrow beam across the porch: the glider, the wing-back chair. On the far railing, a row of potted violets with a gap for the one now spilled on the boards as if by someone vaulting the rail but dragging one heel. . . .

"Didn't hear it fall," the policeman muttered, clacking open the car door. The dome light spilled a startling yellow pool across the two men. As it did so, white motion trembled half a block down Rankin Street.

"Fucker!" Ben said. "He couldn't jump across the street, he threw something so it flashed." Ben was back in the car.

Lorne squinted, furious at being blinded at the critical instant. "Sarge, I'll swear to God he headed for the church." Lorne strode stiffly around the front of the vehicle and got in on the passenger side.

"Mother-*fuck*!" the stocky policeman snarled, dropping the microphone that had three times failed to get him a response. He reached for the shift lever, looked suddenly at Lorne as the slender man unclipped the shotgun. "Where d'ye think *you're* going?"

"With you."

Ben slipped the transmission into Drive and hung a shrieking U-turn in the empty street. "The first one's birdshot, the next four are double-ought buck," he said flatly.

Lorne jacked the slide twice, chambering the first round and then shucking it out the ejector. It gleamed palely in the instrument light. "Don't think we're going after birds," he explained.

Ben twisted across the street and bounced over the driveway cut. The car slammed to a halt in the small lot behind and shielded by the bulk of the old church. It was a high, narrow building with two levels of boarded windows the length of the east and west sides; the square tower stood at the south end. At some time after its construction, the church had been faced with artificial stone. It was dingy, a gray mass in the night with a darkness about it that the night alone did not explain.

Ben slid out of the car. His flash touched the small door to the right of the tower. "Nothing wrong with the padlock," Lorne said. It was a formidable one, set in a patinaed hasp to close the church against vandals and derelicts.

"They were all locked tight yesterday, too," the patrolman said. "He could still be getting in one of those windows. We'll see." He turned to the trunk of the car and opened it, holding his flashlight in the crook of his arm so his right hand could be free for his drawn revolver.

Lorne's quick eyes scanned the wall above them. He bent back at the waist instead of tilting his head alone. "Got the key?" he asked.

The stocky man chuckled, raising a pair of folding shovels, army surplus entrenching tools. "Keep that corn-sheller ready," he directed, holstering his own weapon. He locked the blade of one shovel at 90 degrees to the shaft and set it on top of the padlock. The other, still folded, cracked loudly against the head of the first and popped the lock open neatly. "Field expedients, snake," Ben laughed. "If we don't find anything, we can just shut the place up again and nobody'll know the difference."

He tossed the shovels aside and swung open the door. The air that puffed out had the expected mustiness of a long-closed structure with a sweetish overtone that neither man could have identified. Lorne glanced around the outside once more, then followed the patrolman within. The flames in his mind were very close.

"Looks about like it did last night," Ben said.

"And last year, I'd guess." The wavering oval of the flashlight picked over the floor. The hardwood was warping, pocked at frequent intervals by holes.

"They unbolted the old pews when they moved," Ben explained. "Took the stained glass too, since the place was going to be torn down."

The nave was a single narrow room running from the chancel in the north to the tower which had held the organ pipes and, above, the chimes. The main entrance was by a side aisle, through double doors in the middle of the west wall. The interior looked a gutted ruin.

"You checked the whole building?" Lorne asked. The pulpit had been ripped away. The chancel rail remained though half-splintered, apparently to pass the organ and altar. Fragments of wood, crumpled boxes, and glass littered the big room.

"The main part. We didn't have the key to the tower and the major didn't want to bust in." Ben took another step into the nave and kicked at a stack of old bulletins.

White heat, white fire— "Ben, did you check the ceiling when you were here last night?"

"Huh?" The narrow Gothic vault was blackness forty feet above the ground. Ben's flashlight knifed upward across painted plaster to the ribbed and paneled ceiling that sloped to the main beam. And—"Jesus!"

A large cocoon was tight against the roof peak. It shimmered palely azure, but the powerful light thrust through to the human outline within. Long shadows quivered on the wood, magnifying the trembling of the policeman's wrist as the beam moved from the cocoon to another beside it, to the third—

"Seven of the fuckers!" Ben cried, taking another step and slashing the light to the near end of the room where the south wall closed the inverted V of the ceiling. Above the door to the tower was the baize screen of the pipe loft. The cloth fluttered behind Mrs. Purefoy, who stood stiffly upright twenty feet in the air. Her face was locked in horror, framed by her tousled white hair. Both arms were slightly extended but were stone-rigid within the lace-fringed sleeves of her dress.

"She—" Lorne began, but as he spoke and Ben's hand fell to the butt of his revolver, Mrs. Purefoy began to fall, tilting a little in a rustle of skirts. Beneath the crumpled edge of the baize curtain, spiked on the beam of Ben's flashlight, gleamed the head and fore-claws of what had been clutching the woman.

The eyes glared like six-inch opals, fierce and hot in a dead white exoskeleton. The foreclaws clicked sideways. As though they had cocked a spring, the whole flat torso shot down at Ben.

An inch long and scuttling under a rock it might have passed for a scorpion, but this lunging monster was six feet long without counting the length of the tail arced back across its body. Flashing legs, flashing body armor, and the fluid-jeweled sting that winked as Lorne's finger twitched in its killer's reflex—

Lorne's body screamed at the recoil of the heavy charge. The creature spun as if kicked in mid-air, smashing into the floor a yard from Ben instead of on top of the policeman. The revolver blasted, a huge yellow bottle-shape flaring from the muzzle. The bullet ripped away a window shutter because a six-inch pincer had locked Ben's wrist. The creature reared onto the back two pairs of its eight jointed legs. Lorne stepped sideways for a clear shot, the slide of his weapon slick-snacking another round into the chamber. On the creature's white belly was a smeared, multi-brancate star—the load of buckshot had ricochetted off, leaving a trail like wax on glass.

Ben clubbed his flashlight. It cracked harmlessly between the glowing eyes and sprang from his hand. The other claw flashed to Ben's face and trapped it, not crushingly but hard enough to immobilize and start blood-trails down both cheeks. The blades of the pincer ran from nose to hairline on each side.

Lorne thrust his shotgun over Ben's right shoulder and fired point blank. The creature rocked back, jerking a scream from the policeman as the claws tightened. The lead struck the huge left eye and splashed away, dulling the opal shine. The flashlight still glaring from the floor behind the creature silhouetted its sectioned tail as it arched above the policeman's head. The armed tip plunged into the base of his neck. Ben stiffened.

Lorne shouted and emptied his shotgun. The second dense red bloom caught like a strobe light the dotted line of blood droplets joining Ben's neck to the withdrawn injector. A claw seized Lorne's waist in the rolling echo of the shotgun blasts. His gunbutt cracked on the creature's armor, steel sparking as it slid off. The extending pincer brushed the shotgun aside and clamped over Lorne's face, half-shielding from him the sight of the rising sting.

Then it smashed on Lorne's neck brace, and darkness exploded over him in a flare of coruscant pain.

The oozing ruin of Mrs. Purefoy's face stared at Lorne through its remaining eye when he awoke. Everything swam in blue darkness except for one bright blur. He blinked and the blur suddenly resolved into a street-light glaring up through a shattered board. Lorne's lungs burned and his stiffness seemed more than even unconsciousness and the pain skidding through his nerve paths could explain. He moved his arm and something clung to its surface; the world quivered.

Lorne was hanging from the roof of the church in a thin, transparent sheath. Mrs. Purefoy was a yard away, multiple wrappings shrouding her corpse more completely. With a strength not far from panic, Lorne forced his right fist into the bubble around him. The material, extruded in broad swathes by the creature rather than as a loom of threads, sagged but did not tear. The clear azure turned milky under stress and sucked in around Lorne's wrist.

He withdrew his hand. The membrane passed some oxygen but not enough for an active man. Lorne's hands patted the outside of his pockets finding, as he had expected, nothing with a sharp edge. He had not recently bitten off his thumbnails. Thrusting against the fire in his chest, he brought his left hand in front of his body. With a fold of the cocoon between each thumb and index finger, he thrust his hands apart. A rip started in the white opacity beneath his right thumb. Air, clean and cool, jetted in.

"Oh, Jesus," Lorne muttered, even the pain in his body forgotten as he widened the tear upwards to his face. The cocoon was bobbing on a short lead, rotating as the rip changed its balance. Lorne could see that he had become ninth in the line of hanging bodies, saved from their paralysis by the chance of his neck brace. Ben, his face blurred by the membrane holding him next to Lorne, had been less fortunate.

Ten yards from where Lorne hung and twenty feet below the roof beam, the baize curtain of the pipe loft twitched. Lorne froze in fearful immobility.

The creature had been able to leap the width of

a street carrying the weight of an adult; its strength must be as awesome as was the rigidity of its armor. Whether or not it could drive its sting through Lorne's brace, it could assuredly rip him to collops if it realized he was awake.

The curtain moved again, the narrow ivory tip of a pincer lifting it slightly. The creature was watching Lorne.

Ben carried three armor-piercing rounds in his .357 Magnum for punching through car doors. Lorne tried to remember whether the revolver had remained in Ben's hand as he fell. There was no image of that in Lorne's mind, only the torchlike muzzle blasts of his own shotgun. Slim as it was, his only hope was that the jacketed bullets would penetrate the creature's exoskeleton though the soft buckshot had not.

Lorne twisted his upper torso out of the hole for a closer look at Ben, making his own cocoon rock angrily. The baize lifted further. The street light lay across it in a pale band. Why didn't the creature scuttle out to finish the business?

Brief motion waked a flash of scintillant color from the pipe loft. The curtain flapped closed as if a volley of shots had ripped through it. Lorne recognized the reflex: the panic of a spider when a stick thrusts through its web. Not an object, though; the light itself, weak as it was, had slapped the creature back. Ben's bright flashlight had not stopped it when necessity drove, but the monster must have felt pain at human levels of illumination. Its eyes were adapted to starlight or the glow of a sun immeasurably fainter than that of Earth. "Where did you come from, you bastard?" Lorne whispered.

Light. It gave him an idea and he fumbled out his butane lighter, adjusting it to a maximum flame. The sheathes were relatively thin over the victims' faces to aid transpiration. At the waist, though, where a bulge showed Ben's arm locked to his torso, the membrane was thick enough to be opaque in the dim light. Lorne bent dangerously over, cursing the stiffness of his neck brace. Holding the inch-high jet close, he tried to peer through Ben's cocoon. Unexpectedly the fabric gave a little and Lorne bobbed forward, bringing the flame in contact with the material sheathing Ben.

The membrane sputtered, kissing Lorne's hand painfully. He jerked back and the lighter flicked away. It dropped, cold and silent until it cracked on the floor forty feet below. Despite the pattern of light over it, the curtain to the loft was shifting again. Lorne cursed in terror.

A line of green fire sizzled up the side of Ben's cocoon from the point at which the flame had touched it. The material across his face flared. The policeman gave no sign of feeling his skin curl away. The revolver in his hand winked green.

Lorne screamed. His own flexible prison lurched and sagged like heated polyethylene. Ben was wrapped in a cancerous hell that roared and heaved against the roofbeams as a live thing. Green tongues licked yellow-orange flames from the dry wood as well. Lorne's cocoon and that to the other side of Ben were deforming in the furnace heat. Another lurch and Lorne had slipped twenty feet, still gripped around the waist in a sack of blue membrane. He was gyrating like a top. The loft curtain had twitched higher each time it spun past his vision.

The bottom of Ben's cocoon burned away and he plunged past Lorne, face upward and still afire. Bone crunched as he hit. The body rebounded a few inches to fall again on its face. The roar of the flames muffled Lorne's wail of rage. His own elongated capsule began to flow. Flames grasped at Lorne's support. Before they could touch the sheathing, the membrane pulled a last few inches and snapped like an overstretched rubber band. The impact of the floor smashed Lorne's jaw against his neck brace, grinding each tortured vertebra against the next. He did not lose consciousness, but the shock paralyzed him momentarily as thoroughly as the creature's sting could have done.

Bathed in green light and the orange of the blazing roof panels, the scorpion-thing thrust its thorax into the nave. Its walking legs gripped the flat surface, dimpling the plaster. The creature turned upward toward the fire, three more cocoons alight and their hungry flames lapping across the beams. Then, particolored by the illumination, its legs shifted and the opal eyes trained on Lorne. The light must be torture to it, muffling in indecision its responses, but it was about to act.

A small form wrapped in a flaming shroud dropped to thump the floor beside Lorne. His arms would move again. He used them to strip the remaining sheathing from his legs. It clung as the heat of the burning corpse began to melt the material. Something writhed from a crackling tumor on the child's neck. The thing was finger-long and seemed to paw the air with a score of tiny legs; its opalescent eyes proved its parentage. The creature brought more than paralysis to its victims: it was a gravid female.

Green flame touched the larva. It burst in a pustulent smear.

The adult went mad. Its legs shot it almost the length of the nave to rebound from a sidewall in a cloud of plaster. The creature's horizontally-flattened tail ruddered it instinctively short of the fire as it leapt upward to the roof peak. It clung there in pale horror against the wood, eyes on the advancing flames. Three more bodies fell, splashing like ginko fruits.

Lorne staggered upright. The fire hammered down at him without bringing pain. His body had no feeling whatever. Ben's hair had burned. His neck and scalp were black where skin remained, red where it had cracked open to the muscle beneath. The marbled background showed clearly the tiny, pallid hatchling trying to twist across it.

Lorne's toe brushed the larva onto the floor. His boot heel struck it, struck again and twisted. Purulent ichor spurted between the leather and the boards. Lorne knelt. In one motion he swung Ben across his shoulders and stood, just as he had after their helicopter had nosed into the trees and exploded. Logic had been burned out of Lorne's mind, leaving only a memory of friendship. He did not look up. As his mechanical steps took him and his burden through the door they had entered, a shadow wavered across them. The creature had sprung back into the loft.

Lorne stumbled to his knees in the parking lot. The church had been rotten and dry. Orange flames fluffed through the roof in several places, thrusting corkscrews of sparks into the night sky. Twelve feet of roof slates thundered into the nave. Flame spewed up like a secondary explosion. There were sirens in the night.

Without warning, the east facade of the tower collapsed into the parking lot. Head-sized chunks of Tennessee-stone smashed at the patrol car, one of them missing Lorne by inches. He looked up, blank-eyed, his hands lightly touching the corpse of his friend. Of its own volition, the right hand traced down Ben's shoulder to the raw flesh of his elbow. The tower stairs spiraled out of the dust and rubble, laid bare to the steel framework when the wall fell. On the sagging floor of the pipe loft rested a machine like no other thing on Earth, and the creature was inside it. Tubes of silvery metal rose cradleform from a base of similar metal. The interstices were not filled with anything material, but the atmosphere seemed to shiver, blurring the creature's outline.

And Lorne's hand was unwrapping Ben's stiff fingers from the grips of his revolver.

Lorne stood again, his left hand locking his right on the butt of the big magnum. He was familiar with the weapon: it was the one Ben had carried in Nam, the same tool he had used for five of his thirteen kills. It would kill again tonight.

Even in the soaring holocaust the sharp crack of Lorne's shot was audible. Lorne's forearms rocked up as a unit with the recoiling handgun. The creature lurched sideways to touch the shimmering construct around it. A red surface discharge rippled across the exoskeleton from the point of contact. Lorne fired again. He could see the armor dull at his point of aim in the center of the thorax. Again the creature jumped. Neither bullet had penetrated, but the splashing lead of the second cut an upright from the machine. The creature spun, extending previously-unglimpsed tendrils from the region of its mouth parts. They flickered over a control plate in the base. Machinery chimed in response.

The shivering quickened. The machine itself and the thing it enclosed seemed to fade. Lorne thumb-cocked the magnum, lowered the red vertical of the front sight until it was even with the rear notch; the creature was a white blur beyond them. The gun bucked back hard when he squeezed; the muzzle blast was sharper, flatter, than before. The first of the armor-piercing bullets hit the creature between the paired tendrils. The exoskeleton surrounding them shattered like safety glass struck by a brick.

The creature straightened in silent agony, rising onto its hind legs with its tail lying rigidly against its back. Its ovipositor was fully extended, thumb-thick and six inches long.

"Was it fun to kill them, bug?" Lorne screamed. "Was it as much fun as this is?" His fourth shot slammed, dimpling a belly plate which then burst outward in an ugly gush of fluids. The creature's members clamped tightly about its spasming thorax. The tail lashed the uprights in red spurts. The machine was fading and the torn panelling of the loft was beginning to show through the dying creature's body.

There was one shot left in the cylinder and Lorne steadied his sights on the control plate. He had already begun taking up the last pressure when he stopped and lowered the muzzle. No, let it go home, whatever place or time that might be. Let its fellows see that Earth was not their hunting ground alone. And if they came back anyway—*if they only would!*

There was a flash as penetrating as the first micro-second of a nuclear blast. The implosion dragged Lorne off his feet and sucked in the flames so suddenly that all sound seemed frozen. Then both side-walls collapsed into the nave and the ruins of the tower twisted down on top of them. In the last instant, the pipe loft was empty of all but memory.

A fire truck picked its way through the rubble in the parking lot. Its headlights flooded across the figure of a sandy-haired man wearing scorched clothing and a neck brace. He was kneeling beside a body, and the tears were bright on his face.

—————————*End note to* The Hunting Ground

I attended Duke Law School in 1967–9, and 1971–2, graduating in 1972. While I was at Duke my wife and I lived on Watts Street in Durham, NC, in a house which had been split into three furnished apartments.

The two year gap in my law school attendance was filled by the US Army, culminating with a motorized tour of Viet Nam and Cambodia. You could say this contributed to my education in other fashions.

In 1975 Ramsey Campbell asked me for a story for the horror anthology he was editing. I wrote "The Hunting Ground," setting it on Watts Street where I'd lived. Lorne isn't me. But he's not *not me* either, if you see what I mean.

The veterans will understand.

THE FALSE PROPHET _____

The big young man, grinning at Dama through the doorway of the City Prefect's private office, had the look of a killer.

Dama knew the fellow's name, Lucius Vettius—and knew that he was an officer in the imperial guard, though at the moment he wore a civilian toga.

Dama smiled back.

"The virtuous Marcus Licinius Dama!" bellowed the nomenclator in a strong Syrian accent. Why couldn't Gaius Rutilius Rutilianus—who was, by Mithra, City Prefect of Rome—buy servants who at least pronounced Latin properly?

"He didn't mention that you're only a merchant!" Menelaus whispered to Dama in amazement.

"No, he didn't," Dama agreed without amplifying his response.

The nomenclator was wearing a new tunic. So was the doorkeeper who'd let Dama and his older companion into Rutilianus's reception room with a crowd of over a hundred other favor-seekers. The tunics were best-quality Egyptian linen and represented a hefty outlay—

Even to Dama, who imported them along with the silks which were his primary stock in trade.

"His companion," cried the nomenclator, "the learned Faustus Pompeius Menelaus!" The nomenclator paused. "Known as 'The Wise.'"

Menelaus suddenly looked ten years younger. He straightened to his full height and fluffed his long gray beard.

Though Dama said nothing as the pair of them stepped into Rutilianus's private office, the nomenclator had earned himself a bonus by the degree to which his ad-libbed comment had brightened the old man's face.

Menelaus and Dama's father had remained friends throughout the latter's life. Dama stopped visiting his parent when disease and pain so wracked the older man that every conversation became a litany of insult and complaint; but Menelaus continued to come, to read aloud and to bear bitter insults because to do so was a philosopher's duty—and a friend's.

"Well, he sure looks the part, doesn't he?" quipped Caelius, one of the four civilians standing around the Prefect's couch. "Got any owls nesting in that beard, old man?"

"Looking the part's easy enough," countered Vulco. "If you want a philosopher of *real* learning, though, you'll hire Pactolides."

"I think it's unchristian to be hiring *any* sort of pagan philosopher," said Macer. "Severiana won't like it a bit."

"My wife doesn't make the decisions in *this* house,"

the Prefect said so forcefully that everyone listening knew that Rutilianus was as much voicing a wish as stating a fact.

The Prefect shifted his heavy body on the couch and scratched himself. Though the morning air was comfortable by most standards, Rutilianus was sweating despite having dispensed with the formality of his toga while handling this private interview.

The men were the Prefect's friends, advisors, and employees—and wore all those separate masks at the same time. Except for Vettius (who was about Dama's age), they'd accompanied Rutilianus during his governorships in Spain and North Africa. They carried out important commissions, gave confidential advice—and picked up the bits and scraps which form the perquisites of those having the ear of high office.

"Anyway," offered Sosius, "I don't think that there's anything sinful about hearing advice on living a good life, even if it does come from a pagan."

For what Dama had paid Sosius, he'd expected more enthusiastic support. Pactolides was getting much better value for his bribe to Vulco.

"Well, let's hear what he says for himself," the Prefect said, still peevish at the mention of his wife. He nodded toward Menelaus. "You *can* speak, can't you?" he demanded. "Not much use in having a personal philosopher who can't, is there?"

"Pactolides can speak like an angel," muttered Vulco. "Voice like a choirboy, that man has. . . ."

Dama prompted his friend with a tap on the shoulder. Menelaus stepped forward and bowed. "If ever there was a man who was rightly afraid when called to speak in your presence, noble Rutilianus," the old philosopher boomed, "it is I; and I sense—" he made a light, sweeping bow to the Prefect's companions "—that those who participate in your counsels are well able to see my distress."

Menelaus was a different man as soon as he began his set oration—confident, commanding; his tones and volume pitched to blast through the chatter filling a rain-crowded basilica when he addressed his students in one corner. Dama had worried that the old man's desperate need for a job would cause him to freeze up when the opportunity was offered. He should have known better.

"—for my heart is filled with the awareness of the way you, armed like Mars himself, preserved the liberty of this Republic; and now, wearing the toga, increase its civil glory. For—"

The soldier, Vettius, crooked a finger toward Dama and nodded in the direction of the garden behind the office.

Rutilianus's other councilors looked bored—Vulco was yawning ostentatiously—but the Prefect himself listened to the panegyric with pleasure. He nodded with unconscious agreement while Menelaus continued, "—while all those who have borne the burden of your exalted prefecture are to be praised, to you especially is honor due."

Vettius, waiting at the door into the garden, crooked his finger again. Dama pursed his lips and followed, walking with small steps to disturb the gathering as little as possible—though Menelaus in full cry couldn't have been put off his stride by someone shouting *Fire!* and the Prefect was rapt at the mellifluous description of his virtues.

The garden behind Rutilianus's house had a covered

walk on three sides, providing shade at all times of
the day. The open area was large enough to hold a
dozen fruit trees as well as a small grape arbor and a
variety of roses, exotic peonies, and other flowers.

Military equipment was stacked beside the door: a
bronze helmet and body armor modeled with ideal-
ized muscles over which a pair of naiads cavorted; a
swordbelt supporting the sheathed dagger and long,
straight-bladed spatha of a cavalryman; and a large,
circular shield in its canvas cover.

Vettius followed Dama's eyes toward the gear and
volunteered, "I'm army—seconded to the City Prefect
for the time being."

There were two ways for Dama to handle his
response. He made the snap decision that concealing
his knowledge from this big, hard-eyed soldier couldn't
bring any dividends equal to getting the man's respect
from the start.

"Yes," he said. "A decurion in the squadron of
Domestic Horse."

Vettius was surprised enough to glance sideways to
make sure that canvas still covered the gilt spikes and
hearts against the blue background of his shieldface.
"Right, that's me," he agreed mildly. "The Prefect's
bodyguard, more or less. The name's Lucius Vettius—as
I suppose you knew."

There was no question in the final clause, but
Dama nodded his agreement anyway. He'd done his
homework—as he always did his homework before a
major sale.

This business, because it was personal and not
merely a matter of money, was the most major sale
of his life. . . .

"Let me hope," rolled Menelaus's voice through the open door and window of the office, "that my words today can be touched by a fraction of the felicity with which all Rome greeted the news that you had been appointed her helmsman."

"I was wondering," Vettius said, "just how much you'd paid Sosius?"

Dama prodded the inside of his cheek with his tongue.

"The reason I'm wondering," the soldier continued, "is that he's taking money from Pactolides too." He laughed. "Vulco's an unusually virtuous councilor, you know."

Dama grimaced bitterly. "Yeah," he agreed. "Vulco stays bought."

"My words are driven out under the compulsion of the virtue and benignity which I see before me . . ." Menelaus continued in an orotund voice.

"I hadn't thought," continued Dama, choosing his words carefully, "that a decurion was worth bribing. Until now that I've met you."

"I'd have taken your money," Vettius said with the same cold smile as before. "But it wouldn't've gained you anything. What I'd really like from you, Citizen Dama . . ."

Dama nodded his head upward in agreement. "Go ahead," he said.

If not money, then a woman? A *particular* woman to whom a silk merchant might have access . . . ?

". . . is information." The flat certainty with which the words came out of Vettius's mouth emphasized the size and strength of the man speaking. He had black hair and spoke with a slight tang of the Illyrian frontier.

"Go ahead," Dama repeated with outward calm.

From the office came, ". . . though I fear that by mentioning any particular excellence first, I will seem to devalue. . . ."

"I can see why the old man wants to be Rutilianus's tame philosopher," Vettius said. "It's getting harder and harder to scrape up enough pupils freelance to keep him in bread, onions, and a sop of wine. . . ."

Dama nodded.

"Thing is, I'm not quite clear what *your* part in the business might be, Citizen."

This time the soldier's smile made Dama measure in his mind the distance between him and the hilt of the sword resting against the wall. Too far, almost certainly.

And unnecessary. Almost certainly.

"Menelaus was a friend of my father's," Dama said. "A good friend. Toward the last, my father's only friend. Menelaus is too proud to take charity from me directly— but he was glad to have me stand beside him while he sought this position in the Prefect's household."

Vettius chuckled. "Stand beside him," he repeated ironically. "With a purse full of silver you hand out to anybody who might ease your buddy's road."

". . . speak of the River Tagus, red with the blood of the bandits you as Governor slaughtered there?"

"He doesn't know that," snapped Dama.

"But you do, merchant," the soldier said. "You take your family duties pretty seriously, don't you?"

"Yeah, I do," agreed Dama as simply as if he didn't know he was being mocked . . . and perhaps he was not being mocked. "Menelaus is my friend as well as my duty, but—I take all my duties seriously."

The big man smiled; this time, for a change, it gave his face a pleasant cast. "Yeah," he said. "So do I."

"I can see that," Dama agreed, feeling his body relax for the first time since his interview with this big, deadly man began. "And it's your duty to guard Rutilianus."

"More a matter of keeping things from hitting the Prefect from somewhere he's not looking," Vettius said with a shrug. "So I like to know the people who're getting close to him."

He grinned. "Usually I don't much like what I learn. Usually."

Dama nodded toward the office, where Menelaus's measured periods had broken up into the general babble of all those in the room. "I think we'd better get back," he said. "I'm glad to have met you, Lucius Vettius."

And meant it.

The Prefect called, "Ah, Vettius," craning his neck to see over his shoulder as Dama and the soldier reentered the room. "We rather like Menelaus here, don't we, gentlemen?"

Yesyes/Wellspoken indeed/Seems solid for a pagan—

"Well, being able to spout a set speech doesn't make him learned, sir," crabbed Vulco.

He fixed Menelaus with a glare meant to be steely. Vulco's head was offset so that only one eye bore, making him look rather like an angry crow.

"Tell me, sirrah," he demanded, "who was it that Thersites fed his sons to? Quick, now—no running around to sort through your books."

The philosopher blinked in confusion. Dama thought for a moment that his friend had been caught out, but Menelaus said, "Good sir, Atreus it was who murdered the sons of his brother Thyestes and cooked them for their father."

Dama suppressed a laugh. Menelaus had paused in order to find a way to answer the question without making his questioner look *too* much of a fool.

Vulco blinked. "Well, that seems all right," he muttered, fixing his eyes on his hands and seeming to examine his manicure.

"Yes, well," Rutilianus agreed. "But you, Lucius Vettius. What information do *you* have for us?"

Everyone else in the room looked at the tall soldier: Menelaus in surprise, the Prefect and his companions with a partially-concealed avidity for scandal; Dama with a professionally-blank expression, waiting to hear what was said before he decided how to deal with anything that needed to be countered.

Vettius glanced at Dama. "I'd suggested to his excellency," he said, "that he let me see what I could learn about the learned Menelaus."

"Of course," Rutilianus agreed, lifting his eyebrows. "After all, we need to be sure of the man who's going to be responsible for the moral training of my children."

His companions bobbed and muttered approval.

Vettius took a bi-fold notebook of waxed boards from the wallet in the bosom of his toga, but he didn't bother to open the document before he said, "Menelaus comes from Caesarea in Cappadocia where his father was one of the city councilors."

Like Dama's father.

"Was schooled in Gaza, then Athens. Returned home and taught there for most of his life. Moved to Rome about five years ago. Gives lessons in oratory and philosophy—"

"Epicurean philosophy," the subject of the discussion broke in before Dama could shush him.

"Epicurean philosophy," Vettius continued, giving Dama—rather than Menelaus—a grin that was not entirely friendly. "In the Forum of Trajan; to about a dozen pupils at any one time. Doesn't get along particularly well with the other teachers who've set up in the same area. For the past three months, he's been attacking one Pyrrhus the Prophet in his lectures, but the two haven't met face to face."

Dama was ready this time. His finger tapped Menelaus's shoulder firmly, even as the older man opened his mouth to violently—and needlessly—state his opinion of Pyrrhus.

"Well, we *know* he's a philosopher!" Caelius said. "What about his personal life?"

"He doesn't have much personal life," Vettius said. He betrayed his annoyance with a thinning of tone so slight that only Dama, of those in the office, heard and understood it. "When he's a little ahead, he buys used books. When he's behind—"

Menelaus winced and examined the floor.

"—which is usually, and now, he pawns them. Stays out of wineshops. Every few months or so he visits a whore named Drome who works the alleys behind the Beef Market.

"These aren't," Vettius added dryly, "expensive transactions."

Dama looked at the philosopher in amazement. Menelaus met his gaze sidelong and muttered, "Ah, Dama, I—thought that when I grew older, some impediments to a calm mind would cease to intrude on my life. But I'm not as old as that yet, I'm ashamed to admit."

Macer opened his mouth as if about to say something. Lucius Vettius turned toward the man and— tapped his notebook, Dama thought, with the index finger of his left hand.

Dama thought the soldier's gesture might be only an idle tic; but Macer understood something by it. The councilor's eyes bulged, and his mouth shut with an audible clop.

"Last year," Vettius continued calmly, "Menelaus moved out of his garret apartment at night, stiffing his landlord for the eight-days' rent."

"Sir!" the philosopher blurted in outrage despite Dama's restraining hand. "When I moved there in the spring, I was told the roof tiles would be replaced in a few days. Nothing had been done by winter—and my books were drenched by the first heavy rains!"

"The pair of Moors sharing the room now—" said Vettius.

"If you want to believe—" Vulco began.

"—say the landlord told them when they moved in that the roof tiles would be replaced in a few days," Vettius continued, slicing across the interruption like a sword cutting rope. "That was three months ago."

He turned to the philosopher and said coldly, "Do you have anything to add to *that*, Faustus Menelaus?"

Menelaus blinked.

Dama bowed low to the soldier and said, "My companion and I beg your pardon, sir. He did not realize that the life of an exceptionally decent and honorable man might contain, on close examination . . . incidents which look regrettable out of context."

"Well, still . . ." Rutilianus said, frowning as he shifted on his couch. "What do you fellows think?"

All four of his civilian companions opened their mouths to speak. Macer was fractionally ahead of the others, blurting, "Well, Severiana certainly won't be pleased if an opponent of Pyrrhus the Prophet enters your household!"

"Didn't I tell you to leave my wife out of this?" Rutilianus snarled.

Macer quailed as though he'd been slapped. The other civilians froze, unwilling to offer what might not be the words the aroused Prefect wanted to hear.

Vettius looked at them with cool amusement, then back to Rutilianus. "If I may speak, sir?" he said.

"Of course, of course, Lucius," Rutilianus said, wiping his forehead with a napkin. "What do you think I should do?"

Dama squeezed Menelaus's shoulder very firmly, lest the old philosopher interrupt again—which Dama was quite sure would mean disaster. The soldier wasn't the sort of man whose warnings, voiced or implied, were to be ignored without cost.

"I can't speak to the fellow's philosophy," Vettius said.

He paused a half beat, to see if Menelaus would break in on him; and smiled when the philosopher held his peace. "But for his life—Citizen Dama stated the situation correctly. The learned Menelaus is an exceptionally decent and honorable man, fit to enter your household, sir—"

Vulco started to say something. Before the words came out, the soldier had turned and added, in a voice utterly without emotion, "—or your council. From a moral standpoint."

Vulco blanched into silence.

Dama expressionlessly watched the—almost—
exchange. This Vettius could go far in the imperial
bureaucracy, with his ability to gather information and
his ruthless willingness to use what he had. But the
way the soldier moved, his timing—thrusting before his
target was expecting it, ending a controversy before it
became two-sided—those were a swordsman's virtues,
not a bureaucrat's.

Dama's right palm tingled, remembering the feel
of a swordhilt. In five years, he'd turned his father's
modest legacy into real wealth by a willingness to go
where the profits were as high as the risks. He knew
swordsmen, knew killers. . . .

"Even with the . . . ?" the Prefect was saying. His
eyes looked inward for a moment. "But yes, I can see
that anyone's life examined closely might look—"

Rutilianus broke off abruptly as if in fear that his
musings were about to enter territory he didn't care
to explore.

"Well, anyway, Menelaus," he resumed, "I think
we'll give you—"

"Gaius, dearie," called a silk-clad youth past the
scowling nomenclator, "there's somebody here you
just *have* to see."

Rutilianus looked up with a frown that softened when
he saw the youth—the boy, really—who was speaking.
"I'm busy, now, Ganymede. Can't it wait . . . ?"

"Not an eensie minute," Ganymede said firmly,
lifting his pert nose so that he looked down at the
Prefect past chubby cheeks.

"Oh, send him in, then," Rutilianus agreed with
a sigh.

The nomenclator, his voice pitched a half-step up

with scandal and outrage, announced, "The honorable
Gnaeus Aelius Acer . . ." he paused ". . . emissary of
Pyrrhus the Prophet."

"*That* charlatan!" Menelaus snapped.

"It ill behooves a pagan to criticize a Christian,
you!" Macer retorted.

"Pyrrhus is no Christian!" said Menelaus. "That's
as much a sham as his claim to know the future
and—"

Dama laid a finger across his friend's lips.

A young man whose dress and bearing marked his
good family was being ushered in by the nomenclator.

Rutilianus glanced from the newcomer to Menelaus
and remarked in a distant tone, "A word of advice,
good philosopher: my wife believes Pyrrhus to be a
Christian. A belief in which I choose to concur."

He turned to the newcomer and said, "Greetings,
Gnaeus Acer. It's been too long since you or your
father have graced us with your company."

Instead of responding with a moment of smalltalk,
Acer said, "Pyrrhus to Gaius Rutilianus, greetings.
There is—"

There was a glaze over the young man's eyes and his
voice seemed leaden. He did not look at the Prefect
as his tongue broke into sing-song to continue:

"—one before you

"With whose beard he cloaks for boys his lust.

"Cast him from you hastily

"And spurn him in the dust."

Pyrrhus's messenger fell silent. "I think there's a
mistake—" Dama began while his mind raced, searching
for a diplomatic way to deny the absurd accusation.

Menelaus was neither interested in nor capable of diplomacy. "That's doggerel," he said, speaking directly to the Prefect. "And it's twaddle. I've never touched a boy carnally in my life."

After a pause just too short for anyone else to interject a comment, the philosopher added, "I can't claim that as a virtue. Because frankly, I've never been tempted in that direction."

"Vettius?" the Prefect asked, his eyes narrowing with supposition.

The soldier shrugged. "I can't prove an absence," he said—his tone denying the possibility implicit in the words. "But if the learned Menelaus had tastes in that direction, *some* neighbor or slave would surely have mentioned it."

"In his wallet—" Acer broke in unexpectedly.

"—the debaucher keeps

"A letter to the boy with whom he sleeps."

"That," shouted Menelaus, "is a lie as false and black as the heart of the charlatan whose words this poor deluded lad is speaking!"

Vettius reached toward the bosom of the philosopher's toga.

Menelaus raised a hand to fend off what he saw as an assault on his sense of propriety. Dama caught the philosopher's arm and said, "Let him search you now. That will demonstrate the lie to all these gentlemen."

Vettius removed a cracked leather purse whose corners had been restitched so often that its capacity was reduced by a third. He thumbed up the flap—the tie-strings had rotted off a decade before—and emptied it, item by item, into his left palm.

A stylus. A pair of onions.

"I, ah," Menelaus muttered, "keep my lunch. . . ."

Dama patted him to silence.

A half-crust of bread, chewed rather than torn from a larger piece. The lips of Rutilianus and his companions curled.

A tablet, closed so that the two boards protected the writing on their waxed inner sides. All eyes turned to the philosopher.

All eyes save those of Gnaeus Acer, who stood as quietly as a resting sheep.

"My notebook," explained Menelaus. "I jot down ideas for my lectures. And sometimes appointments."

Vettius dumped back the remainder of the wallet's contents and opened the tablet.

"It's in Greek," he commented. He shifted so that light from the garden door threw shadows across the marks scored into the wax and made them legible.

"Yes, I take my notes—" the philosopher began.

"'Menelaus to his beloved Kurnos,'" Vettius said, translating the lines rather than reading them in their original. "'Kurnos, don't drive me under the yoke against my will—don't goad my love too much.'"

"What!" said Dama.

"*Oh . . . !*" murmured several of the others in the room.

"'I won't invite you to the party,'" the soldier continued, raising his voice to a level sufficient to bark commands across the battlefield, "'nor forbid you. When you're present, I'm distressed—but when you go away, I still love you.'"

"Why, that's not my notebook!" Menelaus cried. "Nor my words. Why, it's just a quotation from the ancient poet Theognis!"

Dama started to extend a hand to the notebook. He caught himself before he thought the gesture was visible, but the soldier had seen and understood. Vettius handed the tablet to Dama open.

Pyrrhus's messenger should have been smiling—should have shown *some* expression. Gnaeus Acer's face remained as soft and bland as butter. He turned to leave the office as emotionlessly as he'd arrived.

Menelaus reached for Acer's arm. Dama blocked the older man with his body. "Control yourself!" he snarled under his breath.

The message on the tablet couldn't have been written by the old philosopher . . . but the forgery was very good.

Too good for Dama to see any difference between Menelaus's hand and that of the forger.

"Lies don't change the truth!" Menelaus shouted to the back of Gnaeus Acer. "Tell your master! The truth will find him yet!"

"Citizen Menelaus," the Prefect said through pursed lips, "you'd better—" his mind flashed him a series of pictures: Menelaus brawling with Pyrrhus's messenger in the waiting room "—step into the garden for a moment while we discuss matters. And your friend—"

"Sir," Vettius interjected, "I think it might be desirable to have Citizen Dama present to hear the discussions."

"We don't owe an explanation to some itinerant pederast, surely?" said Caelius.

Rutilianus looked at him. "No," he said. "I don't owe anyone an explanation, Caelius. But my friend Lucius is correct that sometimes giving an explanation can save later awkwardness—even in matters as trivial as these."

For the first time, Dama could see that Rutilianus had reached high office for better reason than the fact that he had the right ancestors.

A momentary tremor shook Menelaus's body. The philosopher straightened, calm but looking older than Dama had ever seen him before.

He bowed to the Prefect and said, "Noble Rutilianus, your graciousness will overlook my outburst; but I assure you I will never forgive my own conduct, which was so unworthy of a philosopher and a guest in your house."

Menelaus strode out the door to the garden, holding his head high as though he were unaware of Caelius's giggles and the smug certainty in the eyes of Vulco.

"Citizen Dama, do you have anything to add?" the Prefect said—a judge now, rather than the head of a wealthy household.

"There is no possibility that the accusation is true," Dama said, choosing his words and knowing that there were no words in any language that would achieve his aim. "I say that as a man who has known Menelaus since I was old enough to have memory."

"And the letter he'd written?" Macer demanded. "I suppose *that's* innocent?"

Dama looked at his accuser. "I can't explain the letter," he said. "Except to point out that Pyrrhus knew about it, even though Menelaus himself obviously had no idea what was written on the tablet."

Caelius snickered again.

"Lucius Vettius, what do you say?" Rutilianus asked from his couch. He wiped his face with a napkin, dabbing precisely instead of sweeping the cloth promiscuously over his skin.

"In my opinion," the soldier said, "the old man didn't know what was on the tablet. And he isn't interested in boys. In my opinion."

"So you would recommend that I employ the learned Menelaus to teach my sons proper morality?" Rutilianus said.

For a moment, Dama thought—hoped—prayed—

The big soldier looked at Dama, not the Prefect, and said, "No, I can't recommend that. There're scores of philosophers in Rome who'd be glad of the position. There's no reason at all for you to take a needless risk."

And of course, Vettius was quite right. A merchant like Dama could well appreciate the balance of risk against return.

Pyrrhus the Prophet understood the principles also.

"Yes, too bad," Rutilianus said. "Well-spoken old fellow, too. But"—his eyes traced past the nomenclator as if hoping for another glimpse of the boy Ganymede—"some of those perverts are just too good at concealing it. Can't take the risk, can we?"

He looked around the room as his smiling civilian advisors chorused agreement. Vettius watched Dama with an expression of regret, but he had no reason to be ashamed of what he'd said. Even Dama agreed with the assessment.

The wheezing gasp from the garden was loud enough for everyone in the office to hear, but only Vettius and Dama understood what it meant.

Sosius was between Vettius and the garden door for an instant. The soldier stiff-armed him into a wall,

because that was faster than words and there wasn't
a lot of time when—

Vettius and Dama crashed into the garden together.
The merchant had picked up a half step by not having
to clear his own path.

—men were dying.

It looked for a moment as though the old philosopher were trying to lean his forehead against the wall
of the house. He'd rested the pommel of Vettius's
sword at an angle against the stucco and was thrusting
his body against it. The gasp had come when—

Menelaus vomited blood and toppled sideways
before Dama could catch him.

—the swordpoint broke the resisting skin beneath
Menelaus's breastbone and slid swiftly upward through
the old man's lungs, stomach and heart.

Vettius grabbed Menelaus's limp wrist to prevent
the man from flopping on his back. The swordpoint
stuck a finger's breadth out from between Menelaus's
shoulder blades. It would grate on the stone if he
were allowed to lie naturally.

Dama reached beneath the old man's neck and
took the weight of his torso. Vettius glanced across
at him, then eased back—putting his own big form
between the scene and the excited civilians spilling
from the office to gape at it.

"You didn't have to do that, old friend," Dama
whispered. "There were other households . . ."

But no households who wouldn't have heard the story
of what had happened here—or a similar story, similarly
told by an emissary of Pyrrhus the Prophet. Menelaus
had known that . . . and Menelaus hadn't been willing
to accept open charity from his friend.

The old man did not speak. A trail of sluggish blood dribbled from the corner of his mouth. His eyes blinked once in the sunlight, twice—

Then they stayed open and began to glaze.

Dama gripped the spatha's hilt. One edge of the blade was embedded in Menelaus's vertebrae. He levered the weapon, hearing bone crack as the steel came free.

"Get back!" the merchant snarled to whoever it was whose motion blurred closer through the film of tears. He drew the blade out, feeling his friend's body spasm beneath his supporting arm.

He smelled the wastes that the corpse voided after mind and soul were gone. Menelaus wore a new toga. Dama'd provided it "as a loan for the interview with Rutilianus."

Dama stood up. He caught a fold of his own garment in his left hand and scrubbed the steel with it, trusting the thickness of the wool to protect his flesh from the edge that had just killed the man he had known and respected as long as he had memory.

Known and respected and loved.

And when the blade was clean, he handed the sword pommel-first to Lucius Vettius.

There were seats and tables in the side-room of the tavern, but Vettius found the merchant hunched over the masonry bar in the front. The bartender, ladling soup from one of the kettles cemented into the counter, watched hopefully when the soldier surveyed the room from the doorway, then strode over to Dama.

The little fella had been there for a couple hours. Not making trouble. Not even drinking *that* heavy . . .

But there was a look in his eyes that the bartender had seen in other quiet men at the start of a real bad night.

"I thought you might've gone home," Vettius said as he leaned his broad left palm on the bar between his torso and Dama's.

"I didn't," the merchant said. "Go away."

He swigged down the last of his wine and thrust the bronze cup, chained to the counter, toward the bartender. "Another."

The tavern was named *At the Sign of Venus.* While he waited for the bartender to fill the cup—and while he pointedly ignored Dama's curt demand to *him*—Vettius examined the statue on the street end of the counter.

The two-foot high terracotta piece had given the place its name. It showed Venus tying her sandal, while her free hand rested on the head of Priapus's cock to balance her. Priapus's body had been left the natural russet color of the coarse pottery, but Venus was painted white, with blue for her jewelry and the string bra and briefs she wore. The color was worn off her right breast, the one nearer the street.

Dama took a drink from the refilled cup. "Menelaus had been staying with me the past few days," he said into the wine. "So I didn't go back to my apartment."

The bartender was keeping down at the other end of the counter, which was just as it should be. "One for me," Vettius called. The man nodded and ladled wine into another cup, then mixed it with twice the volume of heated water before handing it to the soldier.

"Sorry about your friend," Vettius said in what could have been mistaken for a light tone.

"Sorry about your sword," Dama muttered, then took a long drink from his cup.

The soldier shrugged. "It's had blood on it before," he said. After a moment, he added, "Any ideas about how Pyrrhus switched the notebook in your friend's purse?"

Like everyone else in the tavern, the two men wore only tunics and sandals. For centuries, togas had been relegated to formal wear: for court appearances, say; or for dancing attendance on a wealthy patron like Gaius Rutilius Rutilianus.

Dama must have sent his toga home with the slaves who'd accompanied him and Menelaus to the interview. The garment would have to be washed before it could be worn again, of course. . . .

"It wouldn't have been hard," the merchant said, putting his cup down and meeting Vettius's eyes for the first time since walking behind his friend's corpse past the gawping servants and favor-seekers in the reception hall. "In the street, easily enough. Or perhaps a servant."

He looked down at the wine, then drank again. "A servant of mine, that would probably make it."

Vettius drank also. "You know," he said, as if idly, "I don't much like being made a fool of with the Prefect."

"*You're* still alive," Dama snapped.

Vettius looked at the smaller man without expression. The bartender, who'd seen *that* sort of look before also, signaled urgently toward a pair of husky waiters; but the soldier said only, "Yeah. We are alive, aren't we?"

Dama met the soldier's eyes. "Sorry," he said. "That was out of line."

"Been a rough day for a lot of people," said Vettius with a dismissive shrug. "For . . . just about everybody except Pyrrhus, I'd say. Know anything about that gentleman?"

The merchant chuckled. "I know what I've heard from Menelaus," he said. "Mostly that Pyrrhus isn't a gentleman. He's a priest from somewhere in the East—I've heard Edessa, but I've heard other places. Came here to Rome, found an old temple that was falling down and made it his church."

Dama sipped wine and rolled it around his mouth as if trying to clear away the taste of something. Maybe he was. He'd felt no twinge at mentioning Menelaus's name, even though his friend's body was still in the process of being laid out.

Menelaus had always wanted to be cremated. He said that the newer fashion of inhumation came from—he'd glance around, to make sure he wasn't being overheard by those who might take violent offense—mystical nonsense about resurrection of the body.

Vettius looked past Dama toward the bartender. "You there," he called, fishing silver from his wallet. "Sausage rolls for me and my friend."

To the merchant he added, as blandly as though they *were* old friends, "There's something about a snake?"

"Yes . . ." Dama said, marshalling his recollections. "He claims to have one of the bronze serpents that Christ set up in the wilderness to drive away a plague. Something like that. He claims it talks, gives prophecies."

"Does it?"

Dama snorted. "I can make a snake talk—to fools—if there's enough money in it. And there's money in this one, believe me."

He bit into a steaming sausage roll. It was juicy; good materials well-prepared, and the wine was better than decent as well. It was a nice tavern, a reasonable place to stop.

Besides being the place nearest to the Prefect's doorway where Dama could get a drink.

He poured a little wine onto the terrazzo floor. The drops felt cool when they splashed his sandaled feet. Vettius cocked an eyebrow at him.

"An offering to a friend," Dama said curtly.

"One kind of offering," the soldier answered. "Not necessarily the kind that does the most good."

Dama had been thinking the same thing. That was why he didn't mind talking about his friend after all. . . .

For a moment, the two men eyed one another coldly. Then Vettius went on, "Happen to know where this temple Pyrrhus lives in might be?"

Dama hadn't mentioned that Pyrrhus lived *in* his church. It didn't surprise him that the soldier already knew, nor that Lucius Vettius probably knew other things about the Prophet.

"As it happens," the merchant said aloud, "I do. It's in the Ninth District, pretty near the Portico of Pompey. And—"

He popped the remainder of his sausage roll into his mouth and chewed it slowly while Vettius waited for the conclusion of the sentence.

An open investigation of Pyrrhus would guarantee the soldier an immediate posting to whichever frontier looked most miserable on the day Rutilianus's wife learned what he was doing to her darling.

You know, I don't much like being made a fool of with the Prefect.

Vettius wasn't going to get support through his normal channels; but it might be that he could find someone useful who took a personal interest in the matter. . . .

Dama washed down the roll with the last of his wine. "And since it's a Sunday," he resumed, "they'll be having an open ceremony." He squinted past Venus and the smirking Priapus to observe the sun's angle. "We'll have plenty of time to get there, I should think."

He brought a silver coin from his purse, checked the weight of it with his finger, and added a bronze piece before slapping the money onto the counter. "To cover the wine," Dama called to the bartender. "Mine and my friend's both."

The two men shouldered their way into the crowded street, moving together as though they were a practiced team.

They heard the drum even before they turned the corner and saw the edges of a crowd which Vettius's trained eye estimated to contain over a thousand souls. Dusk would linger for another half hour, but torches were already flaring in the hands of attendants on the raised base of a small temple flanked by three-story apartment buildings.

"Are we late?" the soldier asked.

Dama dipped his chin in negation. "They want places near the front, and a lot of them can't afford to buy their way up."

His eyes narrowed as he surveyed the expensively-dyed cloaks and the jewelry winking in ears and coiffures of matrons waiting close to the temple—the church—steps. "On the other hand," he added, "a lot of them *can* afford to pay."

The crowd completely blocked the street, but that didn't appear to concern either the civic authorities or the local inhabitants. Vettius followed the merchant's eyes and muttered, "Pyrrhus himself owns the building across the street. He uses it to house his staff and put up wealthy pilgrims."

A flutist, playing a counterpoint on the double tubes of his instrument, joined the drummer and torch-bearers on the porch. Two of the attendants at the back of the crowd, identifiable by their bleached tunics and batons of tough rootwood, moved purposefully toward Vettius and Dama.

The merchant had two silver denarii folded in his palm. "We've come to worship with the holy Pyrrhus," he explained, moving his hand over that of one of the attendants. The exchange was expert, a maneuver both parties had practiced often in the past.

"Yes," said the attendant. "If you have a request for guidance from the holy Pyrrhus, give it on a sealed tablet to the servants at the front."

Dama nodded and reached for another coin. "Not now," said the attendant. "You will be granted an opportunity to make a gift directly to the divinity."

"Ah . . ." said Vettius. "I don't have a tablet of my own. Could—"

The other attendant, the silent one, was already handing Vettius an ordinary tablet of waxed boards. He carried a dozen similar ones in a large scrip.

"Come," said—ordered—the first attendant. His baton, a dangerous weapon as well as a staff of office, thrust through the crowd like the bronze ram of a warship cleaving choppy waves.

There were loud complaints from earlier—and

poorer—worshippers, but no one attempted physical opposition to the Prophet's servant. Vettius gripped Dama's shoulder from behind as they followed, lest the pressure of the crowd separate them beyond any cure short of open violence.

"Pyrrhus's boys aren't very talkative," Vettius whispered in the smaller man's ear. "Drugs, perhaps?"

Dama shrugged. Though the attendant before them had a cultured accent, he was as devoid of small-talk and emotion as the messenger who brought deadly lies about Menelaus to the Prefect. Drugs were a possible cause; but the merchant already knew a number of men—and a greater number of women—for whom religious ecstasy of one sort or another had utterly displaced all other passions.

Pyrrhus's converted temple was unimposing. A building, twenty feet wide and possibly thirty feet high to the roof-peak, stood on a stepped base of coarse volcanic rock. Two pillars, and pilasters formed by extensions of the sidewalls, supported the pediment. That triangular area was ornamented with a painting on boards showing a human-faced serpent twined around a tau cross.

The temple had originally been dedicated to Asklepios, the healing god who'd lived part of his life as a snake. The current decoration was quite in keeping with the building's pagan use.

There were six attendants on the temple porch now. The newcomers—one of them was Gnaeus Acer—clashed bronze rattles at a consistent rhythm; not the same rhythm for both men, nor in either case quite the rhythm that the staring-eyed drummer stroked from his own instrument.

The guide slid Vettius and Dama to within a row of the front of the crowd. Most of the worshipers still ahead of them were wealthy matrons, but a few were country folk. Vettius thought he also saw the flash of a toga carrying a senator's broad russet stripe. More attendants, some of them carrying horn-lensed lanterns rather than batons, formed a line at the base of the steps.

Dama had paid silver for a second-rank location. The first rank almost certainly went for gold.

The merchant had opened a blank notebook and was hunching to write within the strait confines of the crowd. The tablet Vettius had been given looked normal enough at a glance: a pair of four- by five-inch boards hinged so that they could cover one another. One of the boards was waxed within a raised margin of wood that, when the tablet was closed, protected words written on the soft surface. A cord attached to the back could be tied or sealed to the front board to hold the tablet shut.

Dama finished what he was doing, grinned, and took the tablet from Vettius. "Shield me," he whispered.

Vettius obediently shifted his body, though the two of them were probably the only members of the crowd who weren't focused entirely on their own affairs.

Dama had been scribbling with a bone stylus. Now, using the stylus tip, he pressed on what seemed to be a tiny knot through the wooden edge of the tablet supplied to Vettius. The knot slipped out into his waiting palm. A quick tug started the waxed wooden back sliding away from the margin of what had seemed a solid piece.

"Pyrrhus the Prophet has strange powers indeed,"

Vettius said as he fitted the tablet back together again.
"Let me borrow your stylus."

He wrote quickly, cutting the wax with large, square
letters; not a calligrapher's hand, but one which could
write battlefield orders that were perfectly clear.

"What are you asking?" Dama whispered.

"Whether Amasius will die so that I get promoted
to Legate of the Domestic Horse," the soldier replied.
He slapped that tablet closed. "I suppose the attendants seal these for us?"

"Ah . . ." said Dama with a worried expression. "That
might not be a tactful question to have asked . . . ah, if
the information gets into the wrong hands, you know."

"Sure wouldn't be," Vettius agreed, "if I'd signed
'Decurion Vettius' instead of 'Section Leader Lycorides.'"

He chuckled. "You know," he added, "Lycorides is
about dumb enough not to figure how a question like
that opens you up to blackmail."

He grinned at the pediment of the church and said,
"Pyrrhus would figure it out, though. Wouldn't he?"

Dama watched a heavy-set woman in the front rank
wave her ivory tablet at an attendant. She wore a
heavy cross on a gold chain, and the silk band which
bound her hair was embroidered with the Chi-Rho
symbol. Menelaus may not have thought Pyrrhus was
a Christian; but, as the Prefect had retorted, there
were Christians who felt otherwise.

"Hercules!" Vettius swore under his breath. "That's
Severiana—the Prefect's wife!"

He snorted. "And Ganymede. That boy gets around."

"Want to duck back now and let me cover?" the
merchant offered.

Vettius grimaced. "They won't recognize me," he

said in the tone of one praying as well as assessing the situation.

An attendant leaned toward Dama past the veiled matron and her daughter in the front rank who were reciting prayers aloud in Massiliot Greek.

"If you have petitions for advice from the Prophet," the man said, "hand them in now."

As the attendant spoke, he rolled a lump of wax between his thumb and forefinger, holding it over the peak of the lantern he carried in his other hand. Prayers chirped to a halt as the women edged back from the lantern's hissing metal frame.

Dama held out his closed notebook with the cord looped over the front board. The attendant covered the loop with wax, into which Dama then firmly pressed his carnelian seal ring. The process of sealing Vettius's tablet was identical, except that the soldier wore a signet of gilt bronze.

"What're you asking?" Vettius whispered under cover of the music from the porch and the prayers which the women resumed as soon as the attendant made his way into the church with the tablets.

"I'm asking about the health of my wife and three children back in Gades."

"You're not from Spain, are you?" the soldier asked—reflexively checking the file of data in his mind.

"Never been there," Dama agreed. "Never married, either."

The door of the church opened to pass an attendant with small cymbals. He raised them but didn't move until the door shut behind him.

The music stopped. The crowd's murmuring stilled to a collective intake of breath.

The cymbals crashed together. A tall, lean man stood on the porch in front of the attendants.

"Mithra!" the merchant blurted—too quietly to be overheard, but still a stupid thing to say here.

Dama understood about talking snakes and ways to read sealed tablets; but he didn't have the faintest notion of how Pyrrhus had appeared out of thin air that way.

"I welcome you," Pyrrhus cried in a voice that pierced without seeming especially loud, "in the name of Christ and of Glaukon, the Servant of God."

Vettius narrowed his eyes.

Dama, though he was uncertain whether the soldier's ignorance was real or just pretense, leaned even closer than the press demanded and whispered, "That's the name of his snake. The bronze one,"

"Welcome Pyrrhus!" the crowd boomed. "Prophet of God!"

A double *crack!* startled both men but disturbed few if any of the other worshipers. The torch-bearing attendants had uncoiled short whips with poppers. They lashed the air to put an emphatic period to the sequence of statement and response.

Pyrrhus spread his arms as though thrusting open a double door. "May all enemies of God and his servants be far from these proceedings," he cried.

"May all enemies of Pyrrhus and Glaukon be far from these proceedings!" responded the crowd.

Crackcrack!

"God bless the Emperors and their servants on Earth," Pyrrhus said. Pyrrhus *ordered*, it seemed to Vettius; though the object of the order was a deity.

"Not taking any chances with a treason trial, is he?" the soldier muttered.

"God bless Pyrrhus and Glaukon, his servants!" responded the crowd joyously.

The merchant nodded. Those around them were too lost in the quivering ambiance of the event to notice the carping. "What I want to know," he whispered back, "is how long does this go on?"

"Pyrrhus! Liar!" a man screamed from near the front of the gathering. The crowd recoiled as though the cry were a stone flung in their midst.

"Two months ago, you told me my brother'd been drowned in a shipwreck!" the man shouted into the pause his accusation blew in the proceedings.

The accuser was short and already balding, despite being within a few years of Vettius's twenty-five; but his features were probably handsome enough at times when rage didn't distort them.

"Blasphemer!" somebody cried; but most of the crowd poised, waiting for Pyrrhus to respond. The attendants were as motionless as statues.

"His ship was driven ashore in Malta, but he's fine!" the man continued desperately. "He's home again, and I've married his *widow*! What am I supposed to do, you lying bastard!"

Pyrrhus brought his hands together. Dama expected a clap of sound, but there was none, only the Prophet's piercing voice crying, "Evil are they who evil speak of God! Cast them from your midst with stone and rod!"

What—

"You've ruined my—" the man began.

—*doggerel*, Dama thought, and then a portly matron next to the accuser slashed a line of blood across his forehead with the pin of the gold-and-garnet clasp fastening her cloak. The victim screamed and stumbled back, into the clumsy punch of a frail-looking man twice his age.

The crowd gave a collective snarl like that of dogs ringing a boar, then surged forward together.

The paving stones were solidly set in concrete, but several of the infuriated worshipers found chunks of building material of a size to swing and hurl. Those crude weapons were more danger to the rest of the crowd than to the intended victim—knocked onto all fours and crawling past embroidered sandals, cleated boots, and bare soles, all kicking at him with murderous intent.

Vettius started to move toward the core of violence with a purposeful look in his eye. The merchant, to whom public order was a benefit rather than a duty, gripped the bigger man's arm. Vettius jerked his arm loose.

Tried to jerk his arm loose. Dama's small frame belied his strength; but much more surprising was his willingness to oppose the soldier whom he knew was still much stronger—as well as being on the edge of a killing rage.

The shock brought Vettius back to present awareness. The accuser would probably survive the inept battering; and one man—even a man as strong and determined as Lucius Vettius—could do little to change the present odds.

The mob jostled them as if they were rocks in a surf of anger. "Two months ago," Dama said, with his lips close to the soldier's ear, "he'd have been one of those kicking. That's not why we're here."

The victim reached the back of the crowd and staggered to his feet again. A few eager fanatics followed some way into the darkness; but Pyrrhus spread his arms on the porch of the church, calming the crowd the way a teacher can appear and quiet a schoolroom.

Whips cracked the worshipers to attention.

"Brothers and sisters in God," the Prophet called, clearly audible despite the panting and foot-shuffling that filled the street even after the murderous cries had abated. "Pray now for the Republic and the Emperors. May they seek proper guidance in the time of testing that is on them!"

"What's that mean?" Dama whispered.

The soldier shrugged. "There's nothing special *I* know about," he muttered. "Of course, it's the sort of thing you could say anytime in the past couple centuries and be more right than wrong."

Pyrrhus's long prayer gave no more information as to the nature of the "testing" than had been offered at the start, but the sentences rambled through shadowy threats and prophetic thickets barbed with words in unknown languages. On occasion—random occasions, it seemed to Vettius—the Prophet lowered his arms and the crowd shouted, "Amen!" After the first time, the soldier and merchant joined in with feigned enthusiasm.

Despite his intention to listen carefully—and his absolute need to stay awake if he were to survive the night—Vettius was startled out of a fog when Pyrrhus cried, "Depart now, in the love of God and his servants Pyrrhus and Glaukon!"

"God bless Pyrrhus, the servant of God!" boomed the crowd, as though the meaningless, meandering prayer had brought the worshipers to some sort of joyous epiphany.

Whips cracked. The musicians behind Pyrrhus clashed out a concentus like that with which they had heralded the Prophet's appearance—

Pyrrhus was gone, as suddenly and inexplicably as he'd appeared.

The crowd shook itself around the blinking amazement of Vettius and Dama. "I don't see . . ." the merchant muttered. The torches trailed sparks and pitchy smoke up past the pediment, but there was no fog or haze sufficient to hide a man vanishing from a few feet away.

"Is this all—" Vettius began.

"Patience," said Dama.

The attendants—who hadn't moved during the near riot—formed a double line up the stepped base of the building to where the drummer opened the door. Worshipers from the front of the crowd, those who'd paid for their places and could afford to pay more for a personal prophecy, advanced between the guiding lines.

Vettius's face twisted in a moue as he and Dama joined the line. *He* shouldn't have to be counseled in patience by a silk merchant. . . .

The private worshipers passed one by one through the door, watched by the attendants. A man a couple places in front of Vettius wore an expensive brocade cloak, but his cheeks were scarred and one ear had been chewed down to a nub. As he stepped forward, one of the attendants put out a hand in bar and said, "No weapons. You have a—"

"Hey!" the man snarled. "You leave me—"

The attendant on the other side reached under the cloak and plucked out a dagger with a wicked point and a long, double-edged blade.

The pair of women nearest the incident squealed in horror, while Vettius poised to react if necessary. The man grabbed the hand of the attendant holding his dagger and said, "Hey! That's for personal reasons, see?"

The first attendant clubbed the loaded butt of his whip across the back of the man's neck. The fellow slumped like an empty wineskin. Two of the musicians laid down their instruments and dragged him toward the side of the building. Twittering, the women stepped past where he'd fallen.

Vettius glanced at Dama.

"I'm clean," the merchant murmured past the ghost of a humorless smile. He knew, as Vettius did, that the man being dragged away was as likely dead as merely unconscious.

That, along with what happened to the fellow who'd married his brother's wife, provided the night's second demonstration of how Pyrrhus kept himself safe. The Prophet might sound like a dim-witted charlatan, and his attendants might look as though they were sleep-walking most of the time; but he and they were ruthlessly competent where it counted.

As he passed inside the church, Dama glanced at the door leaves. He hoped to see some sign—a false panel; a sheet of mirror-polished metal; *something*—to suggest the illusion by which Pyrrhus came and left the porch. The outer surface of the wooden leaves had been covered with vermillion leather, but the inside showed the cracks and warping of age.

These were the same doors that had been in place when the building was an abandoned temple. There were no tricks in them.

A crosswall divided the interior of the church into two square rooms. The broad doorway between them was open, but the select group of worshipers halted in the first, the anteroom.

Crosswise in the center of the inner room, Pyrrhus the Prophet lay on a stone dais as though he were a corpse prepared for burial. His head rested on a raised portion of the stone, crudely carved to the shape of an open-jawed snake.

Behind the Prophet, against the back wall where the cult statue of Asklepios once stood, was a tau cross around which twined a metal-scaled serpent. The creature's humanoid head draped artistically over the crossbar.

Pairs of triple-wick lamps rested on stands in both rooms, but their light was muted to shadow by the high, black beams supporting the roof. A row of louvered clerestory windows had been added just beneath the eaves when the building was refurbished, but even during daylight they would have affected ventilation more than lighting.

Vettius estimated that forty or fifty people were allowed to enter before attendants closed the doors again and barred them. The anteroom was comfortably large enough to hold that number, but the worshipers—he and Dama as surely as the rest—all crowded toward the center where they could look through the doorway into the sanctum.

Bronze scales jingled a soft susurrus as the serpent lifted its head from the bar. "God bless Pyrrhus his servant!" rasped the creature in a voice like a wind-swung gate.

Vettius grabbed for the sword he wasn't carrying

tonight. He noticed with surprise that Dama's arm had curved in a similar motion. Not the sort of reflex he'd have expected in a merchant . . . but Vettius had already decided that the little Cappadocian wasn't the sort of merchant one usually met.

"God bless Glaukon and Pyrrhus, his servants," responded the crowd, the words muzzed by a harshly-echoing space intended for visual rather than acoustic worship.

"Mithra!" Dama said silently, a hand covering his lips as they mimed the pagan syllables.

He knew the serpent was moved by threads invisible in the gloom. He knew one of Pyrrhus's confederates spoke the greeting through a hole in the back wall which the bronze simulacrum covered.

But the serpent's creaking, rasping voice frightened him like nothing had since—

Like nothing ever had before.

Goods of various types were disposed around the walls of the anteroom. Sealed amphoras—sharp-ended jars that might contain anything from wine to pickled fish—leaned in clusters against three of the four corners. From wooden racks along the sidewalk hung bunches of leeks, turnips, radishes—and a pair of dead chickens. In the fourth corner was a stack of figured drinking-bowls (high-quality ware still packed in scrap papyrus to protect the designs from chipping during transit) and a wicker basket of new linen tunics.

For a moment, Vettius couldn't imagine why the church was used for storage of this sort. Then he noticed that each item was tagged: they were worshipers' gifts in kind, being consecrated by the Prophet's presence before they were distributed. Given the

number of attendants Pyrrhus employed in his operation, such gifts would be immediately useful.

Pyrrhus sat up slowly on the couch, deliberately
emphasizing his resemblance to a corpse rising from
its bier. His features had a waxy stillness, and the
only color on his skin was the yellow tinge cast by
the lamp flames.

"Greetings, brothers and sisters in God," he said.
His quiet, piercing voice seemed not to be reflected
by the stone.

"Greetings, Pyrrhus, Prophet of God," the crowd
and echoes yammered.

A pile of tablets stood beside the couch, skewed and
colorful with the wax that sealed each one. Pyrrhus
took the notebook on top and held it for a moment
in both hands. His fingers were thin and exceptionally
long, at variance with his slightly pudgy face.

"Klea, daughter of Menandros," he said. The elder
of the two praying women who'd stood in front of
Vettius during the open service gasped with delight.
She stepped through the doorway, knelt, and took the
tablet from the Prophet's hands.

"Remarriage," Pyrrhus said in the sing-song with
which he delivered his Verses, "is not for you but
faith. You may take the veil for me in death."

"Oh, Prophet," the woman mumbled as she got to
her feet. For a moment it looked as though she were
going to attempt to kiss Pyrrhus.

"God has looked with favor on you, daughter," the
Prophet said in a distant, cutting voice that brought
the suppliant back to a sense of propriety. "He will
accept your sacrifice."

From the bosom of the stola she wore, Klea took a

purse and thrust it deep within the maw of the stone
serpent-head which had served Pyrrhus as a pillow.
The coins clinked—gold, Dama thought; certainly not
mere bronze—beneath the floor. The bench served as
a lid for Pyrrhus's treasury, probably a design feature
left from the days the building was a temple.

"Oh, Master," the woman said as she walked back
to her place in the anteroom.

Tears ran down her cheeks, but even Vettius's experience at sizing up women's emotions didn't permit him
to be sure of the reason. Perhaps Klea cried because
she'd been denied remarriage during life . . . but it was
equally likely that she'd been overcome with joy at
the prospect of joining Pyrrhus after death.

The Prophet took another from the stack of tablets.
"Hestiaia, daughter of Mimnermos," he called, and
the younger of the pair of women stepped forward
to receive her prophecy.

Pyrrhus worked through the series of requests tablet
by tablet. A few of the responses were in absolute
gibberish—which appeared to awe and impress the
recipients—and even when the doggerel could be
understood, it was generally susceptible to a variety of
meanings. Dama began to suspect that the man who'd
been stoned and kicked from the gathering outside
had chosen the interpretation he himself desired to
an ambiguous answer about his brother's fate.

A man was told that his wife was unfaithful. No
one but the woman herself could know with certainty
if the oracle were false.

A woman was told that the thief who took her
necklace was the slave she trusted absolutely. She
would go through her household with scourge and

thumbscrew . . . and if she found nothing, then wasn't her suspicion of this one or that proof her trust hadn't been complete after all?

"Severiana, daughter of Marcus Severianus," the Prophet called. Vettius stiffened as the Prefect's simpering wife joined Pyrrhus in the sanctum.

"Daughter," said Pyrrhus in his clanging verse, "blessed of God art thee. Thy rank and power increased shall be. Thy husband's works grow anyhow. And morrow night I'll dine with thou."

Dama thought: Pyrrhus's accent was flawless, unlike that of the Prefect's nomenclator; but in his verse he butchered Latin worse than ever an Irish beggar did. . . .

Vettius thought: Castor and Pollux! Bad enough that the Prefect's wife was involved with this vicious phony. But if Pyrrhus got close to Rutilianus himself, he could do real harm to the whole Republic. . . .

"Oh beloved Prophet!" Severiana gurgled as she fed the stone serpent a purse that hit with a heavier *clank!* than most of the previous offerings. "Oh, we'll be so honored by your presence!"

"Section Leader Lycorides!" Pyrrhus called.

Vettius stepped forward, hunching slightly and averting his face as he passed Severiana. The timing was terrible—but the Prefect's wife was so lost in joy at the news that she wouldn't have recognized her husband, much less one of his flunkies.

Though Pyrrhus's thin figure towered over the previous suppliants who faced him one-on-one, Vettius was used to being the biggest man in any room. It hadn't occurred to him that he too would have to tilt his head up to meet the Prophet's eyes.

Pyrrhus's irises were a black so deep they could

scarcely be distinguished from his pupils; the weight
of their stare gouged at Vettius like cleated boots.

For a moment the soldier froze. He *knew* that
what he faced was no charlatan, no mere trickster
preying on the religiously gullible. The power of
Pyrrhus's eyes, the inhuman perfection of his bearded,
patriarchal face—

Pyrrhus was not merely a prophet; he was a *god*.

Pyrrhus opened his mouth and said, "Evil done
requited is to men. Each and every bao nhieu tien."

The illusion vanished in the bath of nonsense syllables. Vettius faced a tall charlatan who had designs on
the official whom it was Vettius's duty to protect.

Rutilianus would be protected. Never fear.

"God has looked with favor on you, son," Pyrrhus
prodded. "He will accept your sacrifice."

Vettius shrugged himself to full alertness and felt
within his purse. He hadn't thought to bundle a few
coins in a twist of papyrus beforehand, so now he had
to figure desperately as he leaned toward the opening
to the treasury. He didn't see any way that Pyrrhus
could tell if he flung in a couple bits of bronze instead
of real payment, but. . . .

Vettius dropped three denarii and a Trapezuntine
obol, all silver, into the stone maw. He couldn't take
the chance that Pyrrhus or a confederate *would* know
what he had done—and at best expose him in front
of Severiana.

He stepped back into place.

"Marcus Dama!" the Prophet called, to the surprise
of Vettius who'd expected Dama to use a false name.
Diffidently lowering his eyes, the little man took the
notebook Pyrrhus returned to him.

"God grants us troubling things to learn," the Prophet sing-songed. "Sorrows both and joys wait your return."

A safe enough answer—if the petitioner told you he'd left his wife and three minor children behind in Spain months before. Dama kept his eyes low as he paid his offering and pattered back to Vettius's side.

There were half a dozen further responses before Pyrrhus raised his arms as he had before making an utterance from the porch. "The blessings of God upon you!" he cried.

A single tablet remained on the floor beside the stone bench. Vettius remembered the well-dressed thug who'd tried to carry in a dagger. . . .

"God's blessings on his servants Pyrrhus and Glaukon!" responded that majority of the crowd which knew the liturgy.

"Depart in peace . . ." rasped the bronze serpent from its cross, drawing out the Latin sibilants and chilling Dama's bones again.

The doors creaked open and the worshipers began to leave. Most of them appeared to be in a state of somnolent ecstasy. A pair of attendants collected the tablets which had been supplied to petitioners who didn't bring their own; with enough leisure, even the devoutest believer might have noticed the way the waxed surface could be slid from beneath the sealed cover panel.

The air outside was thick with dust and the odors of slum tenements. Dama had never smelled anything so refreshing as the first breath that filled his lungs beyond the walls of Pyrrhus's church.

❖   ❖   ❖

Almost all of those who'd attended the private service left in sedan chairs.

Vettius and Dama instead walked a block in silence to a set of bollards protecting an entrance to the Julian Mall. They paused, each lost for a moment in a landscape of memories. No one lurked nearby in the moonlight, and the rumble of goods wagons and construction vehicles—banned from the streets by day—kept their words from being overheard at any distance.

"A slick operation," Vettius said.

The merchant lifted his chin in agreement but then added, "His clientele makes it easy, though. They come wanting to be fooled."

"I'm not sure how . . ." Vettius said.

For a moment, his tongue paused over concluding the question the way he'd started it: *I'm not sure how Pyrrhus managed to appear and disappear that way.* But though he knew that was just a trick, the way some sort of trick inspired awe when Pyrrhus stared into the soldier's eyes . . . neither of those were things that Vettius wanted to discuss just now.

". . . he knew what your question was," Vettius's tongue concluded. "Is the tablet still sealed?"

"Sealed again, I should guess," Dama said mildly as he held the document up to the fall moon. "They could've copied my seal impression in quick-drying plaster, but I suspect—yes, there."

His fingertip traced a slight irregularity in the seal's edge. "They used a hot needle to cut the wax and then reseal it after they'd read the message."

He looked at his companion with an expression the bigger man couldn't read. "Pyrrhus has an exceptional memory," he said, "to keep the tablets and responses

in proper order. He doesn't give himself much time
to study."

Vettius gestured absently in agreement. The soldier's
mind considered various ways, more or less dangerous,
to broach the next subject.

Three wagons carrying column bases crashed and
rumbled past, drawn by teams of mules with cursing
drivers. The loads might be headed toward a construction site within the city—but more likely they were
going to the harbor and a ship that would carry them
to Constantinople or Milan.

Rome was no longer a primary capital of the empire.
It was easier to transport art than to create it, so Rome's
new imperial offspring were devouring the city which
gave them birth. All things die, even cities.

Even empires . . . but Lucius Vettius didn't permit
himself to think about *that*.

"It doesn't appear that he's doing anything illegal,"
the soldier said carefully. "There's no law against lying
to people, even if they decide to give you money for
nothing."

"Or lying about people," Dama said—"agreed" would
imply there was some emotion in his voice, and there
was none. "Lying about philosophers who tell people
you're a charlatan, for instance."

"I thought he might skirt treason," Vettius went
on, looking out over the street beyond. "It's easy to
say the wrong thing, you know. . . . But if Pyrrhus told
any lies—" with the next words, Vettius would come
dangerously close to treason himself; but perhaps his
risk would draw the response he wanted from the
merchant "—it was in the way he praised everything
to do with the government."

"There was the—riot, I suppose you could call it," Dama suggested as his fingers played idly with the seal of his tablet.

"Incited by the victim," the soldier said flatly. "And some of those taking part were—very influential folk, I'd estimate. There won't be a prosecution on that basis."

"Yeah," the merchant agreed. "That's the way I see it too. So I suppose we'd better go home."

Vettius nodded upward in agreement.

He'd have to go the next step alone. Too bad, but the civilian had already involved himself more than could have been expected. Dama would go back and make still more money, while Lucius Vettius carried out what he saw as a duty—

Knowing that he faced court martial and execution if his superiors learned of it.

"Good to have met you, Marcus Dama," he muttered as he strode away through a break in traffic.

There was a crackle of sound behind him. He glanced over his shoulder. Dama was walking toward his apartment in the opposite direction.

But at the base of the stone bollard lay the splintered fragments of the tablet the merchant had been holding.

The crews of two sedan chairs were dicing noisily— and illegally—beside the bench on which Vettius waited, watching the entrance to Pyrrhus's church through slitted eyes. Business in the small neighborhood bath house was slack enough this evening that the doorkeeper left his kiosk and seated himself beside the soldier.

"Haven't seen you around here before," the doorkeeper opened.

Vettius opened his eyes wide enough to frown at
the man. "You likely won't see me again," he said.
"Which is too bad for you, given what I've paid you
to mind your own business."

Unabashed, the doorkeeper chewed one bulb from
the bunch of shallots he was holding, then offered
the bunch to the soldier. His teeth were yellow and
irregular, but they looked as strong as a mule's.

"Venus!" cried one of the chairmen as his dice came
up all sixes. "How's *that*, you Moorish fuzzbrain?"

"No thanks," said Vettius, turning his gaze back
down the street.

The well-dressed, heavily-veiled woman who'd arrived
at the church about an hour before was leaving again.
She was the second person to be admitted for a private consultation, but a dozen other—obviously less
wealthy—suppliants had been turned away during the
time the soldier had been watching.

He'd been watching, from one location or another
in the neighborhood, since dawn.

"I like to keep track of what's going on around
here," the doorkeeper continued. He ate another
shallot and belched. "Maybe I could help you with
what you're looking for?"

Vettius clenched his great, calloused hands, only
partly as a conscious attempt on his part to warn this
nuisance away. "Right now," he said in a husky voice,
"I'm looking for a little peace and—"

"Hey there!" one of the chairmen shouted in Greek
as the players sprang apart. One reached for the
stakes, another kicked him, and a third slipped a
short, single-edged knife from its hiding place in the
sash that bound his tunic.

Vettius and the doorkeeper both leaped to their feet. The soldier didn't want to get involved, but if a brawl broke out, it was likely to explode into him.

At the very best, that would disclose the fact that he was hiding his long cavalryman's sword beneath his cloak.

The pair of plump shopowners who'd hired the sedan chairs came out the door, rosy from the steam room and their massages. The chairmen sorted themselves at once into groups beside the poles of their vehicles. The foreman of one chair glanced at the other, nodded, and scooped up the stakes for division later.

Vettius settled back on the bench. Down the street, a quartet of porters were carrying a heavy chest up the steps of the church. Attendants opened the doors for the men.

Early in the morning, the goods Vettius had seen in the building's anteroom had been dispersed, mostly across the street to the apartment house which Pyrrhus owned. Since then, there had been a constant stream of offerings. All except the brace of live sheep were taken inside.

Pyrrhus had not come out all day.

"A bad lot, those chairmen," the doorkeeper resumed, dusting his hands together as though he'd settled the squabble himself. The hollow stems of his shallots flopped like an uncouth decoration from the bosom of his tunic. "I'm always worried that—"

Vettius took the collar of the man's garment between the thumb and forefinger of his left hand. He lifted the cloth slightly. "If you do not leave me alone," he said in a low voice, "you will have something to worry about. For a short time."

Half a dozen men, householders and slaves, left the bath caroling an obscene round. One of them was trying to bounce a hard leather ball as he walked, but it caromed wildly across the street.

The doorkeeper scurried back to his kiosk as soon as Vettius released him.

Three attendants, the full number of those who'd been in the church with Pyrrhus, came out and stood on the porch. Vettius held very still. It was nearly dusk—time and past time that the Prophet go to dinner.

If he was going.

Pyrrhus could lie and bilk and slander for the next fifty years until he died on a pinnacle of wealth and sin, and that'd still be fine with Lucius Vettius. There were too many crooked bastards in the world for Vettius to worry about one more or less of 'em. . . .

Or so he'd learned to tell himself, when anger threatened to build into a murderous rage that was safe to release only on a battlefield.

Vettius wasn't just a soldier any more: he was an agent of the civil government whose duties required him to protect and advise the City Prefect. If Pyrrhus kept clear of Rutilianus, then Pyrrhus had nothing to fear from Lucius Vettius.

But if Pyrrhus chose to make Rutilianus his business, then. . . .

A sedan chair carried by four of Pyrrhus's attendants trotted to the church steps from the apartment across the street. A dozen more of the Prophet's men in gleaming tunics accompanied the vehicle. Several of them carried lanterns for the walk back, though the tallow candles within were unlighted at the moment.

Pyrrhus strode from the church and entered the sedan chair. He looked inhumanly tall and thin, even wrapped in the formal bulk of a toga. It was a conjuring trick itself to watch the Prophet fold his length and fit it within the sedan, then disappear behind black curtains embroidered with a serpent on a cross.

Three attendants remained on the porch. The remainder accompanied the sedan chair as it headed northeast, in the direction of the Prefect's dwelling. The attendants' batons guaranteed the vehicle clear passage, no matter how congested the streets nearer the city center became.

Vettius sighed. Well, he had his excuse, now. But the next—hours, days, years; he didn't know how long it'd take him to find something on this "Prophet" that'd stick. . . .

The remainder of the soldier's life might be simpler if he didn't start at all. But he was going to start, by burglarizing Pyrrhus's church and private dwelling while the Prophet was at dinner. And if that didn't turn up evidence of a crime against the State, there were other things to try. . . .

A hunter learns to wait. It would be dead dark soon, when the sun set and the moon was still two hours beneath the horizon. Time then to move to the back of the church which he'd reconnoitered by the first light of dawn.

Men left the bath house, laughing and chatting as they headed for their dinners. Vettius watched the three attendants, as motionless as statues on the church porch; as motionless as he was himself.

And he waited.

❖   ❖   ❖

When Vettius was halfway up the back wall of the church, a patrol of the Watch sauntered by in the street fronting the building.

Watch patrols were primarily fire wardens, but the State equipped them with helmets and spears to deal with any other troubles they might come across. This group was dragging the ferrules of its spears along the pavement with a tremendous racket, making sure it *didn't* come across such troubles . . . but Vettius still paused and waited for the clatter to trail off in the direction of the Theater of Balbus.

Back here, nobody'd bothered to cover the building's brick fabric with marble, and the mortar between courses probably hadn't been renewed in the centuries since the structure was raised as a temple. The warehouse whose blind sidewall adjoined the back of the church two feet away was also brick. It provided a similarly easy grip for the cleats of Vettius's tight-laced boots.

Step by step, steadying himself with his fingertips, the soldier mounted to the clerestory windows beneath the transom of the church. Each was about three feet long but only eight inches high, and their wooden sashes were only lightly pinned to the bricks.

Vettius loosened a window with the point of his sword, then twisted the sash outward so that the brickwork continued to grip one end. If matters went well, he'd be able to hide all signs of his entry when he left.

He hung his cloak over the end of the window he'd swung clear. He'd need the garment to conceal his sword on the way back.

The long spatha was a terrible tool for the present

use. He'd brought it rather than a sturdy dagger or simply a prybar because—

Because he was still afraid of whatever he thought he'd seen in Pyrrhus's eyes the night before. The sword couldn't help that, but it made Vettius *feel* more comfortable.

There was a faint glow from within the building; one lamp wick had been left burning to light the Prophet's return home.

Vettius uncoiled his silken line. He'd thought he might need the small grapnel on one end to climb to the window, but the condition of the adjoining walls made the hooks as unnecessary as the dark lantern he'd carried in case the church was unlighted. Looping the cord around an end-frame of the window next to the one he'd removed, he dropped both ends so that they dangled to the floor of Pyrrhus's sanctum.

He had no real choice but to slide head-first through the tight opening. He gripped the doubled cord in both hands to keep from plunging thirty feet to the stone floor.

His right hand continued to hold the hilt of his naked sword as well. Scabbarded, the weapon might've slipped out when he twisted through the window; or so he told himself.

Pyrrhus's bronze serpent gaped only a few feet from Vettius as he descended the cord, hand over hand. The damned thing was larger than it had looked from below, eighteen—no, probably twenty feet long when you considered the way its coils wrapped the cross. Shadows from the lamplight below drew the creature's flaring nostrils into demonic horns.

At close view, the bronze head looked much less

human than it had from the anteroom. There were six vertical tubes in each eye. They lighted red and green in alternation.

Vettius's hobnails sparked as he dropped the last yard to the floor. The impact felt good.

Except for Pyrrhus's absence, the sanctum looked just as it had when the soldier saw it the night before. He went first to the couch that covered the Prophet's strongbox. It was solid marble, attached to the floor by bronze pivots. Vettius expected a lock of some sort, but only weight prevented the stone from being lifted. So. . . .

He sheathed his sword and gripped the edge of the couch with both hands. Raising the stone would require the strength of three or four normal men, but—

The marble pivoted upward, growling like a sleeping dog.

The cavity beneath was empty.

Vettius vented his breath explosively. He almost let the lid crash back in disgust, but the stone might have broken and the noise would probably alert the attendants.

Grunting—angry and without the hope of immediate triumph to drive him—Vettius lowered by main strength the weight that enthusiasm had lifted.

He breathed heavily and massaged his palms against his thigh muscles for a minute thereafter. Score one for the Prophet.

Vettius didn't know precisely what he'd expected to find in the crypt, but there *had* to be some dark secret within this building or Pyrrhus wouldn't have lived in it alone. Something so secret that Pyrrhus didn't dare trust it even to his attendants. . . .

Perhaps there was a list of high government personnel who were clients of Pyrrhus—or who supplied him with secret information. The emperors were—rightly—terrified of conspiracies. A list like that, brought to the attention of the right parties, would guarantee mass arrests and condemnations.

With, very probably, a promotion for the decurion who uncovered the plot.

If necessary, Vettius could create such a document himself; but he'd rather find the real one, since something of the sort *must* exist.

The bronze lamp had been manufactured especially for Pyrrhus. Counterweighting the spouts holding the three wicks was a handle shaped like a cross. A human-headed serpent coiled about it.

Vettius grimaced at the feel of the object as he took it from its stand. He prowled the sanctum, holding the light close to the walls.

If there was a hiding place concealed within the bricks, Vettius certainly couldn't find it. The room was large and clean, but it was as barren as a prison cell.

There was a faint odor that the soldier didn't much like, now that he'd settled down enough to notice it.

He looked up at the serpent, Glaukon. Lamplight broke the creature's coils into bronze highlights that swept from pools of shadow like great fish surfacing. Pyrrhus might have hidden a papyrus scroll in the creature's hollow interior, but—

Vettius walked through the internal doorway, stepping carefully so that the click of his hobnails wouldn't alarm the attendants outside. He'd check the other room before dealing with Glaukon.

He didn't much like snakes.

The anteroom had a more comfortable feel than the sanctum, perhaps because the goods stored around the walls gave it the look of a large household's pantry. Vettius swept the lamp close to the top of each amphora, checking the tags scratched on the clay seals. Thasian wine from the shipowner Glirius. Lucanian wine from the Lady Antonilla. Dates from—Vettius chuckled grimly: my, a Senator. Gaius Cornelius Metellus Libo.

A brace of rabbits; a wicker basket of thrushes sent live, warbling hopefully when Vettius brought the lamp close.

In the corner where the stacks of figured bowls had been, Vettius found the large chest he'd watched the porters stagger in with that evening. The label read: *A gift of P. Severius Auctus, purveyor of fine woolens.*

A small pot of dormice preserved in honey. Bunches and baskets of fresh vegetables.

The same sort of goods as had been here the night before. No strongbox, no sign of a cubbyhole hidden in the walls.

Which left Vettius with no better choice than to try that damned bronze serpent after—

Outside the front doors, the pins of a key scraped the lock's faceplate.

Bloody buggering Zeus! Pyrrhus should've been gone for hours yet!

Vettius set down the lamp with reflexive care and ran for the sanctum. Behind him, the key squealed as it levered the iron dead-bolts from their sockets in both doorframes.

He'd be able to get out of the building safely enough, though a few of the attendants would probably fling their cudgels at him while he squirmed through the window. The narrow alley would be suicide, though. They'd've blocked both ends by the time he got to the ground, and there wasn't room enough to swing his spatha. He'd go up instead, over the triple-vaulted roof of the warehouse and down—

The door opened. "Wait here," called the penetrating, echoless voice of Pyrrhus to his attendants.

Vettius's silken rope lay on the floor in a tangle of loose coils. It couldn't have slipped from the window by itself, but. . . .

The door closed; the bolts screeched home again. Vettius spun, drawing his sword.

"Beware, Pyrrhus!" cried the bronze serpent. "Intruder! Intruder!"

Vettius shifted his weight like a dancer. Faint lamplight shimmered on the blade of his spatha arcing upward. Glaukon squirmed higher on the cross. Its somewhat-human face waved at the tip of the bar, inches from where the rope had hung. The creature's teeth glittered in wicked glee.

A chip of wood flew from the cross as Vettius's sword bit as high as he could reach; a hand's breadth beneath Glaukon's quivering tail.

"Come to me, Decurion Lucius Vettius," Pyrrhus commanded from the anteroom.

He couldn't know.

The flickering lamplight in the other room was scarcely enough to illuminate the Prophet's toga and the soft sheen of his beard. Vettius was a figure in shadow, only a dim threat with a sword even when he spun again to confront Pyrrhus.

Pyrrhus couldn't know. But he knew.

"Put your sword down, Lucius Vettius," the Prophet

said. For a moment, neither man moved; then Pyrrhus stepped forward—

No, that wasn't what happened. Pyrrhus stepped *away* from himself, one Pyrrhus walking and the other standing rigid at the door. There was something wrong about the motionless figure; but the light was dim, the closer form hid the further . . .

And Vettius couldn't focus on anything but the eyes of the man walking toward him. They were red, glowing brighter with every step, and they were drawing Vettius's soul from his trembling body.

"You are the perfect catch, Lucius Vettius," Pyrrhus said. His lips didn't move. "Better than you can imagine. In ten years, in twenty . . . there will be no one in this Empire whom you will not know if you wish to, whom you cannot sway if you wish to. On behalf of Pyrrhus the Prophet. Or whatever I call myself then.

"Put your sword down, Lucius Vettius."

The hilt of Vettius's sword was hot, as hot and glowing as the eyes of the approaching Pyrrhus. He couldn't hold the blade steady; light trembled along its sharp double edges like raindrops on a willow leaf.

But it didn't fall from his hand.

Pyrrhus stepped through the doorway between the rooms. His shoulder brushed the jamb, brushed through it—form and stuccoed brickwork merging, separating; the figure stepping onward.

"I will have this empire," Pyrrhus said. "And I will have this world."

Vettius stared down a black tunnel. At the end of the tunnel glared Pyrrhus's eyes, orange-hot and the size of the universe. They came nearer yet.

"And when I return to those who drove me out, when I return to those who would have *slain* me, Lucius Vettius," said the voice that echoed within the soldier's skull, "they will bow! For mine will be the power of a whole world forged to my design. . . .

"Put down your sword!"

Vettius screamed and swung his blade in a jerky, autonomic motion with nothing of his skill or years of practice to guide it. Steel cut the glowing eyes like lightning blasting the white heart of a sword-smith's forge—

The eyes gripped Vettius's eyes again. The Prophet's laughter hissed and bubbled through the soldier's mind.

"You are mine, Lucius Vettius," the voice said caressingly. "You have been mine since you met my gaze last night. Did you think you could hide your heart from me?"

Vettius's legs took a wooden, stumbling step forward; another step, following the eyes as they retreated toward the figure standing by the outer door. The figure of Pyrrhus *also*, or perhaps the only figure that was really Pyrrhus. The soldier now understood how the Prophet had appeared and vanished on the church porch the night before, but that no longer mattered.

Nothing mattered but the eyes.

"I brought you here tonight," said the voice.

"No . . ." Vettius whispered, but he wasn't sure either that he spoke the word or that it was true. He had no power over his thoughts or his movements.

"You will be my emperor," the voice said. "In time. In no time at all, for me. With my knowledge, and with the weapons I teach you to build, you will conquer your world for me."

The glowing eyes shrank to normal size in the sockets of the thing that called itself Pyrrhus. The bearded phantasm moved backward one step more and merged with the figure that had not moved since entering the church.

"And then . . ." said the figure as all semblance of Pyrrhus drained away like frost in the sunshine, ". . . I will return home."

The toga was gone; the beard, the pudgy human cheeks. What remained was naked, bone-thin and scaly. Membranes flickered across the slit-pupiled eyes, cleaning their surfaces; then the reptilian eyes began to carve their path into Vettius's mind with surgical precision.

He heard the creak of hinges, a lid rising, but the sound was as faint and meaningless as a seagull's cry against the thunder of surf.

"Pyrrhus!" shrieked the bronze serpent. "Intruder! Guards! Guards! *Guards!*"

Vettius awakened, gasping and shaking himself. He felt as though he'd been buried in sand, a weight that burned and crushed every fiber of his body.

But it hadn't been his body that was being squeezed out of existence.

The chest—*A gift of P. Severius Auctus, purveyor of fine woolens*—was open. Dama was climbing out of it, as stiff as was to be expected when even a small man closed himself in so strait a compass. He'd shrugged aside the bolt of cloth that covered him within the chest, and he held the scabbard of an infantry sword in his left hand.

His right drew the short, heavy blade with a musical *sring!*

"Guards!" Glaukon shouted again.

The serpent had left its perch. It was slithering in long curves toward Dama.

Pyrrhus reached for the door-latch with one reptilian hand; Vettius swung at him off-balance. He missed, but the spatha's tip struck just above the lock plate and splintered its way deep into the age-cracked wood.

Pyrrhus hissed like tallow on a grill. He leaped toward the center of the room as the soldier tugged his weapon free and turned to finish the matter.

Glaukon struck like a cobra at Dama. The merchant, moving with a reflexive skill that would have impressed Vettius if he'd had time to think, blocked the bronze fangs with the scabbard in his left hand. Instead of a clack as the teeth met, light crackled like miniature lightning.

Dama swore in Greek and thrust with his sword at the creature's head. Glaukon recoiled in a smooth curve. The serpent's teeth had burned deep gouges into the scabbard's iron chape.

Vettius pivoted on the ball of his left foot, bringing his blade around in a whistling arc that would—

Pyrrhus's eyes blazed into the soldier's. "Put down your sword, Lucius Vettius," rang the voice in his mind. Vettius held as rigid as a gnat in amber.

There were shouts from outside. Someone knocked, then hammered the butt of his baton on the weakened panel. Splinters of gray wood began to crack off the inside.

Glaukon was twenty feet of shimmering coils, with death in its humanoid jaws. Dama feinted. Glaukon quivered, then struck in earnest as the merchant shifted in the direction of Pyrrhus who was poised in the center of the anteroom as his eyes gripped Vettius.

Dama jumped back, almost stumbling over the chest in which he'd hidden. He was safe, but the hem of his tunic smoldered where the teeth had caught it.

Put—

Several batons were pounding together on the door. The upper half of a board flew into the room. An attendant reached through the leather facing and fumbled with the lock mechanism.

—down your sword, Lucius Vettius.

Dama's sword dipped, snagged the bolt of cloth that had covered him, and flipped it over the head of the bronze serpent. Wool screamed and humped as Glaukon tried to withdraw from it.

Dama smiled with cold assurance and stabbed where the cloth peaked, extending his whole body in line with the blow. The sharp wedge of steel sheared cloth, bronze, and whatever filled the space within Glaukon's metal skull.

The door burst inward. Pyrrhus sprang toward the opening like a chariot when the bars come down at the Circus. Vettius, freed by the eyes and all deadly instinct, slashed the splay-limbed figure as it leaped past.

The spatha sliced in above the chin, shattering pointed, reptilian teeth. *Down* through the sinuous neck. *Out,* breaking the collar bone on the way.

The blood that sprayed from the screaming monster was green in the lamplight.

Attendants hurled themselves out of the doorway with bawls of fear as the creature that had ruled them

bolted through. Pyrrhus's domination drained with
every spurt from his/its severed arteries. Men—men
once more, not the Prophet's automatons—hurled
away their cudgels and lanterns in their haste to
flee. Some of the running forms were stripping off
splattered tunics.

The point of Dama's sword was warped and blackened. The merchant flung his ruined weapon away as
he and Vettius slipped past the splintered remnants
of the door. Behind them, in the center of a mat of
charred wool, the serpent Glaukon vomited green
flames and gobbets of bronze.

Pyrrhus lay sprawled in a green pool at the bottom
of the steps. The thin, scaly limbs twitched until Vettius, running past, drove his spatha through the base
of the creature's domed skull.

The soldier was panting, more from relief than
exertion. "Where did he come from?" he muttered.

"Doesn't matter." Dama was panting also. "*He* didn't
expect more of his kind to show up."

"I thought he was a phony. The tablets—"

They swung past the bollards where they'd talked
the previous evening. Dama slowed to a walk, since
they were clear of the immediate incident. "He was
a charlatan where it was easier to be a charlatan.
That's all."

Vettius put his hand on the smaller man's shoulder and guided him to the shadow of a shuttered
booth. "Why didn't you tell me you were coming back
tonight?" the soldier demanded.

Dama looked at him. "It was personal," he said. Their
faces were expressionless blurs. "I didn't think somebody
in the Prefect's office ought to be involved."

Vettius sheathed his blade and slid the scabbard parallel to his left leg. If the gods were good, the weapon might pass unnoticed on his way home in the cloud-swept moonlight. "I was already involved," he said.

The merchant turned and met Vettius's eyes. "Menelaus was my friend," he replied, almost too softly to be heard. "Lucius Vettius, I didn't come here with a sword tonight to *talk* to my friend's killer."

In the near distance, the night rang with cries of horror. The Watch had discovered the corpse of Pyrrhus the Prophet.

_____*End note to* The False Prophet

August Derleth of Arkham house put the check for my story "Black Iron" in the mail on July 3, 1971. It was my fourth sale, to him and in total; and also the last to Mr. Derleth, because he died of a heart attack the next morning.

"Black Iron" was the first of my stories that I would now call fully publishable. It wasn't perfect, but it could've appeared in a newsstand magazine without causing readers to shake their heads at the editor's judgment. The story was in the form of a traveller's tale (I don't know why I thought I needed a frame; maybe because I'd recently read a collection of Lord Dunsany's Jorkens stories) and introduced a couple Roman citizens of the 4th century AD: a merchant named Dama and his friend, a soldier named Gaius Vettius. This was the first of many times I've used a Roman setting for my fiction.

I went back to Vettius and Dama a number of times in later years. Their adventures were my first series, intended as such from the beginning. (I more or less accidentally turned "The Butcher's Bill" into the Hammer's Slammers series a couple years later.)

In 1990 I collected the Vettius and Dama stories (along with a few other pieces with ancient settings) as *Vettius and His Friends*. For that collection I wrote "The False Prophet." Much of the setting is drawn from the essay on Alexander of Abonoteichus by Lucian of Samosata, though I used additional material from various sources including Ammianus Marcellinus, Juvenal and other essays by Lucian.

The previous Vettius and Dama stories were fantasies. This one is SF, though I don't suppose the protagonists would've recognized the distinction.

A GRAND TOUR

AUTHOR'S NOTE: *Readers may be amused to learn that both the climax of this story and the archeological methods described therein are closely modeled on real events which took place in the eastern Mediterranean in 1795.*

Edith Mincio waited as her friend and employer, Sir Hakon Nessler, stepped from the hatch of the small starship onto the soil of Hope. He stumbled. Nessler was a good sailor, so good that his body had adjusted to the rhythmic fluctuations of the battered vessel's artificial gravity during the five-day journey.

"Oof!" he said. The doubled sound reminded Mincio they still wore the plug intercoms they'd needed to speak to one another over the noise of the small freighter. She took hers out of her left ear canal and returned it to its protective case.

Hope had little to recommend it as a planet, but at least its gravity remained at a constant level. Nessler's quick adaptation was now playing him false, though

Mincio knew he'd be back to normal in a few hours. Not for the first time she envied the tall youth. She was only ten years older than her pupil, but sometimes he made her feel ancient.

Mincio disembarked with only a little more dignity than the luggage the crew began to toss through the hatch as soon as she'd cleared it. She wasn't a good sailor by any stretch of the imagination, and the sort of vessels Nessler had to hire here on the distant fringes of the Solarian League would make almost anybody queasy.

Her breath caught. On the distant horizon winked a line of six crystal pylons, just as Kalpriades had described them in his *Survey of the Alphane Worlds*— written five hundred years ago and still the most comprehensive work on the vanished prehuman star-travellers. If dizziness and a stomach that would take days to settle down were the prices required to see the remnants of the Alphane civilization in person, then she'd pay willingly.

The landing field was dirt blackened by leaked lubricants where spaceships had hammered low spots into the ground. Half a dozen other vessels were present, most of them intrasystem freighters without Warshawski sails. At the far end of the field sat a large cutter with worn hints of gold-leaf decoration. A dozen men and women in baggy gray uniforms got up from the cutter's shade and slouched toward the Nessler and Mincio.

Hope's planetary capital and the League Liaison Office were here at Kuepersburg. From the field all Mincio could see in the way of civilization were houses roofed with heavy plastic a kilometer to the north.

The remainder of Nessler's party had waited to disembark until the freighter's crew had dumped the luggage in a large pile. Maginnes, Nessler's personal servant, was green rather than his ruddy norm; Rovald, the recording technician, looked as though she'd been disinterred after a week of burial. Mincio was queasy, but at least she could tell herself that she was a better traveller than those two.

Nessler extended his imaging goggles to view the Six Pylons. Kalpriades claimed the towers had once been connected by a bridge of gossamer crystal, but there were no signs of it from this distance. The pylons stood in the middle of a plain with no obvious reason to exist.

"Hope!" muttered Maginnes. He was a stocky little man of fifty, a dependant of the Nesslers of Greatgap as every male ancestor of his back to the settlement had been. "Damned little of that here that I can see."

"It was originally named Haupt when it was the capital of the Teutonic Order," Mincio explained. "The pronunciation decayed along with everything else associated with the Order."

"And a good thing, too," Nessler said, closing his imager with a snap. He was twenty-two T-years old and had a good mind as well as a fierce enthusiasm for whatever he was doing. When he took up his tutor's interest in the Alphanes, that enthusiasm translated itself into a tour of the Alphane Worlds for both of them. On their return Sir Hakon would enter into the stewardship of one of the greater personal fortunes of the Manticore system. "Quite a knot of vipers, that lot. Although . . ."

His eyes drifted toward the plastic-roofed shacks of

Kuepersburg and toyed with the imager, though he didn't reopen it. "I wouldn't say that League membership has done a great deal for any of the worlds that we've visited in this region."

Rovald found the cases holding her equipment, but she didn't have the strength or enthusiasm at the moment to lift them from the pile. She was a slight woman of sixty with an intuitive grasp of electronic circuitry but no pretensions.

There was nothing wrong with Rovald's health, but events had shown that she wasn't really mentally resilient enough for the rigors of travel here at the edge of the settled universe. Mincio was afraid that they'd have to send the technician home soon, and there wasn't a chance they'd find anyone as good to replace her.

"Region Twelve's been a backwater ever since the Alphanes vanished," Mincio agreed. "The League uses it as a dumping ground for personnel who might do real harm if they were anywhere important."

Maginnes spat. "Which *this* sandbox sure ain't," he said.

Hope—Haupt as it then was—had received one of the earliest generation ship colonies. After a brief spell under the Teutonic Order—"flowering" was too positive a term to describe the era during which those psychopathic brutes ruled four neighboring star systems—the planet had sunk to near barbarism before rediscovery early in the Warshawski period.

Hope joined the Solarian League in the belief that this would aid its advancement, but nothing much had changed. Hope had no unique mineral or agricultural resources. The soil and climate permitted growing

Earth-standard crops with ground-water irrigation, so Hope fed the small-scale mines and manufacturing complexes in neighboring systems. The whole region was singularly devoid of wormhole junctions, and since it was on the edge of the human-settled sphere there wasn't even the chance of through-trade stopping over.

The Alphane civilization was the only reason anybody from the advanced worlds would be interested in Hope, and the difficulties of travel to the region meant that such interest normally remained a distant one. No one knew what the Alphanes looked like: even the name was one coined by Kalpriades because he believed they were the first star-travelling race in the Milky Way galaxy.

Alphanes had built in crystal on at least a score of worlds known to humans, vast soaring structures which survived only as shattered remnants. Lava that overflowed an Alphane city on Tesserow had been dated to 100,000 T-years Before Present. How much older the ruins might be was anybody's guess.

Besides their structures, the Alphanes had left nut-sized crystals which formed holograms in the air above them when subjected to alternating current. Kalpriades claimed the crystals were books, and most scholars following him had agreed. Few of the crystals thus far found were whole, and the patterns varied according to the frequency and intensity of the current.

To decipher the patterns a scholar first had to determine the correct input, and there were as many theories about that as there were scholars. Books the crystals might be, but they gave no more information about the Alphanes than did the gleaming skeletons of Alphane cities.

The four-man crew of the Klipspringer freighter

began to walk away. They'd secured their vessel by running a heavy chain around the hatch release and through a staple welded to the hull, then padlocking it. Even so they eyed the people shambling from the cutter askance.

"Captain Cage?" Nessler called sharply to the owner. "Can we expect port officials to arrive shortly?"

"Naw, you have to see the League boss yourself," Cage mumbled. He'd filled his mouth with a wad of chewing tobacco as soon as the vessel touched ground and he had a place to spit. "There's a merchant named Singh who looks after folks like you from the Inside Worlds. I'll tell him there's a Manticoran arrived at the field and he'll send somebody out for you."

"Sod that for a lark," Maginnes muttered, his hands on his hips as he faced the people from the cutter. "Who're you?" he demanded of the squat, gloomy woman in the lead.

"Please, good sir," she said. "Can you give us food? We are very hungry."

"All right, here's the plan!" Maginnes said. "Sir Hakon could buy this whole planet if he felt like it. If you pick up his baggage and take it to Mister Singh's, you won't be the worse for it."

He clapped his hands. "But hop to it!"

"One moment, Maginnes," Nessler said with a slight frown. "Madam, are you League officials?"

The woman patted her eyes, her ears, and finally her mouth with both hands in a gesture of abject submission. "Good sir," she said, "I am Petty Officer Royston. We are Melungeon sailors from the *Colonel Arabi*. Please, we will carry your bags. Mister Singh is a good man. He gives us food often."

"Were you shipwrecked?" Nessler said in growing puzzlement.

The Grand Duchy of Melungeon lay to the galactic south of the Solarian League. Melungeon was an occasional tourist destination for wealthy Manticorans, particularly those who liked to hunt wild animals in conditions in which all the comforts were available to those who could pay for them, but from everything Mincio had heard it was an exotic rather than a really civilized place.

The petty officer started to repeat her salute. Mincio caught her hand to prevent a degradation she found creepy.

"No, good sir," Royston said with a worried look to be sure Nessler wasn't going to strike her. "The ship is in orbit. We are to stay with the cutter while the rest of the crew digs for Lord Orloff, but there is no food for us."

Nessler grimaced. "Yes, all right," he said. "Take our luggage to Mister Singh and I'll see to it you're fed."

With a glance toward Mincio to make sure they were together, Nessler set off for Kuepersburg at his usual long-limbed saunter. Mincio kept up easily though her legs scissored at three strides to Nessler's two. She proceeded through life with a fierce drive that contrasted with her pupil's apparent relaxed ease, but both of them managed to reach their goals.

"I was hoping to see growlers," Nessler said. "Kalpriades said they were common on Hope. Of course, five hundred years . . ."

"Relatively common," Mincio corrected judiciously. "I wouldn't expect to find them near the landing field. They seem to dislike petroleum smells, and ships always leak oil and hydraulic fluid."

Nessler sighed. "I suppose," he agreed grudgingly. "And I don't suppose they can really be the Alphanes, much as I'd like to believe they are."

Growlers were scaly, burrowing herbivores with an adult weight of about thirty kilograms. They were found on most of the worlds with Alphane material remains—and vice versa. Growlers were sweet-tempered and fairly sluggish, with no means of defense. That they were able to survive was due to the fact that no carnivore larger than a dachshund remained on any world where growlers lived. That wasn't an accident, because in many cases the fossil record contained major predators.

Kalpriades took as an article of faith that the growlers were themselves the descendants of his Alphanes; other scholars—almost everybody else who'd visited the Alphane worlds—believed that the growlers had been pets or even food animals rather than the Alphanes themselves.

Mincio had kept an open mind on the question until she'd seen the creatures herself for the first time. If the growlers were the offspring of star-travelling builders in crystal, then the process of descent had been going on for much longer than a hundred thousand years.

Nessler looked over his shoulder to be sure the rest of the entourage was behind them. The dozen Melungeons clomped along stolidly with the luggage while Royston called cadence.

Rovald was at the end of the line. The technician still looked wan, but she managed a smile when Nessler called, "We're almost there!" in encouragement.

To Mincio in a low voice Nessler said, "We'll be

spending a little time here on Hope. If she doesn't get her feet back under her, though, I'm afraid I'll have to arrange her return home."

Maginnes trotted up to Nessler and Mincio, pumping his arms in time with his strides. "It's a crying shame the way those poor devils is treated," he said as he came abreast. "Royston says Lord Orloff, that's the captain, just left them to fend for themselfs and they're six months behind in their pay. They've been *begging.* Can you imagine it? What kind of navy puts its sailors to begging on a dirtpile planet like this one?"

"Navy?" Nessler said in surprise. "The *Colonel Arabi* is a Melungeon naval vessel?"

Maginnes nodded briskly. "It surely is," he said. "A light cruiser, though I don't know what that means where they come from. The captain's a great curio fancier, Royston says, and he's come out here to haul an Alphane building back to the Duke's museum on Tellico."

Mincio missed a step in surprise. "Take a building?" she said. "Good God almighty! Surely they can't do that?"

Maginnes shrugged. "She says Orloff's got most of the crew digging around one of them towers on the horizon," he said. He hooked his thumb in the direction of the Six Pylons. "They didn't bring any equipment, just bought shovels and picks here because that's all there is to be had on Hope."

He spat dismissively into the blowing dust. "Some expedition, huh? Orloff sounds like a thick-headed barb to me, for all he's got 'lord' in front of his name."

"Watch your tongue, Maginnes," Nessler said with

what was for him unusual sharpness. "Persons may be gentlemen even though they don't come from the Manticore system."

"Indeed they may, sir," the servant said in a chastened voice. He bobbed his head. "I beg your pardon."

"I can't believe that someone would try to move one of the pylons," Mincio murmured. "And to Tellico, of all places."

"Not exactly a galactic center of scholarship, is it?" Nessler said in a tone of quiet disapproval. "The Melungeon nobility is given to whims, I'm told. It's perhaps rather unfortunate that Lord Orloff seems to have a whim for Alphane artifacts." He wouldn't stand for his servant calling a fellow nobleman a thick-headed barbarian, but Mincio suspected that he privately agreed with Maginnes' assessment of someone trying to move one of the largest and finest surviving Alphane structures. Certainly Mincio agreed.

They'd reached the outskirts of Kuepersburg. Up close the buildings were more substantial than they looked at a distance. They were built of sandy loam stabilized with a cellulose-based plasticizer, a material as permanent as lime concrete and a great deal easier to shape before it set. Many of the locals had brightened the natural dun color with dyes or exterior paint.

Children played in the street among the pigs, chickens, and garbage. They came crowding around with excited cries as soon as they saw that the travellers were well-dressed strangers. The heavily-laden Melungeons and Rovald were far to the rear.

"Half a Solarian franc to the child who leads Sir

Hakon to Merchant Singh's!" Maginnes called, holding high a plastic coin with a coppery diffraction grating at its core. "Hop it, now! Sir Hakon's too important a person to wait."

Nessler met Mincio's eyes with a wince. He didn't call Maginnes down since the boast was already spoken. Mincio shrugged and chuckled.

The children screamed and leaped for the coin like so many starving rats desperate for a tidbit—though in fact none of them looked undernourished. Maginnes chose a tall girl with an exceptional willingness to elbow clear the space about her. With the guide strutting in the lead and Maginnes obsequiously in the rear, the party turned right on a cross-street nearly as wide as the track from the landing field.

The girl halted in front of a compound. Windblown dirt dimmed the wall's white paint and several patches had flaked away, but somebody'd recently cleaned the surface with a dry broom.

The gate was open but a husky servant sat across it polishing scale off a screen of nickel filigree. He rose when he saw the mob of children and strangers coming toward him.

"Here's the Singhs!" the girl caroled. "Give me the money! Give me the money!"

A middle-aged man stepped out the front door of the largest of the three buildings within the compound. He had a full beard and wore a dark velvet frock coat of the type that was almost a uniform for respectable small businesspeople in the League's hinterlands.

"Yes?" he called in a resonant voice. Two women, one his own age and the second a twenty-year-old of exceptional beauty, looked out the door behind him.

"I'll handle this, Maginnes," Nessler said with quiet authority. "Mister Singh? I'm Sir Hakon Nessler, travelling with a party of three from Manticore to view Alphane sites. I was given to understand that you might be able to help us to accommodations and supplies here on Hope?"

The gatekeeper immediately lifted his bench out of the passage. He watched his master out of the corner of his eye to be sure that he wasn't misinterpreting his duty.

He wasn't. Singh strode forward and clasped hands with Nessler. "Yes, please," he said. "I am consular agent for Manticore on Hope."

Singh grinned. "Also for a dozen other worlds. The duties don't take much time away from my own export business, you understand, and I take pleasure in the company of travellers from more settled regions. I like to believe that I am able to smooth their path on occasions. You will stay with me and my family, I trust?"

"We would be honored, but you must permit me to pay all the household expenses during the time we're imposing on you," Nessler said. "In particular—"

He glanced down the street to call attention to the arriving baggage carriers. "—I've promised these persons that I'd feed them in exchange for carrying our traps. I'd like to fulfil that promise as soon as possible."

"Morey," Singh said to the gatekeeper, "go to Larrup's and tell her to ready . . ." He glanced out the gate to check the count. The gray-clad sailors halted, standing as silently as so many beasts of burden; which indeed they were, ". . . twelve dinners on my account. The parties will be along as soon as they have brought Mister Nessler's goods into the house."

"I'll direct them, dear," the older woman said. In a tone of crisp command she went on, "Come along, Mistress Royston. I'll show you where to put the parcels and then you can go to Larrup's for a meal."

She went inside. Maginnes trotted in also. The servant began introducing himself to the woman of the house in terms that indicated he'd decided the Singhs were gentry to be flattered instead of common folk he could badger on the strength of his connection to Nessler. Mincio sighed, but she knew that the little man wouldn't have been nearly as useful a servant here in the back of beyond if he'd been less pushy.

"Are they really from the Melungeon navy?" she asked Singh in a low voice as the last of the sailors disappeared into the house.

"Yes, indeed," Singh agreed. He gave a faintly rueful shrug. "Maxwell, Lord Orloff, arrived in a warship three weeks ago. He and his cronies as well as most of his crew are at the Six Pylons twenty-five kilometers from here. You've seen the pylons, no doubt?"

"From a distance," Nessler said. "We hope to visit the site ourselves tomorrow, if transport can be arranged. But why doesn't his crew have food?"

Singh shrugged again. "You'd have to take that up with Lord Orloff, I'm afraid," he said. "I've had very little contact with him. He pays quite well for the needs of his immediate entourage, but the common sailors appear to be destitute. Kuepersburg isn't a wealthy metropolis—"

He and the two Manticorans exchanged tight smiles, "—but we can't very well let fellow human beings

starve. We've been providing basic requirements to
the poor fellows, and they sometimes find a taker for
a bit of their vessel's equipment."

"They're stripping their own ship to buy food?"
Mincio said in surprise. "Surely that costs Melungeon
more than it would to pay their crews properly—or
at least to provide rations?"

"Sometimes what officials think are pragmatic decisions seem remarkably short-sighted to others," Singh
said. "That was as surely true when I was home on
Krishnaputra as it appears to be among the Melungeons. And certainly—"

Before continuing he glanced both ways down the
street, empty except for the playing children again.

"Certainly it is true of the way the League deals
with all the worlds of this region, particularly in the
choice of officials the League sends here."

"There's also the matter that the cost of the policy
is generally borne by a department other than the
one which makes that policy," Nessler said drily. "The
phenomenon isn't unique to the Melungeon navy."

His eyes narrowed. Mincio had found her pupil to
be a generally cheerful youth, but he had the serious
side to be expected in a responsible heir to a great
fortune. "Though I must say," Nessler added, "I might
wish that we had the Melungeon navy to fight rather
than that of the People's Republic of Haven." The
Melungeon sailors filed from the house, moving more
briskly than Mincio had seen them do previously.
Royston was in the lead; she held a chit written on a
piece of coarse paper. Singh's wife shepherded them
out with a proprietary expression.

The younger woman remained beside the doorway.

She gave Mincio a shy smile when their eyes met. She was clearly Singh's daughter, though the greater delicacy of her similar features made her strikingly attractive.

"From what the Manticore captains on Klipspringer and Delight told us," Mincio said, "the ships of the Expansion Navy of the People's Republic aren't a great deal better."

Nessler nodded, a placeholder that wasn't really an agreement. To Singh he explained, "Once an assembly line's set up it's actually easier to build ships than it is to provide crews for them. The Peeps thought to get around the problem by drafting able-bodied personnel from the Dole list to crew what they call their Expansion Navy. As Mincio says, the result was less than a first-rate combat fleet. *But*—" He turned his glance toward his tutor.

"You'll recall that the freighter captains who sneered so enthusiastically at the 'Dole Fleet' were nonetheless holding their own vessels in League sovereign space. Expansion Navy ships are quite adequate for commerce raiding, and they provide the Peeps with a presence in far corners from which our very excellent navy lacks the numbers to sweep them."

"You speak like an expert, sir," Singh said. The Krishnaputran merchant had to be a sharp man to have created a comfortable life for himself and his family in a location that didn't encourage commercial success.

"Scarcely that," Nessler said with a deprecating smile. "I spent two years as a midshipman of the Royal Manticoran Navy, and a less than brilliant example of that very junior rank. I resigned my commission when my father and elder sister drowned in a boating accident and I became perforce head of the family.

While I regret the death of Dad and Anne more than I can say, I'm better qualified as an estate manager than I was as a naval officer."

He grinned at Mincio. "And I like to think I'm a gentleman scholar."

"Certainly a scholar to have come so far for knowledge, sir," Singh said. "And a gentleman, also certainly, for that I see with my own eyes." He looked toward his wife and said, "My dear?"

"The rooms will be ready in a few minutes," she replied, "and water for the bath is heating. Will you introduce me, Baruch?"

Singh bowed in apology for forgetting the lack of introductions. "Dear," he said, "this is Sir Hakon Nessler. Sir Hakon, may I present my wife Sharra and our daughter—"

The younger woman came down from the open porch to stand at her father's side.

"—Lalita, of whom we're very proud."

Nessler bowed and took Lalita's fingertips between his. "May I in turn present my friend Edith Mincio?" he said. "She tutored me through university and has kindly consented to accompany me on my travels before taking up a post as Reader in Pre-Human Civilizations at Skanderbeg University on Manticore."

A post which only Sir Hakon's influence gained me, Mincio thought as she touched fingertips with father and daughter. *For all that I was the most qualified applicant.*

Sharra Singh smiled but didn't offer her hand. While she was clearly a person of independence and ability, her idea of a woman's place in society was not that of Manticore or of her own daughter.

"Father, can we have a dance tonight?" Lalita said with kittenish enthusiasm as she hugged Singh's arm close. The girl might well be two T-years younger than Mincio had first judged. "Please Father? They'll have all the most exciting new music, I just know it!"

She looked up at the Manticorans. "Oh, you will let me invite my friends to meet you, won't you? They'll be ever so excited!"

"I'm sure our guests are exhausted from their journey," Singh said with a serious expression. "Dear—"

"Oh, not at all," Nessler rejoined cheerfully. "As soon as I've had a bath and a bit of dinner, there's nothing I'd like more than some company that isn't ourselves and a quartet of sailors from Klipspringer. Isn't that so, Mincio?"

"Yes indeed," Mincio agreed. She wasn't nearly as social a creature as her pupil, but his statement had been basically true for her as well. In any case, it was the only possible answer to make to Lalita's desperate longing.

Rovald and Maginnes came out the side door. Maginnes held a bun and a glass of amber fluid. Rovald wasn't to the point of being ready to eat and drink yet, but at least her face had color and animation again.

"As for music, though," Nessler continued with a frown, "I'm afraid I've brought only a personal auditor with me on my travels. You're more than welcome to listen to the contents, mistress, but I'm afraid we won't be able to dance to it."

"They have an amplifier and speakers, sir," Rovald said unexpectedly. "With your permission, I can run the auditor's output through their system."

"Your equipment will fit ours?" Singh said. "Really, I don't think . . . My set is very old and came from Krishnaputra with me, you see."

"I can couple them, I think," Rovald said with quiet assurance. "It'll help if you have a length of light-guide, but I can make do without it."

"Rovald's the best electronics technician on Manticore," Nessler said. "If she says she can do it, consider it done."

Rovald beamed with pardonable pride as she and Lalita went inside. The technician had been an object of pity through the uncomfortable voyage and after landing; now at last she was able to show herself as something better than a queasy wreck.

"Would our guests care to come in, now?" Mistress Singh said, ostensibly to her husband. "The bath water should be hot."

"Go ahead, Mincio," Nessler said. "I took the last of the warm water on Klipspringer, as I recall."

"Well, if you don't mind . . . ?" Mincio said. Regular hot baths were the one luxury that she really missed in these hinterlands of human habitation.

"You know . . ." Nessler said. Mincio paused, thinking for a moment that he was responding to her immediate question rather than returning to a subject they'd been discussing earlier. "There isn't any complicated difference between the Royal Manticoran Navy and the Dole Fleet or even the Melungeons. It's just a matter of constant effort by all those concerned, the officers even more than the men. If my sister had inherited as she should have, I would have been one of those officers—and I'm very glad I'm not. I'd much rather do something I was good at."

✧   ✧   ✧

Wearing formal dress that—except for the footgear—would have passed muster at a royal levee on Manticore, Nessler and Mincio approached the League Liaison Office. Their boots were a concession to streets whose sandy muck would have swallowed the iridescent slippers which should have completed their outfits.

Singh had given them directions, but relations between League officials and the commercial elite of most worlds in this region were about as bad as they could be. The League personnel were the dregs of a very advanced bureaucracy; the merchants tended to be the most dynamic citizens of the tier of worlds marginally more developed than, say, the systems once controlled by the Teutonic Order.

Singh's native Krishnaputra was a typical example. The planet had a local electronics industry, but half the people didn't have electricity in their homes. League officials could sneer at the local elites as being unsophisticated products of dirty little worlds: mushrooms springing from dungheaps. The local population in general regarded most of the liaison officers sent to them as dense, grasping failures with an overdeveloped sense of their own importance. From everything Mincio had seen or heard, the League Liaison Officer on Hope, the Honorable Denise Kawalec, fell into the expected category.

The League offices on Hope comprised three rectangular buildings touching at the corners like dominoes spilled on a table. They were flat-roofed modular constructions cast from cold-setting ceramic.

Each slab was a different saturated color. Though

the structure was probably a standard bureaucratic design from the generation in which Hope first joined the League, Nessler and Mincio hadn't seen anything like it before on their travels. It wasn't something one would forget. The corner where walls of lime green and royal blue met was particularly eyecatching.

The offices were intended for total climate control. The only original opening on this side was the double main door, though there were probably emergency exits in the rear as well. Plastic panes in frames of native wood now covered window openings crudely hacked through the walls to provide light and ventilation during the power failures. Mincio guessed that outages were more probable than not, given Hope's technological level and the quality of the League personnel who'd have to maintain a separate generator.

"Will you show us in to Officer Kawalec, lad?" Nessler said to the urchin sprawled in the building's doorway. He'd been watching them approach with an expectant sneer.

"Why should I?" the boy said without getting up. His clothing was cut down from pieces of Liaison Service and Gendarmerie uniforms.

Nessler flipped him a small coin. The boy jumped to his feet and ran around the building. "Sucker!" he called over his shoulder. "Find her yourself!"

"I suppose we'd better do that." Nessler said without expression, pushing open the door.

The hallway was dim but the room at the east end had a light which pulsed at the cyclic rate of the current feeding it. They turned in that direction. Two men wearing black Gendarmerie uniforms walked out of one room and into another, ignoring the visitors.

The Gendarmes were supposed to uphold League regulations on the less-developed worlds which had a Liaison Officer instead of a League High Commissioner. Every contact with Gendarmes during this tour had convinced Mincio that the service attracted people who did little for the reputation of the League, or for law and order more generally.

"Carabus!" a woman shouted from the lighted room. A paper placard tacked to the half-open door read CLO2 DENISE KAWALEC. "Damn you, what have you done with the bottle?"

Mincio entered the room on Nessler's heels. Kawalec glared up from her search in the bottom drawer of a cabinet for filing hardcopy. When she saw strangers rather than whoever she expected, her expression quivered between fear and greed. While Kawalec wasn't precisely ugly, Mincio had never before met a human being for whom the word "plain" was a better fit.

"Who are you?" Kawalec demanded, sliding back behind her desk. Its surface was littered with orange peel and fragments of less identifiable food; local scavengers the size of a fingerbone wriggled their single antennae at the newcomers, then went back to their meal.

"Officer Kawalec," Nessler said, "we're Manticore citizens touring Alphane sites. My name is Nessler and my friend is Mistress Mincio."

Mincio handed Kawalec the travel authorization from the League's Ministry of Protectorate Affairs both in the form of a read-only chip and a stamped and sealed off-print. The hardcopy had generally proven more useful in Region Twelve, where chip readers—particularly working chip readers—were conspicuous by their absence.

Kawalec flicked the hardcopy and said, "It doesn't cover Hope by name."

"It covers the whole of Region Twelve—" Mincio began hotly.

"A moment, Mincio," Nessler said. "May I see that again, officer?" He took the document from Kawalec's hands, folded it over a gold-hued coin he'd palmed from his purse, and handed it back. "I believe you'll find the mention if you check now."

Mincio stared stone-faced at the wall-hung hologram of the League Palace in Geneve. Bribes were only to be expected when dealing with officials on undeveloped worlds, but *League* officials shouldn't be pocketing them. Nessler could easily afford the expense, but when the representatives of developed civilizations were on the take, then the barbarians were truly at the gates.

"Right, I see it now," Kawalec said with an approving nod. She returned the authorization to Nessler, but her right hand remained firmly closed over the coin. When her eyes narrowed, she looked even more ratlike than before. She continued, "Now of course there'll be fees for any antiquities you discover. Port duties as well if you ship them out."

"Of course," said Nessler blandly, as though he were unaware that League regulations specifically forbade private traffic in Planetary Treasures—a category covering Alphane artifacts as well as the vestiges of early human settlements. "Payments should be to your office rather than to the government of Hope?"

"There *is* no government of Hope except for me!" the liaison officer snapped. "These savages can't wipe their own bums without help!"

"I was wondering about the arrangements you've made with the Melungeon expedition," Mincio said. "Are they really going to take one of the Six Pylons offworld with them?"

"That bastard Orloff!" Kawalec said. "He's going to take any damn thing he pleases, it seems like, and not so much as kiss-my-hand to me!"

"Because he has approval from the Ministry of Protectorate Affairs on Earth?" Nessler asked.

"Because they've got a bloody cruiser in orbit!" snarled the League official. "I'd complain to Geneve, but Orloff'll be gone by the time a courier gets there and back. And that's *if* anybody on Earth gives a hoot whether I starve here on this pisspot planet."

She glared at Nessler with transferred fury. "But you, boyo," she said. "You're going to pay!"

"I'm sure we will, if we choose to remove any artifacts," Nessler said calmly. He tipped his beret to Kawalec. "Thank you for seeing us, madam," he said.

Mincio was out of the office ahead of him. People like Denise Kawalec made her angry in a quite unscholarly fashion, but an insult to the bureaucratic highwayman wouldn't help matters.

Besides, it was unlikely that there was anything Mincio could say that Kawalec hadn't already heard.

Edith Mincio finished her third *estampe* of the evening with a pirouette that she couldn't have managed in a million years if she'd paused to think about it. Usually she danced merely as a social obligation: mating rituals weren't one of her interests in either the abstract or the specific. This party at the Singhs

was genuinely pleasant, though; not least because
she was a center of attention instead of a wallflower
as usual.

The dance steps that had been current on Manticore when she and Nessler left were years ahead of
anything the young people of Hope had seen. At least
one man had cut in every time Mincio was on the
floor, and the belles of Kuepersburg society stared at
her with undisguised envy.

A servant handed Mincio a glass of punch; she
downed it in three quick gulps. The room was hot
despite the open door. This was the most exercise
Mincio had gotten in the weeks since she and Nessler
climbed the Bakersfield Cordillera on muleback in
search of the Crystal Grotto.

Somebody offered her another glass. She started
drinking before she realized that the Singhs' daughter,
not one of the servants, had given it to her.

"Oh!" Mincio said. "I'm sorry, I've been spinning
around so fast that my head hasn't settled down yet.
I do apologize, Lalita."

"Oh, please," the girl said with a blush. "We are so
honored to have you here." Mincio eyed the line of
men circling just beyond Lalita, preparing to pounce
on the Manticoran guest. Across the room Nessler
stood at the center of a similar bevy of local girls,
visible only because he was a full head taller.

"Lalita," Mincio said, "would you care to get some
fresh air for a moment? I'm not up to another dance
just now, and I'm afraid I'll be trampled if I try to
sit one out inside here."

Lalita turned. To the largest of the young men she
said brusquely, "Carswell, Mistress Mincio and I will

be taking a turn outside. She would prefer not to be bothered. See that everyone understands, please."

Carswell nodded with a look of grim determination. The men and boys around him were already backing away. Lalita acted like a ten-year-old when dealing with the visitors from Manticore, but her authority among her fellows was as assured as Sir Hakon Nessler's own.

The two women walked out of the sliding doors. A group of men stood near the entrance, talking and chewing tobacco, but Lalita's steely glance parted them.

Inside the sound system broke into a spirited *gavotte*. Rovald presided proudly over the jury-rigged apparatus. The link between the amp and Nessler's personal auditor worked perfectly, and Mincio was willing to bet that in addition the Singhs' speakers had never sounded better.

The dance was being held in a warehouse which Singh's laborers had emptied during the afternoon. There wasn't a hall on the planet large enough to hold the crowd, all the "best people" who could reach Kuepersburg in time. Some of them had arrived by mule-drawn carriage, but there were motorized vehicles also and half a dozen aircars—perhaps all the private aircars on the planet.

The breeze was dry and cool, at least compared to the atmosphere inside the warehouse. The grit it picked up as it sailed between the town's dingy, ill-lit buildings was an acceptable price to pay.

"I so envy you," Lalita said wistfully. "I don't see why someone as rich and wise as you are would want to come here, Mistress Mincio."

"Call me Edith, please," Mincio said, a little more

forcefully than the number of times in the past she'd made the same request. "I don't claim to be wise, Lalita, though I'm knowledgeable about a few things that don't matter in the least to most other people. As for rich, though—your father could buy or sell me a dozen times over, I suspect. I'm here very much at Sir Hakon's expense. Don't let the fact that we're friends mislead you into thinking that we're equals in the economic or even social spheres."

"Oh, you can say that," Lalita said dismissively. "You have the whole galaxy at your fingertips and you don't know what it's like for us living on a pile of, of dirt."

The warehouse was on the east side of town, at a distance from the landing field but perhaps more secure for being near the Singh dwelling. The two women walked along the sidewalk of stabilized earth a handsbreadth above the cracked mud of the street proper. Lalita picked her way over the irregular surface without a skip or stumble, despite pools of shadow which the lights of neighboring buildings didn't reach. Hope's three moons were scarcely brighter than planets.

Three people approached from up the street in the direction the women were walking. There was laughter and a snatch of song in which Mincio recognized Maginnes' voice.

"Lalita," Mincio said, "it's never a good thing to feel trapped. Believe me, poverty is just as confining as . . . as a planet which is a long way from the centers of development. After this tour I'll have a position that will provide for me all the rest of my life without any need for concern on my part. That security is as close to paradise as I ever expect to come."

She smiled faintly. *And if I die before returning to Manticore, then that's security of another sort.*

"But don't let the fact that you feel trapped make you blind to the beauties of Hope," Mincio went on fiercely. "And to the beauties of your life here. There are many, many women on Manticore who'd trade their lives in a heartbeat to be as lovely and *central* as you are here."

"Ah, Mistress Mincio?" Maginnes said. A lamp over the adjacent house cast its light through the bars of the fenced courtyard in front of the dwelling. The servant stepped close while his two companions kept a little behind in the shadows. "Good evening, Maginnes," Mincio said coldly. Maginnes was with a pair of female sailors from the Melungeon vessel; they were carrying bottles. Mincio assumed their association with Maginnes was a mercenary one. She didn't approve, but it wasn't her place to object; anyway, that would be a waste of breath.

"I've arranged to borrow an aircar for you and the master tomorrow," Maginnes said. "A farmer named Holdt's staying in town and lent it. I was coming to tell him that, but I wonder if you'd . . . ?"

"Yes, all right," Mincio said. There was no telling when Maginnes would get back to the Singh compound, and there was no need for him and his presumed whores to come any closer to the party in his master's honor.

"Thank you, mistress," Maginnes said, tipping his hat and returning to his companions. "We'll be off, then."

Maginnes seemed to like Mincio well enough, and he never failed to treat her as the gentlewoman she was by birth. There was always an undercurrent of amused contempt when he spoke to her, though. Maginnes knew *his* status: Mincio was neither fish nor fowl. As she'd said to Lalita, poverty was as surely a trap as any backward planet could be.

"We should get back anyway," Mincio said. "Though I don't know that I'm going to be ready for anything faster than a saraband."

They turned together, putting the breeze behind them. It felt cool now. Snatches of Maginnes' song reached them; Mincio hoped that the girl couldn't understand the words, though she didn't suppose anyone on Hope could be described as "delicately brought up."

Two figures came up the alley just ahead of them. *A man and a boy,* Mincio first thought; then realized she'd been wrong in both identifications. The first growler she'd seen on Hope was following an old woman who wore a cloak and floppy hat as she plodded steadily toward the dance.

"Oh, it's Mistress deKyper," Lalita said, her lips close to Mincio's ear so as not to be overheard. The old woman was only a few steps ahead. "She's from Haven. She's been here *oh!* so many years, studying the Alphanes like you. She used to be rich, but something happened back home and now she just scrapes by."

"I'd like to meet her," Mincio said. "If she's as expert as you say, she'd be a perfect guide for the time we're on Hope."

"Mistress deKyper?" Lalita called. "May I introduce our guest, Mistress Mincio of Manticore?"

"Oh my goodness!" deKyper said. She swept her hat off as she turned; a thin, tired woman of at least seventy whose eyes nonetheless sparkled in the area light flooding from the compound across the street. "I'm honored I'm sure. I came as soon as I heard that scholars touring the Alphane worlds had arrived."

Her face hardened in wooden disapproval. "You're not, I trust," she said, "associated with Lord Orloff and his fellow savages?"

"We are not," Mincio said, her tone an echo of the older woman's. They touched fingertips. "While my friend and pupil Sir Hakon Nessler may gather a small souvenir here or there, for the most part we view and record artifacts with the intention of recreating some of them on his estate."

The growler stuck out a tongue almost twenty centimeters long and licked Mincio's hand. The contact was rough but not unpleasant, something like the touch of a dry washcloth. It was completely unexpected, though, and Mincio jerked back as if from a hot burner.

"Oh, I'm very sorry!" deKyper said. "She's quite harmless, believe me."

"I didn't know what it was," Mincio said in embarrassment. "I was just startled."

The growler's broad forehead tapered abruptly to the nose and jaws from which the tongue had snaked. Its skin was covered with fine scales; they showed a sheen but no particular color under the present dim light. According to images and travellers' descriptions, growlers were generally gray or green.

Mincio reached tentatively to stroke the beast's head; it began to purr with the deep buzzsaw note that had gotten the creatures their common name. The sound was a shock to hear even though she knew it was friendly, not a threatening growl.

"Does he have a name?" Mincio asked. The growler licked her wrist as she petted it. The tongue was remarkable, virtually a third hand in addition to the four-fingered appendages on the ends of the arms.

"She, I believe," deKyper said, "but I don't know her name." She straightened and added with the emphasis of someone who knows she's making an insupportable statement, "There's no doubt that growlers are the real Alphanes. I can tell by the way she attends when I play Alphane books."

"Can you read Alphane crystals, Mistress deKyper?" Lalita said. "Oh, that's wonderful! I didn't know that."

"Well . . ." the old woman temporized. "I've discovered the frequency at which the crystal books are intended to be played, but I haven't deciphered the symbology as yet. I'm sure that will come in time."

And so will Christ and His angels, Mincio thought. *Another enthusiast who's discovered the key to the universe by studying the site of the Great Sphinx of Giza; or here, its Alphane equivalent.*

Aloud she said, "Mistress, would you care to meet my companion Sir Hakon Nessler? We like to have a guide knowledgeable about local sites when we visit a planet. Of course there'd be a special honorarium for a scholar like you, if you wouldn't be embarrassed."

The growler stopped licking Mincio and shuffled close to deKyper again. Though its hind legs were short, the beast was fully bipedal. It leaned its head against deKyper's chest and resumed its thunderous· purr.

"I long ago stopped being embarrassed at honest ways to receive money," deKyper said with a wan smile. "And it doesn't happen so frequently that I'm apt to get bored with the experience, either. In any case, I'd be proud to accompany real scholars."

Her resemblance to her pet went beyond a degree of physical similarity that itself was surprising in members of such different species. They both shared a dreamy harmlessness, and neither really belonged—here or perhaps anywhere. Mincio could empathize with the lack of belonging, but she herself was unlikely ever to be mistaken for a dreamer.

Perhaps deKyper understood Mincio's guardedly neutral expression; wistful the old woman might be, but she certainly wasn't stupid. "It's of particular importance that we translate Alphane books," she said. "The knowledge and the public *excitement* that will generate in the developed regions will bring tourists to the Alphane worlds in large numbers."

"You want mass tourism?" Mincio said. "I would have thought . . ."

"Mistress Mincio," deKyper said, "if only scholars like you and your companion toured the Alphane worlds, I would be delighted. But for every pair like yourselves there's a party which knocks chunks off the pylons with a hammer—and now we have the unspeakable barbarians from Melungeon who plan to spirit a pylon clean away! Only large-scale interest among civilized peoples will permit arrangements that will save the remaining artifacts for future generations."

"I see," Mincio said. She fully empathized with the old woman's hopes, but wishful thinking about the translation of Alphane books wouldn't bring those hopes to fruition. "Let's go see Nessler, Mistress deKyper. And perhaps tomorrow while the three of us visit the Six Pylons, our technician Rovald can stay behind to take a look at the crystals in your collection. She has an absolute genius at anything to do with electronics."

The three women walked toward the music and the fan of light spilling through the warehouse doorway. The growler followed with a rumble of soft contentment.

Nessler dropped the aircar skillfully downwind of the long tent with its sides rolled up. The dozen people sitting at cards in its shade turned to watch the vehicle land. A few of them got up.

Hundreds of workers with hand tools continued to toil. Some dug away the ground at the base of the tallest pylon while others carried loosened earth from the pit in baskets to pour in a heap a hundred meters away. The men wore shorts; the women sometimes as little. Mincio frowned at thought of what the sun and gritty wind must be doing to their skin. The burrows in the gully wall east of the site must be housing for the laborers.

"Oh, the barbarians," deKyper whimpered from the back seat. The pylon was the easternmost of the line of six. Almost the entire length of the shaft was covered by contragrav rings like those used for moving torpedoes and other heavy gear aboard a warship. Several of the rings were dark, obviously dead, while others shimmered nervously with a surface discharge that implied incipient failure.

The party—the officers under the tent at least—had arrived on an ornate aircar big enough to carry all of them together. A cutter had landed nearby in the recent past. Despite the skirling wind, the scars from its lift jets remained as pits in the soil.

Nessler shut down the aircar, smiling vaguely in the direction of the Melungeon officers. In a tone much more grim than his expression he said to Mincio, "I really don't believe those grav rings will take the pylon's weight, not unless the ones that haven't failed are all at 100%. But I don't suppose Orloff would thank me for telling him."

"I doubt there are any additional rings available on Hope," Mincio said. "As you say, it's their business." The whole Melungeon operation disturbed her profoundly, but focusing her mind on the details of it wouldn't do any good.

She turned to help deKyper out of the back of the open vehicle. The door was wired shut so the passenger had to step over the side. The old woman was gray with silent despair.

They walked to the tent, Nessler slightly in the lead. The Melungeon officers wore ornate uniforms, but their jackets were mostly unbuttoned and the garments weren't clean enough for Mincio to have imagined putting any of them on. The officers carried sidearms in flap holsters. Sailors, probably thankful that they weren't at the backbreaking labor of the pit, acted as servants.

The half dozen civilians present were obviously prostitutes, though Mincio wasn't sure they were all Hope residents. Four were women, two men.

Nessler approached the big man who'd been sitting at the head of the table. He wore an open white tunic with gold braid most of the way to the elbows. The fellow was completely bald, but he had a full moustache and a mass of chest hair so black that it looked like a bearskin gorget.

"Good morning," Nessler said. "I've been told this is the camp of Maxwell, Lord Orloff. If I may take the liberty of introducing myself, I'm Sir Hakon Nessler of Manticore. I'm a student of Alphane sites as I see you are as well."

Orloff's face split in a broad grin. "I'm Orloff," he said. He ignored the hand Nessler raised to touch fingertips and instead embraced his visitor in a great hug. "Come, have a drink!"

He glanced at Mincio and deKyper and added, "Two women, hey? You Manticorans know how to travel—though I like them with a little more meat myself."

He gave a bellowing laugh and banged Nessler on the back. A servant poured faintly mauve liquid into beakers.

"Permit me to introduce Edith Mincio, my tutor and superior in the study of Alphane remains," Nessler said in a tone of cool unconcern, as though he hadn't heard the last comment, "and Mistress deKyper, a Haven scholar who's studied the Alphanes here on Hope, for many years."

"What you're doing is unspeakable!" deKyper said angrily. "You're desecrating a site that's older than mankind!"

"Oh, you're the crazy old lady," Orloff said with an amused chuckle. "Sure, I've heard of you. Well, have a drink anyway, my dear. We're only taking one pillar, you see. That'll leave five right here for you, but mine will be the only one on Tellico."

There'd been a poker game going on when the visitors arrived. The seven or eight players were using cash rather than chips. The denominations Mincio recognized—the currency of a dozen worlds was on the table—were large ones. Melungeon officers were nobles and either wealthy or at least addicted to the vices of wealth, of which high-stakes gambling was the most common.

Mincio knew the type very well. She shivered. *Sheep for the shearing,* she thought as she glanced at the half-drunk, none-too-bright, faces around the table. She hadn't realized how deeply she'd been infected as a child.

Orloff's officers talked among themselves, not so much deferential to their commander as disinterested in the visitors. One of the men walked to the end of the tent and began to urinate on the dry sand.

Servants filled two more beakers. Mincio took hers; deKyper ostentatiously turned her back and walked toward the pylon fifty meters away. Orloff's face darkened in a brutal scowl before he said, "Maybe you'd like to take a pillar yourself, Nessler? There's plenty for all, it seems to me."

Nessler lowered the beaker from which he'd been sipping. "I'm afraid it'd cost half my fortune to ship home something so huge. My heirs will be disturbed enough at the amount their crazy forebear spent to recreate copies of Alphane artifacts from imagery."

A Melungeon crewman who wore tunic and trousers in token of his higher status—he was however barefoot—clumped up to Orloff. When he caught Orloff's eye he gave the degrading Melungeon equivalent of a salute.

"Please sir," the crewman said. "There's a problem. We can't get the pillar loose."

Orloff rumbled a sound of disgust. "No more brains

than monkeys," he said. "Let's straighten them out, Nessler, and then we'll talk about cards."

He strode toward the pit, pushing the crewman aside as he might have kicked a dog that got in his way. Mincio and Nessler traded expressionless glances as they followed. The remainder of the Melungeon officers trailed after, though Mincio noticed that all the card players put their money in their pockets before leaving the table.

The diggers had lowered the ground at the pylon's base by a distance of three meters, laying bare the natural substrate. Though most of the crystal shaft was hidden behind contragrav rings, the tip forty meters in the air caught the sun and wicked it down through the base. Light spilled in dazzling rainbows across the pit and those laboring in it.

"It appears that the Alphanes didn't set their pylons on the bedrock, Lord Orloff," Mistress deKyper said with dispassionate clarity. "They fused them *to* the rock. I dare say your peons here will be some while chipping away at the granite, don't you think?"

Orloff ripped out a series of oaths that were both blasphemous and disgusting. Mincio kept her face studiously blank and her eyes focused on the pylon. It would be ill-bred to let Orloff know what she thought of him. There was enough ill-bred behavior here already.

She wondered how the Alphanes had managed the attachment. Crystal had flowed down into the dense rock, but streaks of granite wove upward into the pylon's base as well. The zone of contact looked as though colored syrups had been stirred into a mixture, then frozen.

In a mood swing as abrupt as sun after a rainsquall, Orloff draped his big arm over Nessler's shoulders and walked the Manticoran back to the tent with him. "Well, I'll have to get some equipment from the ship, but tomorrow will be time enough for that. Shall we have a friendly game of poker?"

Orloff pointed to one of the servants and said, "Alec! The new cards in honor of our visitor!" His index finger jerked from the man to an ornate wooden storage chest which showed the marks of hard travelling.

"And one of you dogs bring some more liquor!" he added in a bellow. In a friendly, almost wheedling, voice he went on to Nessler, "It's Musketoon. Have you had it before? It's our Melungeon national drink, brandy distilled from the wine of the Muscadine grapes our ancestors brought from Earth."

Mincio had sipped at her beaker and hoped to avoid further contact with the fluid within. Musketoon's cloying sweetness tried to conceal an alcohol content sufficient to strip paint. She tipped the remaining contents onto the roots of a spiny bush.

"I think I've got enough in my glass for now," Nessler said mildly. His host had brought him to the card table with as little ceremony as a policeman conducting a drunk. The servant handed Orloff a flat case from the storage chest. "And as for cards—"

Orloff opened the case; Mincio felt her face harden. Inside were two decks with mottled designs on the back: one vaguely blue, the other a similarly neutral green. They were made of thin synthetic, not paper, and looked pristine.

Pocketed incongruously with them in the case was a meerschaum tobacco pipe whose stem was of black composition material. The intricately-carved bowl of porous stone was white, unused.

"I think that'll have to wait for another time," Nessler continued. Mincio's muscles relaxed, though she still felt cold inside.

Nessler rotated himself out of Orloff's grasp; the motion seemed intended only to let him gesture toward the line of pylons. "We'd like to see the remainder of this site yet during daylight. Tomorrow we'll come back with our imaging equipment to record them, this pylon in particular, and perhaps we'll have time for cards." He handed his beaker—still full—to a servant, bowed to the Melungeon captain, and said, "Good day, sir!" He turned on his heel before the other could respond.

Orloff stood with a slight frown. He'd taken the pipe from its case and was twiddling the stem with his powerful fingers. "Yes, all right, tomorrow," he called to Nessler and Mincio. Mistress deKyper was already in the aircar, sizzling in fury at the Melungeon sacrilege.

The next pylon was almost half a kilometer away, sufficient distance to free their party from the Melungeons' presence. Nessler landed, downwind as before, though sand spurting from beneath the aircar wouldn't do any significant harm to the crystal shaft.

Mincio got her breath. She found she was more angry, not less, now that her conscious mind had processed the information to which she'd reacted instinctively on first receipt.

"Nessler," she said, breaking into deKyper's litany of displeasure, "under no circumstances should you play cards with that man. The deck he brought out is fixed. The cards broadcast their values. Orloff picks up the signals in clicks through the stem of his pipe."

Nessler raised an eyebrow as he got out of the air-car. "Cheating at cards would be in keeping with the rest of the man's character, wouldn't it? I, ah . . . I'm glad you recognized the paraphernalia. I wouldn't have done so."

Mincio tried to stand. She failed because her muscles were trembling. She covered her face with her hands.

Nessler helped deKyper from the vehicle. The two of them spoke for a moment in low voices; then deKyper said, "I'll be on the other side of the pylon," and her feet crunched away.

Nessler cleared his throat. "Ah, Mincio?" he said.

Mincio lowered her hands. Without meeting Nessler's eyes she said, "I never talked about my father. He was a professional gambler. My earliest memories are playing cards with my father. He punished me when I made a mistake. I was three years old, maybe not even that, and he whipped me for drawing to an inside straight."

"I'm sorry that this matter arose," Nessler said quietly. "We needn't go anywhere near the Melungeons tomorrow. Perhaps Rovald can get some imagery."

"It doesn't bother me to see people play," Mincio said. She smiled wanly in the direction of the far horizon. "Really what it does is excite me. My father taught me very well, but I haven't touched a deck of cards since the day he died."

She stood and looked directly at her friend and employer. She smiled again, though the corner of her lips wobbled. "He was shot dead when I was sixteen. It wasn't a duel—merely a murder, a contract killing.

Given that several of the victims he cheated had committed suicide, I suppose justice was done."

Nessler shook his head slowly. "I'm sorry about your father's death, Mincio," he said. "Also about the way he chose to live his life. But that wasn't your choice. I'm honored to have been your pupil in the study of the Alphane culture, and I remain in awe of your learning."

"I hope you're not so great a fool to be awed by mere knowledge," Mincio said tartly. "Any more than I am by mere wealth. Let's take a look at this pylon, shall we? I want to see whether all six are the same molecular composition."

They'd dropped deKyper off at the pair of storage sheds in which she lived on the edge of Kuepersburg. Nessler brought the borrowed aircar down in Singh's courtyard. Generator-powered electric lights were on all over the complex of buildings, and dozens of people had to crowd out of the way to permit the vehicle to land.

"Sir!" Maginnes said as soon as Nessler shut off the motors. "There's a lifeboat landed here from a Manticore navy ship that a Peep cruiser blasted on Air. They're hoping that, you know, you being a gentleman—"

Nessler rose with a subtly changed expression. "A gentleman I hope," he said, "and a reserve naval officer beyond question. May I ask who's in charge of this party?"

Singh stood at his front door but didn't interfere in what he hoped was no longer his business. Mincio moved from the car to a corner where she'd be out of the way while she observed what was happening.

The people who nearly filled the courtyard wore either utility uniforms of the Royal Manticoran Navy or loose locally-made garments which must have been provided by the consular agent. Some of the castaways had been injured; most had sallow, hollow-eyed expressions which were more than a trick of the low-voltage lights that illuminated them.

"Sir!" said a powerfully-built woman who planted herself in front of Nessler and threw a crisp salute. "Leona Harpe, Bosun, late of His Royal Manticoran Majesty's corvette *L'Imperieuse*. There's thirty-seven of us, everybody who survived."

"Stand easy, Harpe," Nessler said in a tone of calm authority very different from that of his normal discourse, and different even from his dealings with servants like Maginnes. "Now, what are your primary needs?"

"Mister Singh fed us right after we landed in the pinnace," Harpe said. She rubbed, her eyes. Mincio couldn't imagine a pinnace having room for thirty-seven people, except wedged too tightly together to sleep. "He doesn't have tents for shelter and I don't know how long we're going to be stuck here."

"We need a way to get to a navy ship big enough to serve out the Peep bastards who whacked us!" somebody called from a rear rank.

"Belt up, Dismore!" Harpe snapped without turning her head. "Though I'm looking forward to that too, sir. After a torp sent the fusion bottle climbing toward failure, all the survivors got off in the two cutters and the pinnace. The Peeps had a heavy cruiser. They lasered the blue cutter under Mister Gedrosian, the XO. Mistress Arlemont, she was Engineering Officer, tried to ram them with the red cutter. They lasered them too."

Harpe swallowed. "The captain loaded the navigational computer before he died," she said. "I couldn't have done it myself. He'd lost his legs from the hit on the bridge but I don't think it was that what killed him. He just gave up."

"Yes, all right," Nessler said. "Wait here for a moment while I consult with Mister Singh."

Nessler stepped toward Singh on the porch. The shipwrecked sailors parted with mechanical precision. They'd lost everything but the clothes they stood in—and clothes as well in some cases—but their discipline held. Mincio had always considered herself a scholar and above petty concerns of nationality, but in this moment she was proud to be a citizen of the Star Kingdom of Manticore.

"Excellent!" Nessler said after a brief conversation. Mister Singh disappeared into the house, calling half-heard orders.

"Bosun Harpe," Nessler continued, still on the porch which put him a head higher than the sailors he was addressing. "You and your people will be billeted in a warehouse and provided with rations during the period you're on Hope. I'll defray Mister Singh's expenses and be repaid on my return to Manticore. Mister Singh is summoning a guide right now."

Mincio doubted that Nessler would even request reimbursement for an amount that was vanishing small in comparison to his annual revenues. Government paperwork was a morass, and she suspected that the navy was worse even than the kingdom's civilian bureaucracy. The comment was his way of not seeming to boast about his wealth.

"We really do want to get back for another crack

at those Peeps, sir," Harpe said. "They took us down, that's war. But the lifeboats. . . ."

"We'll deal with that, bosun," Nessler said sharply, "but first things first." Nodding toward the servant who'd appeared at the door behind him he continued, "You're to report to your new quarters until seven hundred hours tomorrow. A delegation of petty officers will wait on me here at that time. Dismissed!"

"*Hip-hip—*" called a rear-rank sailor.

"*Hooray!*" shouted the whole body, sounding to Mincio like many more than thirty-seven throats in the echoing courtyard.

As crewmen filed from the courtyard behind Harpe and the servant guiding the party, Mincio moved to where Nessler was talking to Maginnes. "This war is horrible," she said.

"The other side of the Dole Fleet not being very competent at waging war," Nessler said without emphasis, "is that they're willing to commit acts that would be unthinkable to a professional force. Like destroying lifeboats."

Mincio nodded. "I'd think that any war was bad enough without people trying to find ways to make it worse," she agreed, "but as you say—failed people are desperate to have *anyone* else in their power."

"I was just pointing out to the master," Maginnes said, "that with the Peeps being the sort they is and Air being so close by to Hope, maybe it'd be a good idea if we cut things short in this sector and got back to systems where the navy shows the flag with something more impressive than a corvette."

He spat. "To take on a heavy *cruiser*, for chrissake!"

"The normal problem in League Sector Twelve is piracy," Nessler said in a voice as flat and hard as a knifeblade. "But I agree that it might have occurred to someone in the Ministry that when the Peeps began sending out cruisers for commerce raiding, our anti-piracy patrols should have been either reinforced or withdrawn. No doubt the Navy Board had other things on its mind."

Rovald came out of the house with a hologram projector, part of the extensive suite of equipment she'd brought on the voyage. She started to speak but stopped when she realized Nessler and Mincio, though silent, were focused on more important matters.

Maginnes had no such hesitation. "So shall I see about arranging transport, say, to Krishnaputra?" he said. "Captain Cage hasn't lifted off yet. It might be three months before another Warshawski ship touches down here!"

Nessler shook his head no. He said, "Yes, that's the problem. We can get out of the region, but the survivors of *L'Imperieuse* cannot—certainly not in their pinnace without a navigator, and not with any likelihood on any of the small-capacity vessels which call on a world like Hope."

"Well sir . . ." said Maginnes, looking at the ground and thereby proving he knew how close he was skating to conduct his master would find completely unacceptable. "It seems to me that when they signed on with the Navy, Harpe and the rest, they kinda . . ."

"Yes, one does take on responsibilities that one may later find extremely burdensome," Nessler said in a cold, distinct tone. "As I did when I took the oath as an officer in His Majesty's navy. Nothing that touches you, of course, Maginnes. I'll send you and Rovald—"

"Sir!" Maginnes said. With a dignity that Mincio had never imagined in the little man he continued, "I don't guess anybody needs to teach his duty to a Maginnes of Greatgap. Which it may be to keep his master from getting scragged, but it doesn't have shit to do with leaving him because the going got tough."

Nessler made a sour face. "Forgive me, Maginnes," he said. "This isn't a good time for me to play the fool in front of the man who's looked after me for all my life."

"Sir?" said Rovald, perhaps as much to break the embarrassing silence as because she thought anybody cared about what she had to say. "As Mistress Mincio instructed, I've analyzed the damaged crystals in the deKyper collection to find a common oscillation freq—"

"A moment please, Rovald," Nessler said, raising his hand but looking at Mincio rather than the technician. "Mincio, would it be possible for you to win a great deal of money at poker from Lord Orloff? More money than he could possibly pay?"

"No," Mincio said her words as clipped and precise as the click of chips on hardwood. She and Nessler were no longer tutor and pupil, though she didn't have the mental leisure to determine what their present relationship really was.

Ignoring the chill in Nessler's expression she continued, "He wouldn't play with me for amounts in that range. If I have the complete cooperation of Maginnes and Rovald, however, I think I might be able to arrange for you to—" She smiled like a sharp knife, "—shear him like a sheep yourself in a day or two."

Maginnes guffawed. "Who d'ye want killed, boss?" he asked; not entirely a joke from the look in his eyes, and the sudden tension in Rovald's thin frame.

"Just a matter of borrowing a deck of cards from Orloff's camp," Mincio said. "It shouldn't be difficult, given your contacts with the Melungeon crew; and perhaps a little money, but not much."

She turned to the technician. "As for you, Rovald," she continued, "I'll want you to reprogram the deck's electronic response. I could probably do the job myself with your equipment, but I couldn't do it as quickly and easily as I'm sure you can." Rovald let out her breath in a sigh of relief. "I'm sure it won't be a problem, mistress," she said.

"I'm going to win at poker?" Nessler said. "That'll be a change from my experience at school, certainly."

He chuckled. "But you're the expert, of course. And Maginnes? Before I surrender your services to Mincio, be a good fellow and find my alcohol catalyzer. Orloff's bound to be pushing his horrible brandy at me, and I wouldn't want him to think I had a particular reason to keep a clear head."

It was midmorning before Reserve Midshipman Nessler finished his meeting with the ranking survivors of the *L'Imperieuse*. That suited Mincio much better than an early departure for the pylons. She was still feeling the effects of the dance two nights before.

Besides letting her muscles work themselves loose, the delay permitted Mincio to examine Rovald's work of the previous day. The technician had calculated the range of resonant frequencies for the four least-damaged Alphane "books" from deKyper's collection.

The next step would be to calculate the frequency of common resonance, then finally to determine the factor by which that prime had to be modified to properly stimulate the crystals in their present damaged state.

If Rovald was successful—and that seemed likely—the breakthrough in Alphane studies would be the high point of Mincio's scholarly life. She wasn't really able to appreciate it, though, because for the first time since her father died Edith Mincio wasn't primarily a scholar.

Nessler lifted the aircar. He and Mincio were in the front seats; Maginnes and Rovald shared the back. There was space for a fifth passenger, but none of them cared to chance adding even deKyper's slight additional weight. The drive had labored just to carry three the day before.

They'd barely cleared the walls of Singh's courtyard before they saw the Melungeon aircar curving down toward the landing field. Lord Orloff's vehicle had a fabric canopy with tassels which whipped furiously in the wind of passage.

"Ah!" said Nessler as he leaned into the control yoke to turn the car. "I think we'd best join them before going on. You may have to drive Rovald to the site yourself, Maginnes."

"I guess I can handle that," the servant said. "Seeings as I've been driving aircars since I was nine. And didn't your father whip my ass when he caught me, sir."

Orloff and his entourage were about to enter the Melungeon cutter when Nessler settled his borrowed car nearby, Orloff beamed at them and cried, "Nessler!

Come and see my *Colonel Arabi*. Then the two of us can go back to the camp and play cards, not so?"

"Mincio and I would be delighted to visit your ship, Captain Orloff," Nessler said cheerfully. He strode to the Melungeon and embraced him enthusiastically. Mincio noticed that this time Nessler's arms were outside Orloff's instead of being pinned to his chest by the Melungeon's bear hug. "There's no problem with my servant and technician going to your camp to record the pylon before you remove it, is there?"

"Foof!" said Orloff. "Why should there be a problem? Alec, go back to camp with my honored guest's servants and see to it that the dogs there treat them right. It's only the other ranks there now you see."

"And perhaps tomorrow when we've had a chance to rest," Nessler added, "I'll be in a mood for some poker. I hope you don't have a problem with high stakes?"

Lord Orloff's laughter thundered as he patted Nessler ahead of him into the pinnace.

Mincio had no naval experience, so the view of the approaching cruiser wouldn't have meant anything to her even if the cutter's viewscreen had been in better condition. If the fuzzy image was an indication of the *Colonel Arabi*'s condition, the cruiser was in very bad condition indeed.

"Why, if I didn't know better," Nessler said as he looked over the coxswain's shoulder, "I'd have said that was a *Brilliance*-class cruiser of the People's Republic of Haven! That's *very* good. Did the Grand Duchy purchase the plans from the Peeps, or . . . ?"

"Not plans, no," Orloff said from the command

seat to the right of the coxswain. "We bought the very ship! Nothing is too good for Melungeon, and nothing on Melungeon is too good for Maxwell, Lord Orloff."

He pounded his broad chest with both fists. "My very self!" The cutter passed through an open lock and clanged down. Mincio felt the seat cushion lift her as the cruiser's artificial gravity, 30% weaker than the cutter's, took hold.

The sale of warships to minor states would be a useful profit center for a government like that of Haven which needed massive production capacity for its own purposes. Post-delivery maintenance wouldn't be part of the deal however. "We bought the *Colonel Arabi* not twenty years ago," Orloff continued as crewmen manually opened the cutter's hatch. The powered system didn't work. "Direct from the yard on Haven, not some dog of a castoff. Have you ever seen so lovely a ship in your life, Sir Hakon Nessler? *My* ship!"

The view of the hold through the hatchway didn't strike Mincio with anything but an awareness of squalor, but Nessler seemed genuinely impressed as he followed Orloff out of the cutter. "This is much more than I'd expected," he said. "Lord Orloff, I'll admit that I didn't think the Melungeon navy had so very modern a vessel in its inventory."

Orloff's officers were obsequious to both him and Nessler, but they showed no such reserve toward Mincio or one another. After Mincio'd been pushed aside by a woman with three rings on her sleeves and a dueling scar across her forehead, she waited to disembark after all the ship's officers.

"Get to work on the forward lasers, Kotzwinkle,"

Orloff said. "Whichever one you think. And I don't want to spend all day here, either! A drink, Nessler?"

"So . . ." Mincio said as she caught up with the others as they left the docking bay. The Melungeons were intent on their own business; she was in effect speaking only to Nessler, though without any suggestion of secrecy between them. "This ship is actually the equal of the Peep vessel on Air?"

"Oh, good God, no!" Nessler said in amusement. "This is a light cruiser. The ship on Air is a heavy cruiser, quite a different thing, and newer as well. Though—" In a lower voice, still amused.

"—there may not be a great deal to choose between the professional standards of the crews. And it *is* a great deal better than I expected."

Orloff turned and thrust one of the two beakers of brandy he now held into Nessler's hand. "Come! Look at my lovely ship."

Mincio followed the pair of them, glad not to have more Musketoon to deal with. Nessler had swallowed a catalyzer before boarding. It converted ethanol to an ester which linked to fatty acids before it could be absorbed in the intestine. So long as Nessler had a supply of suitable food—the bowls of peanuts on the Melungeon card table would do fine—nobody could drink him under the table.

The catalyzer didn't affect the *taste* of Musketoon, however. If Mincio had a choice, she'd prefer to drink hydraulic fluid.

Several of the officers went off on the business of the ship, shouting angry orders at the enlisted personnel still aboard. With Nessler at his side, Orloff led the rest of his entourage on a stroll through the vessel. Mincio followed as an interested though inexpert observer.

The voyage from Melungeon to Hope was long and presumably a difficult piece of navigation, so the officers and crew had to have at least a modicum of competence. More than a modicum, given the *Colonel Arabi's* terrible state of repair.

No expertise was needed to notice the ropes of circuitry routed along the decks, sometimes to enter compartments through holes raggedly cut in what had been blast-proof walls. Equipment didn't fit the racks and was interconnected by exposed cables. Sometimes a replacement unit was welded on to the case of the original.

Above all, everything was filthy. Lubricants and hydraulic fluids were certain to bleed over every surface within the closed universe of a starship. Only constant labor by the crews could remove the slimy coating. There was no sign that anybody aboard the *Colonel Arabi* even made the effort. Mincio saw 20-centimeter beards of gummy lint wobbling everywhere but in the main traffic areas.

They entered an echoing bay. For the most part the *Colonel Arabi* had given Mincio the dual impressions of being very large and simultaneously very cramped. This was the first time she had the feeling of real volume. Crewmen flitted half-seen in the shadows; only a fraction of the compartment's lighting appeared to function.

"Here we will store the pillar," Orloff said, gesturing expansively with both hands. "Three months it took to open the space! Our dockyard on Melungeon, it's shit!"

He spat on the deck at his feet. "Cheating crooks, just out to line their pockets!"

"That bulkhead separated the forward torpedo magazine from a main food storage compartment, did it not?" Nessler said. "Removing the armor plate from a magazine would have been a serious job for any dockyard, Lord Orloff. And I wonder . . . don't you have flexing problems as a result of the change? That was the main transverse stiffener, I believe."

"Faugh!" Orloff said. "We had to have room for the pillar, did we not? What use would it be to come all this way if we couldn't carry the damned pillar?"

As Mincio's eyes adapted to the lack of lighting she made out the forms of two huge cylinders, each nearly the size of the *Colonel Arabi*'s cutter. They were torpedoes, spaceships in their own right, each with a nuclear warhead as its cargo.

Perhaps a nuclear warhead. Based on the rest of what she'd seen of the Melungeon navy, the warhead compartment might be empty or hold a quantity of sand for ballast.

"You've had to remove most of your torpedoes to make room to store Alphane artifacts, I gather, Lord Orloff?" Mincio said. In fact she didn't think anything of the sort. Close up she could see that the cradles which should have held additional torpedoes were pitted with rust. It had been years if not decades since they'd last been used for their intended purpose.

"This is just the forward torpedo magazine, Mincio," Nessler said quickly. "There's the stern magazine as well, and it hasn't been affected by these modifications."

"Faugh!" Orloff repeated. "What do we need

torpedoes for? Are the Alphanes going to attack us, my friend?"

He whacked Nessler across the back and laughed uproariously. "Besides, do you know how much one of those torpedoes costs? Much better to spend the naval appropriations on pay for deserving officers, not so?"

A bell chimed three times. A voice called information that Mincio couldn't understand: the combination of loudspeaker distortion, echoes, the Melungeon accent, and naval jargon were just too much for her.

"Hah!" Orloff cried. "Kotzwinkle is ready so soon. I'll have to apologize for calling him a lazy dog who'd rather screw his sister than do his duty, will I not?"

His laugh boomed again as he shooed both Manticore visitors ahead of him toward the hatch by which they'd entered the bay. "Another drink and we go back to the camp and play poker, not so?" he said.

"Another drink," Nessler agreed. "And tomorrow I'll come out to your camp and we'll play poker, yes."

It had rained at the campsite during the night, a brief squall that seemed to have done nothing to lay the dust. Tiny shoots sprang up from what had been bare soil. The vegetation was an unattractive gray hue and it had spikes capable of piercing the fabric sides of Mincio's utility boots. She'd need to get tougher footgear if they were to stay on Hope any length of time.

Maginnes was erecting a small tent beside the Melungeons' own shelter. Rovald carried her gear to the spot, making a number of trips rather than chance dropping a piece and damaging it. Mincio'd offered to help, but the technician didn't trust anybody else with the equipment. They hadn't been able to bring the protective containers in which the pieces normally travelled. Even now the borrowed aircar was only marginally flyable with four people aboard and the minimum additional weight.

"So," said Orloff cheerfully. "You didn't bring your old fool deKyper to watch? I thought she'd want to say goodbye to her precious pillar."

"She wanted to stay home and check some values Rovald here has calculated for Alphane books," Nessler lied. His smile looked as bright and natural as sunrise. You had to know him as well as Mincio did to notice the vein throbbing at the side of his neck. "That would be a wonderful thing, wouldn't it, if we could actually decode their records?"

"Books are all well and good," Orloff said dismissively. He gestured toward the pylon in its wrapper of contragrav rings. "But this, *this* is what will knock their eyes out!"

Maginnes had the tent up. It was of Manticore manufacture, a marvel of compactness and simplicity. It would sleep four and even hold a portion of their personal property if necessary. Some of the lodgings Nessler's party had found on the tour were rudimentary, but this was the first time they'd actually used the tent.

Crewmen had unloaded the laser they'd stripped from the cruiser's defensive armament. Under Kotzwinkle's shrill commands they were manhandling it the ten meters from the cutter to the edge of the pit where it could point at the rock on which the pylon rested.

The weapon didn't have a proper ground carriage: it lay in the bed of an agricultural cart purchased from a nearby latifundia. Mincio supposed that was all right since a laser wouldn't recoil, but both Nessler and Rovald had warned her not to get near the power cable which connected the weapon to the cutter's MHD generator. Neither of them thought the wrist-thick cable would hold up to the current for long.

A Melungeon servant huddled for a moment with Maginnes. The officers paid no attention: those who'd gotten bored with watching the preparations were playing a half-hearted game of snap. It wouldn't have mattered if they'd all been staring at the servants. Even knowing what to expect, Mincio couldn't tell when Maginnes passed the reprogrammed deck of cards back to the Melungeon.

"I wonder, Lord Orloff," Nessler said loudly enough to be heard by most of the officers. "Might I borrow a pistol from one of your men to do a little target shooting? At one time I used to be pretty good."

"Sure, use mine," Orloff said, pulling a gleaming weapon from the holster on his belt. It was a little thing, almost hidden in Orloff's hand, a symbol rather than a serious weapon which would weigh the wearer down uncomfortably.

"But say," he added. "Don't shoot more than a dozen or so of my dogs of crewmen, will you? We still need to get the pillar aboard!"

Orloff doubled over with the enthusiasm of his laughter. Nessler chuckled also as he examined the borrowed pistol.

He turned and brought the weapon up. It *whacked*, an angry, spiteful sound, and the short barrel lifted in recoil. Dirt spewed fifty meters from where Nessler stood.

"What are you trying to hit?" Orloff asked genially. Several other officers walked over, some of them drawing their own sidearms in the apparent intention of joining in.

Nessler fired again. There was no flash or smoke from the muzzle so Mincio supposed the weapon used electromagnetic rather than chemical propulsion. A second geyser of dirt sprayed from the same bit of ground.

"Seems to group nicely," Nessler said. "If it was mine, I'd adjust the sights; but so long as it groups, I don't mind holding off."

He fired a third time: a fist-sized rock, half a meter from the original point of impact, sprang into the air. He hit the rock twice more before it disintegrated as it bounced across the landscape.

"You meant to do that?" a Melungeon officer said in amazement.

"Of course," said Nessler. He picked up a pebble with his left hand. Mincio noticed that despite Nessler's seeming nonchalance he never let the muzzle waver from the stretch of empty landscape toward which he'd been shooting. "Watch this."

He tossed the pebble skyward. It disintegrated at the top of its arc. The *whack* of the pistol and the *crack* of rock being hammered into sand were almost simultaneous.

"Hit *this*!" said Orloff. He hurled a pebble no larger than the first toward the horizon with all his strength.

Nessler's body swung onto the new target, the pistol

an extension of his straight right arm. The pebble was a rotating reflection forty meters from Nessler when it vanished in a spark and a spray of white dust.

"Yes, very nice," Nessler said as he turned to the astounded Melungeons. He offered the pistol, its muzzle in the air, to Orloff between thumb and forefinger. "Haven't done any shooting in a very long time. Haven't dared to, really."

"Where did you learn to shoot like that?" Orloff said. Though he closed his hand over the pistol, he seemed completely unaware of what he held.

"Well, it wasn't my first love," Nessler said airily. "But after a while people refused to fight me with swords so I had to learn to shoot. I was a terror at school, I'm afraid. How many did I kill in duels, Mincio? It must have been near twenty, wasn't it?"

"More than that," Mincio said, shaking her head sadly. "It was quite a scandal."

Nessler nodded. "Yes," he agreed, "I was on the verge of being sent down. My sainted mother on her deathbed made me swear never to fight another duel. I've kept that oath thus far. But I must say, when I hold a weapon in my hand again it makes me wonder if a little hellfire for a broken oath would really be so bad."

He gave the Melungeons a bright smile. Orloff rubbed his moustache with his fist, trying to process the unexpected information.

"We're ready!" Kotzwinkle called from beside the laser. A crewman murmured a protest, his head abjectly lowered. "We're ready, I say!" the officer roared.

Everyone moved toward the edge of the pit. Orloff had his arm around Nessler's shoulders. He fumbled the pistol into its holster with his free hand.

"The best thing I could say about the master's mother," Maginnes whispered into Mincio's ear, "is that after she ran off with the undergardener ten years ago she never troubled the family again. And Sir Hakon never fought a duel in his life."

"He never had to fight," Mincio whispered back. "He made sure that everyone at school knew he was as deadly a marksman as ever walked the Quad. He gave trick-shooting demonstrations to entertain the bloods. Nobody would have thought of calling him out."

She nodded toward Nessler, listening to their host's expansive boasting. "And he's just done the same thing again, Maginnes."

The big laser was aimed at bare granite beside the pylon's crystal shaft. Some of the Melungeon crewmen were directly across the pit, itself less than thirty meters in radius.

"I wonder if we should be standing so close?" Mincio observed aloud. Everyone ignored her, though she noticed Nessler was covering his eyes with his left forearm. She did the same.

Kotzwinkle signalled a crewman who switched on the cutter's MHD generator. Its roar overwhelmed any chance for further conversation.

The laser's oscillator whined up into the reaches of inaudibility. When the weapon fired, the sound of the beam heating the air was lost in the crash of granite shattered by asymmetric heating.

Bedrock exploded into secondary projectiles ranging in size from sand to head-sized rocks. Most of them flew into the side of the pit, but crewmen on the other side were down and the stone that howled past Mincio's ear could have knocked her silly if not worse.

At the same time as the bedrock disintegrated, a varicolored short circuit blew out the side of the laser. The cable had proved more durable than the weapon it fed. Kotzwinkle fell shrieking into the pit with his tunic afire. His roll down the gritty slope smothered the flames.

Mincio lowered her protective arm; Nessler had done the same. Everybody was shouting, mostly in delight and wonder. The fireworks had been the most entertainment the Melungeons, officers and sailors alike, had seen in a long time. The pylon wavered, then started to tilt. The rock to one side of the crystal was broken into fragments but the granite shelf on the other side remained whole; the base was partly supported, partly free.

The shaft tilted minusculely farther. The entire pylon disintegrated into shards no bigger than a fingernail with a trembling roar like that of ice breaking in a spring freshet.

The contragrav rings flew loose, freed when the shaft they bound dribbled out of their grip. Glittering ruin filled the pit with the remnants of an object that had survived longer than men had used fire. Kotzwinkle had started to climb up the sandy slope. The crystal flowed over him. The Melungeon's screams continued for a little longer than even his outstretched arm was visible.

Mincio swallowed. Her eyes were open, but tears blinded her. From her side Nessler said in a low voice, "I'm glad we didn't bring Mistress deKyper. It'll be bad enough that she has to hear about it."

The last fragments tinkled down. In the silence to which even his own personnel had been struck, Orloff

said, "Well, shall we play poker, Sir Hakon? Let's see
if things go right for at least one of us this day!"

"Yes," said Nessler. "I think we should play cards."

"I've always loved poker, but I'm afraid I'm not very
good at it," Nessler said as he sat in the indicated chair
to Orloff's left. Two other Melungeon officers took their
places at the table; the remainder watched with greedy
expressions, some of them toying with the prostitutes as
they did so. Enlisted personnel drifted to their burrows
or sat stolidly around the glittering wreck.

Mincio stood at the flap of the Manticore tent.
She heard Nessler's voice through the intercom in
her left ear canal and, a half-beat later, via the air
in normal fashion.

"Hah, don't worry," Orloff said, taking the deck of
special cards from his servant. He put the pipe in his
mouth. "We teach you to play good today, not so?"

"If you can hear me," Mincio said softly, "lace your
fingers against the back of your neck and stretch."

Nessler laced his fingers and stretched. "Well, so
long as we play for table stakes," he said, "I don't
guess I can get into any serious problems. Can we
stipulate table stakes?"

"Well . . ." Orloff said.

"I don't mean small stakes, necessarily," Nessler
added. He brought a sheaf of credit vouchers from
his purse and laid them on the table. Each was a
chip loaded by the Royal Bank of Manticore, with
an attached hardcopy of the terms and amount of
the draft.

Orloff picked one of the printouts at random and
looked at the amount it represented. "Ha!" he bellowed.

"I should say not! Table stakes indeed! Let us play, my friends. Sir Hakon thinks he can buy all Melungeon or so it seems!"

"I'm going to check the imagery, Nessler," Mincio called. Everyone ignored her; Orloff was shuffling the cards.

She went into the tent; Maginnes walked over to stand in front of the flap, his eyes on the card game in the adjacent tent.

Rovald had a receiver set up inside. It already displayed the deck's arrangement in the form of an air-projected hologram. The glowing layout shifted instantly every time Orloff mixed the cards.

"All he's got is a code signal through his teeth on the pipestem," Rovald explained as Mincio seated herself before the display. "It tells him what the top card in the deck is. You see the whole thing."

"Yes," Mincio said. "Now, don't move till I tell you, and don't talk." The technician jerked as though slapped. Mincio, though wholly immersed in the job at hand, knew she'd sounded very like her late father. Well, she could apologize later.

Play started with Orloff dealing. Nessler plunged deeply on two pair, losing the hand to another of the Melungeons with three queens.

Mincio said nothing during that hand or any of the scores of hands following. She'd instructed Nessler to bet heavily and to bluff frequently—precisely the sort of mistakes that came naturally to someone rich and unskilled. Mincio needed to get the measure of the opposition, and Nessler had to lose a hefty amount before he could move in for the kill anyway. There was no need to force the pace. "Another drink!" Nessler's voice snarled through the intercom. "Goddammit, isn't it enough that my cards are all shit? Do I have to die of thirst as well?"

He was a good actor; she could almost believe the anger and frustration in her pupil's tone were real. Maybe they were: even though he knew that losing was necessary to the plan, it couldn't be a great deal of fun for somebody like Sir Hakon Nessler. He prided himself on being extremely good at the narrow range of categories in which he chose to compete.

The shifting display was all Mincio's life for the moment. The Melungeons played five-card draw, nothing wild; an expert's game, and Edith Mincio was the greatest expert on Hope.

"Goddammit, I've got to sign over another of these drafts," Nessler's voice snarled. "You'll have my shirt before I leave here, Orloff. And where's that damned bottle? Can't a man get a drink in this place?"

A youth with more money than sense. A bad player growing even wilder as he gulped down brandy. . . .

It took three hours before the deck broke the way Mincio needed it. Orloff was dealing. Even before the second round of cards pattered onto the table, Mincio turned to Rovald. "Switch the signals from these two cards," she ordered.

The technician touched the keyboard. The minuscule cue reprogrammed the chosen pair of cards.

The deal finished. Nessler's hand contained the ten, nine, seven, and six of spades, and the king of clubs. So far as Lord Orloff knew, the top card remaining in the deck was the jack of clubs.

"Nessler, this is it," Mincio said crisply. The bone-conduction pickup was part of the bead in her ear canal. "Bet as high as you can. There won't be another chance. Discard the king and take one card on the draw."

"By God, I'm tired of this penny-ante crap!" Nessler's voice rasped in her ear. "What's the pot? Well, let me sign this over and we'll have a real pot!"

"God and holy angels!" one of the Melungeons said, loud enough to be heard through the tent's insulating walls.

Mincio got up from her chair and wobbled outside. Her legs were so stiff they threatened to cramp. She was dizzy, thirsty, and sick with fatigue. She had nothing more to do, so she might as well watch. Maginnes stepped aside to give her room, but he kept his eyes on the game.

The two officers who'd been makeweights for the game folded their hands immediately. By luck or design the big pots had all gone to their captain. Table stakes meant they had to show the money they were betting, and they simply didn't have it.

"So, we put another of your little chits in to match you," Orloff said genially. "You must have very good cards, my friend. Still, God loves a brave man, not so?"

"From the cards I've been getting, He doesn't love me today," Nessler grumbled. He drank of the rest of a beaker of Musketoon and slapped the king of clubs face down in the center of the table. "One card!"

Orloff slid the top card to his opponent, then set the deck down. "The dealer stands pat," he said. "Perhaps I have very good cards too, or perhaps. . . ."

He laughed loudly to imply he was really bluffing. He wiped spittle from his moustache with the back of his hand. Orloff was nervous despite what must be his certainty that everything was in his pocket. The amount the fool from Manticore had already lost would make Orloff one of the wealthiest men on Melungeon.

"So, are they this good?" Nessler said. He thrust three more drafts onto the table, equalling the full amount of Orloff's winnings and original stake. "Brandy! Somebody give me a glass of damned brandy, won't you?"

A Melungeon officer instantly handed over the full beaker which he'd been holding for the purpose.

"I will see you, yes," Orloff said. His voice was no longer confident. He stared for a moment at the remainder of the deck, but he pushed out the matching bet.

Melungeon officers whispered among themselves; Maginnes was as taut as an E-string. Mincio was relaxed as she watched events roll to their inevitable conclusion.

Nessler slammed down the beaker, empty again. "Then by God I'll raise!" he said. "I'll double the damned pot!"

He pulled another draft from his purse. The printout had red wax seals and the face amount was five times that of any document already on the table. "Do you see me now, Orloff?"

Orloff's bare scalp glistened with sweat. "I see you," he said. "But I call. We would not have it seem that you bought the pot."

"I accept your call," Nessler said. He laid his cards face-up on the table. Orloff displayed his hand with a great sigh of relief. "A full house, jacks over fives," he said. "Which beats your busted flush, I'm afraid, Sir Hakon!"

"It's not a busted flush," Nessler said. "It's complete to the ten of spades. A straight flush to the ten, which beats a full house. My pot, I believe."

"Holy Savior!" a Melungeon officer said, crossing herself. "He's right!" Orloff's face went from red to a white as pale as if he'd been heart-shot. "But I thought . . ." he gasped. He raised the top card on the deck. It was the jack of diamonds which he'd thought was in Nessler's hand.

Nessler stood up and stretched lithely. He didn't look drunk, or young, or foolish, any more. Mincio walked toward the card players, her face calm.

"I don't intend to break the game up now that I'm ahead," Nessler said mildly. "I'll give you a chance to win your money back, of course. But first we'll settle this pot. Table stakes, you'll remember."

Orloff remained in his chair. The other two players rose and stepped quickly away, as though they'd been thrust back by bayonets.

"I'll give you my note," Orloff whispered. He was staring at the cards on the table rather than attempting to meet the Manticoran's eyes.

"No sir," Nessler said in a voice like a whiplash. "You will settle your debt immediately like the gentleman I assumed you were. If you choose instead to affront my honor—"

He left the threat hanging. Half of Orloff's officers stared toward the scarred sand where Nessler had proved he could put a whole magazine through his opponent's right eye if he so chose.

"Actually, Nessler," Mincio said, "this may be all to the good. Why don't you rent Orloff's ship for a month or two in settlement of the debt?"

Orloff looked up, blinking as he tried to puzzle out the meaning of words which seemed perfectly clear in themselves.

"A good thought, Mincio," Nessler said in easy agreement. They hadn't worked out the details of this exchange, but they knew one another well. "That'll serve everybody's purpose."

"But . . ." Orloff said. "The *Colonel Arabi*? I cannot—the *Colonel Arabi* is a duchy ship, I can't rent her to you, Sir Hakon."

"As I understand it, Lord Orloff," Mincio said musingly, "your government put the ship at your disposal to facilitate your collection of Alphane artifacts. Is that so?"

Orloff swallowed. "That is so, yes," he said. His officers were all at a distance, staring at their captain as if he were a suicide beneath a high window.

"I'd say that renting the ship to Nessler here was well within the mandate, then," Mincio said. "After all, old man, you can't collect many artifacts after your brains are splashed over a hectare or so of sand."

Orloff lurched to his feet. Mincio thought he was going to say something. Instead the Melungeon turned and vomited. He sank to his knees, keeping his torso upright only by gripping the card table with one hand.

"Yes, all right," he said in a slurred voice. "The *Colonel Arabi* for a month. And we are quit."

Nessler looked behind him to be sure that Rovald was recording the agreement. "Very good," he said. He picked up his winnings before Orloff managed to tip the table into the pool of vomit beside him. "I suppose the cutter should be part of the deal, but I won't insist on that."

He grinned brightly around the awestruck Melungeons. "I think I'll use the pinnace from *L'Imperieuse* instead."

A few artificial lights were already on in Kuepersburg as Nessler flew them home at a sedate pace. Days were short on Hope, but this one had vanished almost without Mincio's awareness.

She turned to the servants in the aircar's back seat. "Rovald," she said, "this was your win. A child could beat professionals at cards with your help."

"Thank you, mistress," Rovald said. The technician had been unusually stiff and withdrawn ever since Mincio silenced her so abruptly at the start of the game. At last she relaxed—to her usual stiff, withdrawn personality.

"You were both splendid," Nessler said. He sighed. "Now all I have to do is figure out how to get a light cruiser from Hope to Air with thirty-seven sailors and a very rusty astrogator."

Mincio twisted around suddenly in her seat. Stabbing pains reminded her of how tense she'd been as she watched the progress of the card game. "Surely you don't need to go to Air?" she said. "I thought you were going to use the cruiser to frighten away the Peeps if they came here?"

"If we give the Peeps the initiative as well as all the other advantages . . ." Nessler said. He raised the aircar to clear the walls of Singh's courtyard. "Then they'll certainly destroy us. Based on what we've heard of the Dole Fleet, I'm hoping that if we attack and then retreat, they'll make an effort to avoid us thereafter."

The aircar wasn't stable enough to hover. Nessler brought them down in a rush, doing his best to control the bow's tendency to swing clockwise.

They hit and bounced. As the motors spun down he added, "The problem is getting there with a tenth the normal crew, of course."

"You can have all the Melungeons working for you if you like, sir," Maginnes said. "Barring the officers, of course, which I *don't* think is much loss. I'll pass the word that they'll get a square meal every day. They'll trample each other to come along."

Lalita and several household servants came into the courtyard to help if required. Nessler had started to climb out of the vehicle; he paused with his right leg over the side.

"Are you serious?" he said. "I'll certainly do better than a meal a day if you are!"

"Sure you will, sir," Maginnes said with a satisfied smirk. "But I won't tell 'em that, because they wouldn't believe me. You just let me handle this, sir."

He hopped out of the aircar and strolled to the front gate, his hands clasped at the back of his plump waistline. He was whistling.

Nessler watched the little man leave the compound. "I'll be damned," he muttered to Mincio as he finally got out of the vehicle. "There's actually a chance this might work!"

The two ranks of Manticoran sailors in the Singh courtyard looked more professional than they had the last time Mincio had seen them. It wasn't just that they were well-fed and rested: those who'd lost their clothing with the *L'Imperieuse* had now turned local fabric into garments closely resembling the issue uniforms their fellows wore.

"This is a private venture," Nessler said in a carrying tone. "In a moment I will ask those of you who volunteer to board the *Colonel Arabi* with me to take a step forward."

He spoke with the exaggerated precision than Mincio knew meant her pupil was nervous. It was easy even for her to forget that Sir Hakon Nessler, the self-assured youth with all the advantages, had never really felt he belonged anywhere except in his dreams of the distant past.

"I can't order anyone to come," Nessler continued, "because so far as I know my reserve commission is still inactive. Also I'd like to say that we were going to Air to sort out the Peeps who murdered your fellows, but I can't honestly claim I see any great likelihood of success. The ship at our disposal is in wretched shape and has been virtually disarmed besides."

Nessler cleared his throat. The sailors were silent and motionless, their faces yellowed by the courtyard lighting. Naval discipline, Mincio knew, but it still gave her a creepy feeling. It was like watching Nessler declaim to a tray of perch at a fishmonger's.

"Still," Nessler said, "a gentleman of Manticore does what he can. I'll make arrangements for those of you who choose to stay and—"

"Attention!" Harpe said from the right front of the double rank. "On the word of command, all personnel will take one step forward!"

"Wait a minute!" cried Nessler, taken completely aback. "Harpe, this has to be a free choice."

"And so it is, sir," the bosun said. "Mine, as senior

officer of this contingent until we put ourselves under your command."

She turned to the sailors. "Now *step*, you lousy bastards!"

Laughing and cheering, the thirty-six sailors obeyed. Harpe stepped forward herself, threw Nessler a sharp salute, and said, "All present or accounted for, captain."

"Begging your pardon, sir," said a brawny sailor. "But what did you think we were? A bunch of fucking Peeps who were going to argue about orders?"

"No, Dismore," Nessler said as if he were answering the question. "I *don't* think that at all."

"All right, ten minute break!" Maginnes called from the adjacent compartment. "You're doing good, teams. Damned if I don't think I'll be buying beer for both lots of you come end of shift!"

Nessler slid out from beneath a console which he'd been discussing with a Melungeon and a Manticore yeoman who'd crawled under from the opposite side. Mincio had to hop clear. She was standing nearby in a subconscious attempt to seem to have something useful to do. In fact she didn't know the purpose of the console, let alone what problem it was having.

"Mincio, do you know where Rovald is?" Nessler said as he noticed her. His face and clothing were greasy; there was a nasty scratch on the back of his left hand. "The damned intercom system doesn't work, of course."

"I don't—" Mincio began.

"Fetch her here, will you?" Nessler continued without waiting for an answer. "I think she's in Navigation II. All the levels check, but there's no damned display!"

Mincio nodded and trotted into the corridor, thinking

of the curt way she'd acted toward Rovald during the card game. Nessler was focused on putting the *Colonel Arabi* in fighting trim for perhaps the first time since the vessel was delivered to the Grand Duchy of Melungeon. He didn't have time for what anybody else might want.

Parties of sailors—generally a group of Melungeons under the direction of one or two survivors of *L'Imperieuse*—were busy all over the ship, readying her for action. Maginnes had no naval or technical experience, but he'd proven to be a wonder in these changed circumstances. Not only was he acting as personnel officer, he'd formed unassigned Melungeons into teams to clean up the vessel's squalor. Rovald's help was even more crucial. Navies train their sailors to use and maintain equipment, but they don't as a general rule care whether anybody *understands* that equipment. In a ship like the *Colonel Arabi* where so much was jury-rigged and almost none of it was of standard Manticore design, Rovald's ability to trouble-shoot unfamiliar systems was invaluable.

Mincio had no useful skills whatsoever. She'd thought of joining Maginnes' custodial teams, but she decided that she wasn't ready to humble herself completely to so little purpose. She couldn't convince herself she'd be much good at wiping oily scum off the walls.

She stepped aside for six sailors grunting under the weight of a three-meter screwjack. All the cruiser's contragrav rings were down at the pylon site. Nessler hadn't sent for them because he didn't want to discuss with Orloff what he knew about the desertion of the entire enlisted complement of the *Colonel Arabi* and the sabotage of the Melungeon aircar.

"Have you seen Mistress Rovald?" she called to the Manticore sailor at the head of the gang.

"Navigation II!" the man shouted back. "Next compartment to port!" Which didn't mean "left" as Mincio assumed; it meant "left when you're facing the ship's bow" which she was not, but she found Rovald by a process of elimination. The technician sat crosslegged in front of a bulkhead. Before her an access panel had been removed to display a rack of circuitry. The compartment felt cold and musty; the air was still.

"Good day, Rovald," Mincio said. "Sir Hakon needs you in, ah . . . I'll lead you." Rovald didn't stir. Mincio blinked and partly out of curiosity said, "You're fixing the environmental system here?"

"I can't fix that," the technician said in a dead voice. "They used the power cable for the laser, and it's still on the ground at the Six Pylons. Five Pylons."

"Well," Mincio said. "Sir Hakon—" Rovald sucked in a great gulp of air and began to cry. Mincio knelt beside the older woman. "Are you . . ." she said. She didn't know whether to touch Rovald or not. "That is . . ."

"I'm not a soldier, mistress!" Rovald sobbed. "I don't want to die! He doesn't have a right to make me be a soldier!"

"Ah!" said Mincio, glad at least to know what the problem was. "Dear me, Nessler had no intention of taking you with him to Air, mistress," she lied brightly. "You'll be landed as soon as he's ready to, ah, proceed. No, no; you're to continue your work on Alphane books. If worse comes to worst, our names as scholars will live through your work, you see?"

"I don't have to come?" Rovald said. Her tears had streaked the dirt inevitable on anybody working aboard the *Colonel Arabi*. "He just wants me while we're in orbit here?"

"That's right," Mincio said. That would be true as soon as Nessler learned how the technician felt. She stood and gestured Rovald up. "But I think there's some need for haste now."

"Of course," said Rovald as she rose. "They'll be in Generator Control, I suppose."

She stepped briskly off the way Mincio had come to fetch her. Mincio followed, thinking about people. It was easy to understand why Rovald would want to avoid this probable suicide mission. It was much harder to explain why Mincio did plan to go along. . . .

The *Colonel Arabi* shuddered. "The pinnace just docked, sir," Harpe said. "She'll be dogged down in five minutes, and then we're ready."

Mincio completed the statement in her mind: *Ready to depart.* Ready to voyage to Air. Ready to die, it seemed likely. She couldn't get her mind around the last concept, but it didn't seem as frightening as she'd have assumed it would.

"Thank you, bosun," Nessler said. "I'll hold a christening ceremony, then we'll set off."

As if he'd read her thoughts, Nessler turned to Mincio and said, "I don't think we'll have a great deal of difficulty with the drive and navigational equipment. Orloff managed a much more difficult voyage than this little hop to Air, after all. The problem is that the closest thing to an offensive weapon aboard is a broken-down cutter that we've re-engined and hope will look like a torpedo to the Peeps."

"But there *are* torpedoes," Mincio said in puzzlement. "Two of them, at least."

"Ah, yes, there were," Nessler said. "But those we've converted to decoys since there weren't any decoys aboard. Have to think of our own survival first, you know."

He smiled.

If we were thinking of our own survival we wouldn't any of us be aboard, Mincio thought; but perhaps that wasn't true. History was simpler to study than to live.

Maginnes trotted through the armored bridge hatch, holding a suit bag high in his left hand. "Rovald's all happy and digging into them crystals with deKyper," he said cheerfully. "And the folks in Kuepersburg, they sent these up for you and Mistress Mincio. All the ladies in town worked on them with their own hands."

"You were supposed to stay on Hope too, Maginnes," Nessler said in a thin voice.

"Was I, sir?" said the servant as he opened the bag's zip closure. "Guess I musta misheard."

He looked at his master. "Anyhow, I want to make sure these navy types treat my wogs right. Since I recruited them, I figure they're my responsibility."

Mincio winced to hear the Melungeon sailors called wogs; but on the other hand, it was hard to fault the sentiment.

Maginnes flicked the bag away from the garments within. "For you, sir," he said, handing one of the hangers to Nessler. "They worked from pictures of you when you was a midshipman."

"Good God!" Nessler said. "Royal Manticoran Navy dress whites!"

"Close enough, Captain Nessler sir," Maginnes said with a smirk. He turned to Mincio. "And for you—"

"I'm not a naval officer," she protested.

"You are now, Commander Mincio," Maginnes said as he handed over the second uniform. "What's a ship as don't have a second in command, I say?"

Mincio rubbed a sleeve of her uniform between thumb and forefinger. The cloth was of off-planet weave but clearly hand-sewn as Maginnes said. Nessler stared at his lapel insignia.

"Those started out as Gendarmerie rank tabs," the servant explained. "A little chat with a barracks servant and a little work with a file, that's all it took."

A three-note signal pinged from the command console. "All systems ready, sir," Harpe said.

"Then I'll have my little ceremony," Nessler said. He started to drape his uniform over the back of a seat; Maginnes took it from his hand instead.

Nessler rang a double chime, then touched a large yellow switch. Mincio heard carrier hum from the intercom speaker above the hatch.

"This is your captain speaking," Nessler said. His voice boomed from the intercom but it didn't cause feedback. The *Colonel Arabi*'s internal communications system worked flawlessly again. "In a moment we'll get under weigh, but first I wish to take formal possession of this vessel for the Star Kingdom of Manticore."

He took a 100-milliliter bottle from the breast pocket of the jacket he was wearing. "With this bottle of wine from the Greatgap Winery," he said, "I christen thee Royal Manticoran Ship *Ajax*."

He flung the bottle to smash on the steel deck. The intercom managed to pick up the clink of glass.

"May she wear the name with honor!" Harpe cried. There was frenzied cheering from neighboring compartments. From the volume, most of it must be coming from the Melungeons.

"The course is loaded," Nessler said. "Get us under way, bosun." Nessler looked a little embarrassed as he walked over to Mincio at the rear bulkhead. There should probably be a squad of officers at the empty consoles; instead the two of them, Maginnes, and Harpe with a pair of Melungeons were the entire bridge crew. In a dozen other compartments enlisted personnel did work that officers would normally have overseen . . .

Though on the *Colonel Arabi*, perhaps not overseen as closely as all that. The present crew was up to the job, of that Mincio was sure. A Melungeon had already sponged up the splash of wine and thin glass without being told to.

"I was never much of an astrogator," Nessler muttered.

"If Orloff can find Hope," Mincio said, "then you can find Air. You've got proper sailors aboard, besides. A few of them."

"You know," said Nessler, "that's an odd thing. The Melungeons are working harder than I've ever seen sailors do. I think they're trying to prove to the fancy folk from Manticore that they're really good for something. And our people are working doubly hard to prove they *are* fancy folk from Manticore, of course."

The *Ajax* shuddered as systems came on line. An

occasional drifting curse, and clangs that might be hammers on balky housings, indicated that not every piece of equipment was being cooperative. Nevertheless a panel of lights on the main console was turning green bit by bit.

Maginnes walked over to them. "Shall I hang the captain's uniform in the captain's cabin?" he said.

"I . . . yes, that would be a good idea," Nessler said. To Mincio he added, "We should probably sit down. This may be a bit rough. That—" He gestured at the console across the bridge.

"—is the First Officer's station while cruising. Though I don't suppose it matters."

"Of course," Mincio said. She wondered what a First Officer did. Wear a white uniform, at any rate.

"I was wondering, Nessler," she said aloud. "How did you happen to pick that name for the ship? *Ajax*, I mean."

"Well, actually, I'd been given orders to take up the fourth lieutenancy aboard the *Ajax* when I got word of my father and sister," Nessler said without meeting her eyes. "Instead I resigned my commission, of course."

He cleared his throat. Still looking at the deck he continued, "Three weeks later the *Ajax* was lost with all hands. Funny how things work out, isn't it?"

A bell rang three slow peals. Mincio strode to what was apparently her station, the new uniform in her hands. "Yes, isn't it?" she said.

And wondered if Fate was planning to pick up the last of the former *Ajax*' crew, along with all his present associates.

❖   ❖   ❖

The Plot Position Indicator showed the *Ajax* in close conjunction with Air, at least if Mincio understood the scale correctly. Harpe and her Melungeon aides muttered cheerfully as they adjusted controls on a console with a curved bench seat holding three, and Nessler himself was whistling as he eyed the various displays with his hands in his pockets.

In theory the crew of the *Ajax* was at battle stations, but ever since the vessel entered the Air system Maginnes had been leading a stream of Melungeons through the bridge to gape at the optical screen. Mincio knew she was of less use in a battle than the Melungeons were, so she felt free to stroll over to Nessler and say, "I'm not an expert, but it seemed to me to be a nice piece of astrogation."

"Yes, it rather was," Nessler said, beaming. "I'm leaving the pilotage to Harpe and her team, though. The largest craft I've piloted was a pinnace, and my deficiencies then didn't encourage me to try my luck with a cruiser."

He chuckled, embarrassed at being so proud of the dead-on positioning he'd achieved as the *Ajax* reentered normal space. "It may have been luck, my failures cancelling out those of the equipment, of course."

"Stop that, Mister Nessler!" Mincio said. "You'll find no lack of people to criticize your performance unjustly. You should not be one of them."

Nessler straightened and smiled faintly. "Yes, tutor," he said.

A large warship filled the main optical display. Even Mincio could identify the bristling defensive batteries and extrapolate from them to the serious weaponry within the hull. The Melungeon crewmen continued to babble to one another at the clarity of the image even as Maginnes shooed them out to make room for another group of sightseers.

"Have they never seen a ship?" Mincio said. Surely they'd at least have seen the *Colonel Arabi* from the lighters that ferried them aboard. . . .

"The software for this screen was misinstalled," Nessler explained with a grin. "It had never worked until Rovald fixed it—in about three minutes. The equipment is actually brand new and very good, though not of quite the most current design."

He cleared his throat and added, "I hope Rovald's having equal fortune with the artifacts. That's really more important, of course. I've made arrangements for our findings to be returned with her in the event. . . ."

Mincio nodded to the optical screen. "I gather we're still out of range?" she said.

"Oh, goodness no!" Nessler said. "But we can't attack them within the Air system—that's League sovereign space and would be an act of war against the League."

He pursed his lips. "They can't attack us either, in theory," he went on, "but with the Dole Fleet one can't be sure. Our defenses are as ready as they can be." Maginnes guided what appeared to be the last dozen Melungeons off the bridge. "I hope they are, at any rate," Nessler muttered. In a louder voice he said, "Any sign of life from the Peeps, Harpe?"

"Dead as an asteroid, sir," the grizzled woman replied. "I'll bet they're all asleep. Or drunk."

She looked up from the console. "You know, captain," she added diffidently, "what with the condition of our ship, nobody'd be surprised if there was a short-circuit in the fire-control system . . . ?"

"Carry on, bosun!" Nessler snapped. "If we're not in the plotted orbit in three minutes, I'll want to know the reason why."

He turned. Softly he went on to Mincio, "They may all be asleep, but we can't expect them to have disabled their automatic defense systems. And absolutely nothing that could happen to us would be worth the risk of bringing the League into this conflict on the Peeps' side."

Maginnes sauntered over to them, his duties as tour guide completed. "I was wondering, sir," he asked. "Why did they name the place Air? Did they come from a planet that didn't have any?"

"It was Ehre, Honor, when the Teutonic Order named it," Mincio explained. "The League has a sub-regional headquarters here, so it's probably a little more lively than Hope. For the same reason there's not much in the way of Alphane remains, though."

"I'll go down and give the League commander notice to order all combatant vessels to leave League sovereign territory within forty-eight T-hours," Nessler said. "That's proper under international law, but heaven only knows what'll actually happen. Between the Dole Fleet and the sort of people the League sends to these parts. . . ."

"No," Mincio said. "I'll deliver the notice; I dare say it's my duty as First Officer, isn't it? It'll give me a chance to wear my pretty new uniform."

"Well, if you're sure, Mincio . . ." Nessler said.

"I'll set it out for you in your cabin, commander," Maginnes said with an obsequiousness she'd never before heard from the man who was very clearly her *employer's* servant.

The *Ajax* shuddered from a short thruster burn. "Braking into final orbit, sir," Harpe called loudly.

"Besides," Mincio said. "If the Peeps react the wrong way, the *Ajax* can much better spare my expertise than it can yours, Captain Nessler."

Air's landing field was a little more prepossessing than that of Hope. The vessels sat on concrete hardstands—most of them cracked to little more than gravel, but still better than Hope's dirt—and a solid-looking courtyard building stood on the field's western edge. The town of Dawtry, the planetary capital, lay in the near distance to the north and west. Mincio didn't see any aircars, but there was a respectable amount of motorized transport running on paved—mostly paved—roads.

The pinnace cooled with a chorus of pings, chings, and clanks that might even have been pleasant if Mincio hadn't been so nervous. One of the four Manticoran sailors escorting her muttered, "*That* cutter's Peep, and *that* one's Peep, and I figure that big lighter—"

"Belt up, Dismore!" said Petty Officer Kapp, the detachment's leader. She added with a sniff, "And you notice there's not an anchor watch on any of them? That's Peeps for you. Bone idle."

"Right," said Mincio. "Two of you come with me while the others guard the boat."

She strode toward the truck parked beside an intrasystem freighter. A man in greasy coveralls was working on tubing exposed when a panel was removed from the vessel's stern.

"Excuse me, sir!" Mincio called. If Kapp hadn't spoken she wouldn't have known to leave anyone with the pinnace. Dismore would probably have told her even if the petty officer had been too polite. "Will you drive us to the League Liaison Office? We'll pay well."

The mechanic turned with a puzzled expression. "Why d'ye want to ride there?" he said. He gestured toward the building adjacent to the field. "You could just about spit that far, couldn't you?"

"Ah," said Mincio. "Thank you."

"I figured the damned thing was port control," Dismore muttered, immediately making her feel better. "I guess these hicks don't have anything so advanced as that."

"Right," Mincio said, turning on her heel and striding toward the building with what she hoped was a martial air. Dismore was on one side, Kapp herself on the other.

The sailors were armed. The guns were hunting weapons found while ransacking the Melungeon officers' compartments, but fortunately hunting on Melungeon involved weapons that would have been military-use-only in most other societies. Certainly no society Mincio found congenial would hunt goat-sized herbivores with automatic rifles firing explosive projectiles, or with high-intensity, high-pulse-rate lasers—like those which now equipped her escort.

A squad of Protectorate Gendarmes guarded the headquarters entrance. They didn't look alert, but they at least stood up when they saw an armed party approaching.

"Commander Mincio, Royal Manticoran Navy, to see the liaison officer ASAP!" Mincio said in her driest tone. She'd used it only once on Nessler, the time he translated a Latin passage referring to twenty, *viginti*, soldiers as "virgin soldiers."

"I don't have orders to admit anybody to see Flowker," the leader of the gendarmes said. "Maybe we'll mention it to him when we go off shift."

Several of the underlings snickered. Mincio couldn't tell whether the fellow was angling for a bribe or simply being difficult because his own life wasn't what he wanted. A lot of people seemed to feel a need to pass the misery on. Nessler had filled her purse as she embarked in the pinnace. She didn't dare offer a bribe, though, because it would be out of keeping with her claimed authority.

"Listen, you slime," Mincio said. She didn't shout, but her voice would chip stone. "There's a dreadnought in orbit over you. Every moment you piss away is one less moment Officer Flowker has to make up his mind—and believe me, he's going to know who's responsible for that!"

The guard commander backed a step from what he thought was fury. Mincio would have described her emotion as closer to terror, fear that she'd fail in this crucial juncture and destroy the chances of those depending on her. She'd willingly accept a misunderstanding in her favor.

"Allen, take the commander to Flowker's suite," the fellow said. He glared at the sailors. "These other two stay, *and* they give up those guns."

"Wanna bet, sonny?" Dismore said pleasantly.

Allen led Mincio across the courtyard at a brisk pace. She seemed to want to put as much distance as she could between herself and the two armed groups at the gate. Mincio didn't let herself think about that.

Kapp and Dismore were more competent to handle their own situation than she was, and she had enough concerns of her own.

The building—another League standard design, presumably—showed Moorish influences in its arches and coffered ceilings. Mincio could see people in offices to either side of the courtyard. Only half the desks were occupied, and nobody seemed to be doing any work.

There was only one door in the wall facing the outer gateway, and the pointed windows to either side were curtained. Allen opened the door; another gendarme looked up from the chair where she watched a pornographic hologram. "Sarge says let this one see Flowker," Allen said. "But it's your business now." She turned and walked away, letting the door slam behind her. The interior guard hooked a thumb toward the portal beside her. "Why should I care?" she said and went back to watching the imagery. One of the participants seemed to be an aardvark.

Mincio thought of knocking on the door. It was plastic molded to look—when it was newer, at least—like heavy, iron-bound wood. She discarded the idea and simply shoved her way through.

Five people lounged on cushions in the room beyond. Three were women in filmy harem suits. They were pretty enough in a blowsy sort of way and were most probably locals. The heavy man being fed grapes by one of the women wore a sleeveless undershirt and the khaki trousers of the Protectorate Liaison Service: Officer Flowker by process of elimination.

The wasp-thin woman against the other wall was in a black Gendarmerie uniform with Major's collar insignia; like Flowker, she was barefoot. She jumped up when Mincio appeared but remained tangled in the baggy trousers of the girl who'd been entertaining her.

The third girl was by herself, but the blue uniform jacket on the cushion didn't belong to her. A commode flushing in the adjacent room explained where the garment's owner was. The coat sleeves had gold braid, cuff rings with the legend *Rienzi*, and the shoulder flashes of the People's Republic of Haven. As elsewhere in Region Twelve, the Peeps were on very good terms with local League officialdom.

Mincio drew herself up to what she hoped was "Attention." "Sir!" she said. She threw Flowker a salute as crisp as she could make it after fifteen minutes coaching from Harpe—all there'd been time for.

It was a *terrible* salute, just terrible; her right elbow seemed to be in the wrong place and she couldn't for the life of her remember what her left hand was supposed to be doing. The saving graces were that the present audience might never have seen a Manticoran salute delivered properly, and that they couldn't have been more dumbfounded by the situation if the floor had collapsed beneath them.

"Who the hell are you?" Flowker said. He tried to stand but his legs were crossed; he rose to a half-squat, then flopped down on the cushion again.

"Commander Edith Mincio," Mincio said, shifting her legs to something like "Parade Rest." "First Officer of Royal Manticoran Ship *Ajax*, on patrol from our Hope station. I'm here as representative of Captain Sir Hakon—"

A man burst from the commode, holding up with

one hand the uniform trousers he hadn't managed to close properly.

"—Nessler!"

"What's she doing here!" the Peep demanded, looking first to Flowker and then at the Gendarmerie major. "You didn't tell me there was Manticore ship operating on Hope!"

"How the hell would I know, Westervelt?" said the liaison officer peevishly. "Do I look like I know what she's doing here?"

As Flowker struggled to his feet—successfully this time—Mincio said, "Sir, under the Stuttgart Conventions the armed vessels of belligerent powers are to leave the sovereign territory of neutrals within forty-eight T-hours of notice being given by one party to the conflict. I'm here to deliver that notice to you as the representative of the neutral power."

"This is League territory!" Westervelt said. He was a tall, stooping man; soft rather than fat. His hair was impressively thick, but it didn't match the color of his eyebrows. "You can't order me out of here!"

"Of course not," Mincio agreed. The three girls in harem costumes had moved close together and were watching avidly. They'd unexpectedly become the audience rather than the entertainment. "But Officer Flowker will do so under the provisions of the Stuttgart Conventions, and the *Ajax* will most certainly attack your vessel upon the expiry of that deadline whether or not you've obeyed the League authorities."

"Now see here . . ." said Flowker. He bent to grope at the cushion where he'd been sitting. His tunic lay crumpled against the back wall where he couldn't have located it without taking his eyes away from Mincio.

He straightened and continued, "You can't attack the *Rienzi* in League space, and I'm *not* going to order them away. Look, go fight your war—"

"I beg your pardon, Officer Flowker," Mincio said with no more emotion than the blade of a band saw. "If you refuse to give the required notice, Air is no longer neutral territory. If your legal officer can't explain the situation to you, I'm sure your Ministry of Protectorate Affairs will do so in great detail during its investigation."

She drew a chronometer, flat as a playing card, from the outer breast of her tunic. The timepiece was a useful relic of Nessler's naval service. It converted instantly between literally thousands of chronological systems. Mincio entered the present time, then put the chronometer back.

"Good day to you, Officer Flowker," she said, wondering if she ought to salute again.

"We don't need an investigation, Flowker," the Gendarmerie major said, the first time she'd spoken. "If they start looking at the staff payroll. . . ."

"Goddammit, what do you expect me to do?" Flowker shouted. "Does this look like it was my idea? I—"

"Look, Flowker—" said Westervelt with a worried expression.

"You get your ship out of here!" Flowker said. Turning his furious glare toward Mincio he went on, "You *both* get your damned ships out of League space! Forty-eight hours, forty-eight minutes—I don't care, I just want you out!"

"I'll report your cooperative attitude to Captain Nessler, sir," Mincio said. Deciding not to risk another salute, she turned on her heel and strode from the office.

Westervelt spit at her back. He missed.

❖   ❖   ❖

On the *Ajax'* main optical screen a cutter maneuvered to dock with the *Rienzi*; it was the third in the past hour. The image appeared to rotate slowly because the two cruisers were in different orbits. The *Rienzi's* pinnace edged toward the bottom of the display as it dropped for another load of sailors.

Mincio sighed. "I'd begun to think they were going to ignore the deadline," she said to Kapp. "I wondered what would happen then."

"The Peeps never manage to do anything to schedule," the petty officer said, her eyes scanning ranks of miniature displays. She'd set her console to echo all the bridge screens; the other positions had only a Melungeon on duty. "The Dole Fleet, they're even worse than usual. Thirty hours to do what'd take us a day, that's about right."

She and Mincio were the only Manticorans on the bridge. The others and most of the Melungeons were readying more anti-torpedo missiles for use.

At the moment only thirteen missiles were fully operable. Since a Peep heavy cruiser could launch more torpedoes than that in the first thirty seconds of an engagement, the pragmatic reality was more chilling than superstition could be.

The total stock of missiles aboard the *Ajax* was thirty-six. Nessler said they might cannibalize enough parts from the junkers to add five more to the thirteen. After that, defense was up to the lasers. Mincio had already seen the vessel's lasers in operation.

"Well, at least we can make it look like a fight," Kapp said. Somebody reliable had to be on the bridge; Nessler, as captain, had decided it was her. She'd obviously prefer to be getting her hands dirty in a place she didn't have to watch the hugely-superior Peep warship preparing for battle.

"Nessler . . ." Mincio said. "That is, Captain Nessler says we're just going to launch one, ah, torpedo and run. Launch our pretend torpedo, that is. And hope the Peeps choose to give us a wide berth in case we might do better the next time." Kapp snorted. "Right, the next time," she said caustically. She caught herself with a cough. "That is, I think there's a damned good chance it'll work. It's quite, well, possible. Anyway, it's better than what happened to the cutters, and better than what those bastards'd do to us if they found us on Hope." She gave Mincio a lopsided grin. "Besides, it's our job, ain't it?"

"Yes," said Mincio, "it is."

It was the job of every decent human being to fight evil; people who destroyed lifeboats were evil. It was a simple equation.

Unfortunately, Mincio was too good a historian to believe that evil always lost.

The *Ajax* shuddered in dynamic stasis. The planet rotated beneath while the cruiser's engines drove her at 1g into ever-higher orbit. The *Rienzi*'s engines were hot but the Peeps weren't under way yet.

"Counting down," Nessler said. His voice over the ship's address system sounded cool, almost bored. Mincio watched from her console on the other side of the bridge as his long, aristocratic fingers moved. Her display echoed the main optical screen. On its upper left corner the digits 30, 29, 28 . . . began to flip down silently.

"You may launch the decoys, Mistress Harpe," Nessler said in the same disinterested tone. He touched another control.

The *Ajax'* hull rang, rotating minusculely, then rang again in a note that syncopated harmonics of the first. "Decoys away!" the bosun reported from the Battle Center.

That armored citadel at the center of the ship was properly the First Officer's station during combat. Harpe was there instead of Mincio because Harpe knew what she was doing. Edith Mincio might as well have been on the ground for all the good she was now.

She could have stayed on Air when the pinnace lifted Kapp and the sailors back to the cruiser. She would have survived that way, but she wasn't sure she could have lived with herself afterward. It didn't matter now.

Twenty-one seconds to the expiration of the deadline. 20, 19, 18 . . . "Enemy is launching torpedoes!" reported Petty Officer Bowen, who manned the console nearest Mincio's. His voice was higher than it had been when he showed her how to adjust the scale of her display, but he spoke a measurable instant before puffs of gas from the *Rienzi's* open launch tunnels were visible to Mincio.

Two, six, eight miniature starships, reaching for the *Ajax'* life with nuclear warheads. . . .

Because the ships were still within easy optical range of one another, the decoys that mimicked the cruiser's electronic signature were of no defensive value: Peep torpedoes could guide on the visual image of their target. Nessler had kept the *Ajax* close instead of gaining maneuvering room before the deadline as a calculated risk. This way the torpedoes would be at the start of their acceleration curves and vulnerable to lasers.

If the lasers worked, that is.

"Engaging with lasers," reported a laconic female voice that Mincio didn't recognize. The buzz of high-energy oscillators added minute notes to the vibration of a cruiser under weigh with all her systems live. Three torpedoes, then three more, diverged in vectors from the smooth curve they'd been following. Vaporized metal expanded behind the torpedoes at the point they went ballistic and therefore harmless.

Ten seconds. 9, 8 . . .

The *Ajax* rang with a quick shock. Simultaneously the remaining Peep torpedoes failed, one in a low-order explosion instead of mere loss of guidance.

"Number Four battery down!" a voice with a Melungeon accent said. "Five minute, five minute only say Mistress Kapp! We back in five minute!"

"Enemy launching—" said Bowen. His voice changed. "Holy shit! Those are people! They're throwing out bodies!"

"The crew tried to mutiny!" Nessler said, at last sounding excited. "They're throwing out mutineers!"

"Holy shit, that one's *moving*!" Bowen said. "They're alive!" Mincio instinctively increased her display's magnification. She blinked. The victims had been alive when they left the airlock without suits. It seemed very unlikely to Mincio that any of them were still alive by the time the sailor spoke. She felt a little nauseous at the thought, but this was war.

The countdown had reached zero without her

noticing it. She reduced the magnification so that the drifting corpses were merely specks lost against the immensity of the *Rienzi*'s hull.

"Enemy launching!" Bowen said.

"Launch—" Nessler said, professionally calm again.

"They're abandoning ship!" Bowen screamed. "That's their boats! That's not torpedoes!"

"Do not launch!" Nessler said. "I repeat, do not launch the torpedo!" The *Ajax* continued to thrum outward. Her engines gave slightly unbalanced thrust. Occasionally Navigation cued a lateral burn to correct the tendency to rotate. On the optical screen the *Rienzi* lost detail as the *Ajax*' enhancement program segued slowly from sharpening the image to creating it.

"Sir!" called Harpe. "Sir! Those weren't mutineers going out the lock, those were the officers! Those worthless dole-swilling bastards killed their officers rather than fight!"

"Yes," Nessler said. "I rather think they did."

Six smaller craft—pinnaces and cutters—and two great cargo lighters had left the *Rienzi*. As they braked away the cruiser's image started to swell, losing definition. Mincio thought something had gone wrong with her display.

The *Rienzi* brightened into a plasma fireball. A front of stripped atoms swept inexorably across the fleeing light craft, buffeting them from their intended courses for a few moments before the boats' structures and all aboard them dissolved into hellfire.

The bubble of sun-hot destruction continued to expand. Air's upper atmosphere began to fluoresce in response.

"One of the officers survived long enough to scuttle

her," Nessler said. He sounded either awestruck or horrified; Mincio wasn't sure of her own emotions, either.

Bowen stood at his console. "Guess our buddies from the Imp have an escort to Hell, now," he said. He gave the optical screen a one-finger salute. "And a bloody good thing it is!"

Hope was a blue-gray jewel in the main optical screen. Because the *Ajax* was in clockwise orbit, the planet's apparent rotation was very slow. The survivors of *L'Imperieuse* were drawn up in a double rank across the forward bulkhead.

Nessler handed the Melungeon petty officer her wages in currency—a mixture of League and Melungeon bills, the incidental fruits of the poker game that gained him the use of the cruiser. They exchanged salutes which in the Melungeon's case meant the eye, ear, and mouth gesture that Mincio still found unsettling.

"That's the last one, Nessler," she said, then to be sure double-checked the database she'd created during the return from Air. The vessel's computers hadn't contained a crew list when the Manticorans took over. Mincio couldn't pretend that she thought anybody would use the records she was leaving behind, but she'd done what she could.

"Very good," Nessler said. To Mincio his smile looked forced. "Well, I suppose. . . ."

"Excuse me, sir," Harpe said. "We'd like to say something. Ah, the crew, that is."

Nessler raised an eyebrow. "Certainly, bosun," he said. He caught Mincio's eye; she shrugged a reply of equal ignorance.

Harpe bent over the intercom pickup of the command console. "The crew of *L'Imperieuse* would like to thank the crew of the *Colonel Arabi*," she said, her voice booming into every compartment of the ship. "May you some day get officers as good as you deserve."

She straightened and faced the double rank of Manticoran sailors. "Hip-hip—" she cried.

"*Hooray!*"

"Hip-hip—"

"*Hooray!*"

"Hip-hip—"

"*Hooray!*"

From deep in the ship, permeating it, the throats of four hundred Melungeon sailors growled, "*Urrah!*" It was like the sound of the engines themselves.

"Time to board the pinnace, I believe," Nessler said. He'd swallowed twice before he could speak. Mincio blinked quickly, but in the end she had to dab her eyes with the back of her hand.

"I'd almost like to . . ." Nessler continued. "But then, a light cruiser wouldn't be much good to me back on Manticore, and she probably isn't up to the voyage anyway."

"Don't you say that about the *Ajax*, sir!" Dismore said. "She'd make it. She's got a heart, this old bitch has!"

"Dismore—" the bosun snarled in a tone all the more savage for the fact she didn't raise her voice.

"That's all right, Harpe," Nessler said, raising his hand slightly. "Yeoman Dismore is quite correct, you see. I misspoke."

One of the sailors began to whistle *God Save the*

King as the Manticorans marched off the bridge. By the time they'd reached the pinnace that would take them to the ground they were all singing; every one of them, Edith Mincio included.

Because League officials in this region favored the Peeps, Hope's native population was loudly pro-Manticore. The party filling the streets of Kuepersburg had started before the pinnace touched down. It looked to be good for another six hours at least.

Mincio wasn't good for anything close to that. The only thing on her mind now was bed, but the Singh compound was the center of the festivities. She edged her way with a faint smile past people who wanted to drink her health. *She* hadn't taken an alcohol catalyzer, and anyway she was barely able to stand from fatigue.

Chances were there'd be a couple having a private party in her room. If Maginnes was involved, "couple" was probably an understatement. Mincio hoped that by standing in the doorway looking wan, she might be able to speed the celebrants on their way.

The door was ajar; a light was on inside and she heard voices. Sighing, Mincio pushed the panel fully open.

The growler moved aside with grave dignity. Rovald jumped up from the bed on which she'd been sitting; deKyper started to rise from the room's only chair though Mincio waved her back quickly.

"Congratulations on your great victory, mistress!" Rovald said. The technician spoke with a little more than her normal animation, but there was a tinge of embarrassment in her voice also. "We didn't want to intrude during the celebrations, but we hope you'll have a moment to see what we achieved while you were gone."

She nodded toward the equipment she'd set up on the writing desk. DeKyper was standing despite Mincio's gesture. She squeezed against the bed so that Mincio had a better view. The growler wrapped its tail around its midsection and licked the old woman's hand.

"Yes, of course," Mincio said. Actually, this reminder of her real work had given her a second wind. She'd collapse shortly, perhaps literally collapse, but for the moment she was alert and a scholar again.

Gold probes as thin as spiderweb clamped the sharp-faceted "book" into the test equipment. The crystal was one of Rovald's reconstructed copies, not an original from deKyper's collection. Not only was it complete, its structure was unblemished down to the molecular level where the Alphanes had coded their information. Even apart from gross breakage, real artifacts all had some degree of surface crazing and internal microfractures.

An air-formed hologram quivered above the equipment. It was as fluidly regular as a waterfall and very nearly as beautiful.

"That's Alphane writing, mistress," Rovald said. "This is *precisely* the frequency the books were meant to be read at. I'm as sure as I can be."

Mincio bent for a closer look. The crystal was a uniform tawny color, but the projected hologram rippled with all the soft hues of a spring landscape. She could spend her life with the most powerful computers available on Manticore, studying the patterns and publishing weighty monographs on what they meant.

It was the life Mincio had always thought she wanted. She straightened but didn't speak.

"The frequency should be much higher," said deKyper sadly. "I'm sure of it. But it really doesn't matter."

The control pad contained a keyboard and dial switches as well as a multifunction display which for the moment acted as an oscilloscope. She rested her fingers at the edge of it while her free hand caressed the growler's skull. The beast rubbed close to her and rumbled affectionately.

"Mistress," Rovald said. "I've calculated this frequency, not simply guessed at what it might possibly be. This is the base frequency common to all the books in your collection. When they were complete, that is."

Mincio thought of the tomes she had read in which the scholars of previous generations translated Alphane books to their own satisfaction. She would create her own translations while she taught students about the wonders of Alphane civilization. Later one of her own students might take her place in the comfortable life of Reader in Pre-Human Civilizations, producing other—inevitably different—translations.

Rovald and deKyper faced one another. Neither was angry, but they were as adamantly convinced of one another's error as it was possible for a professional and an amateur to be.

DeKyper sagged suddenly. "It doesn't matter," she repeated. "More Orloffs will come to Hope and will go to the other worlds. In a few generations the Alphanes will be only shards scattered in museums. Everyone but a handful of scholars will forget about the Alphanes, and we'll have lost our chance to understand how a star-travelling civilization vanishes. Until we vanish in turn."

Fireworks popped above Kuepersburg. A dribble of red light showed briefly through the bedroom's window. The hologram in the test rig danced with infinitely greater variety and an equal lack of meaning.

Mincio touched the old woman's hand in sympathy. She knew deKyper was right. Destruction didn't require strangers like Orloff and his ilk. Mincio herself had seen worlds where the growing human population broke up Alphane structures that were in the way of their own building projects. People would blithely destroy the past unless they had solid economic reasons to preserve it.

That would require either political will on the part of the Solarian League—a state which hadn't for centuries been able to tie its collective shoelaces—or mass tourism fueled by something ordinary humans could understand.

They couldn't understand a pattern of light quivering above a crystal. Edith Mincio could spend her life in study and she wouldn't understand it either, though she might be able to delude herself to the contrary. "I'm very sorry," she said to deKyper.

"Say!" said Rovald. "Don't—"

The growler touched one of the pad's dials, a vernier control, moving it almost imperceptibly. The beast took its four-fingered hand away.

Instead of a cascade of light in the air above the Alphane book, figures walked: slim, scaly beings wearing ornaments and using tools.

The three humans looked at one another. None of them could speak.

Fireworks popped with dazzling splendor in the sky overhead.

_____*End note to* A Grand Tour

After many years of resisting the friends (including Gordy Dickson and Jim Baen, both of whom read the series repeatedly) who told me how wonderful Patrick O'Brian's Aubrey/Maturin novels were, I read one of them. Then I read all of them. (When I got around to doing it, I found I had a hardcover first of *Master and Commander*, picked up at a yard sale for a quarter in 1971.)

O'Brian's series, though conceived as a knockoff of C.S. Forester's Horatio Hornblower, is really quite a different animal. The Hornblower series has been adapted to SF a number of times (brilliantly by Dave Weber in his Honor Harrington series, of course), but I didn't think anybody was doing Aubrey and Maturin as space opera. I decided to try.

While I was mulling the problems of adaptation, Dave called to ask me to do a story in the Honor Harrington universe. I'd have written a gardening story for Dave if he'd said he really needed one, but this was actually useful: I could use his space opera background as a setting to try the Aubrey/Maturin dynamics.

I based the business of the story on the letters of J.B.S. Morritt, a wealthy young Englishman taking the Grand Tour in the Eastern Mediterranean in 1794–6—at the height of the Wars of the French Revolution. Morritt travelled (as was generally the case) with his tutor and a servant, thus giving me the core characters for the story.

That left a major problem. I've read Dave Weber,

but I didn't have a concordance of the Honor Harrington series in my mind. Further, the physics—which Dave offered in the form of a 70-page background note—of the series lose me quickly. (That doesn't mean I don't appreciate the novels; I know a great deal about firearms, but someone who knows much less can still enjoy a spy novel, for example.)

So Dave and I agreed that I would write the story and that he would go over it and correct details. He did so, making extensive changes including renaming the servant to avoid a conflict with a character in the HH series. (This doesn't prevent avid HH readers who *do* have a concordance from telling me that I got this or that thing wrong: no, Dave Weber got it wrong.)

What I'm publishing here—for the first time—is the story as I wrote it, without Dave Weber's edits. While it isn't part of the Honorverse, I want to emphasize that it would not and could not have been written without Dave's help.

And boy! did I learn a lot that benefited me when I started writing *With the Lightnings*.

WAIT FOR IT . . .

Cabell'd taken a chance when he aimed so close to *Herod* at long range, but a battle's a risky place to be. Buntz wasn't complaining. The tank skidded and jounced outward on the turn. The four Brotherhood APCs sheltered on the reverse slope fired before *Herod* came into sight; the gunners knew that if they didn't cripple the blower tank instantly they were dead.

They were probably dead even if they did cripple the tank. They were well-trained professionals sacrificing themselves to give their fellows a chance to escape.

Bolts rang on *Herod*'s bow slope in a brilliant display that blurred several of the tank's external pickups with a film of redeposited iridium. The Brotherhood commander's vehicles were bunched to escape the tank snipers far to the west, not to meet one of those tanks at knife range.

Buntz fired his main gun when the pipper swung on—on *anything*, on any part of the APCs. His bolt hit the middle vehicle of the line; it swelled into a fiery bubble.

Herod's main gun cycled. Buntz screamed with frustration because his gun didn't fire, couldn't fire. He understood the delay, but it was maddening nonetheless.

The upper half of the APC vanished in a roaring coruscation: the explosion of *Herod*'s target had pushed it high enough that another tank could nail it. Cabell wouldn't have to pay for his drinks the next night he and Buntz were in a bar together.

—From "The Day of Glory"

The RCN Series

With the Lightnings

Lt. Leary, Commanding

The Far Side of the Stars

The Way to Glory

Some Golden Harbor

When the Tide Rises

Hammer's Slammers

The Tank Lords

Caught in the Crossfire

The Butcher's Bill

The Sharp End

Paying the Piper

Independent Novels and Collections

The Reaches Trilogy

Seas of Venus

Foreign Legions, ed.
by David Drake

Ranks of Bronze

Cross the Stars

The Dragon Lord

Birds of Prey

Northworld Trilogy

Redliners

Starliner

All the Way to the Gallows

Grimmer Than Hell

Other Times Than Peace

The Undesired Princess & The Enchanted Bunny
(with L. Sprague de Camp)

Lest Darkness Fall & To Bring the Light (with L. Sprague de Camp)

Killer (with Karl Edward Wagner)

The General Series

Warlord with S.M. Stirling (omnibus)

Conqueror with S.M. Stirling (omnibus)

The Chosen with S.M. Stirling

The Reformer with S.M. Stirling

The Tyrant with Eric Flint

The Belisarius Series with Eric Flint

An Oblique Approach

In the Heart of Darkness

Thunder at Dawn (omnibus)

Destiny's Shield

Fortune's Stroke

The Tide of Victory

The Dance of Time

Edited by David Drake

Armageddon (with Billie Sue Mosiman)

The World Turned Upside Down (with Jim Baen & Eric Flint)